GETTING THERE

Also by Gilda O'Neill

FICTION
The Cockney Girl
Whitechapel Girl
The Bells of Bow
Just Around the Corner
Cissie Flowers
Dream On
The Lights of London
Playing Around

NON-FICTION
Pull No More Bines: An Oral History of East London Women Hop Pickers
A Night Out With The Girls: Women Having Fun
My East End: A History of Cockney London

GILDA O'NEILL

Getting There

WILLIAM HEINEMANN : LONDON

Published by William Heinemann in 2001
1 3 5 7 9 10 8 6 4 2

First published in the United Kingdom in 2001 by William Heinemann

The Random House Group Limited
20 Vauxhall Bridge Road, London, SW1V 2SA

Random House Australia (Pty) Limited
20 Alfred Street, Milsons Point, Sydney,
New South Wales 2061, Australia

Random House New Zealand Limited
18 Poland Road, Glenfield
Auckland 10, New Zealand

Random House (Pty) Limited
Endulini, 5a Jubilee Road, Parktown 2193, South Africa

The Random House Group Limited Reg. No. 954009

www.randomhouse.co.uk

A CIP catalogue record for this book
is available from the British Library

Papers used by Random House
are natural, recyclable products made from wood grown in sustainable forests. The manufacturing processes conform to the environmental regulations of the country of origin

ISBN 0 434 00746 3

Typeset by Palimpsest Book Production Limited,
Polmont, Stirlingshire

Printed and bound in the United Kingdom by
Creative Print & Design (Wales)

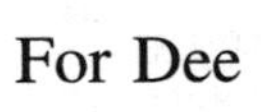

For Dee

Acknowledgements

My thanks, as always, to Lynne Drew
and everyone at Random House.

Part 1

1963

Chapter 1

'Denise. *Denise*.' Lorna Wright was getting more annoyed by the minute. 'I said: can we go now, please?'

Again no response, so Lorna poked her in the back and hissed right into her ear: 'Will you answer me?'

At last, Denise Parker swivelled round; she was grinning like a fool. 'He's fantastic.'

Lorna sighed wearily and let her gaze wander over to the stage where the Spanners, five gawky, teenaged boys, were strangling a tortured rendition of 'From Me To You' out of instruments loaned to them by their music teacher, Mr Hawkins.

Mr Hawkins – a man who believed that wearing a leather jacket and driving a moped made him trendy and, by default, a real favourite with 'the kids'. It was probably best he didn't know their real opinion of him. Since coming to teach in the tough East End school – after having felt called upon to leave a cushy job in leafy Surrey so that he could bring culture to the masses – Mr Hawkins had suffered quite enough disappointments already.

'I suppose that means you expect me to hang around waiting for that lot to finish destroying the Beatles and making complete idiots of themselves?'

Denise shrugged her shoulders and smiled sweetly. 'You don't mind, do you, Lorn?'

Being unwilling to walk home without her best friend to chat to, Lorna leaned back against the wall bars that lined one side of the school hall, folded her arms across her recently developed breasts – it was still something of a shock to find them there; she'd begun to think they would never make an appearance – and made a more critical appraisal of the dodgy-looking herberts plonking away up on the stage. Boys, every one of them, and with enough acne between them to satisfy even the most fanatical of join-the-dots enthusiasts. Whichever one she had her sights on, Denise must be out of her mind.

'I can't wait till next month,' Lorna said to the back of Denise's head. 'Just think about it, Den. No more school. Ever.'

Torn between ogling Terry Robins – he was *so* gorgeous – and reacting to her friend's shocking statement about leaving school, Denise twisted halfway round so she could speak to Lorna while still keeping a watchful eye on Terry. There was always plenty of competition for any boy who was in a pop group, never mind one as adorable as Terry.

'Have you taken leave of your senses?'

'What do you mean?'

'Well, for a start, how about your usual –' Denise put her hands on her hips and started speaking in a singsong whine – '*I really think we should find out about going to college, Den. Could be a right laugh, and we'd get much better jobs if we did. We could even do shorthand*?' Reverting to her normal voice, Denise looked Lorna up and down. 'What about that?'

Lorna shrugged. 'I've sort of decided I don't want to waste my time going to college.'

Denise said nothing; even if she hadn't felt compelled to return her full attention to the stage, for once, in all the years she had been Lorna Wright's friend, she didn't know what to make of her. *College, a waste of time?* It was as if the body snatchers had turned up and swapped her best mate for an alien pod person.

'I just think, you know, at my age, I should be earning some money, acting more sort of grown up. Not like a little kid any more.'

'Yeah, right, good idea,' said Denise flatly, without even looking round. 'Why not think about applying to run ICI?'

As the Spanners' rendition of 'Summer Holiday' came to a straggly, discordant end, Lorna levered herself away from the wall. 'At last. Can we go now?'

'Ten more minutes, Lorna? Go on. I just want to see if he'll talk to me.'

Lorna rolled her eyes. 'It's nearly a quarter to five, Denise.'

'Please?'

'Go on then. But no more than ten minutes, all right? I'll be outside.'

She began to walk away, but then stopped and asked: 'I couldn't have one of your fags, could I?'

Denise spun round and stared into Lorna's face. It took a long moment to find the right words.

'A fag? You want one of my fags? Since when have you been a smoker? You say I stink even if I have a quick drag between lessons.'

'Leave off, Den. Just give me one, and I'll see you outside. Ten minutes, then I'm off.'

Just two minutes later, as Lorna was simultaneously choking and grinding out the barely smoked cigarette under her heel – she really couldn't get the hang of this smoking lark – Denise came rushing up to her, grinning like a monkey, with her cheeks flushed pink, and her eyes wide and bright with total joy.

'Lorn, you'll never guess what: I've only got off with him. Terry flipping Robins! And I've got a date. Tonight. You're coming too. You're going with Paul Miller, his mate from the fifth form over at George Green.' Denise was practically squealing with pleasure. 'I can't believe it. Tonight. And he is just so –'

'Sorry, Den, I can't.'

Denise's eyes widened even further, but this time with alarm. 'But you've got to. I said you would. For his mate, Paul.'

'Honest, Den, I can't.'

'Come on, Lorna. You've got to.'

'No.'

'Look, I know what your mum's like about you not going out with fellers she doesn't know.' Denise nudged her, trying urgently to egg her on, to work her up into some sort of enthusiasm. 'Especially ones who're in the fifth form, eh? But don't worry, Terry said he's not even a whole year older than us.'

Lorna didn't reply.

'Go on, just this once. Please. You can tell your mum you're coming round mine.'

'Sorry, it's nothing to do with Mum. I really can't. I'm busy.'

Denise's look of disappointment slowly changed into a sly smile. 'Here. You crafty cow. Who is he?'

'Don't know what you mean.'

'Lorna. This is me you're talking to. Who is he?'

Lorna shrugged. 'If you must know, it's Richie.'

'Richie?'

'That's right, Den, Richie.'

'Richie who?'

'Blimey, are you thick or what? Richie Clayton.'

'But he's eighteen, *three* years older than us, and he's –'

'Yeah?'

'Look, Lorna, I know I shouldn't interfere, but you know what a reputation he's got.'

'What, for being grown up? For not being a little twerp like Terry Robins?'

'Don't get nasty, Lorna. You know we always said we'd never fall out over a feller.'

'But that doesn't count if the feller's Richie Clayton, eh, Den? We can fall out over him, can we? That all right, is it?'

Denise pressed her lips hard together and tried to think of an answer.

'You don't have to live with him and his temper, and . . . Well, you just don't, that's all,' was her eventual feeble reply.

'You know, Den,' Lorna went on, 'I don't think it's very nice, running down a member of your own family. I mean, if I had a cousin like Richie, I'd never say anything nasty about him. And I certainly wouldn't listen to all the lies and rumours that other people seem to enjoy spreading around the place about him either; because I don't think that would be right. Especially if he'd lived in my house since he was a tiny, little baby, and my mum and dad had brought him up like he was their very own kid, like he was my very own brother.'

Denise stared sullenly at her feet. 'Lecture over?'

'Don't go getting all moody on me, Den. You'll come up with someone else to go with you.' Lorna grabbed her friend's hand. 'Now, are you coming home, or what?'

'You do love me, don't you, Richie?' The fair-haired

girl was really uncomfortable. As Richie Clayton – who everyone knew was the best-looking bloke in the whole of East London – rubbed and kissed and pressed against her, the rough brick scratched her skin through the lawn of her thin summer blouse, and her head kept bumping against the wall. But she didn't dare move in case he got annoyed and lost interest. She had been dying for Richie to take notice of her for months and she wasn't going to risk upsetting him now. 'Tell me you love me.'

'Don't start talking silly.' Richie breathed the words into her neck, then paused. Now what the hell was her name? Christine? Pauline? Something or other –ine . . . Sod it, how was he expected to remember all their names? But they seemed to like it for some reason. Expect it, even. Hang on – Janine. That was it: Janine.

'Course I do, Janine,' he went on as though he hadn't missed a beat. 'You know I do.'

Yeah, course he did. Just like he loved every other girl who let him have a quick feel, or – if his luck was in – a bit of how's-yer-father up against the wall of the huge bonded warehouses that lined the streets surrounding the docks. Richie Clayton loved them all. Each and every one of the silly little tarts, even whingeing, scrawny birds like this one.

'Because if you don't love me, Rich, you do know it wouldn't be right, us doing this, don't you?'

Richie ignored her chattering, and, with practised ease, began undoing the buttons of her school blouse.

The girl half-heartedly brushed at his hands as they insinuated their way into the circle-stitched cups of her pale pink, satinised cotton bra. 'Richie, don't. I can't. It's nearly five o'clock. Mum was expecting me home forty minutes ago.'

Richie tugged open his fly. 'Don't worry, darling. This won't take long.'

Shirley Wright pushed her carefully styled and tinted blonde hair off her face with the back of her wet hand and shook the drips from the saucepan, which she then placed, just so, on the draining rack by the sink. Shirley liked to clear up as she went along, liked to have the kitchen nice – tidy and welcoming – for when her husband, Joe, got in from work, and her daughter, Lorna, got in from school.

Got in from school.

Shirley smiled to herself. She wouldn't be able to say that about her little girl for much longer. Her little Lorna, the light of her and Joe's life, would be going out into the big grown-up world very soon – the first one in their family ever to go to college. Shirley was so proud of her.

She tipped the water from the plastic washing-up bowl into the sink and rinsed it round under the cold tap, dried her hands on her apron, and then took it off and popped it in the dirty linen basket. A quick glance at the kitchen clock. Ten to five.

Lorna was a bit late. Shirley smiled to herself again. She'd be gossiping with Denise as usual; it was a wonder they had anything left to talk about after being at school together all day. Still, Shirley wasn't complaining, it gave her a bit more time to put a comb through her hair and to put on a fresh lick of powder and lipstick before she had to get on with finishing the tea, making the gravy to go with the toad-in-the-hole, one of Joe's favourites. And draining the nice fresh veg. Lovely.

A sudden sharp pain made Shirley catch her breath.

'Don't be silly, Shirl,' she said out loud to herself, gripping the side of the sink until her knuckles whitened. 'You know they said it wouldn't be that sort of a pain if it came back. This is a bit of wind, you daft mare. Shouldn't have kept picking at the food while you were cooking.'

'I mean it, Lorn, I really don't want us ever to fall out over a feller. Any feller.'

Denise and Lorna linked arms as they raced across Penfold Street and then dashed into the courtyard of Lancaster Buildings, the block of flats where Lorna lived with her parents.

'It wasn't me who got all shirty,' said Lorna, unrolling the waistband of her skirt, in her nightly after-school ritual that returned the garment to, what was in her mother's eyes, a respectable length.

'I know, but let's forget it, eh?' Denise didn't bother with the cosmetic lengthening of her skirt; her mum was always too caught up in the general chaos of the Parker household to concern herself over whether her elder daughter was showing a bit too much knee.

'I've forgotten it already.'

Relieved that there was no unpleasantness left between them – Denise could get plenty of that indoors from her little brother and sister – she gave Lorna a peck on the cheek. 'Wish me luck, Lorn. I'm going to get off home and try to persuade Mum it's a good idea to let me go out with Terry tonight.'

'She won't mind you seeing him, will she?' Lorna asked, obviously surprised by such a thought.

She had known Phyllis Parker, Denise's mother, all her young life, and had never found her to be anything other than indulgent and easy-going as far as parenting went.

In Denise's big old three-storey house on the East India Dock Road there was always some sort of a commotion going on, and while it usually blew over as fast as it had blown up, the distraction meant that the kids could get away with all sorts of things. In fact, Denise, and her younger brother and sister, Maxie and Chantalle, never mind her big cousin, Richie, had been allowed an almost free rein when compared to the restrictions that Lorna had always faced as a precious only child.

'No, but you know how she likes to go to the flicks of a Friday with Dad?'

'Yeah.'

'Last week, when her and Dad got home, they found our Maxie had brought in all his mates from the boys' club and they'd eaten the faggots and pease pudding she'd left in the larder for her and Dad's supper. She went bonkers and said if he wanted to act like a little kid, then that's how she'd treat him. Then our Chantalle started laughing at him and Mum turned on her as well.'

'Perhaps the film wasn't any good. You know how easy something like that can give her the hump.'

'Probably. But apart from all that, she's told Maxie I'm going to sit with him and Chantalle to keep an eye on what they get up to tonight, just like they're a pair of five-year-olds.'

'Den, that was a week ago. You know your mum: she'll have forgotten all about it by now.'

'I suppose you're right,' Denise said, pulling the elastic band off her ponytail, and releasing her thick red hair about her shoulders. 'What do you reckon? Up or down?'

'For tonight?'

Denise nodded.

Lorna leaned back and studied her friend's mop of unruly curls. 'It could do with a bit of a shape-up really. Might be better up.'

'That's what I thought. I'll have to get round Dad to treat me to a hairdo. But I won't ask him tonight; it's going to be tough enough getting round Mum to let me go out.' Denise bunched up her hair and refastened it in the band. 'Will you phone Lola's for me when you get home and get me an appointment for tomorrow? Some time after twelve?'

Lorna nodded. 'Course I will, and I'll book myself in as well. I could do with a bit of a trim.'

'I'm so nervous, Lorna. I've been after Terry for months now.'

'How come you never said?'

Denise looked away coyly, a startling addition to her usually uniformly brazen range of expressions. 'Say I mess it up?'

'You won't, Den.'

Despite Lorna's own excitement at being *Richie's girl*, as he had put it when he'd walked her home after she'd bumped into him outside the chip shop in Chrisp Street last week – even though he had stared at her chest all the time he was speaking to her rather than looking into her eyes, and had seemed more interested in her dad's work down the docks than in anything she had to say – Lorna still felt badly about letting down her best friend. She really was surprised at how strongly Denise felt about this Terry Robins.

'So what're you going to do about finding a date for this Paul bloke then?'

'I'll phone someone. No one from school will turn down the chance of a date with one of the Spanners' mates.' Realising what she'd said, Denise held up her hand to stop Lorna from coming back at her with something smart. 'No need to say it, Lorn. I mean *most* girls from school wouldn't turn down the chance . . .'

'All right, you two?'

At the sound of the rough masculine voice – and despite Denise being the redhead and Lorna being the brunette – Lorna blushed bright scarlet while Denise simply rolled her eyes.

'Hello, Richie,' breathed Lorna.

Richie looked her up and down – his gaze settling on her newly filled-out bosom – lit a cigarette and winked salaciously. 'What you girls up to then?'

'We're just on our way home from school.' Lorna's eyes, big and bright blue at the best of times, were now almost completely round, and shining like brand-new sixpenny bits.

'You want to get a move on then, Lorn. You're meeting me outside the Eastern at half-seven.' He blew an expert smoke ring, with his chin lifted to one side, but he was staring straight at her. 'Here, you haven't forgotten, have you?' he asked, mock seriousness making his voice gruffer than ever. 'Wasn't planning to stand me up or nothing?'

'No. Course not.' Lorna hadn't caught the sarcasm in his tone. 'I've been really looking forward to it.'

Denise said nothing, she just glared at her cousin.

'See you later then, darling.' Richie winked again and started to walk away. 'You coming, Den? Auntie Phyllis'll be expecting us for tea and I've worked up quite an appetite this afternoon.' The thought of the little bird he'd just had up against the warehouse wall made him smile with pleasure, and look forward to this evening even more. That Lorna Wright not only had a real nice body on her, her old man was well thought of down at the docks. And everyone knew he idolised his daughter, would do anything for her. If Richie played it right and he got himself well in with them, it could all prove to be a nice little win double. Handsome. Just his sort of thing: a tart just begging for it, and with an old man who could get him an in on all that lovely gear in the docks that was just sitting there waiting for Richie to get his thieving hands on it.

'Well?' he said.

Denise shrugged in supposed indifference, but followed her cousin anyway.

'Here, by the way,' he called back to Lorna, who was watching him walk away with her friend. 'Those Spanners you were talking about when I came along. Who are they then?'

'Just some boys from our class. They're a sort of pop group.'

'Long as that's all they are, Lorna. You're my bird now. I ain't sharing you with no schoolkids.'

Lorna almost fainted with happiness.

'That was lovely, Mum.' Denise smiled winningly at Phyllis as she pushed her empty plate away from her, and rubbed her stomach appreciatively. 'You make the best neck of lamb stew and dumplings in the whole wide world.'

Chantalle tutted spitefully. 'Hark at her. Bloody crawler.'

'Show a little respect, if you don't mind, Chantalle,' said Denise snootily.

'Respect? What, for you? You must be bloody joking.'

Denise narrowed her eyes at her younger sister, and then turned on her brother. 'And don't snatch my plate like that, Maxie. Can't you act like a human being instead of a gorilla?'

'He must take after his big sister,' sniped Chantalle to no one in particular. 'Mind you, I'm not so sure about her acting like a gorilla, but I do know she's ugly enough to frighten one.'

Denise half rose from her chair. 'Mum, tell her!'

'That's enough of that talk, thank you very much, Chantalle.' Phyllis flicked her younger daughter round the head with the back of her hand. 'And get your elbows out of the way so's your brother can clear the table properly.'

With a grimace that showed a combination of displeasure and resignation, Maxie set about collecting and stacking the rest of the plates from the scrubbed deal dining table that had graced the Parkers' big basement kitchen for as long as he could remember; he supposed that doing a bit of clearing-up was a reasonable price to pay for not having to go through the humiliation of being baby-sat by his so-called big sister.

Big sister. It would have been a joke if it hadn't been so completely, sodding annoying. She was fifteen, just one year older than him. It made him sick to see her flouncing about like she was his boss or his teacher or something, and he was a good six inches taller than she was.

'I don't know why we bother sitting round this table like civilised people, Henry,' Phyllis said to her husband. 'We might as well go out the backyard and chuck all the grub in the tin bath and eat like bleed'n pigs round a trough.'

Henry, failing to see the irony in his actions, merely

grunted a swine-like reply, sniffed loudly, and snapped open his copy of the *Evening News*.

'Don't suppose there's a drop more of that stew left, Auntie Phyllis,' said Richie, flashing Maxie a warning look as he wrestled with him for his empty plate. 'That was handsome, that was.'

'Sorry, sweetheart,' said Phyllis, slapping the back of Maxie's hand until he let go of the plate and put it back on the table. 'That bad-mannered little bleeder should have asked you if you'd finished.'

She jerked her thumb towards the door. 'Maxie, go and dish up seconds for your cousin.'

Chantalle, taking the opportunity presented by her mother's anger being temporarily focused on Maxie, pounced immediately. 'Mum?' she said, dragging the word out into three full syllables.

'Yes, love?'

'Why are you letting Denise go out tonight?'

Phyllis, sawing vigorously at the remains of the massive loaf that had all but been demolished during the meal, didn't look up. 'Because I am.'

'But you said she had to stay in and watch what Maxie got up to.'

'Well, I've changed my mind.' Phyllis handed the resulting misshapen doorstep of bread to Richie, who took it with a sickly sweet smile of gratitude.

'But, Mum, if she can go out, why can't I?'

'Because she's nearly sixteen and you're just thirteen; you were a saucy little madam last week, and she wasn't; and I'm your mother and I say so. That's why. That clear enough for you? And anyway, who's she, the cat's mother?'

Chantalle stood up, pushing her chair back with a

dramatic flourish that sent it crashing into the maid-saver. 'I hate you.'

'You're thirteen, you hate everybody. It's your job.'

Shirley, who had been smiling happily as she listened to her husband's tales of what tricks his pals had been up to at work down at the docks that day, suddenly looked concerned.

'Something wrong with your tea, love?' she asked Lorna, who, she realised, had done little more than pick at her food.

'No, Mum, it's smashing.'

Shirley frowned across at Joe, silently signalling at him to find out if he knew what was up with their precious daughter.

Joe flashed a negative reply with a brief shake of his head, a flash of his eyebrows, and a quick downturn of his mouth.

'Me and your dad were really concerned about you, love – you getting in so late from school like that.'

'Blimey, Mum. It was only flipping six o'clock.'

Joe, taken aback, slapped the table with the palm of his hand. 'Don't you dare talk to your mother like that.'

'It's all right, Joe. She's just spreading her wings. You remember what it was like being her age.'

'I know I wouldn't have dared talk back to my mother. I don't know what's got into kids nowadays.'

Shirley put her smile back in place. 'Why don't you go and sit on the sofa with the paper, Joe? And me and Lorna'll go through and make you a nice cup of tea.'

Then she looked at Lorna and jerked her head towards her husband. 'Tell your dad you're sorry, love. Then come through to the kitchen and give me a hand.'

Lorna waited till her mum had left the big back room that served as their flat's living and dining area, then perched herself on her father's lap, threw her arms round his neck and gave him a hug.

'Sorry, Dad.'

He held her at arm's length. 'Now you're not trying to get round me, are you?'

Lorna smiled down at him through her lashes. 'I can't fool you, can I?'

'Cut the toffee, babe. I don't want you upsetting your mum. She's been feeling a bit dodgy again today.'

Lorna gulped. 'I didn't know, it's not –'

'No. She's just a bit tired, that's all. Been doing too much as usual.' The smile softened his big, weather-beaten face into a mature, tougher reflection of the young, handsome boy that Shirley had fallen for when she had been little more than a girl herself working on the buses during the war. 'So, Lorna-Dorna, tell me what you're after.'

'Do you think Mum'll let me go out with my mates tonight?'

'Come on, you know the agreement. She only likes you going out of a Saturday until you leave school. Isn't that enough?'

'I said I'd meet a friend. And I sort of promised.' She bowed her head. 'I'm sorry, I should have asked first.'

'Yes, you should, and don't go too far with the acting, Lorna. I'm your father, not the flaming film critic from the *Daily Sketch*.'

Lorna looked suitably admonished and Joe melted.

'I'll have a word with your mum, but I'm not promising what she'll say. All right?'

Lorna plonked a big, soppy kiss on the top of his head. 'Thanks, Dad, you're the best.'

Lorna's hair was still damp when she arrived, out of breath and panting, at the Star of the East. She'd been too worried about being late to dry it properly. But Richie wasn't there yet. Good. If she was quick she could sort out her face before he turned up.

She rummaged through her bag until she found her blue gingham make-up bag and the little brown plastic wallet that held her hand mirror. Before she'd left home, Lorna had managed to slap on a trace of foundation and a flick of mascara – just enough for her mum not to insist that she go into the bathroom and scrub her face clean of every trace – but she hadn't dared get out her eyeliner or her frosted, pale lilac lipstick.

By the time Richie turned up – twenty minutes late – Lorna had completely made up her face, had adjusted, readjusted and then discarded the tortoiseshell head-band that she had earlier decided should hold back her mid-brown, shoulder-length bob, and had even had enough time left over to begin fretting about being stood up.

But, with a single flash of his knee-weakening dimples, Richie cast all thoughts of humiliating abandonment far from her mind.

'Hello, doll,' he said, offering her his arm in what Lorna found a totally dreamy gesture of gentlemanliness – he cared about her enough to offer her his arm *and* she got to touch him! – 'How's tricks?'

'Great,' was the most Lorna could manage. What with her mouth being so dry it was amazing she'd been able to say even that.

'Come on then. It's a lovely evening, let's go for a walk.'

Lorna was a bit concerned to find herself being steered back across the main road in the direction of the docks. This was far too close to Lancaster Buildings for comfort. If her dad popped out to the Blue Boy for a pint, she'd be for it if he saw her so much as talking to the likes of Richie Clayton.

'Do we have to go this way?' The question needed every ounce of her courage, but this was serious.

Richie stopped at the kerb and grinned at her. 'Mum and Dad don't know you're out with a grown-up?'

Lorna blushed. 'Sort of.'

He flicked her under the chin. 'Don't worry. I know, we'll get a bus up to Vicky Park.'

'Won't the gates be locked?'

He tapped the side of his nose with his finger. 'You're out with Richie Clayton, darling. No one locks me out of anywhere. Ever. But anyway, they won't be shut for hours – not on a lovely summer evening like this.'

Lorna was beginning to panic. It was getting on for eight o'clock. Going over the park at this time of night?

'I promised I'd be back by ten.'

'Stop worrying.'

Still glowing from Richie having paid her fare for the short ride along Burdett and Grove Road – 'I'll get hers,' he'd said to the conductor. 'She's with me' – Lorna was now clutching the skirt of her shirtdress to her thighs as she let Richie boost her over a hedge into the gardens surrounding the boating lake.

'Be nice and private in here,' he'd urged her.

Lorna had been kissed before – she was pretty, bright

and, even before her recent blooming into womanhood, had always been popular with boys – but she had never been kissed by anyone as experienced, or as persistent, as Richie Clayton. It was a strange feeling, as they stretched out, side by side on the sweet-smelling grass: she wanted him to stop – his hands were all over the place – but it felt wonderful, as if Richie had filled up her body with sharp lemonade powder and had then poured sweet cherryade all over her, making her fizz and zing all at the same time. It was all so confusing.

But then Richie went too far.

He rolled over on top of her and started sliding his hand up her thigh, seeking out her stocking top.

Lorna shoved him away.

Richie flopped over onto his back and raised his hands in surrender.

'All right, no need to get nasty.'

Lorna sat up and adjusted her dress, covering her knees demurely.

'I didn't mean to be so rough,' she apologised. 'I'm just a bit . . .'

'New at this?' he offered.

She nodded.

Richie grinned happily. 'We'll soon sort that out, girl.' He sprang easily to his feet. 'Come on, it's gone nine, anyway. We'd better get you home.'

As Richie paid their bus fares, Lorna noticed him eyeing the young bus conductress appreciatively. It made Lorna feel uncomfortable. She didn't like it – she wanted him only to have eyes for her; *she* was his girl, he'd said so.

'I'm leaving school in a couple of weeks,' Lorna said, flashing a glare at the blonde, who, it was obvious when you looked more closely, was just a bit of mousy old mutton done up as a peroxide lamb. 'Mum and Dad still think I'm going to secretarial college, but I'm not. I'm going to get a job, start earning myself some money.'

Richie half raised himself from his seat and slipped his change into his trouser pocket. 'What do you want to do that for?'

'There's loads of jobs around. Everyone says so.'

'I'm sure there are – if you really want one.'

'How do you mean?'

'If your mum and dad'll put up with you poncing about at college, why disappoint them?'

'Because I want to show them I'm not a little kid any more. The way they treat me sometimes, it's like I'm ten or something.'

Richie took his time lighting himself a cigarette. He thought she was a complete mug – who in their right mind wanted to work if they didn't have to? – but he wasn't going to say anything. Richie was planning to be nice to Lorna Wright, really nice. Not only did she have a body on her like a bit of ripe fruit just right for the plucking, but, from how she was acting, he reckoned she was a virgin as well. Plus, there was the added bonus of her old man being well-respected down the docks and therefore trusted with all sorts of information about the cargoes. Spending time being nice to him could prove very useful. Not like wasting his time on his useless Uncle Henry, who nobody trusted as far as they could throw him, or could even bother to give so much as a toss about. The dozy old bastard.

'And it'll be great,' Lorna went on. 'I'll be able to buy new clothes.' She paused, then added shyly, 'I could even get my hair done blonde.'

Richie picked a bit of loose tobacco off his bottom lip. 'I like blondes.'

'Right, I'll get it done then. Denise and me have already got a hair appointment tomorrow at Lola's, but I don't think I'll get it done there. I want it done properly.'

He gave her knee a little squeeze and Lorna beamed with happiness. *He was so nice.*

She might have felt a bit differently about Richie Clayton had she known that as soon as she had shown any signs of resistance to his advances, he had immediately put Plan B into operation.

Having got rid of Lorna, Richie hurried off to a side street in Limehouse to spend the rest of his evening with Li, a rather more willing little fifteen-year-old. Her parents would be far too busy dealing with the Friday night rush in their Chinese restaurant to realise that their daughter wasn't actually upstairs exercising her brains doing her maths homework, but was in fact just round the corner, up past the dock gates, getting up to something altogether more physical with Richie Clayton.

Chapter 2

By the time Denise Parker and Terry Robins reached Denise's house on the East India Dock Road, Lorna was already tucked up in bed over at Lancaster Buildings, but she wasn't anywhere near being asleep.

After having waved goodbye to Richie on the corner of Penfold Street, and then having wiped off every scrap of make-up in the glow of the streetlamp outside the entrance to the flats, Lorna had practically floated up to the top floor, she was so happy. Then she'd stuck her head round the living-room door, blown a kiss and called a hurried 'Night, Mum. Night, Dad' and had gone straight through to her bedroom – to lie in the dark with a grin on her face thinking dreamy thoughts about Richie Clayton.

And while Denise might not have been in bed yet, she was in just as dreamy a mood as her friend.

God, Terry was gorgeous.

'You've gone quiet, Den. You all right?' Terry was standing on the flight of steep stone steps that led to Denise's front door. She was standing on the pavement looking up at him. He had his hands on her shoulders, and was wondering – a bit desperately – what on earth he could say next without sounding like a total wally.

Denise said nothing; she just stared up into his fantastic, gold-flecked, hazel eyes.

Terry racked his brains: what *should* he say next? Something, anything, that wouldn't make him sound like a complete idiot; that wouldn't make her do the hundred-yard dash and leave him standing there like the twit he obviously was.

But why would she run off? This was *her* house. What the hell was wrong with him?

His mouth opened. 'Did you like the film?' he began, and immediately regretted it. He sounded so lame. But hang on . . .

She was smiling at him!

'I loved it,' she breathed. 'Sean Connery's one of my favourites. You know it was me who told everyone to go and see *Dr No* when it first came out? No one else at school had even heard of it till then. But *From Russia with Love* . . . ?' She sighed appreciatively. 'What a title, and what a film. Honestly, I really loved it. And I really loved being with you tonight, Terry. I really did.' As the words came burbling out of her mouth, Denise could have slapped herself round her stupid face. She'd terrify the poor sod, going on like that. He'd run a mile if she didn't cool it a bit. But hold up, what was this? He was looking really chuffed.

He was smiling at her!

'I'm ever so glad, Den, because I had a fantastic time as well. And you really make me laugh. You're not dopey like other girls.'

Denise's smile vanished. 'I make you laugh? And I'm not dopey? You make me sound like one of the bloody lads.'

'Well, you are. You're great.'

'I'll show you one of the lads.' With that, Denise pulled Terry down the steps and onto the pavement, shoved him backwards against the railings, grasped his head in her hands and proceeded – as she would describe her actions to Lorna the next day – to *snog his face off for him.*

'Still think I'm one of the lads, Tel?' she asked when she finally released him from her grip and allowed him to come up for air.

The best Terry could offer was a slow, bewildered shake of his head.

'You two look cosy.' It was Richie.

Just by looking at him, Denise immediately weighed up what he'd been up to that evening: his jacket was slung over one shoulder, his shirt was unbuttoned practically to his waist, and his usually immaculately Brylcreemed quiff was drooping to one side, but, most telling of all, his shiny drainpipe trousers were stained, creased and dusty.

He looked exactly like someone who had been rolling around on the grass in the park and had then finished off his evening by leaning up against the dirty brick wall of one of the local warehouses.

His dishevelment didn't seem to bother him.

He winked at Denise. 'Good job Auntie Phyllis can't see what you're up to, you dirty little cow. You've made me feel quite randy just watching you.'

'Piss off, Richie, you slimy pig,' she hissed back at her cousin.

'Any good, is she?' Richie asked Terry.

'You watch your mouth,' Terry snapped.

Denise put her hand on Terry's arm. 'Leave it, Tel, he's not worth it.'

Richie just laughed and swung past them up the steps.

Denise frowned as he closed the street door behind him. It was well past eleven, almost half-past. Lord knows what sort of an excuse Lorna had given her mum for getting in at this time of night. But, worse than that, judging from the state Richie was in, what would happen to Lorna if her dad found out what his precious little girl had been up to?

Late the next morning – a Saturday lie-in being taken for granted as an automatic teenage right – Denise went to collect her friend. She was hoping desperately that she'd managed to get them both hair appointments at Lola's Exclusive Ladies' Salon in Chrisp Street, because if she was going to carry on charming Terry Robins then she needed to look her very best.

She was surprised to find Lorna already waiting for her, bright-eyed and raring to go, at the bottom of the Buildings, and, from the look on her face, Denise guessed she must have not only got them the appointments they wanted, but that she had come up with one hell of an excuse about where she was last night, as she obviously wasn't in any kind of trouble indoors.

'You're looking very perky.' Denise narrowed her eyes suspiciously, and tucked her arm through Lorna's. It was all she could do to stop her from bouncing along the street like a five-year-old with a new rubber ball. Something *very special* must have happened last night.

'Why shouldn't I be perky?'

'I just thought your mum and dad might have had something to say about you going out when it wasn't even a Saturday night, and what with you getting back so late, and then all those bits of grass on Richie's clothes, and –'

'Late? What gave you that idea? I was in bed by a quarter to ten.' They dodged across the busy junction of the West and East India Dock Roads, with Lorna sniffing the traffic fumes as if they were the purest mountain air. 'And I feel fantastic.' She squeezed Denise's arm excitedly. 'Guess what. He only said he wants to see me again.'

'Right . . .' Denise replied slowly, but her mind was whirring round like the hands of an overwound clock.

Quarter to ten? That bloody cousin of hers.

Lorna was really sweet, everyone said so, a really nice girl, but she could be so naïve and trusting at times that it made Denise's mouth drop open. And now she had gone and fallen for Richie. He would run rings round her. It was obvious he had been out somewhere else last night, with someone else, and up to things that Denise – if not Lorna – could make quite a list of. If Richie hurt Lorna, Denise would kill him – with her bare hands if she had to.

Lorna was still bubbling away like a kettle on full gas. 'Only a couple more weeks to go, Den, then we're free. Just think, we'll be earning enough money to go somewhere decent to get our hair done.'

Denise wasn't in the mood to discuss the comparative merits of hairdressing establishments. 'Lola's is all right,' she said vaguely.

'I suppose it is, if all you want is a trim or something, but I'm thinking about going blonde, and I reckon I'd be better off having it done somewhere a bit more sophisticated. I don't want to end up looking like a tart; Richie would hate that.'

Denise stopped dead, pulling Lorna to a halt beside her. 'Lorna, you might well think this is nothing to do with me, but you are my best mate.' She fumbled around in her bag until she found her cigarettes. 'I don't want you getting mixed up with something you can't handle.'

She ripped angrily at the Cellophane wrapping that for some reason refused to be separated from the packet. 'I know Richie is a right smooth talker, a complete, total bloody charmer, but you've got to realise that when you go out with a feller, especially one as –'

'I'm really sorry, Den,' Lorna interrupted her, a soft smile turning up the corners of her full, pretty mouth. 'I should have realised something was up.'

She took the cigarette box from Denise and opened it with a single deft pull on the tab. 'You're annoyed with me for being so selfish. I've not asked how your date went with Terry last night.' Then she grinned. 'And I won't really be going that blonde, it's just that Richie likes –'

'For Christ's sake, Lorna.' Denise snatched the cigarettes back and flapped her hands in exasperation. 'I don't care if you dye your hair sky-blue flaming pink, and me and Terry got on just great, thank you very much, but it's you going out with Richie, that's what's worrying me. Richie isn't always what he seems. He's –'

'Den, please, don't let's start this again. I really don't want to fall out with you, especially not over a feller. I'm going out with Richie and that's that.'

Lorna couldn't wait for the lift; she took the stairs up to the top floor of the Buildings two at a time – ignoring the taunts of the huddle of little schoolkids, already bored despite it only being Monday afternoon, and the long summer holiday having begun only the Friday before – and came skidding to a halt at the end of the landing. She had no need to hunt around looking for keys, because, as always, the door had been left on the latch.

'Mum! Mum!' she called as she practically threw herself through the doorway. 'You'll never guess what. I've only gone and got it!'

Instead of Shirley Wright stepping out into the hall

from the kitchen, apron on and smiling broadly, Lorna's father appeared out of the back bedroom. He wasn't smiling, and he had his finger to his lips.

'Keep it down, babe. Your mum's having a little rest.'

Lorna felt a chill run down her spine. 'Is she all right?'

'Fine, love.' Joe's expression was strained as he tried to smile. 'Just fine.'

'So she's not –'

'She's fine.'

'I don't know what I'd do if she got ill again.'

'Stop worrying yourself, darling, she just never slept too well last night, that's all. So, when I had the chance to finish early, I took the rest of the afternoon off and came home and made a bit of a fuss of her.'

Lorna sighed with relief. 'We are so lucky having you looking after us,' she said, wrapping her arms round him and pressing her head against his broad, dockworker's chest.

'You daft 'apporth,' he said, stroking her hair, then holding her at arm's length so he could look into her face. 'Now, tell me, what's all this excitement about?'

'The job. I got the job.'

'That's really good news. It'll cheer your mum right up. I know we were disappointed, at first, when you changed your mind about going to college, but, if you're happy . . .'

'There's just one thing that'd make me even happier, Dad.' Lorna flashed him one of her brightest, best-daughter-in-the-world smiles. 'You don't think you could get Denise a job there as well do you?'

'Lorna, it's not that easy, babe.'

'I know, but we've never been apart before. And there's no point her asking her dad if he can do anything for her.'

Joe said nothing. He didn't have to. They both knew that Henry Parker didn't hold any sway down the docks. He was sort of nice enough, but more than a bit on the lazy side. He only had a job there in the first place because his father-in-law had spoken up for him when Henry had married his daughter, Phyllis. Not that his father-in-law ever had much time for him, especially once he saw how the bloke acted in his own home. Henry's philosophy – if he could actually be credited with anything as active as having a philosophy – was that he should do anything for an easy life, and that was usually whatever Phyllis wanted.

Although he had definitely not turned out the way his father-in-law would have chosen, like it or lump it, that was Henry Parker: a man who chose not only not to rock the boat, but who couldn't even be bothered to pick up an oar to make a bit of a splash. So, no, there was no point in Denise asking him to get her a job.

'Go on, Dad, please.'

Joe tipped her under the chin with one big, rough finger. 'If I say I'll see what I can do, will that satisfy you?'

'Thanks, Dad.' She kissed him with a loud smack on the cheek, backed away from him, paused a moment, then said all in a rush, 'I'm going out for a while, to find Richie, so I can let him know my good news.'

There, she'd said it. And the sky hadn't fallen in.

'Richie?'

'Richie Clayton.' Lorna stared down at her new black shoes, the ones her mum had bought her especially for the interview. 'I said I'd see him.'

'You said you'd see Richie Clayton?'

'Yeah.' She lifted her gaze until she was looking directly into her father's eyes. 'I know he's a bit older than me, Dad, but I have left school now, and I'm not a kid any more. And I like him ever so much, and, I promise, I won't ever make you and Mum ashamed of me. Not ever. You've brought me up knowing how important it is to be able to hold your head up, and I won't let you down. Really I won't.'

Joe Wright managed to hold his temper until his daughter had whirled her way out of the flat, and he had heard the lift door clank shut. He then stormed along the balcony to the slightly whiffy space by the rubbish chute, where he knew he would be alone.

He whacked the side of his fist hard against the wall.

Richie Clayton. Why on earth was she interested in that useless, disgusting, verminous piece of crap? What could a beautiful young girl like his little Lorna see in the likes of him?

Joe paced up and down in frustration. How the bloke earned a living was a mystery, but, however he did it, it certainly wasn't by hard work. He was always either in the Blue Boy, knocking back yet another pint as he went through the *Racing Post*, or he was hanging around the dock gates up to who knew what sort of mischief. Probably hoping to get some knocked-off gear from some of the unscrupulous dockworkers, whom Joe despised for giving the rest of them a bad name.

Lorna could have her pick of boys, decent boys, and she had chosen Richie Clayton. Him, of all people.

Hard as it had been for Joe to keep his mouth shut, passing an opinion on what he really thought of the bloke would probably not only have got him nowhere with his obviously besotted daughter, it might even have driven her closer to the little rat. Any other time, he would have asked Shirley what she thought they should do, but he couldn't worry her, not just now, so he'd had to play it by ear. He could only hope he had played it right.

Joe raked his fingers through his thick dark hair, tugging at the roots.

He would also have to hope that Lorna would realise, sooner rather than later, with a bit of luck, what Clayton was really like: a completely worthless, useless –

'Excuse me, mister.'

'Sorry, son.' Joe stepped away from the chute as a young boy tipped a bucket of vegetable peelings, tea leaves and various other bits and pieces of household detritus into the metal hopper. Probably doing it as an errand for one of the old girls along the landing, just as Lorna had done when she was his age. She'd always been willing to help anyone. She was such a good kid.

'Here, take this.' Joe dug into his pocket and handed the child a handful of coppers. 'Get yourself some sweets.'

'Ta!'

Joe watched as the boy walked away, examining his treasure. Lorna would be all right, he told himself. She wasn't only a good kid, she was a bright, clever girl, a daughter to be really proud of, a girl who knew right from wrong.

And anyway, if that flash boy Clayton even looked like so much as getting close to upsetting her, Joe would break every bone in his body.

While Joe fretted about Lorna, Richie, true to type, was propping up the bar of the Blue Boy, enjoying yet another free drink with the landlord, Malcolm Danes.

A squat, brawny man in his mid-forties, Malcolm was celebrating a deal he had just done with Richie, who was going to supply him with four cases of top-of-the-range whisky, at a special knock-down price, no questions asked.

Apart from him and Richie – it being only just gone five o'clock – the only other customer was an elderly, tobacco-stained man, who was nursing a pint of cloudy-looking mild and bitter and muttering darkly as he moaned his way through the early horse racing results.

Malcolm was polishing a mug with a blue and white cloth that looked as if it would add to the greasy smears rather than remove them, and puffing away on a scraggy little roll-up.

'Seen that pretty little brunette from over the Buildings again, Richie? That Joe Wright's girl?' As he spoke, his pathetic excuse for a cigarette waggled up and down between his lips.

Richie shrugged. 'Bit of a disappointment, to tell you the truth, Malc. I've not got anywhere with her. Frigid, I reckon. Don't know if I'll bother with her any more.'

'Frigid? Good-looking sort like her?' Malcolm, shaking his head at the pity of it, put the supposedly clean mug on the shelf above the bar. 'That's a crying shame. She's a very attractive young lady.'

'Think that's half the problem, because you know what they say: the ugly ones are more grateful.'

Malcolm smirked. 'You're right there. You know that barmaid – the one who comes in and helps out of a Friday night? She'll do more than pull a pint for you. She's up for it with anyone, she is.'

Richie grimaced. 'I never said I was desperate.'

'Just trying to do a pal a favour. After all, you've

scratched my back . . . And she's worth considering, at least. I mean, any port in a storm.'

'Tell you what, I'll pop in Friday and work me charms on her.' He swallowed the last of his drink. 'Because I do have an obligation to the rest of womankind to keep the old wedding tackle in good working order. And it wouldn't hurt to do the poor cow a bit of a favour, now would it? Call it my charity work.'

Malcolm laughed coarsely, and Richie, warming to the idea, began suggesting other unpleasantly insulting ways in which he might brighten up the life of the barmaid and women in general, when the door of the pub opened and Lorna Wright, flushed and happy, came rushing in and threw herself into Richie's arms.

Richie wouldn't have been more surprised if Malcolm had told him that the Friday relief barmaid had just been voted Miss Dock-Gate Beauty of 1963.

Richie pushed Lorna away from him. 'How did you know I was in here?'

'Your Chantalle told me.'

Richie slammed down his glass on the counter. 'That meddling little mare wants to keep her nose out. I don't expect birds to come round interfering when I've got business to do. Now if you don't mind . . .'

'I'm sorry, Richie, but I had to tell you my good news.' She nibbled excitedly on her bottom lip and smiled up at him. 'Guess what. I've only got a job!'

'Sod me, girl, you only left school on Friday.'

Malcolm affected deafness at Richie's reference to the presence of an underage girl in his establishment and became suddenly fascinated by the row of optics that lined the shelves behind him.

'I know, and I'm employed already. Brilliant or what?'

Malcolm turned round and flashed his eyebrows in an expression of mature, masculine solidarity with Richie, who, disloyally, returned the world-weary gesture to the landlord.

'If you say so, girl.'

'And you'll never guess where I'm going to work.'

'Surprise me. Woolworth's pick and mix? The knicker and vest counter at Pollard's?'

Lorna stepped further back from him, shook her head and frowned. Why was he being like this? 'No. I told you, even though I've not got shorthand, I'm really good at typing and I got top marks in commerce classes.'

Richie, leaning lazily on the bar, held out his empty glass to Malcolm for a refill. 'So you did.'

'Right. So that's why I got a job in the office.'

She paused waiting for him to say something. But he didn't say a word. He didn't even seem interested.

'Richie? Don't you want to know where I'm working?'

'I'm sure you're gonna tell me.'

Richie's eyes were practically rolling with boredom, while Malcolm simply smirked at the silly, daft tart.

Little did either of them realise, but Lorna was about to set down a royal flush that would knock Richie's arrogant hand for six.

'It's in the dock office, actually,' she said, unable to hide the hurt in her voice, 'doing paperwork to do with cargoes or something. I'm only a junior, but it's a start. A good start. Dad fixed it up for me.'

'The dock office, eh?' A grin was spreading slowly across Richie's handsome chops like dripping on a slice of piping-hot toast. 'Well, I think we ought to celebrate good news like that, darling.'

Lorna was thrilled by Richie's about-turn, but Malcolm had become suddenly flustered. He looked over at the grumpy old man, and gestured for Richie to move along the bar for a private word.

'Sorry, Richie, you know I can't serve her.'

'It wasn't a drink I had in mind, mate. Can't you see how happy she is? A good mood's a better aphrodisiac than that Spanish Fly stuff that Hoppy Cyril was selling out the back of his motor that time.'

Malcolm, not always the quickest off the mark, actually grasped his meaning immediately, and winked knowingly. 'Right, got yer. You'll be after a bit of how's-yer-father with the young lady.'

'You've got it in one there, Malc, but now you mention it, a quart of cider to take away wouldn't come amiss. Birds like all that sweet stuff, don't they?'

Lorna sat down on the grassy bank and brushed the grass clippings from the new plaid skirt her mum had bought for the interview to go with her new black shoes. Lorna had been really pleased with it – even more so when she had been allowed to wear it a full three inches above her knees.

Richie, who was stretched out next to her, reached across and pushed her gently onto her back.

'Lorna,' he whispered into her hair, 'do you like me?'

Lorna swallowed hard, her heart was racing. 'Of course I do.'

'So why won't you let me . . . you know?'

'I've told you: I'm too young.'

He rolled away, turning his back to her.

'Please, Richie. Don't be like that. Don't turn away

from me. I'm sorry, but I just can't. Not yet. I want to, but . . .' She touched him on the shoulder, so desperately wanting him to turn round and smile at her, to tell her it was all right.

To her delighted surprise, that's exactly what he did.

'It's all right,' he said, flipping over onto his stomach, and shuffling across until he was right next to her. 'I was just getting us this.' He held up the paper bag in which Malcolm had discreetly wrapped the cider. 'Thirsty?'

'What is it?' Lorna asked warily.

'Only a drop of apple juice; won't do you any harm. And it's lovely and sweet.' Richie unscrewed the cap, took a swig and then passed it to Lorna. 'Watch the bubbles,' he said, the picture of loving, boyfriendly concern, 'or they'll get up your nose.'

Gingerly, Lorna put the bottle to her lips.

'Go on,' he urged her. 'You must be dry on a lovely warm evening like this, and it's only right we celebrate your new job . . .'

With Richie taking tiny little sips and all the while encouraging Lorna to guzzle it down, it took little more than fifteen minutes to empty the whole quart bottle of extra-strength cider.

Unused to anything more lethal than the occasional sip of something at Christmas time, Lorna was completely sozzled. She puffed out her flushed cheeks and, hardly able to get her words out for giggling, finally managed to say: 'I feel full up with fizz.'

'Lie down then. Go on, stretch out on the grass and enjoy the last of the sun.'

Languidly, Lorna did as she was told. 'I feel all nice and sleepy,' she murmured.

'Good,' Richie breathed into her ear. 'Now close your

eyes and I'll stroke your skin, make you feel really relaxed.'

Lorna giggled again as Richie slowly undid the first of the buttons on her blouse. 'Say the park keeper sees us?'

'What if he does? I'm not doing anything. Well, not anything wrong.'

'But it is wrong.' Lorna was now grinning wonkily as Richie moved on to the second button. 'We're not even engaged.'

His hot breath on her neck and in her ear was making her feel quite woozy. Half-heartedly, she tried to wriggle away, but somehow she just couldn't find the energy; she felt as if she were stuck to the grass with the Cow Gum that they used to use in the infants' when they made cards with bits of shiny paper for Mother's Day.

'Did you used to make cards at school, Richie?' she asked, her eyelids lowering and rising like indecisive shop shutters.

Richie was too busy undoing his fly to answer her.

Phyllis Parker held up the knitting pattern, and studied it more closely in the last of the evening light that was slanting through the high windows into the big, basement kitchen. Why was it that the hardest bit of the pattern always had to have a bit of sticky tape over it so she couldn't read it properly? Perhaps she would buy some new ones. All hers were donkey's years old.

But she didn't know why she was even bothering thinking about it. Henry never noticed what he was wearing; she could have been making this new work jumper for him in fuchsia pink with silver ribbons round the edges and he still would have worn it.

Silly bastard.

But at least when she was busy knitting it meant she didn't have to pay any attention to whatever old nonsense from the paper he was muttering on about.

She had just figured out her plains from her purls, and was negotiating a particularly nifty bit of turning round the V-neck, when there was a loud bashing on the street door that almost had her dropping her stitches.

'For Christ's sake,' she bawled, 'can't they use the flaming bell? Or is that too sensible?'

Henry, who had been able totally to ignore the ridiculously loud knocking, was immediately brought to attention by his wife's furious hollering as swiftly as if he'd been set about with an electric cow prod.

He dropped the evening paper into his lap. 'Who do you think it is, Phyl?'

Phyllis jabbed her needles, hard, into the ball of wool – a bit of displacement activity that probably saved Henry from a serious head wound – and half rose from her chair. 'Do I have to do everything?' Her voice was menacing.

Henry, torn between indolence and fear of one of Phyllis's ruckings, gave in to the latter and hauled himself up the basement stairs to the street door.

'I've just come to borrow a cup of sugar,' Phyllis heard someone yelling from above. 'If you can spare it like. Till the morning.'

It didn't take Sherlock Holmes to work out that it was Mrs Elliot, the Parker's nosy old trout of a next-door neighbour. Nor, as she swung down the steps – particularly athletically for a woman who must have been knocking sixty-five – did it take much of a genius to work out that not only did she not have a cup in which to carry home her borrowed wares, but, from the look of her almost skinny frame, it was clear that not much of the stuff ever passed her lips anyway. And as she lived alone, whatever she wanted with a whole cup of the stuff obviously had more to do with her dedication to her hobby of nosing and interfering than with any culinary or sweetening interests.

'I see you're knitting,' she said to Phyllis, settling herself in Henry's chair.

'I'm off,' was Henry's relieved response to being usurped from his seat.

He grabbed his jacket from the hook behind the door. 'Got to see a man about a dog.'

'Make sure you bring me back a bottle of pale ale,' Phyllis hollered after him. She then stomped over to the long, scrubbed deal table that stood in the centre of the room, picked up the glass sugar basin from the painted tin tray that also held an earthenware teapot and an almost empty bottle of milk, and gestured with it to Mrs Elliot. 'How much do you need?'

Phyllis wasn't at all surprised by Mrs Elliot's reply.

'Actually, dear, it's not really sugar I'm after.'

'*No?*' Phyllis's sarcasm was wasted on Mrs Elliot; she was far too preoccupied for such subtlety. She was a woman with gossip to spread, poison to inject, and stirring to set into action. She was a woman with a mission.

'You see, Mrs Parker,' she began, a vision of concerned neighbourliness, 'it's what everyone's saying about your Denise.'

Phyllis bristled. *Denise?* Whatever nastiness she had been expecting the old cow to spout from out of those mean little lips of hers, it certainly hadn't been anything about one of Phyllis's own daughters. How dare she?

Phyllis slammed the sugar bowl back onto the tray and

stared at her neighbour, who, despite the bombshell of indiscretion she had just dropped, was still looking very nice and cosy, thank you very much, sitting happily in Henry's chair.

'And what exactly is it about my Denise –' slowly, Phyllis moved towards her – 'that is anything at all to do with anyone but this family, never mind the likes of you, you nosy old bitch?'

Mrs Elliot pressed her already narrow lips tightly together until they formed into a wrinkled little cat's bottom. Then she waggled her head indignantly. 'If that's your attitude –' she began, and went to stand up.

But Phyllis was across the room in a flash. She stuck out one of her meat-plate-sized hands and shoved the other woman back onto the chair.

'You were saying?'

Mrs Elliot couldn't resist; this was, after all, what she'd come to say. 'Your daughter, Mrs Parker, is seeing that Terry Robins.'

'And?'

'Well, you know what they say about these pop singers.'

Phyllis shook her head in wonder at the woman's stupidity. 'Don't be so ridiculous, you daft old haddock. The boy sings in a group with another couple of kids a few evenings a week round the local youth clubs. That hardly makes him Elvis the bloody flaming Pelvis, now does it? And I'd rather my daughter was seeing a nice respectable boy who wasn't hanging around street corners getting up to no good. Wouldn't you?'

Undefeated, Mrs Elliot flashed her scraggy eyebrows in a knowing gesture of *you just wait and see if I'm right* and then moved swiftly on to her next topic – no opportunity for muckraking ever being missed by the gossip supremo of Poplar E14.

'And talking about getting up to no good,' her voice was dry and whiny, 'that nephew of yours is getting himself a nasty sort of a reputation.'

Phyllis's usually soft, plump features hardened into stone. 'What did you say?'

'Well, whether what they're saying is true or not – and I'm sure it's none of my business – but I know if I was young Lorna Wright's mother –'

'Lorna? What's she got to do with anything?'

'Didn't you know?' Mrs Elliot smiled nastily. 'She's seeing your nephew. Loads of people have seen them. One night, she was coming out of the park with him, quite late, as a matter of fact. I know if I was her mother, I'd be very concerned. Very concerned indeed.'

Phyllis's mouth felt as if it was stuffed full of feathers. Richie and Lorna? Christ, she could only hope he was behaving himself, but she would rather have poked herself in the eye with one of her knitting needles than let this interfering witch even begin to think she was worried.

'You'd be concerned, would you, Mrs Elliot?' Phyllis could barely spit out the words. 'Well, that's where you're different from other people.' She leaned forward, grabbed hold of her neighbour – encircling the woman's forearm with a single hand – and moved so close to her that their faces were almost touching. 'Because, you see, Lorna's mother – my friend Shirley – knows, like everyone else round here, that we're a respectable family. Got it? And she knows that Lorna's just fine seeing my Richie. So why don't you just get your beaky, rotten snout out of our business, shift your skinny arse out of my old man's chair, and just piss off out of it? Before I chuck you out.'

Despite her rather abrupt ejection from her neighbour's kitchen, Mrs Elliot beamed with pleasure every single step of the way home, and for a good part of the rest of the evening too.

Mission accomplished.

'Do you know, Terry, I must admit I'm a bit surprised that you've not tried the *you would if you loved me* routine on me yet.' As she spoke, Denise was having a bit of difficulty trying to see her reflection in the tiny mirror stuck inside the flap of her handbag. She wanted to check just how badly in need of repair her make-up was before she went back inside. 'I mean, most fellers do.'

Terry, flushed with frustration, tucked his shirt back into his jeans. It had come adrift as he and Denise had been going for the world snogging record round the back of the boys' boxing club where the Spanners had been given permission to practise now that the school was closed for the summer holidays.

'I think more of you than that, Den.'

Denise looked up from her mirror. 'You meant that, didn't you, Tel? You really did?'

'Course I did.'

Denise stepped towards him, and began pulling his shirt back out of his jeans. 'Come here, you.'

'Don't, Den. I don't think I could stand the disappointment.'

'Who said you had to?'

'What? You mean you want to –'

'I *do* want to, but I don't intend to. Not yet anyway. But we will one day.'

'Don't mess around, Den.' Terry twisted away from

her. 'You don't know what it's like. You had me really going there. I thought –'

Denise took him by the elbow and forced him to turn round and look at her. 'Listen to me, Terry Robins, there's plenty of other things we can do, you know. Lots of really nice things I just know you'd really like.'

Terry's look of confusion turned to one of concern. 'How do you know so much?'

'I had a read of this book that Richie keeps in his bedroom.' Denise flashed him a saucy smile. 'And I'm telling you, it definitely wasn't a copy of the Boy Scouts' manual.'

'You awake yet, Shirl?'

Shirley Wright stretched her arms above her head and yawned. 'Hello, Joe. I had a smashing sleep. Everything all right?'

'Yeah. Fine. I brought you in a cup of tea. It's almost seven o'clock, and I didn't want you to sleep too long, or you won't be able to sleep tonight. And I've got some news about Lorna.'

While he was telling her the good bit, about Lorna's job, he was still thinking of a way to break the news about Lorna and that arsehole Richie Clayton.

'Don't fret, Joe.' Shirley was sitting in the living room now, finishing her second cup of tea. 'She's a sensible girl. She's left school and she's just having a bit of fun, that's all. Letting her hair down a bit. You wait and see: now she's got this job, she'll be meeting plenty of nice new people, and she'll soon forget all about Richie Clayton.'

Joe scratched at the dark shadow of bristles on his chin.

'She's asked me to see if I can get Denise Parker a job there too.'

Shirley handed Joe her empty cup, nodding at his gesture offering a refill. 'I know the rest of the family can be a bit much at times, Joe, but I've always liked Denise. She's all right.'

'Yeah, course she is. She's a good kid, always pleasant and that, and you know I've always liked her, but what with Richie being her cousin and everything . . .'

'Look, I know how protective you are, but it'll only be a phase she's going through. You remember what it's like being young.'

'Cheeky so-and-so.' Joe topped up her tea. 'I'm not even forty yet.'

'Almost, you are. Another couple of months, and it's all down hill.'

Joe sat next to her on the sofa and put his arm round her shoulders. 'You'll still think I'm the best-looking bloke in the whole of East London, though, won't you, Shirl?'

'Always did, and always will do. The best-looking of the lot.'

'And the luckiest.' He kissed her gently on top of her sleep-tousled, blonde head. 'You awake enough to fancy coming back to bed for a bit?'

'For a bit of *what* exactly, might I ask, Mr Wright?'

'That's for me to know and you to lie back and enjoy, Mrs Wright.'

Chapter 3

'Only me, darling.' Joe called out his familiar greeting as he pushed open the front door.

'I'm in here, love, in the kitchen.'

Joe stood in the doorway, watching his wife standing at the sink cleaning vegetables; she was looking over her shoulder at him, smiling. To anyone else it might have been just an ordinary, everyday domestic scene, but seeing her there made Joe's heart swell with love and happiness, just as it had over twenty years ago, when, as an exhausted nineteen-year-old dockworker, he had first set eyes on the pretty young bus conductress, and she had smiled that exact same smile at him.

She had taken his fare, as he made his way home on her bus after a hard day grafting in the hold of the *Resolution*. The ship had only just managed to limp its way home to the safety of the docks after surviving a relentless bombing raid in the Channel, and, when Joe had heard the crew's survival stories, he had thought them the luckiest buggers he had ever heard of. But once he had met Shirley he knew no one was as lucky as him, Joe Wright. He was the luckiest man in the world. Usually he would have walked back to his lonely digs in Stepney Green, saving the few coppers' fare for cigarettes, but not that night. After having slogged himself flat out with his gang – frantically unloading the desperately needed cargo of foodstuffs sent all the way from Canada, before anything more happened to spoil what was left in the hold of the badly damaged vessel – he was so exhausted he'd decided to take the bus. And that's when it had happened: the chance meeting with Shirley.

By the time he'd reached his destination he had not only discovered that Shirley Miller was, like him, an orphan, but that she too had lost all her close family – again like him – in the terrifying night raids over London. But it was more than coincidence, more than their shared experience of bereavement, and more than their urgent, human need for love and affection – heightened by the horrors and insecurities of wartime – that had brought the handsome, dark-haired young man, and the lovely, fair-haired young woman together. Theirs was an attraction that had been magical, almost magnetic. And it had increased as the years went by, maturing and mellowing into a deep and enduring love that had impressed even the most cynical and hard-nosed of their neighbours in Lancaster Buildings, the block where they had lived ever since their wedding day in 1944.

Even Doris Barker, a tough, no-nonsense woman, who did things that weren't exactly legal in order to earn her living and didn't give a monkey's who knew it, had taken a shine to the newlyweds. She had insisted, despite their protests, that they accept all kinds of household goods from her that they would have had no chance at all of getting for themselves, what with rationing and all the other shortages.

It was as if their love had been blessed from the day they had met, and Joe had been thankful for that blessing every single day of his life since.

He bent forward and kissed Shirley on top of her head. 'I'll just get myself a bath. It was sweltering down the docks today. Wouldn't surprise me if it storms later.'

'You go and have a nice soak. I put a clean towel in there earlier, and a fresh bar of soap.'

As he went through to the compact little bathroom that the council had recently installed during their refurbishment of the solidly built, but definitely rather elderly, tenement block, Joe was still chatting away to his wife.

'No Lorna yet? She'd already left the dock office when I came away.'

'You just missed her.' Shirley tossed a handful of chopped carrots into the pot as she shouted through to Joe over the roar of the Ascot heater as he filled the bath. 'She rushed in, all of a flap, got changed, and rushed out again. All in a matter of minutes. Never even had a sandwich or a slice of cake. Nothing.'

Joe's whole body stiffened. 'All right, was she?'

'Yeah. Fine. She said she'd have something later on. I didn't say anything – it is Friday, after all.' Shirley laughed, a happy, girlish sound. 'Out with Richie again, of course. All fluttery and jumpy she was. Kids, eh, Joe? I thought she'd be fed up with him by now. Must be, what, a couple of months she's been seeing him?' She laughed again. 'That's the trouble with good-looking young blokes with dark hair: they turn a girl's head for her.'

As he turned off the hot water, Joe nearly wrenched the Ascot off the wall.

Richie and Lorna were sitting in the dank, smoke-filled lounge bar of the Bridge House in Canning Town. Richie had chosen that particular pub because it was not only far enough away from home for people not to know how old – or rather how young – Lorna really was, but also because Richie had made arrangements to meet up with a couple of locals with whom he was going to do 'a bit of business'. When his business was completed, his intention was to round off the evening with Lorna in what had now become the usual way: him having a quick fumble of her breasts, followed by only slightly less speedy intercourse. This either happened in a quiet alleyway down by the river or in the shrubbery over in Victoria Park. The venue depended on where they had started the evening, what his plans were for the rest of the night, and whether he could be bothered – or not – waiting for the bus to take them to the park. Up until now, apart from the odd half-hour or so in various pubs, theirs had been an entirely al fresco relationship. Richie hadn't given any thought to what they'd do when the good weather broke.

If it had been up to Lorna she would have quite liked to have gone to the pictures one evening, or to one of the bowling alleys that were opening all over the place, or, best of all, to have gone dancing at the Ilford Palais or the Tottenham Royal – somewhere nice, where other girls went with their boyfriends. But she was too worried about upsetting Richie to say anything. She didn't want to frighten him off, not when she knew there were so many pretty girls after him. And anyway, now she'd let him 'do it', who else would want her? Richie was now the only one for her, and she had to accept it. Not that she'd have it any other way, of course; she idolised him, she just couldn't help wishing he'd pay her a bit more attention, be a bit kinder, nicer, more like the way he used to be. And not so angry.

She leaned her elbows on the beer-stained tabletop and ran her fingers through her hair. It's bleached stiffness still felt strange to her, but she knew she looked good blonde; Richie had said so himself – finally, when she'd asked him what he thought about it – and she was sure her mum and dad would get used to it eventually.

'I am so hot,' she said, pushing her fringe back off her face. 'And I'm only wearing this thin little dress and you've got a jacket on. Aren't you really stifled?'

Richie didn't reply. Uncharacteristically, he was concentrating on a story in the *Evening Standard*; Lorna had never even seen him so much as glance at anything other than the racing results before.

A middle-aged woman, sitting alone on the bench seat that ran along the wall next to their table, wasn't as unforthcoming as Richie; she had plenty to say on the subject of the uncomfortably sultry weather.

She nodded knowingly at Lorna. 'It'll be a storm coming. You get them in August. There'll be thunder and lightning soon. You just see if there ain't.'

'Maybe that'll cool things down a bit,' Lorna said as pleasantly as she could manage with sweat trickling down between her shoulder blades. She rolled her half-pint glass of cider across her forehead – she couldn't bring herself actually to drink the sweet, sticky liquid – but the glass felt as warm as her clammy skin.

'What're you talking to her for?' Richie spoke to Lorna without looking up from the paper. 'Can't you see she's an old brass?'

'Ssshh, Richie. Keep your voice down,' hissed Lorna. 'She'll hear you.'

'Good, I hope she does.' Richie gripped the paper tightly; he was annoyed. He didn't like anyone correcting him or telling him what he should do. 'Perhaps then she'll piss off. I don't want her sort hanging around while I'm having an important meeting.'

Knowing that this might be her only opportunity to speak to Richie – from experience she knew he could quite easily decide to go off with his 'business' colleagues and leave her to find her own way home – Lorna was about to open her mouth to say the words she had been rehearsing all week, but, at the last minute, good sense got the better of her.

'What are you reading?' she asked instead, in a soft, wheedling voice that she hoped would placate him before she said what she really wanted to say. She couldn't have him losing his temper, not tonight, not when she needed to talk to him about something so important, something that would change the increasingly uncaring way in which he treated her. Something that just had to.

For some reason, her question seemed to please him. He immediately brightened up, snapped open the paper and held it out so she could see what he'd been so engrossed in.

She was taken aback for a moment – why did he seem so pleased she was interested? – but she wasn't complaining. 'Let's see then.'

'The Great Train Robbery.' He spoke in a low, awed tone, practically drooling with admiration as his eyes flicked over the two-page spread, complete with diagrams and photographs of the crime scene. 'Over a million quid, they reckon. Maybe double that. It's fantastic.'

Lorna frowned. 'Fantastic? But didn't they bash that poor man's head in? How is that fantastic?'

'A million quid, Lorna. Maybe more. Are you mad or something? Think about it. A million.'

'No, I can't help it, Richie, I just don't think it's very nice. And anyway, why should I be interested in what a bunch of crooks have been up to?'

She stared down at her lap. She was such a hypocrite. She was passing Richie information from the office, and no matter what he said about it being expected that everyone in the docks would have a 'bit of a fiddle', she still felt like a criminal. But he had been so persuasive, and so nice to her the first time, and then after that it was too late; he said he'd tell everyone what she'd done if she didn't carry on . . .

She gulped. Still, Richie nicking the odd case of Scotch was the least of her worries.

'Anyway, I've got other things on my mind.'

Very deliberately, Richie closed the newspaper, folded it into squares, and then grabbed Lorna by the wrist. 'You have, have you? Now, let's see, what sort of things would they be?' He made a big deal, a real pantomime, out of pretending to try to think what they were. Then he grinned, an ice-cold, threatening grimace.

'Things like being a hypocrite?'

Her eyes widened; it was as if he could read her mind.

'Things like all that stuff you tell me about what's going on at work: what cargoes are coming in and that? Things like when you phone me when the dock coppers have gone for their –' he winked and tapped the side of his nose – '*unofficial* break and have left the coast clear? They the sorts of things you've got on your mind, are they, little Miss Goody Goody Lorna Wright?'

'Richie, please . . .' She felt so ashamed; she'd only told him those things because she loved him, because he'd told her he'd leave her if she didn't. She hadn't meant to do anything wrong, and then, when she said she wouldn't do it any more, he'd told her what he'd do to her if she stopped giving him the information. And now things had got completely out of hand and there was no way out.

'Please, you're hurting me.'

'I'll hurt you even more if you get saucy with me again.'

The middle-aged woman coughed loudly and stared deliberately at Lorna's reddening wrist.

Richie stared back at the woman, let go of Lorna, and then shoved her arm away from him as though he was discarding a particularly disgusting piece of rubbish.

'Just don't start, Lorna. OK?'

She nodded. 'OK.'

'And?'

She didn't understand.

'How about saying you're sorry?'

'Sorry.'

'Say it nicer.'

'You all right, dear?' It was the middle-aged woman again.

'Shut your trap, you interfering old bag,' Richie snapped at her.

Lorna just wanted all this to stop. 'I'm fine, honestly. Thank you.'

'That's better,' Richie said, and, completely unexpectedly, kissed her gently on the cheek.

Lorna stared at him. What was going on now? It was as if the wind had changed and his temper had spun right round from grim to sunny.

She wasn't confused for long. Two well-dressed, powerfully built men were making their way over to the table: Richie was on show to people he thought were worth impressing.

'Hello there.' Richie stood up and shook both men

warmly by the hand. 'This is Lorna, a friend of mine.' He smiled down at her. 'A very special friend, eh, Lorn?'

She managed to smile back at him. Christ, it was so hot, and she was beginning to feel quite dizzy. 'Pleased to meet you.' The words came out as a whisper. Was she really going to have to talk to these people?

'Nice to meet you and all, love,' growled the smaller of the two men. Then, without missing a beat, he said to Richie: 'Let's talk in private.'

Despite being treated as if she no longer existed, Lorna couldn't have been more relieved when Richie and the two men went over to a table in the far corner of the bar, the bigger of the two following them, protecting their backs.

She could hear Richie laughing – too loudly – almost every time the smaller man said something, but she couldn't make out any of the words; it was as if their conversation was going on a thousand miles away.

'You sure you're all right?' It was the woman again. 'Only you're looking a bit peaky, sweetheart.'

Slowly, Lorna lifted her head. 'I'm not feeling that good, to tell you the truth.'

'Can't blame you,' said the woman, sliding along the bench until she was sitting right next to Lorna. 'It's sweaty enough to melt the rouge right off your kisser.' She took out a grubby-looking, screwed-up handkerchief and wiped it across her forehead, leaving a pasty trail of bare flesh in her otherwise bright orange face.

'I can tell you, I'm glad I never put on that bloody panty girdle of mine tonight. I'd have been sitting here in a pool of liquid blubber.'

Lorna really didn't need that image being put into her mind. Offering a shadow of a smile to the woman, she rose unsteadily to her feet and found her way over to where Richie was still howling with exaggerated laughter.

'Sorry to interrupt you,' she said to the tabletop, her voice wobbling, 'but this heat's really getting to me. I think I'd better get off home.' She glanced at Richie to check his reaction, and noticed the briefest flash of anger before he returned to his teeth-baring grin. 'If you don't mind, that is,' she added politely.

'Course you'd better get off home,' he said, copying the actions of the other two men, who had stood in deference to the presence of a lady. 'Course you had.'

'Would you like me to get you a cab, love?' asked the smaller of the two men.

'I was just going to say that,' Richie said, but then hurriedly calculated that he would be expected to hand over the fare to her. 'But you enjoy a little stroll of an evening, don't you, Lorn?'

'Yeah, that's right, I do. And thanks all the same, it's ever so kind of you, but I do need a bit of air.'

'Do you want Archie here to see you home?' asked the smaller man, looking first at Richie then at Lorna. 'Can't be too careful, a pretty girl like you walking about alone of a night.'

Lorna didn't have to look at Richie to imagine how he was panicking about what she might say next.

'Honestly,' she said. 'I'll be fine. Thanks again, but I've got plenty of money to get a cab if I want one.' Then she added, 'Richie always gives me cab money if he knows he's going to be doing business, and his meeting might go on a bit late.'

Richie beamed with pleasure as both of the men nodded their approval at the lie Lorna had just told them.

'So, if you don't mind, I'll be getting off.' She lowered her chin again and said, 'See you then, Richie.' She actually meant it as a question, but she knew she shouldn't push it.

'Yeah, see you, Lorn.' Richie didn't notice the men frown in response to his casual dismissal of his girlfriend.

Outside the Bridge House it was no cooler, but at least there wasn't the heavy fug of cigarette smoke and beer fumes hanging in the air.

Lorna leaned back against the wall and took a deep breath. It wasn't exactly a million miles that she had to walk, but she knew it was going to be a real effort. She just didn't feel up to it, especially with this energy draining humidity, but the thought of getting on a stuffy, crowded bus made her feel even worse.

As Lorna was making her sticky, lonely way home, Terry and Denise, oblivious of the oppressiveness of the rising temperature outside, were generating some heat of their own, entwined as they were, in one another's arms, snogging in the back row of the Mile End Odeon.

As far as Terry Robins was concerned, Elizabeth Taylor, up there in front of him on the big silver screen, draped in all her Hollywood-styled Cleopatra finery, doing her very best seductive stuff for Richard Burton, couldn't hold a candle to Denise Parker. Denise was flaming gorgeous. Terry was just chuffed he'd picked such a long film.

They were still too busy – wrestling and writhing in an ever more passionate embrace – to even notice the tragic ending. The only tragedy for Terry and Denise was that the lights had come on and they were being told by a self-important usherette, who had the classic look of a bulldog chewing on a wasp and obviously no romance in her soul, that it was time for them to leave their cosy, velveteen-covered nest.

Still, there would be plenty of opportunities to stop for a snog on the way home.

With a sarcastic smile at the bulldog, Terry draped his arm around Denise's shoulder. Denise responded by putting her arm around his waist and tucking her hand into his back pocket. Then they left the squint-inducing bright lights of the auditorium, and joined the rest of the home-going crowd in the softer lit street outside the cinema.

'Happy, Den?'

'Yeah.' She leaned her head against his shoulder. 'But do you know what would make me even happier?'

Terry really hoped he did, but he thought he'd better ask before he jumped to any potentially embarrassing conclusions.

'What's that then?' he asked, pulling her closer to keep her safe as they crossed over to Burdett Road.

'I wish Mr Wright could have got me a job with Lorna.'

'Aw.' Terry tried to hide his frustration at her answer, and tried even harder not to show that what he had been really hoping for was Denise suggesting that he should sneak her up to his bedroom and –

Sod it. Be nice. He had to keep reminding himself that it was probably just as tough for Denise.

Probably.

'You really disappointed?' he asked, brushing the top of her head with his lips.

'Yeah. I know it sounds childish, but I am. And it's

not because I don't like working in the City; I do. It's a good job, and the money's decent and everything. But if I was in the dock office at least I'd get to see something of Lorna. I really miss her, Tel. All she ever seems to do lately is go off with Richie or hang around her flat waiting for him to call. Honestly, Terry, I know he's my cousin, but he's, well, horrible. She shouldn't be involved with him.'

'Don't get upset, Den.'

'I won't,' she said with a sad little sniff. 'But he *is* horrible.'

If Denise could have seen her friend at that precise moment, her language would not have been quite so restrained when talking about Richie Clayton – cousin or no cousin.

It wasn't bad enough that Lorna felt so rough or, worse, so badly treated by Richie, but now the heavens had it in for her as well. They had opened their gates and were emptying their overfull buckets all over her.

Raindrops the size of shilling pieces soaked right through her as she trudged, exhausted, along the hot pavement. Her carefully styled hair was now stuck flat to her head and the sides of her face, her thin cotton dress had moulded itself to her body like a plaster cast on a broken limb, and the strappy patent sandals that Richie had said were sexy were cutting into her toes like sandpaper that had been especially sharpened for foot-torturing purposes.

And it wasn't as if the rain was even cooling her down.

The sky was boiling over, and every few seconds there was an ominous rumbling of low, faraway sounds that gathered into loud, metallic cracking crashes of thunder and wild zigzags of orange, yellow and blue lightning that ripped their way down through the blackness of the sky, making Lorna jump and cringe and blink.

And cry.

She didn't have a hankie, not even a screwed-up old tissue in the bottom of her shoulder bag. So her tears and snot mixed in with the rain on her already dripping wet face, just adding to all her other humiliations.

She felt so abandoned, so sorry for herself, it was all she could do to stop herself from sitting down in the middle of the road and waiting for a passing lorry to do the decent thing and put her out of her misery.

How had this happened? Richie had been so lovely when she'd first started seeing him, and now he was being so vile to her. But she really cared for him. Perhaps if she explained that to him . . . ?

Of course, that must be it: he just didn't understand how much she cared. That's what was wrong. She'd just talk to him and explain.

Suddenly everything didn't seem so bad. It was like her mum always said – things are never as bad as they seem.

She could almost feel a smile coming on.

'Oi! Lorna! Drowned-rat features!'

Lorna looked round and saw Denise's younger sister, Chantalle, sheltering in a shop doorway with a group of boys. They were all smoking and laughing. They made Lorna think of the troop of screeching, teeth-baring monkeys she had been so frightened of at the zoo when she had gone there with her dad. She had only been about seven; her mum had been taken into hospital for the first time and she and her dad hadn't known what to do with themselves. It wasn't a memory she treasured.

'All right?' Lorna greeted Chantalle.

'Where's Richie?' Chantalle asked from the dry haven of the doorway. 'Finally dumped you for someone who doesn't moan all the time?'

'Sorry?'

Chantalle flashed her teeth in a grin that would have done justice to the most aggressive troop-leading baboon warning off would-be attackers, and said to one of the boys, 'She's been seeing my cousin. He says all she does is whine and moan. Poor bloke can't do anything right as far as she's concerned. He'll be relieved to be shot of her.'

Lorna took a few cautious steps nearer, and stopped a couple of feet from the doorway.

'That's not fair,' she said quietly, as if only Chantalle could hear her. 'You shouldn't tell such spiteful lies. You know Richie wouldn't say things like that about me.'

'Oh, wouldn't he?' Chantalle took a drag of her cigarette and blew the smoke directly at Lorna, who was now oblivious of the pelting rain. All she wanted was to set Chantalle straight, but she didn't give her a chance.

'You tried smoking, didn't you, Lorna?' Again the grin for the benefit of the boys, her peeled-back lips contorting her otherwise pretty face. 'He told me you couldn't even get that right. And as for doing the other, he reckons you're a joke. Like doing it with a rag doll without the stuffing.'

Lorna tried to swallow, but her mouth was too dry, and she just made a strange, strangulated sound that came out as a sort of whimpering gulp.

'You can get pills for that,' said one of the boys, setting the group off into yet another fit of laughing.

Lorna, with her cheeks burning and her eyes stinging with tears of shame and despair, walked away without another word.

'So who's she, Chantalle?' asked the boy who had given the medical advice.

'Some dopey tart.' Chantalle stubbed out her cigarette with an unnecessarily vicious grind of her heel, and stared along the rain-slicked street, watching the slowly retreating figure of Lorna Wright.

'You seemed to know her well enough.'

'She's my sister, Denise's, mate, if you must know. Don't know what our Richie sees in a pathetic cow like her, except she works in the dock office. I reckon he'd fancy any old dog if she could get him in there.' Chantalle gave a nasty little laugh. 'Way she goes on you'd think he was bloody in love with her or something.'

One of the other boys nudged Chantalle in the ribs. 'Here, he never said those things about her, did he? You made them all up.'

'So?'

'So you fancy your own cousin.'

'I do not, Martin O'Brien.'

'Yes you do. Eeuggh! You're weird, Chantalle, really weird.'

By the time Lorna reached the Buildings she was desolate; her dreams had been shattered.

She wasn't even worried about what her dad would have to say when he saw her in such a state. Well, not until she was standing outside her actual flat, and then she did begin to panic.

She eased open the front door and crept along the hall, intending to slip into her bedroom for some quick emergency repairs, before facing her parents with a story that she would have to come up with while changing into something dry, explaining why her hair was soaked and why Richie hadn't sorted out a way for her to get home without getting wringing wet.

The real answer, of course, was that he had abandoned her.

Lorna couldn't help herself; she stood in the hall weeping pitifully.

'Lorna!' Shirley appeared from the living room. She held her arms wide. 'Whatever's wrong, darling? How long have you been standing out here?'

Lorna fell, wailing and sobbing, into her mother's embrace like a petrified four-year-old trying to hide away from a fearsome combination of the night terrors, a wet bed, and the bogey man leaping out of the wardrobe.

'Let's get you dried off and a nice hot drink.'

Lorna was rooted to the spot. She shook her head anxiously. 'I don't want Dad seeing me like this. He'll go mad and –'

'Don't fret.' Shirley held her daughter close and smoothed her dripping hair from her forehead. 'Your dad popped over the Blue Boy for a pint. You come with me.'

When the men had finished their business with Richie, they left the Bridge House to keep an appointment elsewhere. Richie had been so chuffed with the outcome that he had actually gone outside to wave them off, like a fond auntie bidding farewell to two of her favourite nephews. He had watched enviously as they disappeared into the filthy night in a sleek, brand-new Daimler that purred away from the kerb like a gorgeous black cat, sending sprays of water shushing high into the air. He'd have a car like that one day. And a minder.

He was now sitting alone at the bar of the crowded pub, a whisky in one hand and a panatella in the other, looking as if he'd scooped the Littlewood's jackpot. And in a way he had. The smaller of the two men was the owner of a string of private – that is to say unlicensed, and therefore illegal – drinking clubs that ran right across East London from Shoreditch to East Ham, and he had struck a deal guaranteeing to take all the knocked-off spirits that Richie could lay his hands on. It was exactly the direction that Richie had been longing to move into.

This was his first step towards the *Big Time*.

And he'd get there, he just knew he would; stuff Malcolm Danes and his occasional cases of Scotch. It was like he was doing Richie a favour or something, taking a dozen bottles here and there. He could get his own hooky supplies from now on. Richie would be far too busy. And who knew where it might lead.

He could be a face, a face to be reckoned with. A face no one would dare mess around with. Blokes would point him out in the street and say they wanted to be like him. Say they were afraid of him. Show him respect.

'Excuse me, anyone sitting here?'

Richie blinked out of his reverie to see a petite, smiling brunette with twinkling green eyes, pointing to the empty bar stool beside him.

She was young-looking; Richie liked that in a bird. He stood up politely, in a conscious imitation of his new business partner's manners. 'Please,' he said, nodding towards the stool, and, taking her hand, helped her up.

She smiled again.

Christ, she was sexy. She was what, sixteen? Maybe even younger under all that make-up. Very nice. And a tasty pair of knockers into the bargain.

Richie bought her a vodka and lime.

'There you are . . . ?'

'Pauline. Pauline Carver.'

'There you are, Pauline Carver.'

She sipped the drink with practised ease, flapping her lashes at him across the rim of the glass.

He was still standing up, leaning with one elbow on the bar, and with his body turned into her – very close, intimate. He flashed her a smile in return. 'I think it might be worth my while coming over Canning Town way a bit more often, Pauline Carver.'

She giggled, very prettily. 'I don't come from Canning Town. I was just over here with some of my mates.' She gestured to a group of girls roaring with laughter at the suggestive antics of the singer and the three-piece band crammed onto the little stage.

'I come from Poplar, not that far from you, as a matter of fact.'

'You know where I live?'

'All the girls know where you live, Richie.'

Richie glowed with a combination of pride and a few too many Scotches. 'And you know my name.'

'Course I do. Why do you think I came over to try my luck? I'm the sort of girl who has a very particular taste in fellers. I don't go with just anyone, you know.'

Christ, she made a change from that clingy bloody Lorna.

Lorna – what a bloody fly in the ointment that one

was turning out to be, but he knew he had to keep her sweet: she was his route to the cargoes of booze, tobacco and all sorts of other good things he needed to supply his new customer; she was his route to money and success. A route he was determined to take. A route, in fact, he was already on.

Richie Clayton was on his way.

Joe stood outside on the landing, shaking his jacket over the balcony to get off the worst of the rain.

'Sorry I was a bit longer than I said, Shirl,' he called over his shoulder. 'I waited for the storm to let up a bit. Never seen anything like it. That lightning was like a firework display.'

Shirley came out of the living room and stood in the hall. She tipped her head towards their daughter's bedroom, the door was ajar, and the light was off.

'Come through so we can talk without waking Lorna,' she said.

He followed her into the sitting room and they cuddled up on the sofa.

'Well?'

'I think Lorna's split up with Richie Clayton. Judging by the state she was in, they must have had one hell of a row.'

'Thank Christ for that.'

'Joe!'

'I didn't mean that the way it came out. You know I didn't. I don't want to see her upset, but I'm just relieved she's shot of him, that's all. Good riddance, if you ask me.'

But Lorna wasn't asleep, she was wide awake, and, in the

dark silence of her room, she could make out every word of her parents' conversation.

She lay there, staring blankly up at the ceiling, tears trickling down her cheeks and into her ears, listening to them.

When her mum had questioned her earlier, she hadn't been able to bring herself to tell her that they hadn't argued, that Richie just wasn't interested in her any more, and that Chantalle had told her exactly what Richie really thought about her. He wasn't even interested enough in her to waste his energy having something as passionate as a row.

Not now she'd let him do those things to her. The things she'd promised her mum she would never do until she was sure she had really found the right one, and not the first good-looking bloke who came along and smiled at her and gave her stupid bloody cider to drink.

But she hadn't been drunk the second time. Or the third. Or the . . .

She covered her face with her hands. What could she do now? If her mum ever found out what she'd been up to, she'd feel so let down by her, so ashamed of her. And it would be sure to make her ill again. Dad was always saying they mustn't do anything that might upset her, that they had to look after her if she was going to keep well.

Lorna turned over and buried her head in the pillow to muffle her sobs.

Eventually she fell asleep – exhausted, humiliated and scared. She had done something very, very stupid, and now she would have to pay the price.

Chapter 4

Instead of just walking into the Wrights' flat with her usual, cheery, 'Morning, everyone, it's only me,' Denise took a deep breath, pushed the door right back on its hinges, and called – tentatively for her – along the hall: 'I've come to see, Lorna, Mrs Wright. Is she up yet?'

Denise was acting oddly because she knew this wasn't any ordinary Saturday morning. Actually, she knew by the sick feeling in her stomach, it was going to be a totally bloody awful one.

Why couldn't she have just stayed in bed, all nice and cosy and tucked up in the blankets, dozing in and out of sleep, listening to the disc jockeys yammering away on the radio?

Because she was Lorna's best friend, that was why, and because this was the least she owed her.

Owed her? Did she really owe Lorna anything?

Course she did, selfish cow. Lorna had been a good mate to her, a really good mate, so how could she even think about not being there to help her deal with all this?

Whatever *all this* might be.

Denise was so wrapped up in her own thoughts as she stood there at the front door that when a reply came, she jumped with as much surprise as if she had just been goosed by someone whose nails could have done with a good trim.

'What? I only . . . I never meant . . .'

'What's got you going, Miss Parker?' Shirley called out

to her, with laughter in her voice. 'You sound just like a young woman with a guilty conscience. Fancy telling me what you've been up to?'

'Sorry, Mrs Wright,' Denise called back, still not making a move away from the front door.

'Don't hang around out there, love. Come through. Lorna won't be long.'

Denise shuffled into the kitchen. It wasn't only the three gin and bitter lemons that Terry had sneaked her from his mum's cocktail cabinet the night before that were befuddling her mind and playing around with her sense of balance, it was the terrible tension of knowing *something was very wrong*.

She tried a wan, and, she guessed, a rather unconvincing, smile.

Shirley responded to Denise's patently feeble efforts with a broad and very genuine beam of welcome – anything to try to lighten things up a bit – while Joe, who was sitting at the table like a bad advert for family breakfast togetherness, merely nodded. He was polite enough, but considerably cooler than Denise was used to when she came round to the Wrights' flat. In fact, after his initial brief nod, he ignored her completely and just got on with demolishing his plate of bacon, eggs and tomatoes.

'Lorna's just finishing in the bathroom,' Shirley said, checking her reflection in the small, plastic-framed mirror over the sink, as she put on her lipstick and examined her T-area – a recently learned of target for concern from one of Lorna's fashion and beauty magazines – for unwanted shine.

'There's plenty of tea in the pot, Den, but you'll have to help yourself; I'm off to the hairdresser's in about one minute.'

Shirley's Saturday wash and set – complete with scalp-spiking rollers, dehydrating, baking hot, space helmet hair dryer, and lethal-smelling chemicals – was as much part of her weekly ritual as was painting her nails pearly pink, just as it was for many of the women who lived in Lancaster Buildings, and, for that matter, throughout the whole of the East End.

Regardless of whether you had the money to afford luxuries such as hairdos or just enough to pay your electric bill, looking nice, being smart, and showing that you cared about yourself, counted for a lot in their community.

In any one of the street-corner salons, with their often surprisingly fancy names over the door, a woman could have a cup of instant coffee, a morning's entertaining gossip, and the opportunity to be transformed into a beautifully coiffed sophisticate – all for as little as seven shillings and sixpence, with a tip thrown in if you were feeling a bit flush.

And it was money well spent; with the help of a hairnet, a couple of Kirby grips, and a bit of strategic lacquering, your 'do' could easily last the week round, until the whole process began all over again.

'Your hair always looks lovely, Mrs Wright.'

'Thank you, Denise. You know, since it went all thin that time,' she said, referring lightly to one of the aftereffects of the treatments for her illness, 'I appreciate being able to look after it all the more now.'

'What do you think of Lorna going blonde then?' Denise, feeling more relaxed, due to the warmth of Shirley's welcome, sat down at the table across from Joe, and considered helping herself to a bit of his fried bread. 'I think she's really brave,' she went on, eyeing the eggy plate longingly. 'I'd never have the guts to do something as drastic as that.'

Joe muttered something dark and scornful under his breath, clattered his knife and fork down onto his plate, and snapped open his *Daily Mirror* – the perfect screen for a man who didn't even want to begin getting involved in such a conversation.

Denise was glad her usual impetuosity hadn't got the better of her, and that she'd left the fried slice well alone: the mood he was in, he'd have sawn off her fingers with the bread knife.

Shirley took a moment putting her lipstick away, flashed a quick glance in her husband's semi-obscured direction, and then took another moment to ponder Denise's question.

'I think,' she said thoughtfully, 'that pretty girls like you and Lorna – especially at your age – can get away with just about anything. And I also think that it's at your age that you have to try out all sorts of things. I just hope neither of you tries out anything too daft, that's all.'

'What do you mean, *too daft*?'

It was Lorna. She had appeared in the kitchen doorway behind her mother, and was now hovering there, all hooded eyes and tight lips, like the angel of doom about to claim a soul.

'All right, grumpy drawers,' said Denise, a bit too brightly, and with a pathetically false attempt at a light little laugh. 'Don't go tying yourself up in knots. We were only talking about doing our hair.'

'That's right,' smiled Shirley. 'I was just hoping Denise wasn't going to spoil that gorgeous auburn hair of hers.'

Denise pulled a face, putting on what she thought would be a suitable reaction of: '*What, this old hair?*'

mixed with *'I know, it really is gorgeous, isn't it, and I'd be mad to even think about touching it.'*

Lorna looked infinitely less enthusiastic about anything either of them had to say; she just stood there in gloomy, thin-lipped silence.

'Well, that's me finished; can't stand around chatting with you girls any longer or I'll be late.' Shirley hoiked out her bag from under the kitchen table and checked she had her purse and keys.

'Tell you what, you two, you wouldn't be a pair of loves and get a bit of shopping in for me, would you? Only Joe's taking me to the flicks tonight, aren't you, sweetheart? And then we're going round to the New Friends for a Chinese, and I quite fancy getting myself a dress to wear.'

There was absolutely no response of any kind from Joe, who was still hiding behind his paper. This was despite the fact that the headlines on all of the first eight pages were yelling, yet again, about the latest revelations in the Profumo affair. This time the sub-editors were being jaw-droppingly shocked about an incident involving a supposedly aristocratic man, stark naked except for a mask, acting as a waiter at a posh dinner party.

Such a juicy story would usually have had Joe tutting angrily about the spoiled upper classes and the arrogant ways of the Establishment, while Shirley hid her shocked giggles and tried to be kind about human frailty, and the girls skittered off to guffaw about it in secret in the seclusion of Lorna's bedroom. But there just wasn't the will for that sort of behaviour on this particular Saturday morning.

'I'd really appreciate it, girls, if you would pick up a few bits for me. If I go to look for an outfit I just won't have time to get anything in for Sunday dinner.'

'Course we'll do the shopping, Mrs Wright,' chirped up Denise, all jolly Girl Guide helpfulness. She had to say something or, the way things were going, they'd all be in tears or having a fight. 'We've got nothing else to do, have we, Lorn?'

'No,' her friend answered flatly. 'Nothing. I'll go and get my shoes.'

As soon as her daughter was out of the room, Shirley leaned close to Denise and said quietly: 'I'm so glad you're doing this. I've got plenty of time to do the shopping, but Lorna really needs to get out of the house for a couple of hours, have something to do, and have someone her own age to talk to. She's so upset about Richie.'

Upset over Richie? Denise might have guessed, but all she said was an enigmatic 'Right', as though she knew all about it.

Joe's reaction was for his nostrils to flare and his chest to heave – the mature stallion facing a challenge from a young mustang – then he grunted nastily, snapped his paper shut and folded it into tight, angry little squares. 'I'm going round to see Harry Martin.'

'So, are you going to tell me what's wrong, Lorn, or have I got to carry on playing Twenty Questions?'

The girls were standing in the queue at one of the greengrocer's stalls in Chrisp Street market, the one they had been specifically instructed by Shirley to patronise; loyalty, even to the person who supplied your vegetables, was important to Shirley Wright.

'Nothing's wrong with me, Den.' Lorna's voice was

dull, unconnected. 'I don't know why you keep going on about it.'

'Well, I came round first thing this morning, Lorna – instead of having my Saturday lie-in, I might add – because I'm worried about you, and –'

'Worried about me? Why?'

'I'll tell you, shall I?' She didn't wait for an answer. 'Because Chantalle took great pleasure in staying awake until I came in last night. And why did she stay awake? So she could tell me, at great length let me add – and I'd had a few drinks and just wanted to get my head down – that she'd seen you walking along, all by yourself, right up the other end of the East India Dock road. In the pouring rain. No, not in the rain. During a bloody storm that would have driven flipping ducks indoors.'

'She didn't mention what colour knickers I had on, by any chance, did she? The nosy mare. Hasn't she got anything better to do with her time?'

'Look, Lorna, I don't want to make a big deal out of all this. Just tell me you're all right. I know what fellers are like, especially ones like our Richie. I mean, it's bad enough with Terry. He's as soft as butter, but I've still had to be right careful with him. He's tried it on, in his own quiet way, to persuade me to . . . you know . . . have a bit of the other. And it's not easy saying no. It's flattering, of course, when there are so many girls who fancy him because he's in a group, but I'm going to make him wait. I want him to respect me, I'm not going to –'

'So, this is all about you, is it?' Lorna interrupted her with a loud sobbing cry.

'Lorna,' Denise stroked the side of her friend's face, 'don't get yourself all upset. I only –'

'Upset?' Tears were now streaming down Lorna's

cheeks. 'Why shouldn't I get upset? I've been having sex with Richie, and now he doesn't want to know, and I think I'm pregnant.'

Denise closed her eyes and shook her head. 'Fuck. You'll have to let me think about this one.'

'It's too bloody late for thinking,' wailed Lorna, much to the interest of the huge, mutton-armed woman serving on the saveloy and pease pudding stall behind them.

'Calm down and listen to me, Lorna. We'll just have to –'

'What? We'll have to do what?' She couldn't help herself, she was now yelling wildly. 'If you're so bloody clever, you tell me what.'

'Leave it to me.'

Lorna's tears were now coming in an uncontrollable flood. 'What am I going to do, Den?'

'For Gawd's sake,' hollered Mutton Arms, 'tell her what she's going to do so she'll shut up that bloody weeping and wailing. She sounds like a pissing tomcat with its tail stuck in the door, and she's disturbing all my customers.'

'She's not disturbing me,' said a weedy little man, waiting patiently to be served.

'Who asked you, pipe-cleaner?' barked the stallholder.

Denise glared at the unsympathetic woman and steered Lorna over to a low wall that ran along the side of the market. 'You sit there a minute. I'll get your mum's shopping, and then we'll sort this out. OK?'

'OK? How can it be OK? I'm fifteen years old.'

Denise slumped down beside her. 'Christ, Lorn, it don't sound very good when you put it like that.'

Chantalle was leaning against the cold, hard edge of the

butler sink with her arms folded tightly across her chest, staring contemptuously at Lorna's tear-stained face, as Denise repeatedly assured her friend that Richie was definitely not hiding anywhere in the house.

Finally, having convinced Lorna that Richie really wasn't about to jump out and surprise her, Denise turned to her mother.

Phyllis was sitting at the table in the big basement kitchen, drinking tea, knitting and trying to make sense of what was going on. It didn't take a genius to work out it had something to with Richie, but what the hell had he been up to now?

'We need to talk to you in private, if you see what I mean, Mum,' Denise said to Phyllis, emphasising her words, 'with no one else around. So if you could get rid of –' she jerked her head first at Chantalle then at Maxie – 'the kids . . .'

Before Phyllis could even open her mouth, Maxie was already protesting at the very idea.

'You've got some chance, Denise,' he said, holding up a loaf by way of evidence for the defence. 'I'm not going anywhere, I'm making myself a sandwich.'

'And who's she calling a bloody kid?' snapped Chantalle, bumping irritably back and forward against the sink.

'Chantalle,' Phyllis's voice was low and threatening, 'you watch your sodding language, if you don't mind. And, Maxie, you fetch me my bag from the hook behind the door, and I'll give you both money for some chips.'

Maxie brightened up no end – chips, what a result, better than a mouldy old chopped pork and marge sandwich any day – but Chantalle took the offer of fried potatoes as a personal insult.

'What, so I'm a flipping child who's supposed to get

all excited over a couple of pennies' worth of chips, am I?'

'Give me strength.' Phyllis cast her eyes heavenwards. 'What have I done in my life to deserve all this?'

Maxie, keen for Phyllis not to change her mind, handed his mother her handbag with what he hoped was a winning smile. 'There you are, Mum. There's your bag.'

Phyllis glowered doubtfully at her son, but she decided against commenting on his miraculous transformation from an irritating, lippy little git into a sweet, compliant angel. Challenging him would only kick off another row, and all she wanted to do was get shot of him and his sister for half an hour.

She scooped out a handful of loose change from her purse, turned to Chantalle, slapped it down on the table, and jabbed her finger at it. 'Take that, and get out of my sight, the pair of you. Go and buy some chips or whatever else you want. That all right with you, is it?'

The way Phyllis put it, it definitely wasn't a question.

While Maxie was making his way to the chip shop, deciding whether he should spend his share of the spoils on just chips, or chips and crackling, or on a combination of chips, crackling and a pickled onion, and Chantalle was doing her best to persuade the local newsagent to sell her four loose cigarettes from a packet of ten Weights, Denise, considering the circumstances, was speaking to her mum in a surprisingly steady voice. Lorna, on the other hand, just sat there, pale, shaking and silent, staring down at her lap.

And Richie, the topic of Denise's conversation with the now thunder-faced Phyllis, was hanging around on the corner of Ricardo Street, where he had agreed to see

Pauline Carver, the girl he had met in the Bridge House pub over at Canning Town.

'Hello, Richie,' breathed Pauline, 'sorry I'm a bit late, but I've got a really good excuse.'

'You'd better have. I don't like birds wasting my time.'

She smiled up at him with her big, sexy green eyes; she was a real little stunner.

'You remember at the pub, when I said I didn't go with just anyone?'

Richie shrugged. 'Might do.'

'I wasn't exactly telling the truth.'

'No?'

'No.' She dipped her chin and peered up at him through her lashes. 'I've not gone all the way before with anyone.'

Richie brightened up even more than Maxie had when he had been offered a bag of chips. 'That so?'

'Yeah, but look what I got out of my dad's bedside cabinet.' She held out her hand, and slowly opened her fingers to reveal a packet of Durex.

'And guess what else? Dad's taken Mum out shopping for the afternoon. She's after a new three-piece for the front room, and, knowing her, she won't be happy till she's gone round every shop in East London. Maybe even as far away as Harrison Gibson's in Ilford. They'll be gone for hours.'

'No brothers and sisters indoors then?' Richie asked casually.

Pauline shook her head very slowly, all the while gazing up at him. 'All left home. So there's only little me, the baby of the family.'

Richie couldn't hide his grin any longer. 'I think I'm going to like you, Pauline Carver.'

*   *   *

Phyllis marched purposefully into Shirley Wright's kitchen.

'Is Joe in, Shirl?'

'No, he's gone round to see Harry Martin. He's racing his pigeons today and they've had a few bob bet on the outcome, but he shouldn't be too long. Anything I can help you with in the meantime?' She rubbed an itch on the end of her nose with the back of her flour-covered hand. 'I'm just knocking up a beef and onion pie for Lorna's tea. Me and Joe are going out tonight, so I want her to have something she can pick at if she fancies it. She's not got much of an appetite lately, but I always think a pie –'

'Look, Shirl, I don't mean to be rude,' Phyllis cut in, 'but it's you I want to see, not Joe. Hang on a minute.' She walked out to the balcony and shouted over the side, 'Come on up, you two. It's all right.'

Shirley had followed her outside. 'What's going on?'

'We've got to have a talk, Shirl. I'm really sorry, I know you've got a lot on your plate lately, but this is important. Really important. And I've asked the girls up to –'

'That's who you were calling?'

'Yeah, that's right. I've asked them to come up, because they've always been good friends to one another and . . . Look, I think you'll understand when I've finished.'

'Well, whatever it is, Phyl, I'm sure it can't be that bad. I've learned to be a bit philosophical about things over the past few years. No point being anything else, is there? I read in one of those books they gave me in the hospital that this is our only shot at life. It's not a dress rehearsal, that's what it said.' She laughed. 'It was meant to cheer us up, I think. But seriously, it is right, you do have to make the best of things. Don't let them get to you. Well, that's what I like to believe, or else I'd go barmy.'

'OK, Mrs Wright?' said Denise sheepishly. 'Your hair looks nice.'

'Thank you, Denise, kind of you to notice. Now I'll just clear the rest of this pastry away, while you and Lorna make us all a pot of tea, then we can take it through to the sitting room. By the look on your mum's face I think she could do with a cup.'

The four of them sat around the dining table as formally as if they were attending a board meeting.

'It's about Richie,' Phyllis began, fiddling nervously with the teaspoon in her saucer.

Shirley was dreading this. She knew how fond Phyllis was of her nephew, but, no matter how much Phyllis begged her, she wouldn't speak up for him to Lorna. She wouldn't ask her to give him another chance. It would be too hypocritical. Cruel as it sounded, she was glad Lorna had finished with him, or that he'd finished with her, or whatever else had happened between them, even if it had really upset Lorna. She was the only one who really mattered to Shirley, but she was still only a kid; she'd get over it.

'There's something you need to know about Richie being related to me.'

Shirley nodded; this didn't sound too bad, and not even anything very surprising. 'Henry was a good man, doing that for you, Phyl. Taking him in like that.'

'There's no need to pretend, Shirley. We both know

Henry's an idle, useless pillock, who can't even be bothered to argue.'

'Be fair, Phyllis, there's not many would take in their wife's nephew.'

'It was wartime.' Phyllis was suddenly very interested in her teacup; she picked it up and studied it. 'People did a lot of things.'

'I know, but you can't take that away from him – what he did for that boy.'

Phyllis put down her cup and rubbed her hand over her chin as if she were checking that she hadn't suddenly sprouted a beard.

'Look, I've got to tell you the truth, Shirl. You don't understand and it's important that you do.' She paused, took a bit of time to gather her thoughts, and another sip of tea.

'When I was nursing, I met this Frenchman. And I fell in love with him.' She paused for a brief moment, lost somewhere in the past. 'If you believe in such a thing, he was the love of my life.'

'Awww, Mum. He was what?' Denise grimaced, she couldn't help herself: her mum – *her mum!* – had a love of her life. The very thought of it made her stomach turn.

'Don't interrupt, Denise, just let me finish.'

But Denise wasn't one to do as she was told. 'Is that why us lot have all got French names?' She could hardly keep the distaste from her voice. 'In memory of your *long lost love*?'

Phyllis breathed out with a heavy sigh and then snapped sarcastically, 'No. Actually, it was to remind me to always use a French letter in future. Pity I didn't follow my own advice, eh?'

Denise felt her cheeks go blood red. 'Mum!'

'Well, don't be so saucy.'

Shirley didn't like the way this was going. It was all getting very personal, and more than a bit embarrassing. 'Are you sure you want us to know all this, Phyllis?'

'Yes, I do. Richie, he's . . .' Phyllis clasped her hands as if in prayer, 'he's mine. He's my son.'

This time Denise was too stunned to say anything, and Lorna's mouth had dropped open as if the hinge had gone.

Shirley reached across and took Phyllis's hands in hers. 'You've kept this a secret all these years?'

Phyllis nodded. 'I've told no one. No one except Henry, of course. I couldn't hide it from him. Even he's not that stupid.'

Shirley did the only thing she could think of: she poured Phyllis another cup of tea. 'What was his name?'

'Richard. *Reesharr*, he sort of said it. He was so handsome, Shirl. Lovely dark hair, just like Richie's.'

'How did Henry get involved in it all? Were you already seeing him?'

'No, he was just another one of my patients on the ward. But not a war hero, not like Richard.' Phyllis nibbled hard on her bottom lip.

The girls thought she was trying to stop herself from crying, but Shirley could see that, amazingly, she was actually stifling a giggle.

'Henry's army boots were too tight and they'd given him ingrowing toenails. They'd gone all septic and horrible. He was only on basic training. Hadn't heard so much as an enemy voice raised in a bit of a temper, let alone heard a bullet fired in anger.'

Shirley managed to keep up her serious expression, but Phyllis burst out laughing. Lorna and Denise just averted their eyes in sheer mortification. Parents weren't meant to talk like this. Parents weren't meant to have first loves and definitely not – oh my God! – *sex lives*.

'But you know Henry – anything for a quiet life. So long as he can watch the telly, read his paper, and have his pint of a night, I could run a knocking shop from the back bedroom and he wouldn't even notice, let alone complain.' She lowered her voice and spoke to Shirley as if the girls couldn't hear her. 'It's like when I've done business with . . .' she mouthed the next three words, '*old Doris Barker* – you know, a bit of hoisting to help pay the bills, he's not so much as murmured. Probably didn't even notice, silly bugger.' She shook her head at her husband's foolishness.

'Anyway, so there I was, four months gone, and Richard was off in some convalescent home down in the country somewhere. And bear in mind that this is after I'd been personally posting his letters for him back to his loving wife in France to let her know he was all right. And Henry just appeared – not exactly as if by magic, but it did me a good turn. I had him engaged to me within the week and married to me by the end of the month.'

'I can't believe it. Didn't he even –'

'Look, Shirley, you've seen how he is. If life's easy, then it suits Henry. And it would have been harder to argue with me. So we got married.'

'I know, but getting him to take on another man's child . . .'

'You're not judging me, are you, Shirley? I thought we were friends.'

'Course we are, Phyl. I'm just confused where all this is going, that's all. Well, more why you'd tell me in front of the girls, really. I mean, it's not the normal sort of a conversation you'd have with your daughter around, now is it?' Shirley hesitated, but she had to say it. 'If this is a way of trying to get Lorna to feel sorry for Richie, to get her to go back with him, I'm sorry, but it won't work. I've made up my mind, he's not –'

'Mum, please!' Lorna burst into tears and ran out of the room.

Shirley was about to go after her, but Phyllis grabbed her by the hand. 'Please, Shirl, sit down and I'll explain everything. I had to tell you all this because of what it says on his birth certificate.'

'You're losing me again.' Shirley turned to Denise. 'Go and see to Lorna for me, love, while I sort all this out with your mum.'

Denise nodded miserably and went to look after her friend.

'Stupid really,' Phyllis went on. 'I always used to tell him his name was Clayton, after this brother-in-law I made up. I told him his dad got killed fighting in the war, and then my sister – I never even had a sister, let alone a dead brother-in-law – got killed in an air raid on the uniform factory she was working in near Brick Lane. It all got so complicated. It says Benton on his birth certificate. Benton. My maiden name.'

Shirley was now totally confused. 'So what does it say under his dad's name?'

Phyllis shook her head. 'Nothing. The registrar struck it through with a line of ink. Same for under his father's occupation. Just like that, a stroke of ink. No Richard, no nothing.'

'Phyl, I'll help you if I can, but why are you telling me this? And why now?'

Phyllis covered her face with her hands. 'Shirley, Lorna's expecting.'

Shirley felt as if she'd been smacked round the face. 'No. She can't be.'

'Yes she is. She's up the spout. She's got a flaming bun in the oven. She's been well and truly knocked up.' Phyllis sighed wearily. 'That's what I'm telling you: your Lorna is pregnant, and I am just so sorry. It was guilt, you know, about him not having a proper dad, that's what's made me spoil him. He's got away with murder, that boy.'

Shirley stood up, outwardly very calm, and went to fetch the girls, who were now both weeping pathetically. She steered them back to the table, sat them down, and said, almost matter-of-factly, 'It's no good crying, you two. This is the situation we're in, and although it's certainly not what I would have chosen for you, Lorna, we're just going to have to deal with it.'

'But how?' Lorna could barely speak.

'Listen to me, Lorna, you'll be sixteen in the middle of October. That's not even four weeks away. You'll just have to wait till then, then you can get married.'

This time Lorna said nothing; she buried her face in her hands and wept again.

Shirley took Lorna in her arms. 'Make us some more tea, Denise. I'm sure we could all do with some.'

Denise was just topping up their cups, when they heard Joe come in.

'Hello, Shirl,' he called as he hung up his coat on the peg in the hall. 'Only me.'

By the sound of his voice, Shirley guessed rightly that his mood had improved since his trip round to Harry

Martin's, but when he came into the sitting room and he saw Richie's aunt and cousin sitting there, she watched his mouth compress into a tight, angry line and his eyes narrow into a hard expression of irritation.

'What's this, a mother's meeting?'

Lorna turned away so he couldn't see her face.

Shirley stood up. 'Joe do us a favour and go over the Blue Boy for a pint, eh?'

He eyed Phyllis suspiciously. 'But I've only just got back, and how about us going to the pictures and for a Chinese?'

'Joe, believe me, you don't want to hear this. It's *women's business.*'

Now it was a look of panic that clouded Joe's handsome face. 'Not feeling unwell again, are you, Shirl?'

'No, I'm fine. Look, we only need half an hour. Me and Phyllis just want to have a little talk to the girls.' She flashed her eyebrows. 'You know.'

'Right. Right.' Joe was out of the flat before Shirley had a chance to elaborate.

She sat down again and they waited for Denise to finish pouring the tea.

'I'm so ashamed of him,' said Phyllis. It was the quietest Shirley had ever heard her speak. 'It's just like history repeating itself. Just like me all over again.'

'No it's not,' spat Lorna, surprising them all. 'It's nothing like you.'

'Lorna, don't you dare speak to Mrs Parker like that.'

'I'm sorry if you think I'm being rude, Mum, but times are changing.' Lorna was still sniffling, but she was doing her best to sound blasé.

The two women looked at one another, Phyllis shrugged, and then Shirley turned to her daughter. The sight of her child's tearful young face wrenched her heart. 'Things haven't changed that much, love.'

'Yes they have. All I've done is go with my boyfriend. That don't make me bloody Christine Keeler, does it? I'm not like those little whores in the paper, going to parties with naked men in masks, and going with all sorts for money.'

Shirley whacked her hand down on the table. 'No, you're not some little whore, you're Lorna Wright, my daughter, and I'll stand by you whatever you do, but don't you get lippy with me, young lady. And you just watch your language.'

'But she is right, Shirl. Times have changed. There're different attitudes about things nowadays.'

'No there's not, Phyllis, there's still one rule for them and one for us.'

'I'll have to admit that's true.'

'Yeah, and there're plenty of hypocrites out there and all.'

'I admit you're right again. That bloke in the papers is OK resigning over all this scandal he's got caught up in, but he's still a grown man who's been knocking off a seventeen-year-old kid. And what's he going to do now? You wait and see. He'll be a good man and go and work for charity like they all do. And all the papers are going to say *good for him*. But it'll be working with young girls, you just see if it's not. He wants putting away and having his balls chopped off, not a round of sodding applause for doing so-called good works.'

'I agree with every word you're saying, Phyllis, but it doesn't help us, does it? It doesn't help us sort out this mess.' She turned to her daughter. 'And it doesn't excuse Lorna being rude to you.'

'I'm sorry, Mum, but I'm so scared.'

'I know you are.' Shirley patted her hand. 'But come on, we've got to be practical.'

'All right, I'll be practical. What am I going to do about my married name then? Even that's a mess.'

'Married name? My little girl?' Shirley had to gnaw the inside of her cheek to stop herself from crying. 'This is like a bad dream.'

Phyllis sighed loudly and rolled her eyes towards the ceiling as if seeking divine intervention. 'I went into all this before. A year or so ago.'

Lorna lifted her head and stared at Phyllis, but it was Denise who said what they were both thinking. 'Mum, are you saying this has happened before?'

'Please, don't ask, OK? That's all in the past, and Shirley's right, it's not easy, but we've got to be practical.' Phyllis took a deep breath and launched into her explanation. 'What you need to know is that his birth certificate says Benton.'

'Benton?' Shirley looked confused.

'My single name, remember?'

'Right.'

'But there is a complication because I made up that brother-in-law, Eddie Clayton, and a make-believe sister for me, for him to be married to – Iris, I called her. She was supposed to be his mum, if you follow me.'

'I think so,' said Shirley.

The girls just listened.

'Well, that's why he's always been called Richie – I mean Richard – Clayton. So, how it goes is – hang on, let me get this straight – he'll have to register for the marriage as *Clayton, formerly known as Benton*.' Phyllis pinched the bridge of her nose; she had a cracker of a headache coming on. 'It's true what they say: you tell one lie . . .'

'Does that mean she'll have to have the registry office?' Shirley asked.

Phyllis shook her head. 'No. I know that for a fact.'

'Thank God for that. Everyone'd know something was up if we didn't go to St Anne's.'

'They're going to know something's up soon enough, Mum.'

They all now sat in silence with their thoughts for a long uncomfortable moment, until Phyllis dragged them back to the practicalities. 'Denise, you take Lorna through to wash her face. I want a private word with Mrs Wright.'

She waited until the girls were in the bathroom. 'Shirley, I dread to think how Joe's going to take this. I think it'll be best if Lorna comes back with me and has a bit of tea with Denise, while you have a talk to him.'

'No. I don't want to go to yours,' Lorna shrieked from the bathroom. 'Tell her, Mum.'

'Bugger. Me and my big mouth. I forget how small these flats are. You can holler at the top of your lungs in our place and they still reckon they can't hear me calling them.'

Lorna was now standing in the doorway with a flannel in her hand and Denise peering gingerly over her shoulder. 'I mean it, Mum, I don't want to. I don't want to see Richie. Not yet. I can't face him till this is all sorted out. Let me stay here. I'll go in my bedroom and wait until you've told Dad. Please. Don't make me go with Mrs Parker.'

'If that's what she wants, then I think she better had

stay here, Shirl. No good her getting even more upset. Not in her condition.'

Shirley spread her hands. 'I feel like this isn't happening.'

She thought for a moment, imagining Joe's reaction to their daughter not only marrying into a family he disliked, but into a family he would probably actually despise if he knew the full story. Joe was a very proper man, and he had little time for the likes of Henry Parker as it was.

'All right, Lorna, you stay here. And just to keep everything as calm as possible, perhaps we won't mention that Phyllis is really Richie's mum. We can just keep it between us four – and Henry, of course. Agreed?'

Phyllis nodded. Shirley was a sensible woman, everyone knew that, so it would be silly not to agree with her at a time like this. And, on reflection, she thought that perhaps she wouldn't mention that Richie had actually long known the truth about his parentage. Like Shirley had said: best to keep it all as calm as possible.

Joe had stayed in the Blue Boy for almost an hour – just in case they hadn't finished – and had even dragged out the time by walking up the stairs to the fifth floor rather than getting the lift. The last thing he wanted was to go wading in with his size elevens while Shirley and Phyllis were still talking to the girls about *private things*. He had always been very clear about leaving that sort of business to his wife. Give him the hardest, back-breaking cargo to deal with and he was your man, but even hint at Women's Stuff and he'd run a mile. Mind you, he had surprised himself when Shirley was ill. He had faced up to all sorts of things then all right. But that was different, he'd had no choice: Shirley had needed him, so he'd coped. For her.

He would fight wild tigers with his hands tied behind his back for Shirley and for his little Lorna.

'All right, Shirl?' he called along the hall.

'Yeah, you're safe, Joe. I'm in the kitchen. By myself.'

He frowned; Shirley was mashing potatoes. 'I know we've missed the pictures, but we can still go and have a Chinese.'

'Would you mind if we stayed in tonight, Joe?'

'No, not if that's what you want.' He folded his arms round her and hugged her close to him. 'You sure you're not hiding anything from me, babe? You would tell me if you're feeling rough again, wouldn't you?'

'I'm all right, Joe, honest. But there is something I want to talk to you about.' Shirley pulled away from him. 'You go in the other room. I'll just turn down the oven so the pie doesn't burn, then I'll come through.'

Since Phyllis and Denise had gone home, Shirley might have rehearsed a dozen different ways to break the news to Joe, but, in the end, there was only one way to do it.

'Now, don't go losing your temper, Joe, please, but it's Lorna. She's pregnant.'

She would remember the moment she told him as clearly as if it had been photographed, stuck in a frame, and stood on top of the telly. He was in the sitting room, standing with his back to her, looking out of the big picture window. She knew what he was doing – watching the kids downstairs mucking about and having a laugh in the playground at the back of the flats. He often stood there, smiling, watching them enjoying themselves and getting up to all sorts of monkey business.

But this time, as she spoke to him, he turned round very slowly to face her, and he wasn't smiling.

The colour had drained from his face, and, for a moment, she really thought he was going to pass out.

'Lorna?' He sounded like a machine – flat, toneless. 'No. She can't be.'

'Yes, Joe.' Shirley walked over and stood in front of him; she didn't touch him. His eyes were full of tears.

'But she's fifteen years of age.'

His heart was breaking for his little girl, and Shirley's was breaking for him. She couldn't stand it. 'It's all my fault, Joe. I know it is. If she hadn't been an only child, if I'd been able to have more kids, this would never have happened. She wouldn't have been –'

'Don't you dare say that. Of course it's not your fault. We both know whose fault it is and I'm going to kill him.'

'No, Joe, please. Don't do anything to make things worse. Lorna's beside herself as it is.'

'Where is she?'

'In her bedroom.' She grabbed hold of his big muscled arm. 'But wait, listen to me. We can get things organised in no time. She's sixteen next month and –'

'You mean you want her to marry that scumbag?'

'No, Joe, I don't mean that at all. I don't *want* her to marry him, but what choice have we got? I'm not having her going in one of those mother and baby homes like that kid down on the ground floor. She's never got over having them take her baby away, the poor little cow.'

'We can move. Somewhere nobody knows us. Miles away. We can bring it up as ours. Who'd know the difference?'

Shirley shook her head as visions of Phyllis sitting at the table swam before her. 'Lies never lead to anywhere but trouble, Joe. And, anyway, what would you do about work? What would we live on?'

'There's always work if you're willing to look for it. I'd find something.' He raked his fingers through his hair. 'We could go to the country. Have chickens and that. The fresh air would be just right for a baby.'

Baby.

Actually saying the word was the final straw. Joe began to sob.

'What're we going to do, Shirl?'

'We're going to support our daughter, that's what. We're going to make the best of a bad job. Now go through and talk to her. She needs us, Joe, and she needs a cuddle from her dad.'

'Is this what you really want, sweetheart? To marry him?'

Lorna's handkerchief was soaked through; she sniffed and wiped her nose on the back of her hand. 'If he'll have me.'

Joe got up from where he'd been perched on the side of his daughter's pink, frill-covered, little girl's bed. He just about managed a smile. 'What do you mean: if he'll have you? Who wouldn't want to marry a princess?'

'I've got no row with you, Phyllis, but if you don't let me in, I'm going to force me way in. Clear enough for you?'

Phyllis stepped away from the door with a sigh and let Joe into the passage. 'He's down in the kitchen, eating his tea.'

'Thanks.'

Joe took the stairs two at a time, and, ignoring Henry's

cheery 'All right, Joe?', grabbed Richie by the scruff of the neck and hauled him to his feet.

'Put that knife and fork down. We're going out the back-yard. There's something I've got to say to you. Got it?'

As Joe slammed Richie hard against the whitewashed brick wall, Richie was actually stupid enough to object. 'Oi, watch it. That hurt.'

Joe poked him in the chest. 'Good. It was meant to. Now, look here, you little runt, I don't like you, I never have, and I never will. In fact, you could say I can't stand the fucking sight of you, you horrible ponce, but she wants this. So, you're going to marry her, right? But let me tell you something, if you ever hurt her, I'll kill you. Your aunt and uncle might have been soft on you, but I don't take nonsense from anyone. Understand me?'

Richie stared at him. Aunt and uncle? He still didn't know, the thick old bastard. They'd pulled the wool right over his eyes. He was as bad as Henry. A prize, number one, class A mug. Richie's mind was racing like an adding machine on overdrive. Joe was a mug all right, but he was one whose daughter had gained him almost free access to the docks, and to lots of nice, helpful contacts, contacts willing to do anything for a swift two quid in their back breech with no questions asked. But if it got round that he'd upset the old git, that he'd brought trouble to the Wrights' doorstep, they might not be so friendly. For some unknown reason, people seemed to respect Lorna's old man down there. Plus, he certainly didn't fancy the idea of getting himself a good hiding, especially from someone as massive as Joe Wright.

So how best to play this? What should he do?

Joe grabbed him by the collar with both hands and began to shake him. 'Well? I asked you a question.'

Joe's jaw was so rigid he could barely spit out the words. 'I said: *have you got it*, you nasty piece of shit?'

'Course I have. Course I've got it. I can't wait to marry her.'

Joe let him go and Richie straightened his shirt.

'Please, believe me,' he said, burying all traces of sarcasm deep into his coward's chest. 'I love Lorna with all my heart, I swear on my uncle and aunt's lives I do, Mr Wright.' He grinned. 'Or should I say: Dad?'

It was only the thought of Lorna's tear-stained, lovely little face, and his promise to Shirley that he'd behave himself, that held Joe back from knocking Richie Clayton's teeth right down his sewer of a throat.

Chapter 5

'Are you sure I don't look too fat, Mum?' Lorna turned sideways and examined her silhouette in her mother's full-length wardrobe mirror. 'Only I feel like an elephant.'

'You look beautiful, darling.' Shirley fiddled with Lorna's crystal headdress, jiggling it around until it sat more firmly on top of her heavily lacquered, French-pleated, now almost platinum-blonde hair. 'Just like a fairy princess.'

'And you're not really that far gone to show *all* that much. Not really.' Denise was doing her best to cheer up her miserable-looking friend; she had even finally given in over the matter of the hated turquoise satin headbands that Shirley had made for her and Chantalle to go with their matching bridesmaids dresses. That was friendship. In fact, she was so keen to please Lorna that she hadn't so much as murmured her disapproval when the dresses had somehow been translated, from the simple, rather elegant Empire line of the original pattern they'd bought, into vile mock-shepherdess outfits that made her and her sister look like refugees from a particularly unkind spoof book of nursery rhymes.

The awful transformation of the frocks had been the work of an overenthusiastic dressmaker friend of Phyllis's, who had won the commission for the job when she'd come up with such a cheap quote that alarm bells should have begun ringing immediately and very loudly. But Phyllis, in her usual forceful way, had insisted that not only would everything be just fine, but that the woman was practically a genius, and it was a wonder she hadn't been snapped up by Bond Street. And so it was that the tender put in by a woman with the satin and lace equivalent of dyslexia had won.

And, anyway, it had all happened in such a rush, and there were so many more important ways to spend any spare money – most of it Joe's, of course – that correcting fashion mistakes came very low on the list. Money was needed, for instance, to secure somewhere for the 'kids' to live. 'Kids' being how Lorna and Richie had somehow become collectively known to Shirley and Phyllis, their unlikely, but now inevitable mothers-in-law.

This time Phyllis had actually come up trumps; she had persuaded her own landlord, the usually despised Mr Bartelow, to rent Lorna and Richie the top of a house just ten doors along from the Parkers' place in the East India Dock Road.

It might have been only two rooms plus a tiny kitchenette and an even tinier lavatory, but Shirley and Phyllis had been delighted – well, more relieved, really – with the arrangement. Nothing was said in so many words, but it clearly comforted them both to know that the 'kids' were so close at hand, where they could keep a close eye on them both.

'I think you'd better remember to hold your breath, or at least pull yourself in, as you walk down the aisle, though, Lorna.' It was Chantalle; she had edged her way in front of the mirror to check on her own reflection. 'Or everyone's going to guess you're up the stick right away.' She flashed a nasty look at Lorna. 'If they haven't already.' She patted the bounce of her auburn flick-ups. 'What a show-up that'd be, eh, Mrs Wright? Everyone knowing your daughter's been knocked up. And that she must have been under age when she was doing it. A real shamer.'

Before Shirley could say anything, Denise grabbed her sister by the shoulder and spun her round so that they were nose to nose. 'If you've said anything to anyone, Chantalle, anyone at all, I'll tell Mum of you, I swear I will.'

'Oh yeah? Like she'd give two shits who knows.'

Shirley pasted on a smile. God, Chantalle was a handful. 'OK, girls, I know we're all nervous, but don't let's lose our tempers, eh? Not today.'

'What have you lot got to be nervous about?' Lorna was close to tears. 'I'm the one who's . . . Oh, Mum . . .'

'I know, love.' Shirley put her arm round her daughter's shoulders. 'Denise, go through to the sitting room and tell Mr Wright to pour four small port and lemons. I know you're not really old enough, but it is a special occasion.'

As Denise pushed roughly past her scowling sister, Chantalle hissed at Lorna: 'Funny, eh, Lorna? Not old enough to drink, but old enough to have a fu–'

'Need any help with your headdress?' Shirley interrupted the foul-mouthed little madam, twisting her round rather more roughly than was necessary, and then re-pinning her headband with no attention at all to the tenderness or otherwise of Chantalle's scalp.

'Oi!' complained Chantalle. 'That bloody hurt!'

Shirley didn't so much as flinch, but she really didn't know how much longer she could hold her smile. She wasn't a snob – she had nothing to be a snob about – and she had always known the Parkers were rough diamonds, but now that her only child was actually marrying into their unruly clan, Shirley honestly didn't know if she could carry on turning a blind eye to such behaviour.

'Hold on a minute, sweetheart, don't get out just yet.' Joe Wright reached across his daughter's lap, flattening a dozen layers of stiff, bright-white frock, and grasped hold of the door handle of the big black wedding car, effectively blocking the uniformed chauffeur from letting Lorna out onto the pavement.

'This is your last chance, Lorna. You don't have to do this, you know. Me and your mum'll stand by you, no matter what. We'll even move away if you want. Somewhere no one knows any of us. So there'd be no shame. We could make a new start. It'd be easy. We could go right now.'

He ducked his head until he made eye contact with the driver, and then gestured, with a flick of his chin, a mouthed instruction and a splay of his fingers, for the man to leave them alone for five minutes.

Used to anxious fathers' last-minute pep talks, the man did as he was told. After all, all it meant to him was a slightly earlier chance to have a cigarette and a quick glance at the sports pages.

'Just say the word,' Joe went on, 'and I'll go in that church and tell them it's all off. There won't be any problem, I swear on my life there won't.'

Lorna couldn't look at him. 'You'd do that for me, Dad?'

'Course I would, darling; I'd do anything for you and your mum, you know that. I love you both more than I could ever tell you. I'd even kill for you if I had to, and wouldn't think twice about it.'

'And that's why you've got to let me do this, Dad.

I know you don't like him, but I love Richie, and I'm having his baby. And I just want all this to be over and done with, and everything to be all right again.'

'I know you think you love him, Lorna, but you've only just turned sixteen, babe. You've never even had any other proper boyfriends.'

'Mum never had *any* boyfriend but you.'

'No, but . . .' Joe wanted to say that that was different, that Shirley loved him because he was a decent, respectable, hard-working bloke, and not an idle, self-absorbed little prick like Richie Clayton, but when he saw the desperate, appealing look on his little girl's face, he couldn't bring himself to say it, couldn't bring himself to hurt her.

'If you're honestly sure this is what you want . . .'

'I'm sure.'

So that was it. Joe took her hand gently in his great big paw. 'Come on then, angel face, let's go and show ourselves in that church, and let them see what a beautiful daughter I've got.'

The church was packed out with friends, neighbours and family members from both sides. Family members, that is, except Phyllis's elderly parents, and her even more elderly aunties and uncles. They had been invited, Phyllis's pride had seen to that, but they had been adamant that they wouldn't come, their response being that Phyllis had shamed them enough all those years ago. The shaming back then having been a direct result of Henry's genuinely innocent, but totally stupid behaviour.

He had said something about Richie's true parentage when he'd been under the influence of too much drink on the very first Christmas he had spent with his new in-laws and, unfortunately, quite a few of their neighbours

– thoughtless behaviour that had set a template for his lazy thinking and general idiocy throughout the rest of their marriage. The humiliation of seeing the looks on the neighbours' faces had stayed with Phyllis's family like an embarrassing bad smell, and there was absolutely no chance of her nearest and dearest risking having the finger pointed at them ever again, regardless of the free food and drink being laid on courtesy of Joe Wright.

But now, save for the organist tidying away his music, the church was empty; all the guests and the vicar were hanging around outside, shivering in the autumnal dampness of the watery afternoon sunlight, on the steps of St Anne's, while the photographer barked out his orders about who should be standing where and when they should look happy, and when he had finished with them for now, thank you very much.

Young Maxie was one guest who didn't need a bloke with a camera to tell him to look happy. As he towered over his 'big cousin' Richie, Maxie was grinning all over his face. And why shouldn't he be? He was a young, well-built, good-looking best man, wearing his very first grown-up suit, knowing that he would very soon be back at the reception sinking a few illicit beers and making a beeline for any one of a number of cracking-looking girls he already had his eye on. His grin broadened. Just look at them, they were gorgeous, like a row of birthday presents all done up in their sexy little wedding outfits, ready and waiting for him to get his hands on their ribbons and fancy wrapping paper. It was going to be hard to choose which one of them most deserved his attentions. But first things first.

'I'm making a speech later on,' he said to Richie. 'I've written one especially for you and Lorna.'

'Hoo-bloody-ray. I can't pissing well wait.'

Lorna flinched at the harshness of Richie's tone, and all her worries about whether her expanding girth and the goose pimples on her arms would show up in the wedding pictures disappeared. Now she had something serious to worry about – Richie losing his temper.

Not today, she pleaded in her head. Don't start. Please. Not in front of my mum and dad and everyone.

Lorna's silent wish was magically granted. Richie, noticing a familiar face from the docks coming towards him, broke into a warm, welcoming smile, his unpleasant sarcasm melting away like an early frost in the autumn sunshine.

'That'll be great, Max,' he said, slapping the boy on the back. Then he reached out and shook the big stevedore warmly by the hand.

'Here, George, come and meet the new missus, and my young cousin, Maxie. He's the best man, ain't you, Max? Come and get yourself in the snaps next to me, George. Come on. Up here on the steps.'

Lorna relaxed. Richie must be as nervous as she was, that's what was wrong with him. It would be strange if he weren't on his wedding day.

Mrs Elliot, the Parkers' neighbour, had seen George join the happy couple and had decided that she too deserved a place in the front row, so she elbowed her way through the throng and plonked herself next to Phyllis.

'We'll all be invited back to the do then,' she said, putting on what she thought was a suitably wedding-like face for the photographer, but which to everyone else looked more like an appalled grimace of pain.

'I don't even remember inviting you to the church,'

said Phyllis, straightening up the veil of her sunflower-yellow hat for the hundredth time, the sunflower-yellow hat that matched her truly remarkable sunflower-yellow two-piece. Someone in a gown shop, a very long time ago, had – mistakenly as it happened – told Phyllis that sunflower yellow was the perfect colour for her with her auburn hair. She really should have taken the vividness of Phyllis's flushed complexion and the size of her ample frame into consideration before saying such a thing, but then she had wanted to shift the huge sack of a sunflower-yellow frock that had, up until that moment, hung on her rack for months with absolutely no interest from even the most gullible of punters.

But, regardless of what anyone else thought she looked like, Phyllis felt great, really great: the wedding had happened, the kids had a place to live, and the baby was going to have two proper parents. So she could bloody well find it in herself to be pleasant to her bleeding old crab of a neighbour, couldn't she?

'But why not, Mrs Elliot? One more at the reception won't make any difference, now will it? I mean, there'll be plenty of everything.' She patted her sequin-spotted veil with a contented sigh. 'I suppose you already know the reception's over at the Blue Boy?'

'Yeah, and I know you and your old man ain't paying for none of it, and all. Joe Wright is.' Mrs Elliot flashed her rusty railing teeth for the photographer. 'So you can stick your Lady Bountiful act right up your arse.'

Malcolm Danes unlocked the doors of the pub and the wedding party entered with an unseemly rush; a free knees-up was an occasion that everyone knew required a bit of determination if you were going to make the most of it. Getting to the prawns before there were only tails and heads left, and getting to the eels before the bowl could only offer a sloppy pool of leftover jelly was something of an art form requiring swift movement and sharp elbows, and no concern for dignity or causing offence to someone's aunt twice removed. And as for making sure you downed your fair share of drink, a place at the front of the bar and a nice pleasant smile for the landlord was an absolute must – the minimum really; a friendly enquiry after his health and a fag or two passed over at the beginning of the evening could work wonders, and ensure that the spirits would flow freely for the rest of the night.

But at the moment the landlord, Malcolm Danes, was too busy talking to Richie to be susceptible to any little bits of persuasion, and the guests had to negotiate with barmaids they had never met before, an altogether more difficult trick to pull off successfully, but with the tantalising possibility that they wouldn't try to ration how many times you returned for refills as they probably wouldn't remember who you were in the sea of strange faces.

Malcolm lifted the flap in the polished wood counter and beckoned Richie behind the bar.

'Got a little wedding gift for you, Richie, old son. When I got in this extra staff I thought to myself, I know,' he tapped the side of his nose with his index finger and winked, 'I'll get in the Friday relief barmaid to give us a hand as well, if you know what I mean.'

'That's very thoughtful of you, Malc,' Richie grinned. 'And I do you know what you mean. She's given me a hand plenty of times. So where is she then?'

'In the kitchen when you feel the need, old son. You

take your time and enjoy yourself, I'll keep an eye out for the enemy.'

Richie took a quick glance over his shoulder: Lorna was talking to her dad; 'Auntie' Phyllis was jawing away to Lorna's mum; and the rest of the idiots were either stuffing their faces, necking the free booze, or, like stupid Denise, goggling up at the stage as the Spanners tuned up ready to show everyone how crappy they were. Perfect, no one would even notice he wasn't there. With a double thumbs-up to Malcolm, Richie delivered himself into the kitchen and into the very experienced hands of the Friday relief barmaid.

Denise, her hated turquoise satin headband long since discarded, wouldn't have noticed if Richie had decided to do a naked clog dance in front of the vicar, who, as it happened wouldn't have noticed either, as he was already well stuck in at the bar. She stood in front of the stage with a blissful, slightly daft look on her face. Terry – *her* Terry – was so fantastic; there he was, up in front of everyone, with the Spanners. And what were they doing? They were playing all the old standards, that's what, just as Mrs Wright had asked them. They would be playing all the Beatles and the Searchers and that sort of stuff later on, but when Mrs Wright had booked them, she had told Terry that she wanted them to play 'something nice' to begin the evening, so he had persuaded the others to learn some of the old songs their parents liked. Denise could have just jumped up on the stage and hugged him, right there and then. *He was so lovely.*

Terry put down his guitar, leaving the others for a moment to carry on playing one of the Hoagy Carmichael songs they had learned at such short notice, and leaned forward so that Denise could hear him over the music.

'Why don't you go and have a dance, Den? Go and enjoy yourself? You're making me feel guilty, seeing you standing there all by yourself.'

Denise gazed up at him. 'I'd rather be here than anywhere else in the world.'

'Go on, Den, do as he says.' Chantalle had suddenly appeared behind her sister, and was hissing nastily into her ear. 'I'll stay here and take care of Terry for you. Bet he'd like that, wouldn't he?'

Denise didn't bother to turn round, she just kept smiling up at Terry, and made sure she spoke loudly enough so that only her sister could hear. 'Just piss off, will you, Chantalle? The children are all round in the other bar with crisps and lemonade, so why don't you go round there and pick on someone your own age?'

'Not scared of the opposition, are you, Den?'

'Fuck off, Chantalle,' she spat through clenched teeth.

'You two all right?' asked Terry, confused as to what was going on.

'Fine.' Denise arranged her face into a picture of happiness and wellbeing. 'Just fine.'

Terry, realising that whatever was going on was sister stuff, and so, way beyond him, stepped away from the front of the stage and picked up his guitar, and the swaying rhythms of 'Stardust' from the rest of the group, leaving a sour-faced Chantalle to stomp off through the jam-packed pub to find someone else to torment, and Denise deciding, now her kid sister had taken the hint, to go off and look for Lorna.

Lorna was also looking round the pub, but she was looking for Richie.

'You OK, babe?' Joe held his pint well away from Lorna's dress, and planted a gentle kiss on her forehead.

'I was trying to see where Richie had got to. Thought it might be nice if we had at least one dance before the evening's over.' She had only just realised that she had never danced with him – ever – and it felt important that they should dance tonight of all nights. 'But I can't see him anywhere.' Then she added overbrightly: 'Too many people to see anything.'

Joe felt his jaw tighten, but he managed to keep his smile. 'What, are you telling me you don't want to have a dance with your old dad?'

'Course I do.'

Joe managed to find a bit of space on a nearby table for his glass, then he took Lorna by the hand and led her to the middle of the crowd of dancers, who, realising who had joined them, all stepped away to make room for the bride and her father.

As guests oohed and aahed at the two of them, saying what a lovely bride she made and how handsome her dad looked, Chantalle planted herself next to Maxie, who was surreptitiously knocking back the drink with a group of youngsters. She sneered spitefully for the benefit of a particularly good-looking boy who, annoyingly, seemed very taken with Lorna.

'She's not a natural blonde, you know,' Chantalle began, spitting her venom, then finished with the clincher. 'And, don't know if you know, but she's four months gone. Got caught out, she's that stupid.'

'No?'

'My life.' Chantalle lowered her lids and ran her tongue flirtatiously round her lips. 'She's nothing like me. I'm not stupid at all.' She rocked her shoulders slowly from side to side. 'Do you think I'm attract-ive?'

The boy did his best to reply to Chantalle's come on – not easy when his mouth had suddenly become as dry as the sawdust he sprinkled on the floor of the butcher's shop where he worked as an apprentice. Maxie was oblivious of what was going on between his sister and the slack-jawed youth, being too busy gulping down yet another beer. Quite a lot of it was dribbling down his chin.

'You want to watch them two, Mrs Parker.' Mrs Elliot jabbed Phyllis in the back to get her attention.

Phyllis turned round with a frown. 'What two? Who're you talking about?'

'Your Maxie and Chantalle. 'Cos if you don't they'll be bringing even more trouble to your doorstep.'

'Even more trouble?' Phyllis glowered. 'So what sort of trouble am I meant to have already then, Mrs Elliot?' She moved threateningly close to the skinny little woman. 'What sort of trouble would that be then, eh?'

Mrs Elliot wasn't that easily fazed. 'Obvious. What sixteen-year-old girl in her right mind would marry that nephew of yours unless they were in trouble? And what was all that *known as* business when they read the banns? All very fishy, I'd say. And I should think that's more than enough trouble for any wedding, wouldn't you?'

'I haven't got a single clue what you're talking about, Mrs Elliot.'

Phyllis paused and put a finger to her chin as if she were working out a problem. 'Here, have you ever thought that a woman of your age might need her ear holes syringing? They do it round the doctor's for you, you know. Now, if you'll excuse me, I fancy another snowball.' She put her face right up close to Mrs Elliot's. 'I said *snowball*,' she hollered into the woman's ear. 'Got it?'

As Phyllis strode determinedly over to the bar, ready to slaughter anyone who came between her and another advocaat and lemonade cocktail, the Hoagy Carmichael song came to an end and Joe clasped Lorna to his chest. The other people on the crowded floor clapped, smiled and muttered sentimental hopes and good wishes for Lorna's future and about how much her old dad loved her.

Joe wanted to mutter something himself: that Lorna should hitch up her skirts and make a run for it before she got herself stuck with that Clayton bastard for life. But he didn't. He just swallowed the words down into a deep private part of himself and hugged his daughter all the tighter. He hadn't felt so close to despair since Shirley had first got the bad news from the hospital. He had to get away from it, get a bit of fresh air, if only for a couple of minutes.

'Blimey, princess, I never knew this dancing lark was such thirsty work. I'm going to get myself a drink and then nip out for a quiet smoke away from all this noise.'

'All right, Dad. I'll go and see if I can find Richie.'

While they'd been dancing, Joe, a good six inches taller than most of the other people in the pub, had scanned the bar, and he hadn't seen so much as a sign of the little bleeder. He couldn't bear it if Lorna got upset.

'Why don't you go over and have a chat with your mum first, eh, babe? Just a few words. I know she'd really like that. She's going to be lost, not having you at home with us.'

Lorna was suddenly too choked to answer. Things had

all happened so fast, the reality of what it actually meant hadn't really sunk in until now. This was it, her life had changed for ever: she wasn't going to be going home to live in Lancaster Buildings, not ever again, and she wasn't her daddy's little girl any more. Her lips trembled; all she could manage was a nod at Joe before going off to look for her mum.

Shirley, although trying her very best to be positive about everything, was finding the evening very hard going. Like Mrs Elliot, she had been watching what Chantalle and Maxie were up to, and she didn't much like what she saw.

She shook her head. Just look at that Chantalle, already acting like a tart, despite being only thirteen years of age, and Maxie, heaven help him, knocking back drinks like he was a grown man. Well, he might be a physically big lad, but he was still not much more than a child, barely a year older than Chantalle.

Shirley immediately dismissed the disturbing thought that told her that meant he was only two years younger than Lorna – two years, but there she was, a married woman – and turned her attention to Phyllis.

Phyllis was standing by the bar with a group of women, laughing, with her head thrown right back, as if she didn't have a care in the world. She was a good-hearted woman in lots of ways, but – Shirley couldn't help it, she couldn't think otherwise on the evidence – she hadn't done much of a job with her kids.

Shirley had studied the two youngest, and they were a complete nightmare, and now Lorna had got hiked up with Richie. What was she expected to think? Denise was definitely the best of the bunch, but there were times when even she made Shirley squirm, what with her language, and the way she had hung around with the boys.

Shirley felt her cheeks suddenly flame red. Denise might have been the one who always hung around with the boys, but she wasn't the one who was expecting, was she? No, that was Lorna . . .

Shirley wasn't usually much of a one for alcohol, but goodness, she could do with something stronger than a small port and lemon right now.

'Mum?'

Hearing her daughter's voice, Shirley immediately rearranged her weary expression of despair into one of pride and enjoyment, and then turned round to face her with it. She held out her arms in welcome.

'Look at my beautiful girl.'

Lorna gulped back her tears and held on to her mother like a lost soul clinging to the wreckage.

With her daughter in her arms, Shirley was immediately in protective mode. 'Have you had anything to eat yet, love?' she asked, touching her lips to Lorna's cheek. 'What with all the excitement, it's easy to get carried away at a do like this and forget to have even a little sandwich or something.'

'I don't think I could, Mum. My stomach's still doing somersaults.'

'Sure?'

Lorna nodded.

'How about your dad? Has he had anything?'

'Don't know, but he said he was popping out for some fresh air.'

To get away from this lot, more like, Shirley thought. 'And how about Richie? Has he had something?'

'I don't really know where he is.'

'Well, it might be a good idea to go and find him, and make sure he does get a slice of pork pie or something inside him. There's a lot of drink being taken and you don't want him making himself unwell or anything. You know what fellers can be like. They see all this –'

''Scuse me, are you Lorna?'

Lorna and Shirley both looked over their shoulders to see who had spoken. It was a girl of about Lorna's age, maybe a bit older, with her hair bleached to a white, cotton-wool blonde, and wearing a too-tight skirt and frilly blouse combination that did no service at all to her rather chubby figure.

'Silly question,' the girl went on, before either Shirley or Lorna had a chance to reply. 'You are the only one here looking like the bleed'n fairy off the top of the Christmas tree, so I suppose it's got to be you. Unless you've come in fancy dress, of course. At least that'd be an excuse for the frock.'

'Sorry, do I know you?' asked Lorna.

'No, but I know all about you, and I know all about Richie. I'm a right good friend of his as a matter of fact. Pamela's the name. Pamela Logan.' She looked smug. 'Ring any bells?'

'No. None.'

This time, Pamela looked disappointed. 'He's obviously been keeping me a secret.'

Shirley went to say something, but Lorna stopped her.

'No, it's all right, Mum. I can deal with this. What do you mean, *keeping you a secret*?'

'So, you really don't know. I'd better tell you then, hadn't I? Probably best that you know where you stand. You see, the thing is, it should have been me standing there wearing that dress. Well, not that dress exactly – something a bit more stylish would be more my cup of tea.'

'What are you talking about?'

'Me and Richie. We were going to get married, but my mum and dad wouldn't give their permission, even when I told them we'd been having it off for over a year. They said yes at first, they were so scared I'd be left on the shelf when fellers found out I wasn't a good little girl. And we nearly got it all sorted out. But then they changed their minds. When they got to know Richie a bit better, they said he was no good, but we know better than that, don't we, *Lorna*? We know just how good he is, if you catch my drift. So I was waiting – no, me and Richie were waiting – till I was twenty-one. But now you, you scheming little piece of dog shit, you've gone and spoiled everything.'

This time Shirley wouldn't be silenced; she was totally indignant. 'Have you quite finished? There are enough foul-mouthed little madams round here without you joining in.' She stepped closer to the girl. 'Speaking to my daughter like that on her special day. You should go and wash your mouth out with soap and water.'

'It's all right, Mum. She's just jealous. And who can blame her? It must be hard for her, seeing me so happy with Richie.'

'Aw, ain't she sweet? But funny, I can't see him anywhere near you. He must really love you, mustn't he? Not even standing with you on your own *special day*.' With that, Pamela slapped Lorna hard round the face, then grabbed at the short net veil that was attached to her hair by the crystal tiara and tried to rip it from her head. 'Give me that. It's mine.'

'Aowww! You rotten cow!' exploded Lorna, grabbing

Pamela by the wrists. The first slap had taken her by surprise, but now she was ready for her.

As Pamela tried to wrestle herself out of Lorna's grip, Lorna kicked her hard – twice – once on each shin, then she let her go and leaped back out of range while she considered her next move.

Lorna was too busy weighing up the opposition, and Pamela was too preoccupied with her sore legs, for either of them to notice the crowd that had, from out of nowhere, immediately encircled their catfight. As for Shirley, she was so shocked, she could do nothing more than stand there, clutching the side of a nearby table for support.

'You know it's a good do when there's a punch-up,' one of Phyllis's neighbours said approvingly. 'Means there's been no skimping on the booze.'

'It's a good do all right,' snarled Phyllis in reply, pushing up her yellow sleeves, ready to sort out Richie's ex, 'and if that Pamela sodding Logan thinks she's going to ruin it by coming in here, gobbing off, then she's got another think coming.'

But just as Phyllis was about to plunge into the fray, Pamela made a surprise lunge forward, took hold of Lorna by her puffed, net, off-the-shoulder neckline, and sent her reeling. As she stumbled backwards, Pamela still had hold of her and was shaking Lorna like a terrier dispatching a rat. Pamela was a big, powerful girl.

'Let go of me!' screeched Lorna, trying to keep upright, but failing miserably and crashing into a table, sending glasses, ashtrays and plates of discarded chicken drumsticks flying all over the place.

'Make me, you ugly, meringue-frocked mare,' retaliated Pamela, as she fell on top of her.

'Don't let her get away with that, Lorn,' hollered one

of the men in the crowd with a laugh. 'Your outfit might be a bit dodgy, but she's the ugly one.'

By now, everyone in the pub, the band included, was watching the fight. It was hard to resist: two young blondes, one big, white frock, and twenty nice sharp fingernails.

They were at each other like monkeys squabbling over a banana. As for the banana himself, he was still appreciating the attentions of the Friday relief barmaid in the walk-in store cupboard in the kitchen.

The only other person missing out on the entertainment was Joe. He was still outside, smoking and trying to find the enthusiasm for a party supposedly celebrating his daughter's marriage to a piece of rubbish that wouldn't have looked out of place on the bottom of someone's shoe.

Shirley was glad he wasn't there to see such a spectacle. She took a deep breath and began to force her way through the now cheering and whooping crowd. She'd soon put a stop to all this; she had to, before Joe came back in. She'd show that Pamela, or whatever her name was, very firmly to the door.

But Shirley only got as far as the outer circle of the audience, where she was blocked by Phyllis, who was standing there with a hand clamped over her mouth.

Phyllis put her other hand on Shirley's shoulder. 'What can I say, Shirl?' she said with a remorseful shake of her head. 'I know we're a rough mob, but even I feel ashamed that we've brought this on you.'

Shirley said nothing, she just grabbed hold of Phyllis as her legs crumpled slowly under her.

'Shit.' Phyllis scooped her up under the arms as if she weighed little more than a shopping bag full of potatoes and greens, and hauled her over to one of the bench seats that ran along the wall on either side of the door.

With all the performance going on, nobody seemed to notice, or else they thought Shirley must have had one too many. Either way, it suited Phyllis just fine; the last thing she wanted was some busybody like Mrs Elliot sticking her oar in.

Phyllis stretched Shirley out on the leatherette seat, took off her prized sunflower-yellow jacket and bundled it under Shirley's head.

After a moment, Shirley's eyes flickered open. 'Phyl?'

'Ssshh, you just keep still. I'm just making you comfortable, then I'll go and get Joe.'

'No, please . . .' Shirley's voice was weak, but she was insistent. 'Leave him outside to have his smoke. Don't let him see me like this; he'll only worry. Just stop that girl, Phyllis. Please.'

'But you're not well.'

Shirley's face contorted with pain, and her breathing was shallow. 'It's just all this . . . It's made my nerves bad.'

'Look, I'm not stupid, Shirl. I know you're covering up. I was a nurse, remember? But I won't say anything to Joe if you promise me you'll go and see the doctor first thing on Monday morning. All right?'

Shirley nodded.

'Right. Then I'll make sure I sort this lot out before Joe comes back in.'

After having dispatched Denise with a glass of brandy 'to soothe Mrs Wright's nerves', Phyllis, with a new and frightening determination, barged her way into the fray with Henry, whom she had forcibly collected from the crowd, in half-hearted tow behind her.

'Right, you, get them two separated and chuck that bloody Logan girl out in the gutter where she belongs.'

'But, Phyl –'

'Just do it, Henry.'

Henry might have been daft, but he wasn't completely stupid. He knew how far he could go with his wife, and he had just reached the limit. Having a choice between two hysterical, brawling teenagers and one even slightly annoyed Phyllis, Henry made the wise choice and did as he was told.

While he pulled the girls apart – much to the annoyance of those guests who had placed bets on the big, brassy one – Phyllis clambered up on the stage with her yellow frock hauled right up round her thighs.

'Terry, turn on that microphone and give it to me,' she ordered him. 'And you lot, you start playing something jolly that'll make 'em all start dancing.'

The Spanners were reluctant to return to their instruments – they had a bird's-eye view from the stage – but after a muttered discussion they knew they had to obey Mrs Parker, so they struck up the opening chords of the perhaps not entirely appropriate 'She Loves You'.

Phyllis, meanwhile, took it upon herself to address the wedding guests over the mike.

'Show's over, everyone. Now either get yourself on that dance floor and start jigging about or go and get yourselves another drink.' She pointed at Mrs Elliot. 'Look, there's a nice partner if someone fancies a bit of a slow dance and a quick snog round the back later on. And I know Malcolm's got enough barrels stacked up out the back for a siege.'

The thought of wanting to take Mrs Elliot in their arms, and, worse, kissing the shrivelled old bat, had the men making predictably raucous comments, but at least Phyllis had got them all laughing – a neat trick considering that her husband had just ruined their fun by hauling Pamela Logan, arms flailing and legs kicking, bodily out of Lorna's reach.

Then Phyllis dealt the killer blow. 'But if there's no interest in carrying on the jollifications then perhaps it's time to shut the bar and call it a day.'

Satisfied with her work on the stage – the floor was now filled with boppers rather than fight fans, and the sacrilegious thought of a free bar closing before it had actually run out of booze had wedding guests swarming back to the bar – Phyllis went back to check on Shirley.

Denise, having run her errand with the brandy, was now escorting Lorna to the ladies to repair her hair and make-up.

Henry was somewhat less successful in completing his allotted task. Although he had parted the girls easily enough – he was a big man, a docker, after all – he hadn't quite twigged what his job actually was – smoothing things over, keeping things *nice*.

It wasn't just Phyllis's opinion of him, Henry really wasn't that bright, and, having spotted Joe Wright standing across the street from the pub with an empty glass in his hand and a pile of cigarette butts at his feet, Henry had made a beeline for him.

Unfortunately, Henry was still holding Pamela Logan firmly by the arm.

'Bloody women, eh, Joe?' he tutted, with a flash of his brows, a roll of his eyes and a lift of his chin.

'How do you mean?' asked Joe, lighting another cigarette, and wondering what on earth Henry was doing hanging on to one very angry and dishevelled-looking young woman. Surely he hadn't been stupid enough to try it on with her? If he had, Phyllis would rip his head right off his shoulders for him.

'How do I mean?' A slow realisation revealed itself on Henry's blurry-eyed face. 'Don't tell me you missed the fight.'

'Fight?' Joe was immediately on the alert. 'Just spit it out, Henry.'

'It was a right laugh. Young Pamela Logan here used to go with our Richie. They were even talking about getting married at one time, when she thought she was up the –'

'Henry.'

The seriousness of Joe's expression and the tone of his voice was enough to make even an idiot like Henry get on with it.

'Well, to cut a long story short, Pamela here decided that today should have been *her* special day and not your Lorna's. That it should have been her getting married to him. Ain't that right, love?'

Pamela's eyes widened. *His* Lorna's? So this was the rotten little trollop's old man.

'So they had a fight. You should have seen them go. It was a right turnout.'

Joe said nothing; he just swatted Henry out of his way and stormed across the street and through the pub's double doors, sending them crashing back on their hinges like something out of a scene from one of the wild west serials at the Saturday morning pictures.

As Henry, dry-mouthed and not a little worried for his

own safety, watched Joe's departing back, Pamela Logan could hold it in no longer: she exploded into laughter fit to wet her knickers.

'Good old Henry,' she snorted, holding her sides and shaking her head. 'Still as thick as shit and twice as smelly. Don't you ever learn?'

'Learn?' Henry didn't get it. 'Learn what?'

Inside the Blue Boy, Joe was frowning. A fight over that arsehole Richie? What was Henry on about? Everything looked just fine to him: Lorna was coming out of the lavatories with Denise, with not a hair out of place and just as beautiful as she'd been before he'd gone outside for a fag; Phyllis was sitting on one of the benches chatting away to Shirley; and Richie was just appearing from the kitchen behind the bar – he'd probably been up to some no-good, dodgy deals with Malcolm Danes – but there was no sign of any violence, or even any upset. Not that Joe could see.

Bloody Henry, the man was stupid enough when he was sober; when he'd had a drink he was completely bloody useless.

Still, however stupid Henry Parker might be, Joe was so thankful that nothing was wrong on Lorna's big day that he could have kissed the big, hairy ape. He let out a long sigh of relief. 'Time for another pint,' he said to no one in particular.

But if Joe had studied Richie a little more closely he might not have felt quite so calm.

From out of the kitchen, coming up close behind his new son-in-law, was the Friday relief barmaid; she was touching Richie on the shoulder in a very familiar manner, and was whispering into his ear.

'Watch it, lover, here comes the bride. Make sure your flies are done up or it'll be the divorce courts for you before you even get to enjoy your wedding night. And I know you, you wouldn't want to miss out on a bit of the other, even if it is with little Miss Droopy Drawers.'

Richie burst out laughing, just as Lorna and Denise reached the bar.

'What's so funny?' barked Denise. 'She could have been really hurt.'

'Do what?' Richie was baffled. Was she talking about him and the barmaid? No, she had no idea about his special wedding gift of a blow job, she had no idea what they'd been up to. And even if she did it was hardly a threat to the old tart's health, it was what kept her going. No, Denise was bluffing, winding him up as usual. Well, he'd call her bluff this time.

'What're you talking about, Denise? Had one too many shandies, have you?'

'I'm talking about the fight, you moron.'

Lorna touched her on the shoulder. 'Leave it, Den. Please.'

'No, I won't leave it. He's acting like he hasn't got a flaming clue what you've just been through.'

'If you must know, I haven't actually.' Richie's bravado was wearing a little thin. Whatever it was, he just hoped Joe Wright hadn't been upset by it. 'But I'm sure you're gonna tell me.'

'Too sodding right I am.' Denise stuck her fists into her waist. 'That bloody Pamela Logan only turned up and laid into Lorna.'

The barmaid melted away with a barely concealed snigger, and got on with the job she was theoretically being paid to do: serve drinks.

'Pamela Logan,' said Richie, suddenly wistful. 'I've not seen her for bloody months.'

'Aren't you even going to ask if she's OK?' Denise was talking through her teeth. It was all she could do to keep herself from wrapping her hands round his rotten throat; she could bloody well kill the selfish bastard sometimes.

'Why should I ask if she's OK?' Richie smirked nastily. 'Pam'll be all right, she's a big old bird, built like a bloody number fifteen bus.'

Denise was too busy shouting the odds at Richie about his vile, self-centred pig-headedness to even notice the deflated look on Lorna's face as she walked away with her head bowed low and her arms hanging loosely by her side.

She was going to get plastered.

Lorna passed the rest of the evening in much the same way as the guests: in a blur of drink, dancing and increasingly incoherent singing along to the band.

Sharing her daughter's need to anaesthetise herself and to block out the whole horrible nightmare, Shirley had discovered a taste for brandy and lemonade, and Phyllis, willing to do anything to maintain a bit of peace, had been only too happy to keep Shirley supplied with great goblets of the stuff. If it wasn't too much of a contradiction for Shirley to think that being anywhere near such a boozy knees-up could be anything like 'peaceful', never mind the nerve-racking experience of being stuck with being the brand-new mother-in-law of young Richie Clayton.

Phyllis loved Richie as only a mother could, but that didn't mean she wasn't ashamed of him. But then again, maybe marrying into such a nice, decent family would be the making of him.

Right. And maybe Henry would wake up in the morning and announce he was going to paper the front parlour, do a bit of washing up, and whitewash the walls in the backyard, and all before he got in to work nice and early to make sure he had the chance of a full day's casual work in the dock.

It was inevitable, but it still came as a shock to those present: the wedding party had drunk the Blue Boy dry.

Well, as good as. Apart from a few bottles of vicious-looking green and blue liqueurs that had been rejected after some admittedly quite determined tastings, there wasn't anything left. So that was it: the jolly-up was over. It was time to go home.

But no one had given much thought to how the newlyweds would be getting back to their new flat. The few guests who had cars – all of them dockers, the only ones who could afford the luxury of private transport – were all far too gone to drive them. In fact they could hardly stand, let alone operate any sort of machinery. Then it came to someone: Lorna and Richie should be carried through the streets. The idea then evolved, through several increasingly bizarre suggestions, that they should be carried on thrones, or, more realistically, on pub chairs draped with tablecloths from the buffet.

And so, the now very drunken couple were hoisted up to shoulder height by an equally drunken group of men, and were then paraded through the streets accompanied by loudly singing friends and family, most of them banging out an accompaniment on tin trays borrowed from the pub, right round to their little flat on the East India Dock Road.

Only Shirley and Joe, declaring themselves too exhausted for this final stage in the proceedings, declined to take part, and, instead, slipped quietly across the street back to Lancaster Buildings.

Richie might have been drunk – very drunk – but he wasn't so far gone that he would even consider forgoing his full marital rights on his wedding night. Sex was far too important to Richie for him to miss out on that sort of an opportunity, especially with Lorna looking not half bad in that dress of hers, and with her breasts even fuller now she was pregnant.

Richie was going to enjoy himself. And the fact that Lorna was out like a light, almost comatose, stretched out on the bed and still fully dressed, didn't deter him one little bit; actually it turned him on all the more.

But the effect of having Richie pumping away obstinately, relentlessly on top of her – the alcohol was taking its toll – eventually had Lorna beginning to come round.

What the hell was happening to her?

The room was spinning, Lorna knew that, just as she knew her dress was pulled up over her face, and the layers and layers of net were making it hard for her to breathe. But what on earth was going on?

It took her a few befuddled moments to realise what was happening.

He was doing it to her. Doing it to her, while she'd been knocked out from all the drink.

Lorna felt the bile rise in her throat.

He'd have to finish sooner or later.

And he did.

Then he rolled off her onto his side and was asleep in seconds, snoring like a pig, and still wearing his socks and his vest.

Carefully, Lorna got off the bed, and she slipped off one of the pillowcases and took it through to the kitchen.

She stood there in the dark, feeling horribly sick but knowing what she had to do. She ripped off every shred of her clothing and rammed each frothy white stitch of it into the pillowslip.

She'd put it down by the dustbins as soon as it got light.

As she stood at the sink trying to wash herself she knew it would take a lot more than soap and water for her ever to feel clean again.

Chapter 6

When Lorna opened the door to her, Denise gasped in shock at the way her friend looked, and it wasn't just the messy hair and paint-spattered clothing that had so surprised her.

'Christ, Lorn, I know honeymoons are meant to wear you out, but you look really terrible. Like you've not slept for a whole week.'

'Thanks very much.'

'Sorry.'

Lorna managed a smile. 'That's OK.'

'Is this is a bad time? Is Richie still asleep or something?'

'No, he went out ages ago.'

'Can I come in then?'

'Course you can.' Lorna stepped back and ushered Denise in through the flimsy plywood door that stood at the very top of the narrow stairway, the only barrier between the newlyweds and the other two families who occupied the lower floors and basement of the tall, traffic-stained Victorian house.

'Look at all the hard work I've been doing.'

Lorna gave the door a rattling shove, that being the only way to close it properly, she explained, then went on, pointing at the walls of the hallway, and only half-lying: 'This is why I look so tired. I've been working my guts out trying to make this place look nice.' She paused and then added quietly, 'I really want to try and make it into a proper home for us, Den. Somewhere nice.'

'Blimey.'

'Blimey good or blimey bad?'

Denise looked round. 'Blimey flipping amazing. You've never done all this in just a week, Lorn? It must've taken the pair of you working night and day to scrape all that rotten old wallpaper off back to the plaster. I must say Richie's really surprised me this time. And I mean that nicely for once.'

Lorna fiddled nervously with the brush she was holding. 'Richie's been ever so busy, so I did it.'

'All this? By yourself?'

She nodded. 'I've stripped off every last bit. Satisfying, really, now it's all ready for painting. I'd have liked to have put up fresh wallpaper. You know, something nice and bright and modern, but I don't know how.'

'Hang on, you're saying you did all this by yourself? In your condition?'

Lorna nodded again.

'But when? You only had the Friday and Monday off for the wedding.'

'I just fitted it in. Bit before, and a bit after work.'

'I have to say, Lorna, I am well impressed. And like I said before, especially with you expecting and everything.'

'It's because I'm expecting that I want to make this a proper home. A home for the baby to be happy in.'

'That's all very well, Lorna, but don't you think you should at least consider getting someone in to help? I didn't want to sound horrible just now, but you don't half look knackered. You don't want to go taking on too much.'

'I thought about it, but you know how Richie gets.'

'Yeah, won't do anything himself, but thinks you're

criticising him personally if you say someone else can do so much as tie their own shoelaces. He's always been like it.'

'I'm learning that.' Lorna suddenly brightened. 'Tell you what, he wouldn't mind if you gave me a hand.'

Denise pulled a face. Why should she do Richie's work for him?

'I wouldn't expect you to do anything hard or heavy, Den.'

'It's not that. I don't mind a bit of graft. I just don't want to cause any rows between you and Richie.'

'It'll just help pass the time if I have someone to talk to while I get on with it. Look, I've got these little samples from the shop. They're a new idea. You test them out on the walls and see what colour looks nicest. I'm not definite which I prefer yet, but you can tell me if you agree with the ones I think might be prettiest.'

Lorna bent down and picked up a tin tray that had been left at the flat by one of the impromptu wedding procession on the previous Saturday night, then showed Denise the dozen little plastic pots she had set out neatly on their lids.

'What do you think?'

'What does Richie think?'

Lorna looked away and shrugged. 'I told you, he's been busy.'

'But he must at least have –'

'You know him, he doesn't have much to say about this sort of thing.'

'You mean he couldn't care less and he's not interested?'

'I never said that.'

'Right.' Denise could be tough, but she wouldn't be

spiteful, not to Lorna. And she'd be doing this for Lorna, not him. And if Richie did come in and start, at least she had plenty of experience dealing with the miserable git, which was more than Lorna had.

'OK then,' she said decisively. 'If this hallway's going to get painted, I'd better get my sleeves rolled up, hadn't I?'

The look of delight on Lorna's face reassured Denise that she had made the right decision, and anyway, what else did she have to do with herself on a Saturday afternoon? Only shopping for something new to wear, having a nice long bubble bath in Terry's mum's new bathroom, getting ready to go out with Terry tonight while she watched some old rubbish on the telly . . .

Still, what were friends for?

The painting was going surprisingly well. Denise found the swish-swosh of the brush almost hypnotic, and the fumes of the turpentine quite heady. She could have probably fallen into a trance if the chair she was using as a ladder wasn't quite so wobbly.

'Break time, Den.' Lorna was carrying the tin tray. This time it held the two mugs of tea she had just made in the little kitchenette.

'I'll just finish this bit up by the picture rail.' Denise leaned back at a precarious angle to admire her handiwork. 'There, done it.' Then she took Lorna's hand to steady herself, climbed down, sat on the hall floor and got stuck into the tea and KitKats.

She cupped her hand under her chin to catch the chocolate that had melted during dunking, took a big bite, chewed, then let out a deep contented sigh. 'Tell you what, Lorn, I'm enjoying this. Makes you feel like you've achieved something. Once you've had the baby, we'll have to set up our own painting and decorating business.'

Lorna, who had settled down beside her, laughed. 'You're mad, you are. Whatever will you think of next? Can you imagine the look on people's faces if we turned up – female painters and decorators?'

'It'd be just like the look on my face when I saw that tramp Pamela Logan marching in uninvited to the wedding like that. I couldn't believe the cheek on her. But she's always been a slut, that one. No shame.'

'People are probably saying the same about me: that I'm a slut, that I've got no shame.'

'Don't be daft, you're not a tramp, you're a respectable married woman.' Denise shook her head. 'Christ, that sounds weird – *married woman*.'

'Imagine how it feels *being* married.'

'I'll tell you what's really weird, that Pamela thinking she could just barge in and start shouting the odds. Fancy her thinking –'

'Please, Den, don't let's talk about her. Tell me about Terry instead. The Spanners were great at the wedding, everyone said so.' She carefully flattened the silver paper from her KitKat and began shaping it into a ring, then she changed her mind and fashioned it into a little goblet instead, which she handed to Denise. 'There you are, Den, a trophy, for being a champion mate.'

Denise took it with a heavy heart. Champion mate? If she'd been any sort of a mate at all she'd have stopped Lorna going anywhere near bloody Richie, never mind getting knocked up by him and, worse, married to the rotten bastard.

*　*　*

They had long since finished their break and were just putting the finishing touches to the second coat – guilt had spurred Denise to work with even more energy – when the door opened and Richie came in.

Lorna straightened up, paintbrush in hand. 'Look what we've done, Rich.'

Denise noticed three things: Lorna sounded as wary as if she were trying to calm a rabid dog that was about to sink its teeth into her leg; that Richie made no attempt at all to kiss Lorna – his wife of just one week – as he pushed past her and stood in the middle of the hallway, looking about him with narrowed eyes like a monarch surveying his kingdom; and finally that Richie stank like he had put away the best part of a brewery's entire monthly output.

'And while we've been working,' Lorna was speaking quicker and quicker, chattering out the words like a demented mynah bird, 'Denise has been telling me how well Terry and the other Spanners are doing. They're going to be playing at a different pub every weekend, right up until Christmas. And she said that we can –'

'They're playing at a different pub every weekend, Lorna, because no one can stand hearing their shit-hole music twice on the trot.'

'No, Richie, it's not like that.' Lorna couldn't stop herself, couldn't stop saying these things, even though she knew she was making him cross. 'They're doing really well. Den said –'

'Doing well? What, playing guitars like little kids, and earning peanuts like trained monkeys?'

'Lorna,' Denise said calmly, 'I'd love another cup of tea, and I bet Richie wouldn't mind one either.'

Lorna, with a grateful widening of her eyes at her

friend, shot off to the kitchen, like a human cannonball being fired across the big top.

As soon as she heard the tap being turned on and Lorna clattering about with the kettle and cups, Denise moved as close to the beery smell of Richie as she could bear, then retaliated on behalf of Terry, Lorna, and all the years she had spent at home with Richie trying to bully and manipulate her.

'At least Terry's trying to earn an honest living – working during the day, practising at night, doing gigs at weekends –'

'*Gigs?* Hark at you. Anyone would think you're some big flash pop star's groupie, instead of some silly little cow hanging around with a bunch of no-mark kids.'

'When did you last bring in any decent money?'

'I bring in plenty.'

'I said *decent* money. Not knocking out bent gear down the pub, earning a pocketful one night then nothing for the rest of the week.'

Denise folded her arms and leaned back against the doorframe. Pick the bones out of that, Richie, she thought smugly. But when she realised her sweater was stuck to the doorframe – the white gloss paint was still tacky; Lorna must have only just finished it before she arrived – Denise's self-satisfaction vanished and indignation took its place.

That girl was working so bloody hard. No wonder she looked like a sodding ghost. Richie needed more than his fortune telling for him, he needed a kick right up the arse.

'You don't know the meaning of the word decent, do you, Richie?'

'What's that cow been saying?'

'She's not a cow and she'd not been saying anything. Lorna wouldn't hear a single word spoken against you, so she's hardly going to say anything herself, now is she, you thick sod? You don't deserve her, Richie, you really don't. If only you realised how lucky you are, you'd wrap her up in cotton wool and treasure her like she was a flaming precious jewel, not treat her like she was a mangy dog who you can kick whenever you feel like it.'

'Who the hell are you telling anyone how to behave?' He moved as if to push past her, but Denise, despite the stench of beer, stood her ground and blocked him.

He took a deep breath. 'Now you're really beginning to annoy me, Denise. I don't have to put up with this.'

But she was adamant. 'Look, Richie, Lorna's not going to be able to work for much longer, especially not down that dock office with all them blokes round her all day. And that dress she's wearing, it barely does up round her chest. She's over four months gone; she needs proper maternity gear. And a husband earning a regular wage. The heating bills for this damp hole alone are going to be –'

Richie took a single step forward and was now standing right up close to Denise. He jabbed a finger into her face. 'Are you saying I can't provide for my own wife?'

She brushed his hand away. 'Don't be such a prat.'

'What did you call me?'

'Why don't you act like a civilised human being for once, Richie? Go in the kitchen and help her. Make sure she's all right.'

'*You* fucking make sure she's all right. I'm going out. Going out to get some *decent* money. For *my wife*. So just keep that turned-up pig's snout of yours out of my business.'

Richie shoved her out of the way, crashed out of the door, and hammered down the stairs.

'One day, Richie . . .' Denise called after him.

He stopped, halfway down, and looked up at her over his shoulder. 'Aw, don't frighten me, Den, you'll have me cacking my pants.'

Lorna poked her head out of the tiny cubbyhole of a kitchenette. 'What's wrong? What's all the noise?'

'It's all right, Lorn, it was only Richie. He's had to pop out. He said to tell you he had a bit of urgent business he had to get sorted.' Denise hoped that her voice wasn't shaking quite as much as she was. 'Now, where's that tea?'

Richie walked along in the shadows of Commercial Road, avoiding the pools of yellow light from the streetlamps and the on-coming beams of passing cars; his head was bent low as if he were bearing down against the gusts of chilly rain, but he was actually casing each parked vehicle he passed for a potential target.

Bingo! It hadn't taken long.

Some idiot had left a bag on the back seat of a brand-new Zodiac parked near a phone box. Richie stopped on the pretext of lighting a cigarette.

He weighed up the situation: a bloke was using the phone; the car was empty save for the bag. The car was too nice to belong to anyone round there, so it probably belonged to the bloke on the phone.

If he was quick, and didn't make too much noise . . .

Richie pulled off his navy and red striped college scarf. Shame to spoil it – he'd only bought it the other day, and he did like to be in fashion – but needs must, and he had to deaden the noise. He then took the half-brick from out of his overcoat pocket that he had picked up especially off one of the countless demolition sites that scarred so many East End streets. After a quick look round, he gave the side rear window of the car a sharp tap with the scarf-wrapped brick.

The glass crazed and crumpled and Richie gave it a helping hand with a quick smack from the side of his gloved fist. In a flash his hand was in the car and out again, now holding a rather smart calfskin briefcase.

Easy. All over in less than a minute.

With his head well down and the bag tucked safely under his arm, Richie strode off into the rainy night towards the junction with Three Colt Street, where there was a Second World War bombsite still waiting to be cleared.

He clambered and slipped over the rain-slicked rubble until he was well hidden in the lee of one of the derelict houses.

Squatting down, Richie prised open the lock with his flick knife and then proceeded to work his way through the contents of the case.

A pork fucking pie in a Cellophane wrapper? In a poncy bag like this? Was the bloke having a laugh?

Richie tossed the pie angrily over his shoulder.

A sheaf of type-written documents quickly followed the pie in a fluttering arc of paper.

Typical. Bloody City types, they were all the same, all-show snobs with no dough in their bin. He probably had that shiny new motor on the book, and he probably couldn't even afford the payments, but he had to have it to show off to his snot-nosed neighbours just how well he was doing at the office.

Richie was about to send the bag the same way as

the rubbish it contained when he noticed a bulge in the elasticated pocket in the lid. Inside he found a classy-looking, gold-tooled leather box.

What was this then?

He flicked on his lighter to get a better look.

Inside the box was a gold charm bracelet, with a delicately embossed gift card tucked into the little velvet cushion. He ripped the card out and threw it on the debris in the direction of the pork pie and the carefully prepared, half yearly, projected accounts of Joseph, Wood and Pritchett, merchant bankers of Throgmorton Street.

He'd show Denise who could bring home a decent few quid. He'd take his haul straight down the docks to the Cadiz Arms, and find a seaman fresh off a long, lonely voyage, with his wages just burning their way through the pockets in his bell bottoms, begging to be spent.

As Richie loped off towards the pub, two boys, who had been playing Cowboys and Indians in the shell-damaged buildings on the bombsite way past the time they should have been – 'when it gets dark' having being their officially designated, but long since past, curfew – came out to find what sort of treasure the man had discarded.

'What is it? What did he throw away?'

'Dunno? Looks like a load of old papers and . . .' he bent down and retrieved the little card, 'some sort of a tag or something.'

'Show us. What does it say?'

'*For my darling wife on her fortieth birthday.*'

'Ooo! Hark at you! *Darling*!'

'Here, this is more like it,' said the bigger of the two boys. 'I've found a pork pie, still in its plastic and everything.' He unwrapped it, broke it in two and gave half to his little brother.

They stood there in the rain devouring the unexpected pastry-covered treat.

'I reckon he was a robber,' said the bigger one.

'Do you think there'll be a reward if we tell the coppers what we saw?'

'No, but Dad'll tan our arses if he thought we'd ever grassed on someone.'

'Even on someone like stinky Richie Clayton?'

'Even on him, and if we don't get home soon, we'll get our arses tanned anyway.'

With that, Geronimo ran off into the rain, with Zorro in hot, if rather incongruous, pursuit, neither of the two mini-sized heroes giving a second glance or thought to the discarded pie wrapper, or to the small, embossed gift card that they had abandoned on the soaking wet rubble.

On his way to the dockside pub, Richie was having second thoughts – not about the person he had robbed, nor about the birthday he had spoiled, but about the amount of money that the bracelet might be worth.

He had weighed it in the palm of his hand and had realised how heavy it was. There must be a good bit of gold in it, and it wasn't bad to look at either. Pretty in fact. The sort of thing that someone would buy as a present for someone.

The fact that it had already been a present for someone didn't enter Richie's head. What did occur to him was that he would be better off taking it round to Doris Barker, the fence who lived in the same buildings as Lorna's mum and dad. She'd be sure to give him a better price than some sozzled merchant mariner, who just wanted to take home a little softener for his old woman, to make up for going to the pub rather than straight home after so many months away at sea.

Doris was definitely the best bet.

'What do you want?' The formidable Doris Barker, trademark bouffant tangerine curls quivering, stood in the doorway of her flat, glaring at Richie with as much appreciation as if he were a slime-trailing slug crawling out of the boiled cabbage during one of her gargantuan Sunday lunches.

'I've got something to sell you.'

'Sell to me? Why would you sell me something?'

Richie snorted. ''Cos you're a fence.'

'Me? Are you suggesting I'm a receiver of stolen goods?' She gave a shocked little laugh. 'Whoever's been spreading that sort of rubbish? Who on earth could have told you that?'

'Don't play games with me, Grandma. You fucking fence for everyone round here. Including for my own fucking aunt.'

'Whatever you think I do or don't do, Richie Clayton, I don't want anything to do with the likes of you. Got it? Now you just clear off out of it. And while you're about it, ponder on this bit of advice: I'd watch that mouth of yours if I was you. I don't like people who use bad language in front of me, and I like people with loose tongues even less. Your Auntie Phyllis's business is hers, not yours, got it? So, if you know what's good for you, you just remember that. Believe me, it'll be better for your health if you do.'

With that the door was slammed in his face.

He stood there a moment, shaking his head, trying to understand who this pathetic old woman thought she was.

Shutting the door in his face? Was she stupid?

He hammered on the door with the flat of his hand, but to no avail. Then he tried kicking it.

Two things quickly became obvious: firstly, Doris Barker's door was not made of the usual thin wood used by the council, even though it looked just the same as those belonging to all her neighbours; and, secondly, that the door was not going to be opened again that night – not to him, anyway.

By the time Richie finally reached the Cadiz Arms, he was soaking wet and in a stinking, fuming temper.

Did that stupid whore, Doris Barker, really think she could put the frighteners on him? And all that coming-the-innocent about not being a fence. So why did she have a reinforced door on her flat then? Not to keep boyfriends at bay, that was for sure, the ugly old slag.

Women were all the same, scheming conniving cows, every single jack of them. Only good for one thing, and they weren't always much good at that. In fact, much as he needed to have sex with them, Richie hated women. Really hated them. They made him sick. Each and every one of them.

But despite what had been an all-encompassing, blind anger – an anger so acute that, despite his natural cowardice, Richie had been ready to take on anyone who so much as looked at him a bit sideways – after just a few minutes in the Cadiz Arms, his mood, as it so often did, changed dramatically. By the time he had swallowed down his first whisky he was smiling happily to himself, convinced that things had begun to look up.

The cause was simple: Richie had found a mark.

He was a grizzled, grey-bearded merchant seaman,

just back home from the West Indies on that evening's tide, and with lots of lovely back pay to dispose of. He had joined Richie at the bar, looking to strike up a slightly drunken conversation with him. And Richie had been only too glad to oblige.

It hadn't taken much longer for things to progress to the point where they were sharing a discreet table in the corner. Richie opened his newly acquired briefcase with a flourish – noticing for the first time, now that he was in the light, that the case had a set of bold initials tooled in gold along the flap – and the sailor was examining the charm bracelet with admiring attention.

'This'll be a perfect gift for my daughter. Karleen's her name,' he said, swiping his dripping nose with the back of his gnarled, liver-spotted hand. 'Lovely kid, she is. She misses me so much when I'm away, that girl. More than her sour-faced mother ever does. Women, eh? They start off as angels, then, once you do the right thing and marry them, they turn into nags and troublemakers.'

'I won't argue with you there, mate,' said Richie. 'You could have taken the words right out of my mouth.'

'Four of them, I've got.'

'Eh?'

'Four wives.'

'No?' Richie didn't know whether to be impressed, to call him a bloody liar, or to have the bloke committed. Four wives? What was he, a nutcase or something?

'Honest. All in different parts of the world, mind. They don't know about one another.'

Richie grinned. 'I should think not. You'd get your ear hole bent then all right. Imagine them having that as a weapon to use against you.'

'Don't. That's too horrible to even think about. They're

nasty enough separate. I'd dread to think what would happen if they ever got together. Be like bloody witches in a coven.' He took a deep drag on his pipe and then exhaled enough tobacco smoke to cure a kipper.

'Do you know, there's not one I'd bother to piss on if she was on fire. But my kids, they're different. They're the most precious things in my life. Fifteen of them, I've got.' He grinned. 'The ones I know about, that is. And they're not all with my wives either.'

He supped some more of his drink with a satisfied 'Aaahh, that's the stuff', then went on: 'You been blessed with kids, son?'

Richie, steaming nicely in the overheated fug of the public bar, considered for a moment. Why not play along? Who knows, it might be worth a few extra quid on the price if he humoured the pathetic, sentimental old sod.

'Not yet,' he said, holding his empty glass above his head and pointing to the seaman's almost finished beer as a signal to the barmaid to bring them over a couple of refills. 'But, I'm pleased to say, we've got our first little one on the way. We're right chuffed, the missus and me.'

'That's lovely son, right lovely. Here, let me get this one, to celebrate your good news.'

They had another drink. And the seaman had a few more. Richie, having no intention, let alone the head, to match him, was drinking more slowly; he was interested in making a sale, not in getting legless. But by the time the landlady had finally persuaded him and the sailor, the last of her customers that evening, to drink up for the night, Richie had had far more than he'd intended, and he still hadn't closed the deal.

Frustrated, he nodded his obsequious good nights to the

bar staff – who knew when he might want the Cadiz Arms as a bolt hole, or a barmaid as an alibi? – and steered the now tottering and staggering ancient mariner outside into the cold and blustery autumn night.

'So, that'll be twenty quid then,' Richie said, the rain tipping down on them in sheets like the overflow from a blocked drainpipe. 'Briefcase thrown in. Like we agreed.' Richie had no intention of keeping such a traceable bit of evidence, and figured he might as well work it off on the drunken old git as a bit of a laugh. Let him explain that away if he got a tug from the law on the way home.

''Sright. We'greed.' The seaman's words were so slurred, Richie could barely make out what he was saying. 'Twenny. 'Sworth ev'rypenny. See my little girl's face. Daddy wi'presents. Aaahh.'

He took a few moments to find his pocket, then a few more to put in his hand. Then he pulled out everything he had.

'Whoops!' He was grinning and waving two green notes. 'Two quid. Look! Only two left. Where's it all . . . ? You know . . .' His words trailed off into a drunken giggle.

Richie saw nothing to laugh about. His jaw tightened. 'You fucking what?' He slammed the man, double-handed, right in the middle of his chest. He was a fair size, but far too drunk to keep his balance, or even to consider retaliating. His arms flailed around like sails in a brisk northwester, and he went sprawling and stumbling about the slippery flagstones until he landed on his knees. He stayed there for a moment, goggle-eyed and rocking, and then, in almost comic slow motion, he rolled off the pavement and into the rain and muck-filled gutter, landing on his back with the added indignity of a loud fart.

He lay there in the filth, his mouth opening and closing, like a beached haddock.

Richie stood over him, snorting like a bull. All he could see was the cause of his own pockets being empty.

'Useless. Fucking totally useless.' He took aim, threw back his head, then tipped it forward and spat right in the man's face. Then he straightened up and kicked him – hard – in the guts.

The crotch of the man's trousers darkened.

'Jesus, you dirty old bastard, now you've pissed yourself. Your daughter's going to be so proud of you.'

The sound of bolts being shot on the other side of the pub door had Richie back on alert. Realising that when the bar staff had finished clearing up for the night he might well have an audience, he lined up a final departing kick at the man's side, delivered it with clinical swiftness, shoved the bracelet in his own jacket pocket for safekeeping, and dumped the bag across the man's unconscious body. Then he pulled up his overcoat collar and trotted off into the night.

By the time he got home it was a quarter to midnight.

Lorna had waited up for him, but she was so exhausted after all her hard work that she had fallen sound asleep. She lay there, curled up like a little girl in one of the matching armchairs that Phyllis had loaned them from her front parlour.

Richie hardly registered his new wife's presence. He peeled off his wet overcoat and dropped it on the floor at his feet on the ugly swirly patterned carpet, then fished out the bracelet from his jacket pocket and threw it down angrily onto the walnut coffee table.

His aim was good, but he hadn't considered the consequence of throwing a heavy gold bracelet at the glass-covered top. There was a loud crack, and Lorna woke up with a terrified start.

She sat bolt upright, her hair all over the place, and her eyes puffy from sleep. 'What have you done to the table?' she gasped, too dazed to think about what she was saying. 'That's Mum and Dad's. We're only borrowing it.'

'*What?*'

Lorna, waking up very quickly, noticed the bracelet for the first time. She immediately forgot the table.

'That's so lovely, Richie. Really pretty.'

She reached out to touch it, but Richie scooped it up before she had the chance.

'Yeah, it is. So don't go putting them filthy, paint-covered hands of yours anywhere near it.'

Lorna pulled back her hand as if she'd been burned.

'And it's worth a lot money.' He pushed the coffee table back against the wall with his foot. 'Not like that piece of matchwood. Get rid of it, it's a bloody menace.' Without stopping for more than a single beat, he went on: 'So what have I got for tea?'

'Shepherd's pie. I've only got to make a bit of gravy.'

She stood up, denying herself the moment's luxury of a good stretch to ease her aching muscles, and went straight out to the kitchen, leaving Richie sprawled in the other armchair.

'Do you like the colour we did in the hall?' she called, careful not to speak too loudly or to make too much noise with the kettle; she didn't want to wake up the people downstairs. 'Denise said she'd come round to help me with the rest of the flat next weekend.'

Richie was on his feet and out into the hall. He'd had just about enough of bloody women.

'What have you been saying to her?' His voice was low, but she could hear his temper boiling. 'You trying to show me up again?'

Lorna, with a mixing bowl holding a cold paste of gravy powder and water in one hand, and a wooden spoon in the other, came out of the kitchen to join him, praying that he wouldn't start shouting. 'I never meant anything, Rich,' she said gently.

'Getting her to help do up *my fucking home*.' He snatched the bowl from her hand and smashed it against the wall. Shards from the shattered bowl seemed to fly everywhere, while the dark brown, sludgy paste trickled slowly down the fresh, pale cream paint.

'Richie!' Lorna couldn't help herself, she grabbed his arm. 'All our hard work!'

Very slowly, Richie looked down at her hand on his sleeve, and then he plucked it off as if it were no more than an annoying insect. She had her back to the door. He began walking towards her, driving her backwards like a wild creature being netted by a hunter. He didn't say a word, he just bunched up his fist and kept moving towards her.

'Don't, please, you're frightening me.'

Her back was right up against the plywood door

'*Richie, don't!*'

They both knew what he was going to do next, but when it happened, they were still both stunned.

Richie's fist slammed into her stomach; Lorna doubled over and bounced – twice – against the door from the force of his punch. The cardboard-thin plywood buckled, and, on the second impact, folded under her weight.

Backwards down the stairs she went, tumbling and turning like an acrobat, only coming to a halt when she hit the turn in the landing right outside the door of the flat below.

Richie looked down at her from the now doorless threshold of their own flat, his eyes wide, his mouth dry, and his stomach churning. What the fuck had he done? He rubbed his hand over his eyes as though his actions could be erased.

Joe Wright would kill him.

Think, think.

He scrambled down after her. 'I'm sorry, Lorn, really sorry. It was an accident. My foot must have slipped. What can I do? Do you want a drink of water?'

Curled up in a ball on the floor and gasping for breath, Lorna managed to say to him: 'I'm hurt. Get my mum. Get your mum. Get someone. Anyone.'

Richie thought for a moment. Joe Wright would definitely kill him if he went round there. Denise, he'd get Denise.

'You wait there, I'll go and get our Den.'

He stepped over her, and was halfway down the next flight when he stopped and turned. 'Don't you go saying anything silly to anyone, Lorna. Do you understand me?'

'Just get someone, Richie. Please.'

As Lorna lay there, the Dennisons, her downstairs neighbours, were listening from the other side of their door. 'Should I go out and see if she needs help?' said Mrs Dennison. 'Sounds like she had a right nasty fall.'

'Interfere in a married couple's tiff?' Her husband was appalled by the idea. 'You get yourself back in bed and mind your own business.'

*   *   *

Lorna was stretched out on her bed, with one arm thrown back over her face, and the other clutching her middle.

Shirley – who Denise had insisted should come along, after having point-blank refused Richie's ridiculous demands, and then pleas, that Lorna's mother shouldn't be told – knew from bitter personal experience exactly what to do while they waited for the doctor to arrive. She had gone straight into Lorna and Richie's bedroom and had covered their bed with the pile of newspapers she had brought with her, and then spread out a fresh clean sheet. She had then called down for Joe to carry Lorna upstairs to the bedroom.

Shirley, after gleaning only the barest of details from Richie – he was so jumpy he was making no sense – had sent him to fetch the doctor. Not only did her daughter need medical attention, but Shirley also thought it best to keep Richie out of Joe's reach as he paced up and down in the little living room like a caged animal waiting for a haunch of red meat to be thrown in by the keepers.

'Shall I make some more tea, Mrs Wright?' Denise was almost as jumpy as Richie.

'That'd be nice, Den, thank you.' Shirley squeezed Lorna's hand. 'Could you manage a cup?'

Lorna shook her head and started sobbing again.

Shirley's chest felt as if it had been stuffed with bricks. 'Don't keep punishing yourself, darling.'

'Why not? It's all my fault.'

'No, of course it's not.'

'Yes, it is.'

'How is it?'

'I shouldn't have been standing on that chair.'

'I'll go and make just you and Mr Wright a cup then,'

whispered Denise. 'Then I'd better be getting off home, if that's all right. Mum was sound asleep in bed and I never stopped to leave her a note or nothing. I just came straight out when Richie turned up. If she wakes up she'll be worried out of her life.'

'You're a good girl, Denise. Thanks.'

Better than that bloody half-brother of mine, thought Denise as she filled the kettle. It was obvious to her that Lorna had been lying. She hadn't been standing on any chair, the hall was already finished, and as for that sticky brown mess all up the wall and the bits of glass everywhere, Denise didn't even want to start thinking what that was all about. Christ knows what Richie had done this time, but she knew, as surely as if she'd told her, that Lorna was covering up something. She was scared of the rotten bastard. God, Denise hated him.

'Here's your tea, Mr Wright.'

As Joe turned to face her, Denise gulped back the ping-pong-ball-sized lump that rose in her throat. Tears were streaming down his face. She had never seen a grown man crying before. She didn't know what to do.

'Denise,' Joe said, ignoring the tea, 'you're Lorna's best friend. Can't you say something to her? Persuade her to come home with her mum and me? Tell her that little cowson's not good enough for her?'

Denise fiddled with the cup, moving it round and round in the saucer.

'I would, Mr Wright, course I would. But I don't think she'd listen to me. And it makes me ashamed to say it, but I agree with you. I don't think Richie's good enough for her either. But you know how much Lorna reckons she loves him. And she comes over all protective and defensive if anyone dares say anything about him. It's like she's got this blind spot where he's concerned.'

Joe turned away again, and covered his face with his hands.

Denise just stood there, still fiddling with the cup, now not only not knowing what to do, but not knowing what to say either.

Then the silence was broken.

'Joe.' It was Shirley. 'The doctor's here. He says he's going to call an ambulance.'

'I can't tell you how much I appreciate you coming with me, Tel.'

Denise and Terry were making their way through a long, green-painted maternity ward in the London Hospital at Whitechapel. They were heading towards Joe Wright, whom they could see standing, with his hands thrust awkwardly in his trouser pockets, next to a bed that they guessed would be Lorna's.

'I really wanted to come in and see Lorna, but I knew her mum or dad would be here, and I felt so embarrassed about being related to that creep Richie. Honestly, Tel, he's about as much use as an arse with a headache.' She looked at him and gave him a little smile. 'You're my moral support, you are.'

He smiled back, but her own smile disappeared as they walked past yet another bed with a little clear plastic crib by its side.

'I don't think I could have stood it by myself. I'm telling you, I wasn't expecting this.'

'No, nor was I, Den. I would never have thought they'd have put her in here with all these new babies and their mums. This all seems so wrong, like it's a punishment or something. And Lorna's such a smashing girl, so kind and gentle. She doesn't deserve this. I know it's terrible happening to anyone, but . . . Aw, you know what I mean.'

'Yeah, course I do.' She kissed him softly on the cheek. 'I'm so glad you're here with me.'

Terry linked his fingers through Denise's. 'I'll always be here for you, Den.'

She looked away in case she started crying. 'Thanks. That means a lot to me.'

'And I don't blame you for being embarrassed by that cousin of yours either. If only half of what I've heard about him's true . . . How can you possibly be related to him?'

'I know, I feel like that half the time.' Denise had to get off the subject of cousins. 'Look, Tel, over there.'

'What?'

'It's only Mrs Wright. Sitting there, by Lorna's bed.'

Terry frowned. 'Yeah, I can see it is. But why are you so surprised?'

'No reason. And look there's Richie. Standing next to Mr Wright.'

'Yeah, so he is.' Terry shrugged.

She must be in shock, he decided, as he looked at Richie who was standing there, grim-faced, with his hands clasped in front of his crotch as if he were defending the goal from a free kick.

He could think of a million and one other places he would rather be, even on a rainy Sunday afternoon, but Richie wasn't stupid; he had to keep up the appearance of playing happy families, at least while Joe Wright was there, just as he had to be there to hear what Lorna had to say to everyone about the 'accident'.

'Hello, Den. Hello, Tel.' Lorna's voice was husky from weeping and she was almost as pale as the pile of white, starched pillows that were propping her up. She had a drip in one arm, a sling on the other, and a row of stitches in a gash above her left eyebrow. Both her eyes were bruised slits.

'Hello, Lorn.' Denise leaned down and kissed her, dithering for a moment as she found the place that would hurt least from any contact. Not only had Denise not expected to see all the babies in the ward, she hadn't expected to see her friend looking quite as bad as this either. But, no matter how close to tears she felt, Denise knew she mustn't cry, knew she mustn't make things worse for Lorna.

So she straightened up and addressed the other visitors round the bed. 'All right, everyone?'

There were mumbled replies from Richie and Joe, and a 'Not too bad, love, in the circumstances' from Shirley.

'Here's some grapes for you, Lorn. Me and Terry got them down the Lane this morning.'

'That's really kind. Thanks.'

Denise put the brown paper bag she'd been clutching on the bedside locker and then sat down on a big, green leather armchair.

'What have they said?' she asked, and immediately flashed a 'sorry' look at Shirley, who was sitting on the other side of the bed, and added hurriedly, 'I already know about you losing . . . you know . . .'

'Mum said she'd told you.'

'So, what have they . . . ?' Denise really wasn't finding this easy, especially with Richie standing behind her.

'I didn't want to stay in. I said to Richie: I'm all right, I can go home.' She glanced anxiously at him, seeing if she'd said the right thing. He didn't seem even to be listening to her. Was that good or bad? Keep talking, keep things going, make them all think everything was going to be fine. 'But they said I'd lost quite a lot of blood, and they weren't very happy about my shoulder, but I said –'

'Not broken, is it?'

'No, no, nothing like that,' she said hurriedly. 'Just bruised, that's all. But you know what they're like: cautious and that. They want me to rest it. Here, Tel, Den says you're doing really well.' Lorna was as desperate to change the subject as Denise had been earlier, and she felt so dopey with all the drugs, she was terrified that if they kept on asking about her injuries she might say the wrong thing and go upsetting Richie, and then he'd lose his temper and start shouting and hollering, and . . . The thought of the scene, if her dad found out what had really happened, was just too much for her. And, despite feeling as if she had had her heart torn out of her chest, she knew she had to keep everyone sweet, keep things nice. 'Feels like ages since I've seen you to talk to properly, Tel.'

'It is ages.'

Denise smiled at her. 'He was only saying earlier how much he missed having a chat with you, Lorn. How you're about the only one of us lot who ever makes any sense.'

'I don't think so,' said Lorna quietly, dropping her chin. She took a moment to compose herself then looked at Terry again. 'It's really kind of you coming in to see me, especially when you must have been up so late last night.'

Richie sneered dismissively at Terry.

Joe glared at him. 'Something wrong, Richie?'

'No, just holding back a sneeze. Bit of a cold coming on.'

'In that case, perhaps you'd better get off home. Lorna doesn't want a cold on top of everything else now, does she.' It wasn't a question.

'All right, Joe.' Shirley put her hand on her husband's arm. 'Calm down. We're all a bit overtired.'

'I think your dad's right, Lorna.' Right? Richie could have kissed the old bastard for giving him such a first-prize get out. He couldn't wait to get away from this stinking place and all the screaming chavvies in their cots. Kids – who needed all that aggravation? What an escape he'd had.

He pulled out a handkerchief and held it ostentatiously to his face. 'When you're weak like this,' he muttered through the layers of cotton, 'a cold's not going to do you any good, now is it? And nor are having all these people round your bedside.' If he was going, he was going to make damn sure she didn't have anyone left to blab her mouth off to.

He stared at Terry. 'I don't know how these two got in here past that ward sister. Should only be three to a bed, she told us, *and* they're meant to be relatives.'

Denise looked over her shoulder at him. 'We lied,' she said flatly, then stood up. 'But I think me and Terry will leave you in peace now, Lorn. I'll pop in after work tomorrow, if that's all right.'

'I'd love that, Den. See you then.'

'Just one more thing, if it's not too much for you: Mum's waiting outside. She just wanted to pop in to say hello. She won't stay long or anything.'

'Course it's all right. Tell her to come in.'

'See you tomorrow then.' Denise turned to Richie; she could at least get rid of him for Lorna. 'You coming?'

'I'll just wait and see Auntie Phyllis,' he said. Why the hell was she hanging about the place?

'I don't think so,' said Shirley, surprising everyone. 'Not with that cold coming on.'

She stood up and took Richie's arm. 'I'll walk you outside, and then I can bring Phyllis in for a few minutes. Like you were saying, we don't want too many of us round the bed at once, tiring out Lorna and upsetting the sister, do we? Then me and your auntie, and Lorna's dad can all go home together. Now tell your wife byebye, and we can be off.'

Richie was so shocked, he did as he was told and allowed Shirley to steer him out of the ward.

Shirley made sure they were in one of the service corridors, well away from any prying ears, before she let go of Richie's elbow.

'You might have guessed I wanted a private word,' she said.

'I ain't thick.'

'Good, then you'll understand my point very easily. Lorna will be needing time off work, Richie. So if you get a bit short with her on sick pay, we can help you.'

'You can what?'

'Help. With money. I don't want Lorna going without.'

'Have you been talking to Denise?'

'No. But if you do get in trouble without Lorna's wages coming in –'

Richie's teeth were clenched with anger. 'Why does everyone keep on at me about providing for my own wife?

I don't need any help with money, all right? I don't need help with anything.' He pushed Shirley out of the way and ran off towards the exit as if the bloodhounds were closing in on him.

Shirley leaned back against the cold, bare brick of the wall, her eyes wide with shock. He'd actually pushed her.

Why on earth had she ever persuaded Joe to let this sham of a marriage go ahead? She had been so wrong on this one, more wrong than she had ever been about anything in her life. She had just thought he was a bit rough round the edges, but this was the real Richie Clayton, an arrogant bully. No wonder Joe said he felt like throttling him. She felt like doing it herself.

Shirley levered herself away from the wall. She had to pull herself together and go to find Phyllis before Joe and Lorna wondered where she'd got to.

'Hello, Mrs Parker, Mrs Wright. I thought it was you two.'

Phyllis and Shirley, just yards from the maternity ward's swing doors, spun round; unfortunately, the owner of the tinny, irritating voice was exactly who they'd thought it was: Phoebe nose-ointment Elliot, Phyllis's neighbour.

'Hello, Mrs Elliot,' said Phyllis stiffly. 'What you doing here? Practising haunting the wards for Hallowe'en?'

'I'll ignore that remark. If you must know, I'm in for me veins.'

'What, on a Sunday?'

'Special appointment,' she lied, without the slightest hesitation.

The reason she was really there was because she'd

noticed all the activity around Richie and Lorna's place the night before, and then, with all the comings and goings from the Parkers' house, her nosiness had got the better of her. That was why she had decided to sacrifice her usual Sunday afternoon post-prandial kip and, instead, to dedicate herself to a bit of spying. And very successful at it she was too; the culmination of her efforts being the grand prize of not just tracking them all down to the London Hospital, but to outside one of the *maternity* wards.

It was better than getting a full house on the bingo.

'They must be pretty bad,' snarled Phyllis.

'Aw, they are,' said Mrs Elliot, 'and they're giving me such gip. Look, all up here.' She pulled up her calf-length black serge skirt, exposing calves as misshapen and mottled as a wedge of Gorgonzola left by a gas ring. 'I'm a martyr to my legs, I am.'

'Now there's a shame, but, if you don't mind, Mrs Elliot, we're just on our way to visit someone.'

Shirley still hadn't said a word.

'Don't know why you're being so nasty. Thought you might appreciate seeing a neighbourly face, what with all your troubles.'

'And what sort of troubles would they be this particular time then, Mrs Elliot? What sort of nonsense have you got in your head now?'

'Your . . .' she paused pointedly then leaned forward, '*nephew*,' she said conspiratorially, 'bringing more sorrow to your house, Mrs Parker.'

'*Nephew?* Why d'you say it like that? What's that tone of voice supposed to mean?'

'We all lived through the war, Mrs Parker.'

'At your age, you probably lived through the relief

of pissing Mafeking. Now if you don't mind, we're busy.'

'She's pregnant, is she, your daughter, Mrs Wright? Is that why she's in here?'

Phyllis narrowed her eyes. 'No, Shirley's daughter is not pregnant.' Christ, the old bag didn't know how true that was. Poor little Lorna. 'If you really must know, she's had an accident decorating their new home.'

'Are you saying Richie ain't got her knocked up?'

'So daintily put, Mrs Elliot, but that's exactly what I'm saying.'

'So why the hell did they get married then?'

'Because they sodding well, poxy love each other, that's why, you interfering old bastard.'

Mrs Elliot began to walk away. 'Aw, I see. Got better morals than his so-called auntie then, has he?'

'What did you say?'

'Nothing, Mrs Parker. Nothing at all. But perhaps all this *accident* business is really a blessing in disguise, eh?'

That was it. Shirley exploded. Phyllis had never seen her act in any way like it before. She was like a mad woman. She lunged after Mrs Elliot and grabbed hold of her by the coat, stopping her dead in her tracks, then she twisted the woman round until she was facing her.

'You listen to me, you poisonous cow,' she hissed into her face. 'If you say another fucking word about my family, I'll slap your wrinkled rotten chops so bloody hard you won't know whether it's Sunday afternoon or Monday morning. Got it?'

'Charming,' said Mrs Elliot. 'Just like Lady Docker, I don't think. I expect that sort of talk from the likes of Phyllis Parker, but from *you*.'

'I'll show you Lady Docker, if you don't shift that saggy old arse of yours and get out of my sight. *Right now*. I'll punch you right on the nose.'

As Mrs Elliot tottered off with muttered warnings about calling the law, Shirley took the now open-mouthed Phyllis by the arm.

'Come on, Phyl, let's get away from here. I don't like the bloody stink.'

'Blimey, Shirl, I didn't know you knew such words.'

'What words do you expect me to use? We've just lost our first grandchild.'

While Phyllis was still trying to take in the enormity of what Shirley had just said – it wasn't just a miscarriage, something that was sad because it had gone wrong, it had been their *grandchild* – Richie was otherwise occupied.

Almost out of his mind with fury at being picked on, yet again, by a woman, he was climbing in the back window of a house on the Highway.

He had been aimlessly walking the streets, no longer even noticing the rain, kicking stones, and cursing under his breath that he'd agreed to go in the ambulance with Lorna, so leaving the car at home. But then, with his small-time crook's radar, he had spotted the line of washing in someone's backyard. No one would leave stuff out in this weather. Either they were still having a sleep after their Sunday roast, or they had gone out and left the house empty.

Richie decided to investigate.

After a quick look each way along the practically deserted street he slipped down the side alley that led to the back of the grimy Victorian terrace.

He grinned. It was as if someone had set it up especially

for him: one of the windows had been left open a couple of inches.

He had his gloves on – always be prepared – and was over the back wall, and shoving up the sash in a matter of moments.

He listened. Not a sound. Then, with a glance over his shoulder, he put both hands on the windowsill and levered himself up and into the living room.

He had a quick shufty round, and then decided on the big oak credenza that took up almost the whole of one wall.

From the style of the furniture, the china knick-knacks, the photographs, and the junk in the drawers, he guessed an old woman probably lived there. He'd find out once he went upstairs and started going through the more personal stuff.

But Richie's guess was proved right rather sooner than he might have anticipated.

'What are you doing? Get out. Leave my things alone.'

He slammed the drawer and turned round to see an elderly woman in her nightdress standing in the middle of the room. What was wrong with her; it wasn't even seven o'clock in the evening?

Then he noticed the Jack Russell terrier in her arms.

Great, the dog was bloody snarling at him.

Richie very calmly reached out, picked up a heavy cut-glass fruit bowl from the table, emptied out the shiny Cox's apples onto the floor, swung back his arm to build up a bit of momentum, then swung it forward and whacked the dog, with a crunch of bones and teeth, right out of the woman's hands.

'I hate dogs,' he said, then he whacked the woman.

'Jesus!' Richie stepped back hurriedly as she fell

towards him, blood pouring from the side of her head. 'And I hate fucking women as well. Look what you made me do. You all get on my sodding nerves. Why do you always have to interfere?' He shook his head sadly. 'You're all the same. You're your own worst enemies.'

Then he went back to working his way through the credenza drawers.

Outside the hospital, Phyllis and Shirley sheltered on the steps so that Phyllis could have a cigarette, while Joe went down onto the Whitechapel Road to see if he could find them a taxi.

Phyllis threw down her used match, which fizzed and sputtered on the wet stone, took a long, relieved drag, then blew out a plume of lavender-blue smoke with a sigh. 'I needed that.' She took down another, less urgent, lungful. 'This is all so sad, Shirl.'

'Yeah, I know. But it's some comfort to know she's so young. She won't think so now, but she's got plenty of time.'

'*She?* I notice you didn't say *they*.'

'Please, Phyllis, don't. I'm tired.'

'Sorry, Shirl.' Phyllis leaned forward to see how Joe was getting on, but soon ducked back under the canopy. It was pouring down. 'What a lousy evening.'

'I hate it when it gets dark early. You can feel winter drawing in all round you.'

'Shirl.'

'Mmm?'

'Are you going to keep your promise to me and go to the doctor's yourself?'

'I already have.'

'And?'

'I'm all right. There's nothing wrong except I'm a bit tired, that's all. What with the wedding, and now this.'

'You need a rest.'

'And Lorna needs her mum. I feel terrible, leaving her in there. I'll come back later for a few hours. That nice nurse'll let me in.'

'Shirley, you need your rest or you'll wind up in there with her. She'll be OK till the morning.'

But Lorna was far from OK. Despite her shoulder hurting and the drip in her arm tugging, she curled up in a ball and pulled the covers up over her head, desperately trying to block out the sound of newborn whimpering and of mothers soothing and feeding their babies. She felt empty, bereaved, and completely, horribly alone.

'Lorna?'

Someone pulled the blankets away from her face.

Lorna screwed up her sore, puffy eyes against the light. A starched, middle-aged nurse was sitting on the side of the bed.

'I don't want anything. Please, please, leave me alone,' Lorna whispered, her throat raw from sobbing.

'All I'm offering is myself,' the nurse said, in a soft Irish lilt. 'I'm not off shift for another half-hour or so. I've done all my jobs. Staff and Sister are having a conflab in the office. So how about me and you having a little chat?'

The nurse's kindness made Lorna want to weep all the more, but she didn't pull away when the woman brushed the hair away from her face with her big, capable hands.

'Is there nothing you want? A drop of tea, maybe?'

'I don't want anything,' Lorna wailed. 'I didn't even want my baby.'

'Hush, now. Come on.' The nurse handed her a tissue. 'Don't break your heart.'

Lorna carried on, speaking more to herself than to the nurse. 'Not at first I didn't. I really didn't. Now I'd do anything to have my baby in my arms. Anything. And now it's gone. And it's all my fault. I've been so stupid.'

'You mustn't do this to yourself. These things happen. Nature isn't always kind, but, most of the time, it does know best.'

She stroked Lorna's head. God, she was little more than a child herself. How in God's good name did these young girls get themselves into these situations? Heaven knows what sort of a family she came from. But that wasn't her fault. And why torture her all the more by letting her lie here listening to a ward full of mothers and babies?

'Listen to me, love, I know it's early, but I'm going to have a word with Staff, see if she can get the doctor to give you something to help you sleep.'

She stood up, straightened her apron and went off to find her boss, but she never reached the office; on the other side of the ward doors she was hijacked by Mrs Elliot.

'As if you ain't got more to worry about than cheap little tarts getting themselves knocked up, eh, Nurse?'

'May I ask what you're doing here? Visiting time's long over.'

'I've been given special permission,' she said, rather pleased with her inventiveness. 'Visiting my husband, see. Touch and go he is, poor devil. Old war wound. Terrible state the man's in.'

'I'm sorry.'

'He's got no regrets.' She sighed, a picture of martyrdom. 'War hero, see, Nurse? Thank Gawd we had him to protect us all. You must be proud to nurse the likes of them – *him*,' she corrected herself. 'Different to some of them in there.'

'I must say, sometimes I have to agree with you. They come in here with some cock-and-bull story about losing their baby. What do they think I am, straight off the boat from Cork? We all know what they've done – and the risks they take going to these terrible backstreet places. But I don't always blame them. You should see the families they come from. Not a God-fearing soul amongst the lot of them.'

As Nurse Simon strode off, Mrs Elliot melted away into the shadows of the dimly lit, windowless corridor. She was cackling unkindly to herself. 'I knew I was right. She was up the stick, and now she's gone and got rid of it. The dirty trollop.'

Richie considered that he had spent quite enough on the young brunette, and now it was time for her to repay his generosity. She was a bit skinny for his taste, but on a miserable evening like this he had settled for the best offer he'd had, the only offer, in fact. The only other customers in the Porpoise and Anchor in Cable Street that night were male, and interested in sex as he was – well, more obsessed really – Richie had never considered experimenting with a man. And as for the barmaid, she'd made it very clear to him that that was her husband, sitting over there in the corner, keeping his eye out for her safety. It was a tough sort of area for a woman to work in. So, until the brunette had tottered into the pub on her ridiculously high-heeled black patent shoes, making right for him as if he had magnets attached, Richie had been drinking alone at the bar, working his way through the proceeds from his earlier exploits in the old woman's house in the Highway.

'I think you might want to make me a happy man, seeing as I've bought you all those gins.'

The girl smiled flirtatiously. 'I couldn't think of anything nicer.'

'Any ideas where can we go?'

'I know just the place.'

Richie winked at the barmaid, who just rolled her eyes in reply – jealous, Richie reckoned – and followed the girl outside.

'This way,' she said, holding her handbag over her head and making a run for it in the still-teeming rain.

She led him to an alleyway that was just round the back of the pub, but by the time they had scrambled over the crates and barrels that were stored there, both she and Richie were puffing.

'How about this then . . . ?' gasped Richie admiringly as she showed him a tarpaulin-draped niche hidden by a stack of crated-up empties. 'Very cosy.'

Richie was about to go through his usual chat-up lines to charm her out of her drawers, when the girl surprised him again.

'What do you fancy then?' she asked, bending her knees slightly so she could get a better look at his flies, which she then undid with a single, expert slide.

'Blimey,' he laughed, 'you're a bit forward. What can you offer?'

'All the usual for thirty bob, plus a quid extra if you'd rather go to a room, but seeing as it's pissing down out there, we might as –'

'Hang on, are you telling me you're –'

The girl's heavily made-up eyes narrowed. 'Hang on. Didn't you arrange this with Tony?'

'Tony?'

'Tony Diaz. The Maltese bloke who looks after me.'

'You mean your pimp?'

Her mouth contracted into an angry, straight line. 'You're not my punter are you?'

'But you're a brass.' Richie started laughing. 'This is a real first, sweetheart.' He shook his head in appreciative amazement. 'If a bloke like me can almost be conned into paying, I think I'll have to consider getting into this trade myself. I can think of plenty of girls who'd work for me. Don't know why I've never thought about it before.'

'Look, mate, if you don't wanna do business, I'd better get going, and, take it from me, you'd better not let Tony hear you saying anything like that.'

'Why not come back in the pub and have another drink with me? I'll buy you another gin and bitter lemon by way of payment, and you can tell me all about it.'

'You are kidding. But I'll tell you this for free. If I don't go back in there and find the punter I was meant to be doing –'

'That'll be the humpy-looking bastard by the door who couldn't take his eyes off you,' interrupted Richie with a grin. 'I wondered what was up with him. He was right agitated.'

'– then,' she continued crossly, 'get myself back out here and find at least half a dozen more punters tonight, I might as well go and throw my overworked, knackered little body into the Thames before Tony Diaz gets someone to do it for me.'

'Are you saying half a dozen blokes –'

'Yeah, I know, hardly worth coming out on a night like this, but a girl's got to earn a living.'

Richie watched the girl clambering back over the crates, and did a few quick calculations. They must be making a fortune round here. He knew it was notorious for the toms but having never done any business with them himself, he had genuinely had no idea it was so lucrative. And if a rough sort of bird like her could earn, let's see . . . He did a final calculation and let out a long, slow whistle.

Blimey, not bad. He'd be a mug not to be up for this: real money and a bloody sight easier than risking his collar down the docks. He wouldn't get too flash, not at first, and he wouldn't have his girls working round here. Well, not yet. He'd get himself established somewhere else, then he'd move in and show this foreign bastard what was what. This was the way he was going to make his fortune. This would make him a face to be reckoned with. He'd show Joe Wright and the rest of them who could bring in serious dough. And Richie knew exactly who would be the first to hear the good news about his new business.

Richie smirked to himself as she came through the steamed-up glass doors of the coffee bar, with a gaggle of giggling girls in tow, all shaking the rain from their coats and umbrellas.

Pamela Logan spotted him immediately. 'Richie! I've not seen you for ages.'

'Pam, what a smashing surprise.' He smiled boyishly as he made room for her next to him on the leatherette-covered bench. 'Not a surprise really. I knew you and the girls always go to the flicks of a Sunday night, then in here for a coffee after.'

'You remembered!' Pam shrieked, and then turned her head and mouthed to her friends that they should all shove off and leave her alone with Richie.

'Course I remembered. I remember everything about you.' He put his hand under the table and ran it up her nylon-clad thigh until he found her stocking top. 'Everything.'

Pamela glowed. 'You know I turned up at the wedding?'

He flashed her his best smile. 'So I heard.'

'Why didn't you keep in touch?'

'Sorry, Pam, I've been that busy.'

'Up the duff, ain't she?'

'No, whatever gave you that idea?'

'So why did you marry her?'

'Don't get all moody, Pam. I had to do the right thing by the poor mare, didn't I? When her old man found out I'd been schtupping her, he was going to throw her out on the street. I just felt sorry for her. You know how soft I am.'

'So you don't love her?'

'Don't be daft. You know who I love, Pam.'

'Who?'

'You know I've only ever loved one person.'

'Aw, Richie, give us a kiss.'

As Richie took her head in his hands – just like in the films, the way birds always liked it – he knew he had cracked it.

It was too easy for him. She was like putty in his hands. She'd do whatever he wanted.

'If I drink any more tea . . .' Shirley stared into her cup.

'Why don't you go through to bed?' Joe took her hand across the kitchen table. They'd been sitting there for hours, ever since getting back from the hospital. They hadn't said much; there wasn't much to say.

'I can't help thinking about Lorna, lying there in that hospital all by herself.'

'You're going back in tomorrow. But you need your rest first, Shirl, or you won't be any use to yourself, let alone to anyone else. Come to bed, eh?'

'Tell you what, you go through, Joe, and I'll be in in a minute. We went out in such a rush I never had a chance to tidy round. I'll clear up a bit now so I don't have to do it before I go and see Lorna.'

'I'll help you.'

'No, Joe, you go through. Please.'

Joe knew there'd be no arguing with her, so he stood up and kissed her on top of her head. 'Well, don't be long.'

'I won't.'

He went into the bedroom, and lay on top of the bed in the dark, with his hands linked under his head, thinking murderous thoughts about Richie Clayton, believing that even his sweet, loving Shirley was thinking the same.

But she wasn't.

For the first time in two days, Shirley had other things on her mind.

She went to her handbag and took out the envelope the doctor had given her when he had come round to see to Lorna. When was that? Could it really have only been yesterday?

He had taken Shirley to one side, and had spoken to her privately, while they had been waiting for the ambulance, telling her that he had fixed it all up for her, and he was glad to have the opportunity, even at such a difficult time, to stress the importance of it, that she had to take it seriously.

Shirley had put it all to the back of her mind – she'd been far too busy thinking about Lorna – but now she knew she had to acknowledge its existence.

On the front of the envelope there was an appointment time.

Eleven o'clock.

It was to see a consultant in the oncology department at the Poplar Hospital. It was for Tuesday week.

Nine days' time.

Shirley felt as if she'd been handed a death sentence.

Chapter 7

'Shirley Wright?' An exhausted-looking nurse hollered the name over the aggravating buzz of noise that dominated the out patients' waiting room. The combination of crackly, supposedly soothing Muzak, fractious, whining children and grumbling adults, could still, after all these years, put Nurse Taylor's teeth on edge – especially after a double shift, with her legs aching, and the desperate need for a cup of tea and a cheese and pickle sandwich.

'Shirley Wright?' she hollered again.

'What was that name? Who did she say?' The pallid, elderly man who had been sitting next to Shirley, or rather who had been squashed up next to her on the splintery wooden bench, plucked anxiously at her sleeve. 'Did she call me? Was it me she wanted? Is it my turn?'

'No, dear.' Shirley spoke gently but loudly into what she had discovered was the man's one good ear. 'It's me she's calling, but I've already told her your name and who you're here to see, and she's promised she'll come and fetch you herself when they're ready for you. That all right?'

'It would be all right if I had someone here with me. They said they were all too busy. And they know how I hate these places.'

Shirley squeezed his hand; he looked so lost, love him. She could imagine Joe being just as helpless if he'd been here by himself even though he was at least thirty years younger than this poor old chap and at least twice his size. It was strange; men were supposed to be the stronger sex, but Shirley, like most women, knew that just wasn't true.

'Tell you what, I shouldn't be too long, how about if I come back after I've seen the doctor and check everything's OK with you?'

'*Shirley Wright?*' the nurse called for a third, and, from the tone of her voice, final time. She looked round the room and then checked her clipboard; she neither sounded nor looked very happy.

'Over here. Coming,' Shirley called back to her, then she squeezed the man's hand again and followed the now tight-lipped Nurse Taylor along a corridor painted in the particular shade of miserable green only ever seen in schools and hospitals. The stark neon strip lighting overhead, and the overbright, mauve-dominated prints of cottage gardens taped on the walls, somehow managed to make the space seem even gloomier.

'Mr Berkeley doesn't like to be kept waiting,' said the nurse primly without bothering to turn round and look at Shirley, who was having some difficulty keeping up with her.

'You're all like athletes,' puffed Shirley. 'Why do you nurses always walk so quickly?'

The nurse slowed down, turned her head slightly, and offered a brief, but apologetic smile. 'Because of ogres like Mr Berkeley.'

Shirley returned her smile by way of acceptance. 'He's always been lovely to me.'

This time the nurse's smile was more strained, and she said nothing. Instead she kept her thoughts to herself. Of course he's always nice to you, love, she was thinking. If you see Mr Berkeley it's because you're ill, really ill.

The nurse knocked on the door and waited for the

gruff 'Enter', then ushered Shirley inside the softly lit consulting room. She followed her in and said firmly but quietly: 'Mrs Wright for you, Mr Berkeley; Mrs Shirley Wright,' then she melted into the corner, the hospital pecking order being very clear about the lowly position of nurses, but still requiring their presence during the examination of female patients.

'Mrs Wright.' Mr Berkeley pointed to the plain wooden chair that was dwarfed by his huge, padded leather affair. 'Please, sit down.'

'Thank you.'

'Good to see you again. Remind me, when did we last meet?'

'Just last week, Mr Berkeley. Last Tuesday. You did the tests, remember? I've come back for the results.'

He nodded at the nurse, who handed him the buff folder she had been holding in readiness, then he hunted around on his practically empty desk for his glasses – a delaying ritual while he was actually hunting around in his memory for details of Shirley's case – then he flicked through the thick wad of notes.

'Here we are.' He tapped on the papers with his gold fountain pen. 'Mrs Shirley Wright.'

He took a moment to study the top few sheets, and then peered at Shirley over his glasses.

'Do you have someone with you, Mrs Wright?'

'No. My husband and daughter are both working, and I didn't want to bother them. They tend to worry. You know what families are like.'

Mr Berkeley took off his glasses and leaned back in his seat. 'There's something we need to discuss. Something rather serious. Would you prefer, if I wait until . . .' He waved a hand, inviting her to say something.

Shirley struggled to moisten her lips with her tongue; her mouth having suddenly gone very dry. 'No. Go on. Please. Whatever it is. Tell me.'

'Very well.' He clasped his hands, and leaned forward in his chair. 'In my opinion, Mrs Wright, your condition requires further surgery.'

'Further surgery. I see.' Shirley, unable to bear what she was sure was pity in the man's gaze, looked away and focused instead on the shiny, tiled floor, incongruously thinking how hard it must be to keep it so clean, what with all the people walking in and out all day.

'Mrs Wright, do you understand what I've told you?'

'Sorry, I was thinking.' She raised her chin until her eyes met his. 'Is it really necessary? Would you advise me to go ahead, or maybe . . .'

'In my opinion, it would be more than advisable.'

Shirley snapped open her handbag and took out her handkerchief, thinking she might be about to cry, but the tears didn't come. So she dabbed at her nose instead. Rather than tearful she felt numb; there was a curious kind of calmness washing over her. It was as if she knew this was going to happen, and that it was actually a relief to get it all over with, to have someone say the words she had been dreading for the past three months.

'If I do have further . . . another operation, this'll have to be the last one, Mr Berkeley.' Her expression and her voice were dull and vacant. 'I don't think I could go through it all again.'

'Unfortunately, Mrs Wright, I have to agree with you. This probably will be the last time. But the procedure should give you a deal more comfort.'

'For how long?'

'I'm quite certain we're talking years.'

Quite certain? How on earth would Joe and Lorna cope without her? 'How many years?'

'I can't lie to you, Mrs Wright, I'm really not sure, but I'm confident that they'll be good years. And certainly better than you'd experience without having the operation.'

He stood up, consultation over. 'We'll be writing to you very soon. Now if you go with nurse, I'm sure she'll find you a nice cup of tea.'

'No, thanks, Mr Berkeley,' she said politely, as she rose unsteadily to her feet. 'You're very kind, but I've said I'll go and see someone. Thank you for your time.'

'Terry, are you listening to me?'

'Sorry, Den, but I've got to concentrate on these sound checks, we've only got another hour and a bit before we're on.'

'Terry, will you listen to me for just one minute? Please?' She could hear herself whining, which really wasn't like her, but this was important.

'Course, I will. Sorry, I'm just a bit overexcited. They get a big crowd in here, even on a Tuesday night.' He put his guitar down and squatted at the front of the stage. 'Right, I'm all yours and I'm listening. Tell me, what's the big deal?'

'I'm still worried about Lorna.'

She saw the look on his face.

'I know, but . . .' She scratched her head, forgetting all the trouble she'd taken with her hair. 'Look, Tel, you know I asked her to come along tonight?'

'So you said.'

'Well, when I spoke to her this morning – I phoned her at work – it was obvious there was something wrong with her. She was so jumpy and nervous. I reckon it's something to do with her and Richie. I don't want to make too much of it, but I've known her so many years, since we were little kids, I can tell when something's going on with her, when something's not right. What shall I do, Tel? Any ideas? You know what a big mouth I am – I don't want to start mouthing off, and putting my foot in it, and making things worse. That's why I've not said anything up to now. But I'm sure Richie's upsetting her.'

Terry shook his head. Interfere in Richie Clayton's private business? Was she sure? No, thanks very much, the bloke was a nutcase: East Ham, as his dad would say, a stop short of Barking. It was bad enough not knowing where he was with Denise half the time – one minute she was all over him and then she was pulling away again – but he could cope with that because he thought the world of her, but getting involved with her nutty cousin? It was tragic that a really nice girl like Lorna was involved with him, but, in the end, he wasn't about to stick his nose in.

He stood up. 'Look, Den, you know how much I like Lorna, she's really smashing, especially the way she's dealing with . . . you know, losing the baby and that. But it's nothing to do with me. He's your family, and she's your friend. I think you'd be better off working out what you should say to her. Or how about talking to your sister? Girls are always better at this sort of personal stuff than blokes.'

He jerked his head towards Chantalle, who had invited herself along to the gig with Maxie.

Maxie's excuse for being there was that he wanted to be a drummer and needed a few tips; Chantalle didn't have an excuse other than that at thirteen she was trying to pull one of the Spanners. She really fancied the idea of having a boyfriend in a group, so she could show everyone just how grown up she really was. And while the Spanners might not be famous, they did still qualify as a group, and appearing at a venue like the Red Lion, Leytonstone was a definite step up in the world of pop from the little pubs and halls that they had played in up until now.

'As if Chantalle would be any use to anyone but herself,' she said, staring scornfully at her sister, who was smiling up at the bass player with a look that Denise knew was far too knowingly seductive, and therefore bloody dangerous, for a girl of her age. 'And, anyway, it's not family stuff, or personal stuff. Not really. It's more . . . How can I put it, when I don't really know myself? I just feel there's something wrong, something –'

'Den, I don't want to be mean, and I know she's your best mate, but the others are not going to appreciate me standing here chatting to you while they do all the work, now are they? I'll talk to you later, all right?'

'At last,' Shirley said to herself, taking the kettle off the stove. 'I didn't think you'd ever boil.'

She spooned tea leaves into the warmed pot, filled a little milk jug from the bottle, and smiled stiffly to herself.

'Nice cup of tea, Shirley Wright, that's what you need.' She took a spoon out of the drawer. 'With plenty of sugar in it to give yourself a bit of energy.'

'They say that's the first sign of going barmy, talking to yourself. You do know that, don't you, babe?'

Shirley turned round to see Joe standing in the doorway.

'I don't want them men in white coats carting you off,' he grinned. 'I mean, who'd do me tea for me? You know how useless I am at all that domestic stuff.'

Shirley flicked a quick glance at the kitchen clock. Her hand flew to her mouth.

'That can't be the time. I'm so sorry, Joe, I never realised. I've not even thought about what we're going to have to eat. There was this old man, you see, and he had no one with him, no one to help him. He was so lost. So I went back and stayed with him, like I promised, till they saw to him, then I made sure he got home all right. He lived right over Silvertown way. The nurses were really nice, but they're so busy, and . . .' She dropped the spoon onto the table and covered her face with her hands.

'Nurses? Shirl, what're you talking about? What's wrong?'

Shirley had promised herself she wouldn't, but she couldn't help herself, she started crying.

'They want me to have another operation, Joe. But I'm so scared. I don't know if I can go through it again.'

Joe folded his arms round her, wanting to take away her pain and her fear, wanting to take away anything that might harm a single hair of her beautiful head.

They stood there in the kitchen, holding each other, their tears spilling unchecked down their cheeks.

When Lorna heard the street door slam and the sound of footsteps on the stairs – up to the first floor, then to the second, then round past the Dennisons' landing – she hurried into the little kitchenette.

She took Richie's dinner out of the oven and set it, just so, in the centre of the tray she had already prepared with cutlery, salt and pepper, and brown sauce – just the way Richie expected it – and carried it all through to the living room.

She gulped back her nerves as she waited for him to open the front door that her dad had repaired for them while she had been in the hospital.

'Please, let him be in a good mood, please,' she whispered to herself. Not only did she need a rest from his sniping, derisive comments about everything she said or did, she really wanted to go to the Red Lion tonight, to get out for a few hours. It wasn't so bad at work – not when she was busy, anyway. But once she was indoors, all she could think about was the baby – the baby she didn't have, the baby she couldn't hold in her arms.

When Denise had first asked her to go along, Lorna had point-blank refused, but then she had managed to persuade Lorna that it would do her good. And Denise was right: it would take her mind off things for a while. And Denise was also right about her only being sixteen years old. She was entitled to go out, and especially after all she'd been through.

But that didn't mean she was brave enough to say those things to Richie. The bruising and the pains in her shoulder – never mind the emptiness in her heart – reminded her all too clearly of that.

And now here he was.

'Hello, Richie.' She smiled nervously. 'Your tea's ready.'

She sat quietly as Richie wiped his bread round his plate, mopping up every last trace of the juices from the pork chops.

She waited a moment longer, then asked softly: 'Everything all right for you, Rich? Want anything else?'

'You putting a bit of flesh back on them bones of yours would be a start. You must've dropped a stone since you lost the kid.'

Lorna flinched. 'Sorry, I've not had much of an appetite.'

'Well get one. I hate skinny birds.' He put the tray on the floor by his armchair. 'Come here.'

Warily, Lorna did as she was told, doing her best not to tremble. She felt pathetic being so nervous around him, but he was so unpredictable. A raised hand might mean a stroked cheek or a slapped face. Or worse. How had she been so stupid to be taken in by his handsome face and his smooth words? But it was too late for regrets. She was his wife.

She stood in front of him, just out of his reach.

'Closer.'

She took another step forward.

He reached out, pulled open her blouse and then tugged up her bra until her heavy breasts tumbled free.

'Still got good tits, though,' he said, dragging her down on top of him and kissing her roughly.

'Get your gear off, Lorna, you're in luck.'

With his decision made, Richie pushed her down onto the floor. The old carpet that had been left by the previous occupants of the flat was rough and stickily unpleasant against Lorna's back, but she didn't say anything. She just did as she was told, stripping off her clothes and then lying there, naked, as Richie dropped onto his knees, unzipped his fly, and plunged straight into her.

He nuzzled and bit her breasts while he satisfied himself, coming into her with an animal-like grunt and a shudder, his hasty, uncaring excuse for lovemaking over as quickly as Lorna had come to expect. But at least his attentions, however offhand and short-lived, meant he wasn't in a bad mood with her, and that was something.

Richie rolled off her, and did up his trousers. He felt around in his pockets for his cigarettes, lit one, and stretched lazily, making no attempt to get up off the floor. 'I could do with a cup of tea.'

Lorna picked up the tray and took it out to the kitchen.

'Fancy going out tonight, Rich?' she called through to him.

'Out? Where?'

Still naked, she shivered in the chill of the November evening and at the feel of the cold lino under her feet, but she didn't care. He hadn't said no. Get it over with before he changes his mind.

'Denise phoned me at work today. She wanted to tell me about this gig Terry's got. She's invited us along.'

'To see Terry? At a gig? You're joking, right?'

'No, Denise said –'

'Fuck off, Lorna. Why would I want to go out and play with the kiddies?'

Lorna picked up the tea caddy, and took a deep breath. 'I didn't explain properly. It's a really big do, Rich. It's at the Red Lion in Leytonstone, not some little church hall or something.'

'The Red Lion? That sounds much better.'

Was he being sarcastic? It was hard to tell without being able to see his face. She poured milk into his cup. 'Does that mean –'

'It means you do what you want. I'm going out.'

She put down the milk bottle and rushed into the living room, terrified of upsetting him, of the beating she could expect when he came in drunk and angry because of some nonexistent slight from someone or other. Keep him calm. 'I'll go with you.'

'No you fucking won't. It's too late.' He pushed her away from him, picked up his coat from the armchair, and stomped out of the room into the hall. 'You've upset me now.'

Lorna stood in the front doorway, not caring she was naked, watching her husband rush down the stairs two at a time.

'Please, Richie,' she begged him, 'come back. We can go somewhere else. Anywhere you like. I don't care where.'

'Don't kid yourself, Lorna,' he shouted back to her. 'Why would I want to go anywhere with you? You know and I know that if it wasn't for that old man of yours threatening me, I'd be a million miles away from this dump, and at least two million miles away from you. Just the sight of you makes me feel ill.'

He was shouting up the stairs to her from the street door, obviously not caring who was listening.

Lorna stood there impassively, waiting for him to slam the street door, and listening to the muttered disapproval of the Dennisons, the couple downstairs, as they passed their opinions on the latest set-to between the Claytons.

She went back inside and picked up her clothes. She was going to meet Denise.

Why not? What more could he do to her?

Lorna stood in the women's lavatories at the Red Lion, leaning back against the sink, watching Denise applying yet another coat of mascara to her pale auburn lashes.

Lorna hadn't bothered putting on any make-up herself; she hadn't had the heart for it.

'You're so lucky, Den.' She was whispering so that the row of other girls, all concentrating on their reflections as they brushed and patted and combed, couldn't hear what she was saying. 'Everyone out there was so jealous when Terry dedicated that Gerry and the Pacemakers' song to you.'

Denise beamed into the mirror. 'I know, it's because they can all see he loves me so much.'

Lorna nibbled at the inside of her cheek. 'Richie hates me.'

Denise couldn't make out what she said. 'You what?'

'I said: Richie hates me.'

'Don't be so daft.' Denise looked at her friend; there was no colour in her thin, drawn face except for the dark purple smudges under her eyes. She looked bloody awful.

'I'm not being daft. I make him feel ill. He told me. He wouldn't even be with me if it wasn't for my dad. He knows he'd kill him if he ever found out he'd upset me. And while Richie might be a bully with me, he's a coward as far as my dad goes.'

Denise put away her mascara brush and washed her hands. 'I know he's my –' She paused, staring at the water disappearing down the drain hole. 'I nearly said cousin then.'

'Yeah, I know, it's still hard getting used to him being –'

'Don't say it, Lorn, it doesn't exactly thrill me knowing that that arsehole's my flesh and blood.' Realising what she'd said, Denise pulled a face. 'I'm sorry. I didn't mean –'

'It's all right. We both know what he's like.'

'Yeah, we do: useless.' She tucked her make-up purse into her bag. 'Can I say something, Lorn, something that's been on my mind?'

'Course.'

'I know you've only been married a matter of weeks, and, to be honest, I can't even really believe I'm saying this, but why don't you leave him, Lorna? I can tell how unhappy you are. And now you're not . . . you know, any more, no one would blame you. Not even Mum.'

'Do you think I haven't thought about it, Den? I'm telling you, when I'm in bed of a night, staring up at the ceiling, wondering when he's going to come home, *if* he's going to come home, and how drunk he's going to be this time, then it's all I think about. But you're wrong, Den, people would blame me. You know what they're like. Girls don't just walk out on their husbands. Mum wouldn't be able to stand the shame of it. Not with everything she's had to put up with, and everything else I've put her through.'

Denise was frowning. 'I honestly never realised things were that bad, Lorn. I'm sure if she knew, your mum would –'

'But she mustn't know, Den. She couldn't take it. She's not said anything, but she's not been well again. You can see it in her face. She looks ill. And I've just been making things worse, what with getting married on the quick like that, and then losing . . .' She hesitated for a moment, closing her eyes to find the strength to go on. '. . . the baby. I can't do anything else to her, Den. She can't take any more. I know she can't.'

Lorna shook her head, trying to rid herself of all the horrible thoughts and images crowding into her mind.

'It's all such a mess. Why did I ever let him go anywhere near me?'

'I don't know, Lorna. I really and truly don't know.'

All around them, the preening girls were suddenly jolted into scooping up all their cosmetic paraphernalia and hurrying back to their boyfriends, as the main attraction of the evening – a five-piece rhythm-and-blues outfit from Wanstead – began belting out a Howlin' Wolf song.

'Anyway, enjoy the rest of the evening, Den, and tell Terry I thought he was really good.'

'You're not coming back in?'

'No, I'd better be going. It's just like him to be awkward and decide to get back home before the pubs shut. I was risking it coming out at all, but I was so upset with him.'

'Risking it? Upset with him? I know he's got a rotten temper, and that he's a selfish, horrible git, but you can't let him tell you what you can and can't do. That's not right.'

She shrugged. 'I know it's not, but what choice have I got?'

Denise put her hand on her friend's shoulder. 'Tell me the truth, Lorna: are you scared of him?'

Lorna didn't like this. It was getting too close to home. The last thing she wanted was for Denise to go round shouting the odds. Denise's mum would be bound to get involved then everyone in the whole East End would get to hear about it, her own mum included.

'Don't be silly.' Lorna conjured up a fairly convincing smile. 'I just don't like all the shouting and hollering, that's all. I'm not used to it, am I? You know how quiet we are in our family. It's all been a bit of a shock, that's all.'

'Are you sure?'

'Course, you daft thing. Why would I be scared of my own husband?'

Pamela snuggled into Richie's shoulder, and licked the side of his face, not giving a bugger about what the rest of the customers in the Cadiz Arms thought about such behaviour.

'So what do you think of Melanie then?' she asked, stroking Richie's thigh. 'I told you she was pretty, didn't I?'

Richie took a long swallow of his lager. 'I think she's a little cracker, just like you.'

He pinched Pamela's backside, and she giggled appreciatively.

'And I'm telling you two,' he said, winking at Melanie, 'you'll make a right good living working for me. You'll want for nothing. And, let's face it, it's better than giving it away for free, eh, ladies?'

This time both of the girls giggled.

'We weren't objecting to you not paying us just now in the back of the van, were we?' Melanie flashed her eyebrows. 'Here, Pam, shall we still let him have it for nothing once we go professional, or should we start charging him the going rate?'

'You'd better still let me have it for nothing.' Richie reached out and tweaked Melanie's nipple, then cupped his hand round her full, round breast, fully aware of the two sailors standing behind them, who were now practically dribbling with lust. 'You pair of dirty little cows.'

Stupid pair of bitches, more like, thought Richie, his smile not slipping for a second.

'Now, let's have a drink to our new business partnership, and then there are a couple of gentlemen,' he jerked his head in the direction of the sailors, 'who I just know are dying to meet you.'

He raised his glass and sighed contentedly.

Richie Clayton, old son, you are on your way to fame and fortune.

Part 2

1967

Chapter 8

'Might still be over eight weeks till Christmas, but it feels cold enough for snow.' Denise watched as Lorna – who, like her, was still wearing her coat – boiled the electric kettle in the smartly fitted and tiled kitchen.

'I can't believe how fast this year's gone. Must be getting old, eh, Lorn?'

Lorna poured the water into mugs and handed Denise her coffee. 'That'll warm you up.'

'So will this heating. It's fantastic.'

'I know. Every flat in the whole block's got it.'

'Bit different from your old place, eh? It was like a fridge in there. Don't know why you never got Richie to sort it out.'

'He was too busy, Den, wasn't he? Planning the next Mediterranean cruise he was going to take me on. You know how he spoils me.'

Denise pulled a face, acknowledging her stupidity.

Lorna shrugged noncommittally. 'Come on, take off your coat, and let's go through.'

They carried their drinks into the living room and sat on the green Draylon armchairs that Shirley and Joe had bought Lorna and Richie for their new home in the tower block near Chrisp Street market.

'It's really nice you popping in after work like this,' said Lorna, turning on both bars of the inbuilt electric fire for extra heat. 'And good timing, catching me down at the lifts. It would have been a shame if you'd missed me.'

Lorna was chattering away as if she didn't have a

care in the world, but it was obvious to Denise that, as usual, she was just trying to change the subject to something safe.

'Still enjoying the job, Den?

Denise, her hands cupped round her mug, nodded. 'It's great. I love every minute of it.' She grinned. 'And why wouldn't I? Still working in the West End in a record company, but now doing something a bit more than taking calls and saying good morning to people I've never heard of. Now I'm in publicity I'm going to get to meet all the top groups, *and* I'm earning decent money at last. I couldn't believe it last week when I got my first pay packet.' She laughed. 'If only they knew I'd do it for free.'

'I bet you're ever so proud of Terry and the boys.'

'I am. I never thought they'd have been able to give up their day jobs like they have.'

'A proper record deal, eh?'

Denise held up her hand. 'Hold on, Lorna, it's not all confirmed yet, and after that other one fell through that time and they thought they'd have to give it all up . . .' she paused to sip her drink, 'they don't want to get too excited.'

'The time wasn't right then, that's all.'

'Maybe.'

'And the company thinks enough of Terry to try and impress him by making sure they gave you this new job.'

'Thanks.'

'You know what I mean.'

'Yeah, course I do. Anyway, you're not doing so badly, are you?'

'Depends what you mean by badly.' Lorna muttered the words into her coffee.

'Sorry?'

'Nothing.'

'Work's OK, isn't it? I thought you said you were well in.'

'I am, but I sometimes wish I'd gone to college, you know, like I always said I was going to.'

'What, you mean because of all the changes down the docks?'

A feeble smile flickered on Lorna's lips. 'Sort of.'

Sort of? What she really wished was that she'd gone to college, had never met Richie Clayton, not got married at sixteen, and that she was leading the sort of life that most people took for granted: a normal life, with no fear of what some brute might decide to do to you, just because he could, and no way out because there wasn't one for the likes of her.

Denise nodded, not catching the tone in Lorna's voice. 'I know Dad wasn't very happy when they dropped the casuals. Not because he was worried about money, but because Mum made sure he got a job down the market.'

Denise laughed at the thought of her mother dragging her dad from stall to stall all around Chrisp Street until she'd nagged one of the men into putting in a word for him at the Spitalfields wholesale fruit and vegetable market, where he eventually, if rather reluctantly, got himself a job as a delivery van driver – a very early-in-the-morning delivery van driver.

'I'm telling you, he's definitely not chuffed with the hours, or with the fact that it means him working every single weekday. But Mum's made right up with it. He's got a regular wage for once, and she gets as much free fruit and veg as he can nick.'

'I'm glad it's all worked out for him. It's not so easy for everyone down there.'

'But you'll be all right, won't you, Lorn?'

She shrugged. 'Don't really know. Everything's a bit up in the air, really. I know my job's going to be safe for a while, but for how long? There're so many changes going on round here; it's not knowing what's going to happen next, I suppose. It's not a nice feeling.'

She dipped her chin and said quietly, 'It's nothing like when Mum had to go back in for that other operation, but it's not easy. You can tell by looking at Dad's face how worried he is, and so am I, if I'm honest. I really depend on my wages.'

'Don't start fretting, Lorn. It's like when Terry's deal fell through that time: things work out in the end, not always in the way you expect them to, maybe, but they do.'

Denise put her cup down on the floor and took her friend's hands in hers. 'If it had worked out with that first lot, then the Spanners would never have had a chance with this really big company.' She grinned wickedly. 'And I wouldn't be having it off with a bloke who's going to be a famous pop –'

Denise stopped speaking and frowned. 'Whatever's the matter? Your hands, they're trembling.'

'It's nothing. I just heard the front door open, that's all. Made me jump.'

Denise stiffened. 'You've got better hearing than me.' She let go of Lorna's hands and sat very upright in her chair. It must be bloody Richie. Why did he have to turn out to be such a no-good arsehole? Other people grew out of behaving like yobs. Other people grew up. But not him. Why couldn't he either try being nice to Lorna for a change or just clear off out of it and leave her alone? Let her start a new life while she was still young enough? And as for some of the rumours about what he was up to, they made Denise ashamed even to know him, let alone be related to him. Her mum might deny it all, but Denise knew most of it was probably true. It was just a shame Lorna wasn't the sort to stand up to him. Or to not care what people thought about her and her family. Maybe then she would have walked out on him.

'He'll be home for his tea then, eh?' Denise said softly.

'Yeah.' Lorna sounded distracted; she rose to her feet and frantically scanned the room for any signs of mess.

They could now both hear the solid thunk, thunk, thunk as Richie made his way along the parquet flooring in the hall.

'Trouble is, I never know when to expect him, so it's difficult to know what time to get it ready.'

Denise could have cried for her; she looked frantic. 'That's the best thing about still living at home with my mum and dad,' she said, trying to lighten things up. 'Getting everything done for me. Well,' she said, attempting a little laugh, 'I suppose it's the only good thing about still being at home. When me and Terry want to –'

'Good thing about being at home? With that lot?' It was Richie. The shoulders of his raincoat were beaded with raindrops, and his thick black hair was flattened against his head. 'I can't imagine anything being good about living with them.'

He then made a big performance of walking across the living room to kiss Lorna on the cheek.

Denise watched her friend; she didn't pull away from

him, but she visibly flinched at the touch of his lips. God knows what went on when no one was around.

'Being looked after,' Denise said coldly. 'That's what's nice about living at home. Especially after a long day at work.'

Richie threw his coat on the chair, and squatted in front of the electric fire to warm his hands. 'Call what you do work?'

Denise was about to say something, but Lorna flashed her a pleading look to keep quiet.

'Your tea won't be long.' As she spoke, Lorna took her friend's barely touched coffee away from her. 'Denise was just going, weren't you, Den?'

'Don't go on my account,' Richie said unexpectedly. 'In fact, stay for a bit. I wanted to have a word with you.' He straightened up and checked his hair in the gold-framed mirror – another gift from Joe and Shirley – then turned and spoke to Lorna. He was smiling.

Lorna gulped. A kiss, and now a smile? What was he playing at?

'Take this, Lorn.' He handed her a ten-shilling note and a handful of silver. 'Nip out and get the three of us some fish and chips, and I'll have a bottle of pale ale. We can have our tea together. Play happy families, eh, girls?'

Lorna looked imploringly at Denise, her eyes begging her to do what Richie wanted. Although she had no real idea what on earth he could be up to, he wanted Denise to stay, so that's what Lorna wanted too.

'OK, Richie,' Denise said warily. 'That'd be nice. Hang on, Lorn, I'll just get my coat from the kitchen and I'll go down the chip shop with you.'

'No, she'll be fine, and it'll give me a chance to have that word with you.'

* * *

Lorna made her way towards the chip shop that Richie favoured on the East India Dock Road, doing her best to shelter behind her umbrella from the sleeting rain, and hopping out of the way as car drivers made their way back to the warm comfort of their homes, oblivious of the young woman they were spraying with cold, muddy water as they hissed their way through the deep, blue-black puddles.

She couldn't understand what Richie's game was. Why was he being so nice? And why did he want to talk to Denise? It was a real relief having him in such a good mood, and not just coming in, wolfing down his tea in silence, and then clearing off again for who knew how long. But it was also worrying. Lorna could only hope that Denise would keep her lip buttoned and try not to wind him up.

'Make yourself another cup of coffee, if you like, Den.'

Denise looked sceptically at Richie. 'You mean you want one?'

'Well, if you're offering . . .'

Instead of snapping at her, he had flashed her one of his most charming smiles. And when he followed her into the kitchen, she was even more surprised; she would have laid money that, having lived in the new flat for less than a week, her useless creep of a half-brother wouldn't have even known where the kitchen was.

Half-brother.

Even after four years of knowing about her real relationship to Richie, she still couldn't get used to it, because she still didn't like it.

'Den?'

'What?'

'Ever hear of a place called the Canvas?' Richie leaned back against the Formica-clad sink unit and folded his arms across his chest, while Denise got on with the coffee making. 'It's a club. In Soho.'

'Course I've heard of it, it's where all the groups want to play.' She smiled to herself, pleased to know that she was about to get one over on him. 'As a matter of fact, my Terry's playing there next week-end.'

'No? Is he really?' Richie did a good job of looking completely taken aback by such news, despite the fact that he already knew all about Terry's *gig* at the Canvas – Chantalle and Maxie had been going on about nothing else for bloody weeks – but it suited him to play her along.

'That's great, Den, really great. I've heard all about the place. It's supposed to be the right business.' He made a big show of getting the milk from out of the compact little fridge that stood in pride of place beneath the draining board – Phyllis and Henry's contribution to the new household.

'I wouldn't mind going there myself one day. They reckon it's meant to be even better if you're on the special VIP guest list. Apparently you don't have to pay to get in, or for your drinks, or anything.'

He waited for a response, but Denise wasn't playing along. If he wanted to get on the list and go along with them, he'd have to make a bit more effort than handing her a milk bottle.

'Here,' he said, as if he'd just had a bright idea, 'any chance of me and Lorna getting an invite?' Then he added the clincher: 'She's been a right miserable mare lately,

Den. It'd do her good to get out. You know, what with the move and everything.'

Denise glowed smugly. So, she had something that Richie wanted, but he was too proud to ask for it. What a shame.

'I don't know, Rich. I'll have to see what Terry says. I can ask him if you really want to go.'

Richie gripped the side of the table. 'Don't put yourself out, Denise.'

If she hadn't been concerned about leaving Lorna to deal with the aftermath of him losing his temper, Denise would have walked out on him there and then, leaving him to stew in his own stupid juices, but instead she smiled sweetly.

'Course you can come along. I'll tell Terry to get us all special passes. We can make a night of it.' As she handed him his mug, she couldn't resist a final little dig. 'And I'll ask Chantalle and Maxie along as well. You know how kids get excited about that sort of thing.'

'Our Lorna was in a good mood when she popped in after work today.' Shirley lifted her face to her husband for a kiss, and then went back to setting the table ready for their evening meal.

'That's nice to hear, love.' Joe stretched out in his armchair and flicked open the *Evening Standard*. 'With all these changes going on at work,' he held up the paper, showing her yet another story on the changes – both actual and threatened – down at the docks, 'there's so many union meetings being called, I don't get as much time as I used to, to check up on her during the day.'

'Check up on her?' Shirley flicked him affectionately under the chin before going out to the kitchen for the plates. 'You sound just like a dock copper,' she shouted from the other room.

'Don't wish that on me,' Joe shouted back with a good-natured chuckle. 'You'll have all the other blokes at work turning against me.'

Shirley appeared in the door with two plates, one piled high for Joe and the other holding less than half that amount for her. 'Richie's taking her out on Saturday. Up the West End.'

Joe felt himself bristle. A night up West? Who had the nasty little cowson been robbing now? 'Is he, love? That'll be nice. She'll enjoy that.'

'Yeah, Lorna's chuffed. It's not easy for kids starting out nowadays, is it? They deserve a little treat – you know, a break from things.'

Starting out? They'd been married four bloody years. And as for deserving a break . . . Joe gulped back the bile. Lorna certainly needed one, but *him*? Apart from thieving, and a few other things that Joe had heard rumours about – but didn't even want to start thinking about or he wouldn't be able to hold himself responsible for what he might to do him – taking breaks was all that lazy bastard Richie Clayton ever did. After four years they should have had more round them than the few bits of furniture that him and Shirley had bought them. If only Lorna would see Richie for what he was, Joe would take great pleasure in telling the little prick his fortune and giving him such a good hiding he'd never show his face round there again. Bugger the shame of a broken marriage, who cared what people said?

He sighed wearily. Why did it have to be his little Lorna he'd got his claws into?

'Did you hear me, babe?' Shirley set the plates on the table.

'Sorry, Shirl, I must be getting a bit mutton in my old age.'

'I've told Lorna she's to bring Richie round for Sunday dinner, so they can tell us all about their night up West. That'll be nice, won't it?'

Joe's appetite suddenly disappeared, as he did his best to stop his anger erupting. 'Look, Shirl, I don't want to have a go or nothing, but you might be delighted she's still with that useless, lazy whoreson, but not me. I can't be. We all know he's running some kind of a racket, and that I'd grass him – *yes, me, grass him* – if I thought it wouldn't break our baby's heart.' He tightened his hands into fists. 'If it wasn't for Lorna, I'd put my hands round that little fucker's neck, and –'

'Joe!'

'Shirley, I'm sorry, it's just . . .'

'I know. I know. I've hinted to her plenty of times what I really think, but it's like –'

'He's brainwashed her.'

'No, it's not that, Joe. If you want the truth I think it's two things.'

'You really have been thinking about this.'

'Of course I have,' she said, putting down her knife and fork. 'Sometimes I think of nothing else. And what I think is: she's ashamed of the choice she's made, and now she's trying to make the best of it.'

'But no one would think badly of her if –'

'Yes they would, Joe,' she interrupted him – behaviour so unusual as to shock Joe into immediate silence. 'We're ordinary working people, not film stars who change their husbands as often as their mink coats.' She hesitated a brief moment. 'And the other thing: me.' Shirley rubbed her hands over her face. 'She's worried about my health. Doesn't want to upset me, so she pretends everything's lovely, all hearts and flowers. I bet she doesn't even realise we know the horrible little bugger's a crook.'

Shirley dropped her chin and began to weep. 'And what's even more worrying is he's always been so pathetic at it, a real two-bob merchant, but – you must have heard them – there's all sorts of stories going round about how he's involved with other stuff. No one actually spells it out, of course, but they certainly like to hint. God alone knows what he's really mixed up with.'

Joe got up and put his arm round his wife's shoulders. 'Don't worry, Shirl, you know how people waste their time gossiping and telling tales. And at least when they're talking about him, they're leaving decent people alone.'

Shirley took a deep breath. 'I might have been a bit unwell, Joe, but I've not gone stupid; I know they're not just gossiping, I know there's something going on. And I wouldn't give a damn what they were saying, not if Lorna wasn't involved with him.'

She couldn't stomach saying *married to him.*

Joe hugged her close. He knew he was going to have to do something about all this, but what? If only half the rumours that people had been brave enough to hint at to a giant of a man like Joe Wright were true, then the bastard deserved a good hiding at the very least. But then there was Lorna. And that little toerag Clayton knew only too well that she was his protection.

He was a pathetic, crawling coward.

Joe closed his eyes.

What the hell was he going to do?

*   *   *

As Chantalle led the way into the mirror-tiled Soho night spot – the famously, even notoriously, cool Canvas Club – her eyes glittered as brightly as the rows of glass beads that dangled around the neck, wrists and ankles of the extravagantly made-up seventeen-year-old.

Looking round at the other clubgoers, she wished she'd maybe gone for more of the Dolly Bird look than the kooky Weekend Hippy she'd finally decided on, but at least she knew the flowers she'd painted on her cheeks made her look sexier than ever, especially with her fringed, suedette skirt practically showing her knickers.

She made her way straight for the circular dance floor where she could show off her stuff to its best advantage – there were some very tasty-looking blokes around.

Maxie was equally impressed by the club. But he no longer nurtured his ambition to appear in such places as a drummer. When he had investigated the ins and outs of pursuing that particular dream, he had been shocked, to say the least, to discover that he actually needed to learn to play the things, rather than just bash about on them – at the right speed, of course – but sort of willy-nilly.

Drumming lessons? He'd been genuinely knocked for six. Taking time to learn things wasn't for the likes of him.

Maxie now wanted to be a singer, just like Terry, a person he hero-worshipped in the mistaken belief that he found it all so easy, an example of just how possible everything was. But he didn't let himself dwell on the everyday reality of Terry's life, and certainly had no intention of copying him in any other ways, such as investing effort in learning the guitar, or in practising with the rest of the band members almost every night of the week. No, that wasn't Maxie's way. He decided he would thrive on his talent and his good looks alone, because, despite having no idea about their real relationship, Maxie had grown to admire his half-brother Richie's laid-back attitude to life, and there was now more than a touch of Richie Clayton's work-shy, self-seeking ways in the character of young Maxie Parker.

Maxie let his gaze wander around the hedonistic splendours of the Canvas Club – from the projected light shows, with their almost living, pulsating walls of colour, to the flashing strobes and needle spotlights – and then settling on individual young men and women, admiring their peacock clothes, and knowing they were all out for the same thing: a good time and a chance to pull.

He'd been to other clubs, of course, but this was *the* club. It was bloody fantastic, exactly like a scene from a magazine article on Swinging London.

Maxie just knew that pop music would be his future and his saviour. He would become a star, appearing at places like the Canvas as a matter of right, and he would tell the City insurance firm, where he worked as a messenger, just what they could do with their job. And as for that old baggage in the post-room, he'd get his own back on her all right, and she'd have a bigger surprise coming to her than having a few extra parcels to deal with last thing of a Friday night.

He fluffed up the lavishly ruffled front of his new lavender shirt, and strutted over to the bar where two pretty, giggling girls were perched on high chrome stools, flashing enough thigh to make a young man dizzy.

Maxie sighed with the sheer pleasure of it all: his evening was about to begin.

Denise was still standing with Lorna just inside the

entrance, where they were waiting to put their things in the cloakroom.

Despite the freezing weather, Maxie and Chantalle had insisted they didn't need topcoats – the truth being that they didn't have anything they considered stylish enough, and preferred to shiver all the way there rather than spoil their look.

And, in truth, Denise's coat hadn't kept her a lot warmer. She was wearing a short, navy-blue reefer jacket, fine as far as her body went, but her legs were frozen, as, underneath, she had on a psychedelic, bottom-skimming shift dress.

She'd finally found the dress in the Oxford Street branch of C&A, after nearly three hours' frantic, late-night Thursday shopping. It had been a close thing; the shop doors were about to be locked when she grabbed it, in desperation, off the rail. Miraculously, it had turned out to be just what she wanted: up to the minute, outrageous, and a perfect complement to her wild halo of red curls. Fashion had, quite suddenly, freed Denise from spending hours angrily trying to tame the hair, which had, until recently, been the bane of her life. She now proudly referred to her hairstyle as an *Afro*, and happily teased the red corkscrews into ever-bigger extremes. But while Denise looked the genuine, up-to-the-minute part, she was just as wide-eyed about being in the Canvas as were her young brother and sister.

The club might have been only a few miles from where she lived in the East End, and not much more than a gentle stroll from where she now worked in the West End, but, as she'd taken her first glimpse through the doorway, she knew she had never been anywhere like it before. It had a sort of buzz about it, a feeling that was young, exciting, and glamorous. But, best of all, her Terry was actually playing there tonight, and Denise was loving every single minute of it.

Lorna was having a great time too, but she would honestly have been as happy standing in the Blue Boy sipping a half of bitter shandy. This was like the old days, like being with the Richie she had fallen for all that time ago. She couldn't help herself, this was what she had wanted then, and, foolish as it might be, it was what she wanted again now – that charming, funny, handsome Richie, her old Richie. The real Richie, the bloke she had fallen for when she was just a kid.

Her evening had started brilliantly. Before they had left the flat, she had asked him if he liked her dress. It was a floaty, Juliet-style, ribbon-bound, chiffon mini that she'd bought in the Ilford branch of Richards – it was too far for her to get up West in the lunch hour, and going Thursday late-night shopping with Denise would have been pushing her luck – and he had actually said that he thought she looked very tasty.

Very tasty!

Her, Lorna, who he hadn't so much as noticed was even alive for the past . . . who knew how long? She had felt so chuffed, she'd pushed it a bit further and had asked him what he thought of the new hairdo she'd had done just that morning.

She had only gone to Lola's, but Lola had performed miracles on her, copying the picture of Twiggy that Lorna had cut out of the paper. She had kept it bleached blonde, the colour Richie preferred, but it was now cut short at the back and left long at the front so she could tuck it behind her ears.

Richie didn't hesitate when she'd asked. He'd said,

right away, that it was *smashing*. It was all more than Lorna could have hoped for, and she didn't even care what his reasons were for being so nice. She had just stood there in the sitting room, savouring his words and nibbling hard on her bottom lip to stop herself from bursting into tears of happiness. Things would get better from now on. She just knew they would.

For anyone less cowed down than Lorna, or even anyone who had listened to his many whispered conversations on the telephone lately, Richie's motives would have been transparently simple: he was making an effort to keep Lorna sweet – a definitely begrudged but necessary effort – as he needed a legitimate reason to be in the Canvas Club. It represented exactly what he wanted: a successful bit of turf where no one knew him. That was the Canvas, all right, and it suited ideally his purposes of carrying out what he thought of as his *research*, and where he could make the contacts crucial to his plan. And having a personal invitation from one of the band meant that he had a great alibi for being there. The last thing he wanted was to be taken for some little blow-in no-mark from out of town.

In order to blend in convincingly, Richie had made an effort to look the part: a trendy young bloke, totally at ease in Soho, so cool that all this was completely normal for him. He had forked out on a new pair of maroon crushed-velvet loons, and a pink and orange paisley shirt. Teamed with his floor-length Afghan coat, the floppy, cerise silk scarf at his throat, and his dark, handsome looks, Richie, vain at the best of times, was more than pleased with the result.

While he was still giving the club the once-over, Denise and Lorna scampered up to him like a pair of puppies on their first day loose in the park, all eager energy and anticipation.

In response, Richie produced one of his finest teeth-baring smiles, but, not wanting to be distracted from his carefully planned goal, he knew he had to move on to stage two: getting rid of them. So rather than stand there listening to inane, girly chatter about how thrilled they were by everything, how they couldn't wait for the Spanners to come on later, what a fantastic discotheque it was, and what terrific music the DJ was playing, Richie gave Lorna a squeeze, shelled out for a round of exorbitantly priced drinks, and encouraged them to go, glasses still in hand, and have a dance to what he called, without so much as a blush, the *groovy Cream track* that was playing.

Such a comment would usually have had Denise spluttering with mocking, finger-pointing laughter into her Cinzano and lemonade, and Lorna stiffening with terror at what might result from her friend's loud-mouthed, dumb-headed provocation of Richie, but this evening seemed to be having a magical effect on all of them.

Denise simply smiled sweetly at his suggestion, and said 'Good idea, Rich. Come on, Lorn, let's go and show them how it's done.'

Lorna had also smiled, then she'd pecked Richie on the cheek, thanked him for the drink, and – blissfully happy – had trotted off after her friend and joined her on the dance floor.

For his part, Richie hadn't swatted away Lorna's display of affection, but had launched another dazzler of a smile back at both of them, and had even given them the extra pleasure of a broad wink.

With Lorna safely occupied copying her friend's dance

moves – gyrating her body and waving her outstretched arms, just like Denise said she'd seen them do when she'd gone to watch *Blow-Up* at the pictures – Richie parked himself in a dark corner, nice and discreetly, flat against the wall, where he was well out of sight, but had a good view of everything going on around him. He was barely sipping at his Scotch, knowing that if he was going to make a job of this, he had to keep his wits about him and his head clear.

It didn't take him long to spot his target: a slightly anachronistic, very skinny mod, with a bleached-blond crop and a shiny, tonic mohair suit, probably aged around twenty-two, -three – about Richie's own age – who was standing outside the men's lavatory.

He watched and noted as the mod kept popping in and out of the loo, like an indecisive model Tyrolean on a souvenir weather house, followed, each time, by one of a succession of other young men.

It was obvious to Richie what he was up to, and that he was doing it with the full permission of the club's massive bouncers. They could have stopped him in a heartbeat, but, by him not flaunting his activities in their faces, if anything went wrong, both parties could deny all knowledge of the other's complicity. Simple. And they were no doubt getting a nice cut of the action too.

Richie levered himself away from the wall with his elbow, and made his way over to the mod through the now-packed club.

Richie stopped next to him, and spoke, all the while looking out at the crowd rather than in his face. 'All right, mate? Doing business tonight, are you?'

The mod glanced sideways at Richie and hurriedly

stuffed a bulging wallet into his inside jacket pocket. 'Do I know you?'

Still with his body facing the dance floor, Richie turned his head slightly and let him have a smile – more subdued than the one he'd used on the girls, but still chock-full of charm – then held out his hand.

'Richie Clayton. I'm here with the Spanners, the new band that's playing tonight. Everyone says they're going to be massive.'

The crop-haired bloke looked him up and down. 'You want to do business, do you?'

'Certainly do, er . . . ?' Richie paused, with his head cocked on one side, waiting for him to share his name.

'They call me Blond Boy. But Boy'll do. Give me a minute.'

Richie nodded, then, after a thirty-second wait, he followed Boy into the men's lavatory.

It was empty except for Boy, who was leaning against the doorjamb of one of the stalls opposite the far end of the run of urinals.

Richie stood with his back to him, used the urinal, then checked his hair in the mirror.

'When you've finished, what're you after exactly?' Boy's voice was soft, but surprisingly firm and no-nonsense for someone with such a slight build.

Richie turned to face him and took a few steps closer, until he was standing right in front of him, effectively blocking his escape.

He leaned forward until his face was very close to Boy's. 'What I'm after,' he said, with subdued, but obvious excitement, just as if he were asking for something *really lovely in lilac* in a soft furnishers, 'is getting into the retail side of things.'

Boy curled his lip in disgust. 'Get stuffed. And don't try anything stupid, I've got a room full of mates out there.'

He dropped one shoulder and pushed past Richie. He was unexpectedly strong.

Richie grabbed his arm, but Boy shook him off and started for the door.

'Hang on,' Richie said, chasing after him. 'Just listen to me. You'll be sorry if –'

Boy spun round. There was a switchblade in his hand.

'Fucking want some of this, do you?'

Richie, coward that he was, had his hands in the air before the idea of surrendering had even become a conscious thought.

'Don't be silly, say someone comes in? You'll be in right trouble.' Richie's voice was steady but he wasn't that far from losing control of his bowels. 'I really don't think you understand what I –'

'No, mush, *you* don't understand. No one comes in here unless I give the nod to my fellers out there. Without my say so, they use the bogs across the other side of the dance floor. So, we're in here all nice and safe and alone.'

Jesus. 'Look, Boy, I came here especially tonight. See, I've been making enquiries, and –'

Boy touched the knife to the side of Richie's neck. 'Who's been shouting their mouth off?'

'No one. Look, everyone knows this is the place to come for gear. I just thought you might be interested in me doing a bit of sub-contracting for you, that's all.'

Boy frowned; the taut, pale skin on his skeletal face barely wrinkled. 'You having a laugh?'

'No, it's a serious proposition. I come from Poplar, see.

Near the docks, where Fuller controlled all the dealing on the estates.'

'Fuller?' asked Boy.

'Yeah, David Fuller.'

'What do you know about Mr Fuller's business?'

Richie noted his respectful attitude, but this was a chance to get into the big time that he wouldn't throw away.

'What I know is that he's been inside for nearly two years now. That he won't be out for at least another three. That, at first, he had a grip of steel on all the dealing round there, even from inside, but now it's starting to fall apart. There's all sorts of kids and foreigners muscling in. And while all their fighting and rowing about who's in charge takes up all their time, it's leaving the door wide open for the likes of me to approach someone, someone with contacts and a reputation, to start up a nice little business of our own.'

Suddenly the main door opened.

Boy slipped his knife up his sleeve and twisted round to see who had dared come into his place of business.

Richie was probably the more shocked of the two of them to see it was Terry.

'All right, Tel?'

'Richie.'

Another man, twice the size of Terry, appeared in the doorway behind him. 'Sorry, Boy, he –'

'You two know each other?' snapped Boy.

'Sure,' said Richie, using the confusion to his advantage. 'This, Boy, is Terry Robins, lead singer and guitarist with the Spanners. The next big thing, so they reckon, eh, Tel?'

'I don't know about that,' Terry began warily, 'but –'

'What exactly are you doing in here?' Boy interrupted him.

Terry looked very uncomfortable. 'This is the lav.'

'Bands use the one in the dressing room.'

Now Terry looked embarrassed and even more uncomfortable. 'Busy. And the other ones in the club. I was desperate.' He wagged his head towards the man mountain blocking the exit behind him. 'I even got past him. Bit of nerves, see. We're on in five minutes.' He managed a feeble smile. 'Us at the Canvas, eh? Now if you'll just . . .'

With that, Terry disappeared inside one of the stalls and locked the door firmly behind him.

Boy considered a moment then nodded for the minder to take his leave.

Richie, with some of his usual cockiness regained, started chatting to Terry through the door.

'Here, Tel, see them toms outside the front of the club? Right nice, some of them. Not like the old brasses you get round our way. Some right pretty little birds.' He laughed. 'Tell you what, you should introduce me and Boy here to some of them groupies you read about. You do have groupies, don't you, Tel, or does our Denise put the block on them?'

Terry groaned. 'Piss off and leave me alone, Richie.'

'Good advice,' Boy hissed into his ear.

'Don't be so hasty.' Richie slipped his hand inside his shirt and brought out a very thick roll of banknotes secured with an elastic band.

Boy couldn't conceal the flash of greed in his eyes at the sight of so much money in someone else's possession.

Richie, holding it out encouragingly, like a pork chop

to a reluctant mutt, beckoned for Boy to follow him to the far end of the lavatory. He then opened the taps until they were gushing so noisily there was no chance of the conversation being overheard by Terry or anyone else.

'I have my fingers in quite a few pies, Boy,' he said, his voice low but friendly, 'and I'm very keen to find other ways of spreading my interests around a bit. This,' he said, handing Boy the thick wedge, 'is only a little sweetener, a taster to whet your appetite, if you like. Do business with me, and we're both gonna be laughing.'

'I'll have to think about it,' said Boy, counting the money with practised speed and a well-licked thumb.

Richie held out his hand, palm upwards. 'If I might just take some sample merchandise in return . . .'

'How's the young couple?' Mrs Elliot, Phyllis's neighbour, stood at the bottom of the stone steps leading up to the Parkers' front door. She was covered, from neck to ankle, in swathes of black serge. On top of her head sat a strangely fashioned turban affair of dark grey chenille.

'I just came past their place,' she jerked her chin vaguely in the direction of Chrisp Street, where Richie and Lorna had their new flat, 'on my way back from the cemetery – putting flowers on my Stanley's grave, I was – and I noticed their curtains are still drawn.'

She folded her arms. 'I know it's a Sunday morning, but we never slept in like that, not even on the Sabbath, not when I was a young woman. I'd have been out scrubbing my step. Every single day I did that, making my place look respectable. But then that's the sort of person I am. I care what people think about me.'

'You finished, have you?' Phyllis stared down at her; it was bitterly cold, and she was hardly dressed for outdoors, having just popped her head round the door to bring in the milk, but she was buggered if she'd go inside till she got the better of this old faggot.

Mrs Elliot considered for a moment, then waggled her lips and raised her eyebrows to indicate that, yes, she probably had finished, thank you very much.

'Good. Well, for a start, Mrs Elliot, it's beyond me how you think you could pick out their flat from that huge sodding block. But maybe you've got a pair of binoculars in your bag. I must admit, I wouldn't put it past you. But, if their curtains are still drawn, and if they are still asleep, and if you really must know other people's private business, then I'll tell you why. They're tired because they went out and had a lovely time last night. Up West, they went, to a club, where my Denise's boyfriend was playing with his group. Famous, they are. The Spanners, they're called. You might have heard of them if you was forty years younger.'

Now Phyllis folded her arms, clinking the milk bottles together, with a defiant *top that you, old bag* expression on her face.

But Mrs Elliot wasn't so easily beaten; she was a professional.

'Still no sign of them having a little one then? You do know that when they got married everyone was sure that young Lorna Wright was already up the spout.'

Phyllis plonked down the bottles with a dangerously heavy hand, and stomped down the steps. She stuck her finger in Mrs Elliot's face.

'Look, you nosy, rotten trout, them kids married for love, not because she was in trouble. No matter what spiteful, gossiping, poisonous, old bleeders like you have to say. And they'll have a baby when they're good and ready. Got it?'

Mrs Elliot looked Phyllis slowly up and down, taking her time to observe every detail of her mauve nylon housecoat and her pink fluffy slippers, before walking away and sniping over her shoulder: 'I'd be ashamed if that boy was anything to do with my family, the way he carries on, and I'd be ashamed of being seen on the front step in my night things and all. Standards have certainly dropped round here since I was a young woman.'

Phyllis pulled her housecoat tightly about her. The wind was spiteful and right on target. Just like Mrs Elliot's tongue.

Mrs Elliot had been wrong about one thing: Lorna wasn't still in bed – she had been up for ages. After her night at the Canvas Club, dancing and laughing, enjoying seeing Richie have a good time, and him not sneering even once, not even when the Spanners got a rave reception from the crowd, she had been so excited she had hardly slept. This was how it was meant to be when you were married: not just having a good time – that was a bonus – but not being scared of what you said or did, and being told you looked nice, being treated properly. She would have burst into song if she hadn't been worried about disturbing Richie.

She had slipped carefully out of bed and had made sure the entire flat was clean and tidy. Then she'd washed her hair over the sink in their lovely new bathroom – using the ridged, blue rubber hose attachment she'd bought especially in Woolworth's – to get rid of the smell of cigarettes from the club. It was one of the first things Richie had ever said to her, that her hair smelled nice, and Lorna had never, ever forgotten it. She would have liked to have had a bath as well, but the sound of it filling might waken him. Still, she could have a good all-over strip wash, and then she'd put her hair in big, fat rollers to smooth all the ends, and get ready to go round to her mum and dad's for something to eat.

Lorna was really looking forward to it, and not only to the roast dinner that no one could make like her mum, but to her dad seeing her and Richie being happy together. She knew how much her parents worried about her, and that Richie had behaved badly in the past, but she knew they could put all the bad stuff behind them. Perhaps her dad would talk to him about getting a proper job. The docks would be closing soon, and, sad as that was, it meant that she wouldn't have to do those things any more, wouldn't have to get him the information he needed . . . But she didn't want to think about that now. She wanted to think happy, positive thoughts: *maybe about trying for a baby*. That would be fantastic.

She knew she shouldn't get too overexcited, but it was difficult not to. This was their chance to make a fresh start, their chance for happiness.

That chance was short-lived.

When Lorna took a cup of tea through to the bedroom to wake him, Richie refused point-blank even to get up, let alone to get himself ready to go out. Instead, he pulled the blankets up over his head, turned over, and muttered from under the covers that, if she knew what was good for her, she would just fuck off, leave him alone and not disturb him. He'd decide when he was good and ready to get up.

Lorna knew better than to try to persuade him otherwise.

Just as she should have known that being happy was too good to be true, and that things didn't just suddenly work out for the best.

Not for the likes of her they didn't.

In the end, Richie slept the whole day away, only getting out of bed in the late afternoon, when it was already dark again, and only then because he'd caught a whiff of the roast dinner that Lorna had brought him back from her parents' house. It wasn't that he was particularly partial to his mother-in-law's cooking – he couldn't have cared less what he was eating – it was just that he hadn't had anything in his stomach except booze for over twenty-four hours, and he was starving.

'Mum and Dad were disappointed you didn't go round theirs for your dinner,' said Lorna, setting down a cup of tea next to his plate.

'I bet they were,' said Richie, his voice still thick with sleep. He was crouched over the table, shovelling the food into his mouth as though it were more like a fortnight since he'd eaten.

'They said they're popping into the Blue Boy for a drink later on and they wondered if we fancied –'

'Don't be stupid,' he said, tossing down his knife and fork. 'I told you: I'm going out.' He picked up his cup and gulped down the tea.

'No you didn't, Richie, you never said anything about going out.'

Slowly, he lifted his head. 'Are you arguing with me?'

He wasn't inviting an answer.

With that he got up, left the kitchen without another word, and locked himself in the bathroom.

Lorna cleared the table to the sounds of her own tears of disappointment, and of Richie using the lavatory.

Rita Thomas was a slightly dopey, but willing, young bottle redhead, whom Richie had picked up in Victoria Park a few days before. Despite the perishing weather, she and her mates, for want of anything better to do, had been hanging around in the kiddies' playground, messing about on the swings. When Richie had come along and promised her a frothy coffee, the pert little fifteen-year-old – 'I'm almost sixteen' – had trotted after him like a pretty young fawn from the deer enclosure, leaving her friends to make jealous comments and to continue freezing their backsides off in the hope of getting a similar offer from as dishy a bloke. Richie was well pleased with Rita; the only reason he'd been in the park was on the off chance that he'd meet some likely bit of teenage stuff, and the moment he'd seen her, he knew he was on to a winner, knew she'd be a good little earner for him.

His original plans – made nearly four years ago now – to run a whole stable of girls and to take over the turf around Cable Street hadn't exactly taken off in the way he had originally hoped. It had all involved a lot more hard work than he'd expected: keeping the girls he had managed to recruit in some sort of line, and keeping other brasses off their pitch, never mind all the feeble excuses about them not wanting to work outside in bad weather, and that was all before he'd got anywhere near being able to invade the lucrative Cable Street business.

But now, with the money from the docks drying up, and him being left with just Pamela Logan and her silly-as-buggery mate Melanie working for him – and they were both starting to look more than a bit rough – he had no choice. He had to get his act together and sort out something very soon, or he'd be done for. He'd be a no-hoper, stuck at the bottom of the barrel, just like his stupid *Uncle* Henry.

That was why he had had to go to the Canvas last night, and that was why he had to reel in this little cracker, reel her in so far, get her so tied up and done for, that she had no choice in the matter but to do exactly as he told her, and, with a bit of friendly persuasion, to bring some of her peachy little mates along with her.

Rita wiped her sweaty palms down the cheap shiny material of the skintight thighs of her flares.

'I can't do it, Richie. I swear, I can't.'

'Everyone's nervous the first time, Rita.'

As Richie spoke to her, he looked over his shoulder, then at his watch. That silly tart Lorna had better have got this cargo right. If he was taking all these risks for nothing more than a few cases of sweet sherry . . .

'Look, worse way, we've got a clear fifteen minutes before the dock copper starts his next round. But, on a freezing cold night like this, if he's got any brains, he'll be amongst the missing even longer. He'll be round the back, see, by the braziers, having a nice warm kiss and a cuddle with that old slag from the Blue Boy.' Richie grinned in the darkness at happy memories of his own times spent with the Friday relief barmaid. 'That'll put fire in his belly.'

'That's what I feel like. Like I'm on fire.'

Richie ignored her. 'Take this a minute.' He passed her the stubby length of lead pipe he had taken from a deep pocket inside his overcoat, and then produced a jemmy from another pocket. He weighed it, thoughtfully, in his hand, then slipped it into the gap between the two narrow metal gates set into the railings, and levered it back and forth until one of them swung open, leaving the keeper firmly anchored into the cobbles.

Richie grinned, pleased with his expertise. 'There. Easy.'

Rita, despite her earlier reservations, grinned back. She'd never done anything like this before. Her adrenalin had never pumped round her body like this, nor had she ever felt so excited.

Richie winked and, with a jerk of his head, signalled for Rita to wait outside, in the shadows cast by the massive bonded warehouse. 'You wait here and keep an eye on the van.'

'That's it,' gasped Richie, heaving a crate into the back, 'the last one.'

'Richie, hurry up,' Rita pleaded. 'You've been ages. I thought they'd collared you.'

'Calm down, can't you? Everything's fine. We've got ages before he patrols this bit.'

The almost too relaxed tone of Richie's voice was beginning to alarm Rita. 'Honestly, you really were a long time getting that last crate.'

'That's because I've got to make sure I make the most of it. This could be one of the last chances to turn this gaff over.'

He started the engine, let in the clutch, and pulled away from the kerb with a series of kangaroo-like jumps that made Rita grab for the door handle to steady herself.

'And what with all this container nonsense going on down at Tilbury, I'm going to have to find myself some new territory. But now that pathetic old face Fuller has lost his grip on things, I reckon it's about time someone younger took over the job of supplying the estate.'

'Fuller?' Rita asked, glancing sideways at Richie. He was driving really badly, and she could see, reflected in the pool of light as they passed by a lamppost, that his eyes were strange and glassy. And why was he talking to her like this, about things she didn't understand? Something wasn't right, something wasn't right at all.

Richie changed gear with a grinding wrench of metal against metal. 'David Fuller. Used to run the supplies for this whole area.'

'Supplies? What of?'

Richie took one hand off the steering wheel, leaned over alarmingly, and dipped into an inside pocket. 'These.'

She stared at the small, lavender-blue pills he held in his palm. 'What are they?'

'Uppers. They're going to make me a fortune.'

With no warning, Richie suddenly stopped the van.

It was all Rita could do to stop herself from crashing into the windscreen. She was getting scared.

'Here.' He handed her one of the pills, then threw back his head and tossed the rest down his throat. 'Swallow that and get out of the van.'

'But, Richie, it's dark out there and –'

He reached across her and, on the third attempt, undid her door. 'It's all right, you dozy mare, we're going to get in the back. I'm going to give you a treat for being such a big help tonight.'

'But how about all the gear you've just loaded up?'

'You're right. We'll get a bottle of Scotch out of the back and just have to think of somewhere else to do it.'

Lorna lay alone in the dark, in the new double bed she

was still fretting about having to buy on the never-never – it would be two years before it was theirs. She was wide-eyed, watchful, waiting for the light to go on in the hall and for Richie to come home.

She had sat up until ten o'clock, drinking tea and thinking about how her life had turned out like this, oblivious both of the time and of the flickering black and white images on the television screen in the corner of the room.

Then she'd glanced at her watch.

Christ, if he was this late, he was bound to be drunk.

She'd rushed out to the kitchen, rinsed her cup under the tap, prepared him a supper tray in case he came home hungry – some of the cold meat she'd brought back from her Mum's, bread and butter, a slice of egg and ham pie, tomatoes, and a can of lager, with the opener sat on top of it so he could find it easily – and had set it on the coffee table between the armchairs, then she'd got ready for bed. If she were lucky he would think she was asleep, and just eat his supper, and fall into a drunken stupor in the chair.

And the docks might stay open, and everyone down there might keep their jobs, and all be given a massive pay rise for being so loyal to their bosses . . .

She was getting too old for wishing on stars.

It was almost a quarter past eleven, when she heard the sound of the front door opening, followed by Richie, singing a drunkard's muddled and mumbled version of 'Ruby Tuesday', as he stumbled even more noisily along the hallway.

At least, Lorna consoled herself, the neighbours weren't getting the full benefit of all the row he was making, as they would have done in the old flat.

She swallowed hard as she heard him go into the bathroom.

What was he going to do next?

She found out sooner than she'd expected. He just had a quick pee – he hadn't even bothered to close the door, let alone flush the lavatory or hang around washing his hands – and staggered straight into the bedroom.

After a couple of failed cracks at turning on the light, he finally managed to locate the switch.

Lorna blinked and shaded her eyes with her hand.

'Hello, Richie,' she said, in a voice that was surprisingly calm and agreeable, considering she was actually shaking with fear. 'I've put out some supper for you in the sitting room. Shall I make you some tea?'

Still excited from the adrenalin of committing the robbery, pissed on stolen Scotch, and stoned on uppers, food was the last thing on Richie's mind.

'Nah.'

He dropped down onto the bed, struggled out of his overcoat and jacket, ripped off his tie, fumbled around until he managed to undo his flies, then pushed Lorna onto her back, and pulled the bedclothes off her.

Lorna lay there, with her eyes screwed tight, but the tears still found their way down onto her cheeks and into her ears.

As he pumped into her, grunting, and stinking of booze and tobacco, she didn't struggle, she just cried.

This was their so-called love life. It didn't happen very often, but when it did, it was only because Richie was excited or angry about something. It was him forcing himself on her.

It was nothing more nor less than rape.

How could she have even thought of wanting to

have a baby with a life like hers? With a man like this?

'Richie,' it was hard to breathe with him thrusting into her, grabbing at her breasts, but she had to say it before it was too late, 'use a rubber, please. There are some –'

'Scared you might catch something?' he hissed into her ear.

His breath was hot, nasty, but she didn't pull away. She knew she mustn't antagonise him. 'Course not, I just don't want to get pregnant.'

He laughed, an ugly, frightening sound. 'Well, you should be worried. Couple of hours ago I had some little bitch I hardly know up against the wall of the West India Dock.'

Lorna felt nauseous.

'She's going to work for me.' He started giggling.

Lorna was scared. He sounded strange, different.

'I'm going to have twenty girls soon, thirty.' Now, as he continued to force himself into her, the alcohol delaying his usually rapid, self-gratifying climax, he was bragging. 'Like them Maltese down Cable Street.'

Cable Street? Lorna's eyes flicked open. He couldn't mean . . .

'I'm not wasting my time with a girl here and there no more,' he said, rolling off her.

She hadn't even noticed that he'd finished.

'I'm really getting into it big time.' He groped around on the floor for his jacket, searching for his cigarettes.

He flopped back onto the pillows and lit one with a self-satisfied groan.

Lorna just stared up at the ceiling, terrible thoughts running through her mind about the sorts of things that people like old Mrs Elliot had hinted at.

'Here, you can work for me and all,' he said, finding the idea both hilarious and brilliant at the same time. 'With your tits, you're bound to attract the punters.'

He grabbed one of her breasts and squeezed and pinched at it until she was sure he would draw blood.

He was mad. It was the only explanation. She had always been too terrified to leave him before, too scared about how easily he could beat her and destroy her family, but now she was more terrified of staying. She had to get away.

His grasp on her breast gradually lessened, and his snoring began.

He had fallen asleep with the half-smoked cigarette still in his hand.

Let him burn to death was her first thought as she crept across the room and gathered up her clothes from the chair where she'd set them out for work in the morning. But then she thought about the other people in the block.

With her heart racing she managed to take the still-smouldering butt from his fingers and silently stub it out in the ashtray on the bedside rug.

Then she pulled on her clothes, snatched her coat from the wardrobe, and fled.

The rain had turned to watery snow, but Lorna hardly noticed the cold as she ran through the deserted streets. Tears were blurring her vision, but her purpose was clear: she was heading for Lancaster Buildings. The block might be old and patched up, but decent people lived in those flats. Even an old fence like Doris Barker had values – certainly more than Richie would ever have. How had Phyllis ever had a child like him?

When she got there, the lift was out of order, but Lorna

didn't care. She raced up the stairs to the top floor, and along the landing to her old home.

She took a moment to compose herself before she fitted the key into the lock – the key her dad had insisted she keep 'just in case'.

Why hadn't she listened to him?

Then she slipped along the hall and into the living room. She wouldn't disturb them, she would spend the night – or what was left of it – on the sofa, and deal with the explanations in the morning.

But she hadn't been quiet enough for Shirley. Lorna hadn't even sat down when her mother appeared in the doorway.

'Babe?' With her lovely kind face flushed from sleep, she rushed over to her daughter, took her in her arms, and pulled her close. 'Whatever's wrong? It's gone midnight, and it's filthy out there.'

'I'm really sorry it's so late, Mum,' sniffed Lorna. 'Let me stay just for tonight. We've had a bit of a tiff, and I walked out.'

'Ssshh, don't cry.'

Shirley steered her through to her old room – still exactly as Lorna had left it: all pink frills and teddies – flicked on the bedside lamp, and started to peel off her child's wet clothes.

As she pulled the now exhausted Lorna's sweater over her head, she gasped in horror and her hand flew to her mouth.

'What happened?' she demanded, gently touching the welts and bruising on her daughter's breast, but forgetting to keep her voice down.

Lorna, ashamed, covered them with her hands. 'Nothing. Can I go to sleep, Mum, I'm so tired.'

'Shirley?' Now Joe was there too, standing in the doorway in striped pyjama bottoms and a vest. 'Lorna?'

'They've had a few words, Joe,' Shirley said, flashing him a look. 'Go and put the kettle on, and I'll be through in a minute.'

Shirley sat with her beloved daughter until she had cried herself to sleep, then went through to her husband in the kitchen.

'Your tea,' Joe said, his voice strained, helpless. 'It's got cold.'

He was out of his depth, didn't have a clue what to say, just knew he wanted to punch someone, and knew exactly who that someone was.

'Don't really fancy any, Joe. You go back to bed; you've got work in a few hours. I'll warm some milk up for myself and bring it in with me.'

'Sure?'

She nodded.

Shirley waited until she could hear the low, regular breathing coming from both the bedrooms, then she padded softly along the hall, and carefully opened the front door with the quietest of clicks.

She stepped out onto the balcony, heedless of the icy chill beneath her bare feet, and looked across to where she could see the new tower block rearing up in the distance.

That bastard was probably snoring peacefully in his bed, while her baby . . .

Shirley gripped the rail until her knuckles turned white.

This couldn't go on.

Chapter 9

Jimmy Donovan sat waiting: head drooping, hands clasped and hanging loosely between his knees, staring listlessly at the crusty-edged cigarette burns dotted asymmetrically across the grey and yellow Formica tabletop. He was not very happy.

Why did it have to be him doing the bloody visit? Why couldn't Gary have come today of all days, just over a week before sodding Christmas? Fuller liked Gary – well, as much as he liked anyone.

He was going to be in a bad enough mood as it was, knowing he was going to be inside for yet another Christmas, but if he'd caught wind of what was going on outside, he'd be sure to lose his rag, and Jimmy had seen him go potty enough times to know that it definitely wouldn't be a pretty sight.

And who would Fuller be taking it out on? Him, that's who. Jimmy Donovan, the mug who'd be sitting at just about arm's length away from him, perfect for a great big bastard like Fuller, nice and convenient for giving him a right cross – bang! – full on the hooter.

Automatically, one hand went up to his face, and he cupped his nose protectively. His Joanie would go potty and all, if he had a busted snoz and a couple of nice matching black eyes when her pain-in-the-arse of a sister came over for Christmas dinner.

And then there was this lot in here. That'd be all he needed as well, being shown up by Fuller in a visiting room full of old lags, their brassy, frowsy old women, and their snotty-nosed, scabby-kneed kids. He'd be a right laughing stock. By tomorrow morning everyone in East London would have heard: *Dave Fuller gave Jimmy Donovan a whacking in front of everyone during visiting time!* His Joanie would probably give him another just for luck.

The sound of a chair scraping across the cheap lino floor jolted Jimmy back to the present.

He looked up to see David Fuller – a larger-than-life Michael Caine lookalike, right down to the crinkly strawberry-blond hair – with a burly-looking prison officer standing just to one side of him, and about two steps back.

Fuller sat down.

'All right, Dave?' Jimmy greeted him. He spoke warily, as if his thoughts about being punched had somehow been projected outside of his brain.

'Cut the shit, Jimmy.' Fuller leaned forward, his big, broad arms folded in front of him on the table. 'I've heard something that's right upset me.'

Here we go.

'Ain't you interested in what I've heard?'

Jimmy shrugged. 'Sure, Dave.'

'Good, because I'd value your opinion.'

Jesus.

'Now, what I've heard, *Jimmy*, is that there's some little prick, who – for reasons I can't imagine – thinks it's all right for him to muscle in on my interests down by the docks. A little berk who thinks that no one'll mind, no one'll care, if he takes over supplying the estates round there.'

Jimmy tried a smile, flashing a mouthful of gaps

and gold teeth. 'I did hear someone was being a bit silly, Dave.'

'*Silly*?'

'Yeah, you know what it's like. He's some young bloke – Richie Clayton his name is. He's got a couple of toms working for him; he knocks out a bit of bent gear from down the docks now and then. You know, bits and pieces, nothing, two-bob stuff. He's a no-mark.'

'If he's such a no-mark, *Jimmy*, then how come he's getting away with supplying *on my fucking manor*? What, is he planning to move in on the clubs next? Planning on taking over *all* my businesses? All making him nice and welcome, are you?'

He hadn't raised his voice, but the menace was all too clear to his wiry little visitor. Jimmy said nothing; he just shrugged down deeper into his oversized topcoat.

'Two years I've been in here, Jimmy, two long years. And, up till now, nothing's gone wrong outside. Nothing. So what's suddenly gone wrong now? Who's taken his fucking eye off the ball?'

Think, Jimmy, think. Say something. 'I brought you in some snout, Dave. And some –'

Fuller dragged his hands down his cheeks; Jimmy tried to convince himself that he looked more tired than angry.

But Fuller wasn't tired.

'Sort it out, Jim, all right? I've got enough grief in here, and what with that bitch Sonia still laying in the hospital like Sleeping fucking Beauty, I don't want you going jumping in with both feet. Just try and be a bit discreet – if you even know what discreet fucking means. I don't need anyone associating me with anything that looks even a little bit dodgy. I don't even want to hear of any of you lot getting done for speeding. I've got to be seen to be keeping my nose clean. You got that?'

When Jimmy didn't answer immediately, David Fuller's hand shot out across the table and grabbed him by the lapel. 'I said, have you got that?'

Trying to free himself from Fuller's grip, and away from the threat of a yuletide broken nose, Jimmy squirmed and wriggled like a bait worm on a fishing hook.

Not wanting the attention Jimmy's ridiculous antics were attracting, Fuller let him go.

That took Jimmy completely by surprise, and, now jerking around like a fish caught by the worm, Jimmy lost his balance, propelled himself right off his chair and went sprawling under the table.

All eyes in the room were now turned towards the excitement: a welcome relief from the awkward silences of visits to husbands and daddies who wouldn't be at home – yet another year – to hang up the stockings, to decorate the tree, or carve the turkey.

'Right, that's it.' The prison officer clamped his hand over Fuller's shoulder. 'Visit's over.'

'We'd finished anyway, Mr Barr,' said Fuller, standing up and smoothing down his shirtsleeves as though he were wearing Jermyn Street's finest, aware, even without looking, that he was the centre of attention.

'Mr Donovan here's got to be on his way, ain't you, Jim?'

Jimmy, shuffling backwards on his bottom across the floor, nodded.

'You see, Mr Barr,' said Fuller, unable to resist taunting a man who had the power to tell him – *him, David Fuller* – what to do, 'he's putting a deposit on a new motor for me. They've not even gone into production yet, but I'm going to be one of the first to own one. It'll be ready to come over and collect me on the day I get out.' He looked the PO up and down. 'See, some of us get out eventually.' He winked. 'You know I've always had a soft spot for a Jag, I have. And this new model, well, I'm telling you, Mr Barr . . . Here, Mr Barr, you'll have to have a ride in it.' He paused, just long enough to show his contempt. 'If they let you have a day off away from here sometimes.'

Jimmy Donovan, now well out of Fuller's reach, felt as elated as if he'd just been sprung from high security. He scrambled to his feet, and watched as the PO started to lead Fuller back to his cell.

'I'll be off then, Dave,' he said, buttoning up his coat and walking backwards in the direction of the exit.

No reply.

'Oi, Dave,' he called out, just as the guard was unlocking the barred door through which he would lead the prisoner.

Fuller turned round. 'What?'

'I nearly forgot. Happy Christmas, mate.'

The waiting room erupted into laughter.

If it hadn't been for the grip that Mr Barr had on David Fuller's arm, Jimmy Donovan's few remaining natural teeth would now be jammed halfway down his throat.

Lorna, pale and ill-looking, did the washing-up in silence, listening to the sounds of Richie getting ready to go out: taps running, teeth being brushed, sprays of various kinds being squirted.

She said nothing because there was nothing more she could say.

She had been back in the flat with Richie for just

over a week; had returned from her parents when she realised she had no choice; that she had missed two periods; that she was never, ever, late; that she had had to tell Richie the truth about why she had to come back to him.

Simple as that: no choice.

She felt disgusted with herself. She had really thought she had found the courage to leave him for good, to leave behind his vile habits and his worse temper, the constant fear of what he might do next, the knowledge that he was involved with those . . . tarts. But how could she keep away now? What would it do to her mum knowing that, after everything Lorna had put her through, she was even thinking about bringing up a baby on her own?

And how about money? What with the docks going and Dad having no security – that was more than enough for her parents to have to worry about.

If only she could persuade Richie, could find the right words to make him see that things had to change between them.

It was his child that they were talking about, for God's sake.

She wrung out the dishcloth, draped it over the tap to dry and wiped her hands on the tea towel.

She heard the front door open and Richie calling to her as he stepped out onto the balcony.

'Remember what I said: it's up to you. You do as I say or you can piss off back to your old man's. Aw no, I forgot, you can't do that, can you? It upsets your mum to think you're not happy. Makes her all ill again. And we wouldn't want that, now would we, upsetting Mummy?'

'Don't, Richie, please don't make me.' Lorna ran out to him. The icy winter wind, carrying flurries of snow from the grey-yellow sky, cut through the high walkway like a knife. 'I can't.'

Richie grabbed her by the hair, spun her round, and slammed her hard against the safety railing. She felt as if her ribs were going to cave in.

'Don't you dare get lippy with me. You're lucky I took you back, and if you want to stay, then you follow the rules. Things are changing round here. Old geezers like your dad have had it. It's a new world, run by the likes of me. *Me*, not him.'

He let go of her hair and checked his pockets for his keys. 'I'll be back in a couple of days, but then again, maybe I won't. So have a happy Christmas if I'm not here, won't you?'

His expression rearranged itself from a sneer into a nightmarish grin. 'Oh yeah, that address: it's on the table.'

With that parting shot, he shoved her backwards into the flat, and slammed the door in her face.

Lorna leaned against the wall and slid down to the floor. 'You *are* still scared of Dad,' she sobbed into her hands. 'I know that's the reason you had me back.'

Richie had a couple of immediate plans to put into action. First he had to drive along the road to Upper North Street so he could pay the landlady for the room he had taken there for Rita Thomas, and then he would pop upstairs and have a quick word with young Rita herself.

He enjoyed visiting Rita; it had been a real pleasure training her up and getting her used to the idea of working for him. She'd not only taken to sex like the proverbial duck, but she was now so infatuated with him that she would do anything he wanted.

Anything.

He grinned to himself at the thought of the compliant, eager-to-please, young Rita.

He'd had a real result with Mrs Wilkinson, the woman who owned the house, as well. She was a moneylender by profession, and was such a greedy bastard, she couldn't have cared less how many blokes Rita paraded up and down her stairs every night, just so long as she got her weekly bung from Richie.

He used the key Mrs Wilkinson had given him and let himself into the house. He stuck an envelope with the rent and the usual sweetener under Mrs Wilkinson's parlour door, and then ran up the stairs to the top landing. He knocked twice with the flat of his hand.

The door was flung open and Rita appeared: stark naked, arms stretched wide, and squealing with pleasure.

'Richie! I was just redoing my make-up.' She ran her tongue lasciviously around her little rosebud mouth. 'This work doesn't half play havoc with a girl's lipstick.'

'You'll catch your death,' he said, making a grab for her still-immature girl's breasts – her only fault as far as Richie could make out. 'It's bloody snowing out there.'

'Come in and warm me up then.'

'Tempting, very tempting, but I'm just collecting right now. Maybe later, eh?'

Rita was clearly disappointed, but she knew Richie liked her to keep cheerful, so she skipped across the room, took a roll of notes out of the teapot on the mantelpiece and handed it over to him.

He smiled and nodded approvingly. 'You have been a busy girl.'

'I like to keep busy.' She reached inside Richie's overcoat and rubbed her small hand over his already stiffened penis. 'Sure you haven't got time for a quickie?'

Richie's smile broadened. 'Why not?'

He didn't even bother to loosen his tie.

Within ten minutes Richie was back in his car, driving towards Bow Road through what was promising to become a full-blown snowstorm.

He was grinning like a fool. How much better could life get? He was getting there all right. By this time next year he'd be making David Fuller look like the has-been he really was.

He pulled up outside a large, once rather grand house that had a flashing blue neon sign advertising the fact that it was now a nightclub. What wasn't advertised was that it belonged to one of the most feared families in London's East End. That was known only to the manager, to a select group of local villains, and to the bent police officers who turned a blind eye not only to the unconventional hours in which drinking went on in the place, but, more importantly, to the money laundering that went on in there – the actual reason for the club's existence. And they were all only too happy to keep quiet about the infamous owners' identity, and just to get on with availing themselves of their very generous hospitality, and, it had to be said, their protection.

Richie Clayton, full of himself and his big ideas about his future, swaggered into the club as if he were the owner. He made his way straight for the bamboo-clad bar that stood at the far end.

He brushed the snow from his coat, and then tapped a tall, powerfully built man on the shoulder. 'Oi, McGregor, where's my money?'

The man put his drink down slowly, apologised in a low Glaswegian growl to the curvaceous brunette by his side, and turned to face Richie.

'Politeness don't cost nothing, *pal*.'

'But fucking black bombers do, *mate*. Especially in the wholesale quantities I've been letting you have. Now where's my dough?'

The man chuckled as if he couldn't believe what he was hearing. 'I told you when we did the deal: meet me in the Regal tonight and I'll have it for you. So here you are. And here am I.'

'And?' Richie didn't like the way this was going; it was spoiling his good mood.

'Ask nicely, Clayton, and I'll give it to you.'

'Why should I?'

'Because I said so.'

Richie could feel himself colouring. He had no intention of doing anything physical about the situation – he didn't like pain, and this bloke could make two of him – but he couldn't be seen acting like a weakling. 'I want my money, McGregor, you Jock bastard.'

'And I'd like a bit of respect.'

Richie's chest rose and fell as he battled to keep his temper.

'You'll be sorry if –'

'Don't be silly.' The man shook his head in disgust and turned back to his drink and the brunette.

* * *

Richie slammed the car into gear, and drove far too fast through the now snow-covered streets to a house overlooking Victoria Park.

He banged furiously on the door.

'All right, hold your bloody horses,' a female voice hollered from inside. Then an elderly woman with her hair in rollers and a fag in her mouth opened the door.

'Yeah?'

'I need to speak to Herbie, Mrs Johnson.'

'He's watching the telly.'

'It's work.'

The woman, her eyes narrowed against the smoke from her cigarette, jerked her head, indicating he should come in. 'In the front room. And shut that bloody door before all the heat gets out. I'll make some tea.'

'Don't bother on my account.'

'I said: I'll make some tea.' With that she disappeared out to the back kitchen, muttering oaths about missing her programme.

Richie stuck his head round the door. 'Herbie?'

A double-wardrobe-sized man in an incongruously feminine pale blue velvet dressing gown twisted round in his armchair to see who had said his name.

'All right, Richie?'

'I've got a job for you.'

'Sit down. Mum making you tea, is she?'

'Don't worry about that. The job's now.'

'Do us a favour, Rich. I'm watching telly here.'

'I'll pay you double what I did last time.'

'No, sorry, Rich, not tonight. Mum and me are watching this play. Right good it is. How about tomorrow?'

Tomorrow? Richie couldn't let that bastard McGregor think he'd got away with it, even for a single night. 'I'll throw in a nice little bonus as a Christmas present for your mum.'

Herbie dropped his big football head to one side and smiled, flashing two perfect, baby-doll dimples.

'What a nice gesture, Richie. Very nice, and much appreciated. I'll just nip upstairs and get dressed, then we can get a move on.'

Richie and Herbie Johnson sat in Richie's car in the freezing cold, just along the road from the club, waiting for McGregor. They'd been there for over an hour and a half when he finally showed.

He came out of the club, looked up at the sky, swore, turned up his collar, and then slithered along the pavement to his car, which was parked just across the street from Richie's.

He was followed by his dark-haired, now fur-swathed girlfriend, who was complaining about him not waiting for her, and how was she meant to manage in heels like hers?

'I'm getting the bleeding door for you,' he called over his shoulder, brushing off the layer of snow that had settled in a ridge along the cold, chrome handle.

McGregor was just about to open the door for the young woman when Herbie grabbed him from behind.

The girl tried to scream, but Richie was too quick for her. He clapped his hand over her mouth and marched her across the road to his car.

As he bundled her in through the driver's door, across the wide bench seat, and onto the passenger side, she cracked her head on the steering wheel, and he laughed like a maniac.

'Ooops!'

Christ, what was he going to do to her? Rape her?

She threw back her head ready to yell, but stopped when she realised that Richie had a switchblade.

He touched it to her cheek.

'Keep your trap shut, darling, or you'll have a nasty scar down that pretty little face of yours. Understand?'

She nodded, terrified.

Richie was back to being the *big I am*; he didn't need help from Herbie or anyone else to frighten women.

He climbed into the car next to her, drove across to the other side of Bow Road, and pulled into the alley that ran down the side of the club.

He left the engine running so that the wipers could clear the screen, and turned the headlights onto full beam.

The girl gasped as she realised what she was seeing: McGregor, her McGregor, was on his knees in the snow, having seven kinds of tripe kicked out of him by the gorilla of a man who had grabbed him.

'Not a sound,' said Richie, feeling himself getting aroused by the sight of all the blood, and by the knowledge that he had paid one man to pulverise another.

That showed just how powerful Richie Clayton was.

It didn't take long for Herbie Johnson to do his job – to hurt the man, but to keep him conscious for long enough to hear the warning and to hand over the money owed to Richie. Herbie prided himself on his professionalism.

'You owe a friend of mine some gelt, a friend who won't be so generous next time, but who'll make sure you get really hurt. Hand it over.'

McGregor, his breathing shallow and his nose clogged with blood, hugged his broken ribs with one arm, while he found the money in his overcoat pocket.

'You do know,' he panted, giving Herbie the money, 'that he could have had that two hours ago?'

'What did he say?' Richie, having seen the money being produced, was now standing behind Herbie.

McGregor answered for himself. 'That you're a flash little shit who's out of control. I told you I had the money, you cockney arsehole. And I'm telling you this too – for free – you don't know what you've done, Clayton, who you're messing with. The owners of this club are related to me, their ma's my ma's cousin. Family, see? You've messed with the wrong bloke this time.'

'Fuck.' Herbie shook his head. 'Listen, mate, it was nothing personal. I was being paid to give you a going-over.'

He took hold of Richie by the sleeve and dragged him back to the car.

'Get out,' Herbie ordered the brunette, and jumped in her seat.

'Drive,' he snapped at Richie.

Not sure what was going on, Richie just did as he was told, reversing wildly out of the alley and back onto Bow Road; he wasn't about to argue with anyone even half as big as Herbie.

Herbie picked up a copy of the *Racing Post* from the floor of the car, wiped the blood from his hands, then tossed it out of the window.

'Richie, mate,' he said, pulling the wedge of money from his pocket and slamming it on the dashboard, 'I'm going to say this for your own good. I know you're doing well –'

'*Well*?' Richie snatched up the money and kissed it. 'I'm fucking raking it in.'

'I know, but mind you don't go treading on too many

toes, eh? Especially the toes of the sort of nasty bastards who own that club. If he really is part of that family, then you'd better make sure you keep looking over your shoulder. Stick to having kids working for you. They're a bloody sight easier to control than the likes of that lot.'

Richie didn't know what family he was talking about, although he could probably guess if he bothered to put his mind to it – there were really only three families in the East End serious enough to put the wind up hard men like Herbie – but Richie didn't much care. He had dough, and – like all the pills he had started taking – that made him feel invulnerable. He had more than enough to spend, and plenty left over to pay blokes like Herbie to take care of any little problems for him. And if Herbie swallowed because he was too gutless for the job, then there were always plenty of others willing to crack a few heads for a nice fat roll of used notes.

'Don't you worry about me, Herbie. I'll be just fine.'

By the time Richie had dropped Herbie back to his mum's, had popped round to Rita's for a nightcap – a couple of bombers, two glasses of Scotch and a quick blow job – and had driven to Phyllis and Henry's house in the East India Dock Road, it was almost three in the morning.

He still treated their place as if it was his home, even down to keeping spare sets of clothes in his old bedroom.

He stuck his hand through the letter box and hauled up the key by the string.

As he stepped into the hall, Henry was coming downstairs.

'What do you want?' he sneered, dragging his braces up over his shoulders.

'Early mornings down the market obviously still suiting you down to the ground then, Uncle Henry?' grinned Richie.

'Who's that?' Phyllis bawled down from the front bedroom.

'Only me, Auntie Phyllis.'

Phyllis appeared on the landing: a galleon in full mauve nylon sail.

'You and Lorna haven't fallen out again, have you?' she asked, pulling her housecoat more tightly round her as she stomped heavily down the stairs.

'No, but she's got the right hump on her for some reason, so I thought it best to come round here rather than start rowing.'

'Sensible boy,' cooed Phyllis, stroking his cheek. 'I'll make you a nice bacon sandwich.'

'I notice you don't offer to make me no sandwich,' complained Henry.

'You're not a guest,' she snapped, shoving past him. 'Now get that damp coat off, Richie, and come and sit by the stove to warm up.'

The two men followed her through to the kitchen, sat at the table and watched as she lit the gas and propped open the oven door so that it would heat the perishing cold room.

Standing to one side, so she wouldn't scorch her legs, Phyllis dolloped a big glob of lard into the frying pan, and, while it was melting, took the bacon from the larder.

'Shove in a few rashers for me?' Henry asked.

'All right,' Phyllis sighed begrudgingly.

'Got your turkey ordered yet, Auntie?' asked Richie smarmily.

'No, love, not had a minute to get anything done. It

takes all my time just keeping up the housework for this lot.' She prodded the rashers with a fork. 'Denise is no help – she's always out with Terry – and as for Chantalle: that one wouldn't know a vacuum cleaner if it bit her on the arse.'

'Here you are then, Auntie Phyllis,' said Richie, peeling a stack of notes from the roll he had collected from Rita – he made sure he left the even thicker one Herbie had *persuaded* off McGregor safely in his coat; he didn't want Henry telling him hard luck stories and trying to tap him. 'Put that towards your Christmas shopping. It'll help make things a bit easier.'

Phyllis glowed with pride. 'You are a good boy,' she said, shoving it in her pocket, then flipping over the fat-marbled streaky in the sizzling pan. 'Your sandwich won't be long, love.'

'Smashing. I'll just go up and have a slash.'

Henry glowered as Richie left the room. 'He's a bloody parasite, that boy. He's got a brand-new place of his own a smashing little wife, and even a tart shacked up down Upper North Street, according to Malcolm over at the Blue Boy. I wasn't going to tell you, but he's only gone and put her on the game for him – a kid – and that Logan girl and her rough-looking mate.'

'I don't know how you can listen to such wicked lies,' said Phyllis, angrily slamming the kettle onto the gas ring.

'Well, what's he doing round here again?'

'At least he brings in decent money.'

'Don't you ever wonder how?'

'Well, it's obviously not by driving some poxy potato truck.'

'Phyllis, he's a ponce.'

'Don't start, Henry.'

'Don't start? That's been my trouble over the years, not starting. Things are going to change round here, I'm telling you. I'm not putting up with it any more.'

Phyllis rolled her eyes and slapped down the bread knife and a loaf on the table in front of him. 'Shut up, Henry, and get that sliced, will you?'

While Richie was sleeping peacefully in his old bed – his belly full of breakfast and his feet toasty warm from the hot-water bottle Phyllis had filled for him – Lorna was standing in a side street in Catford, shivering in the driving snow.

She stared at the small terraced house, and checked, for the third time, that it really matched the address Richie had left for her.

The curtains looked clean enough.

She opened her bag and looked at the creased brown envelope. In it was every penny of the Christmas money she'd been saving.

The door opened. A motherly-looking woman in a bright, floral print overall, with a neat perm and a friendly smile, stood there expectantly.

'Good morning, dear.'

Lorna said nothing; her mind was reeling with confusing, frightening thoughts. She had to go through with it, she knew that, just as she knew she was too scared of the implications if she didn't: what it would do to her mum; that she would have to give up work, and she certainly couldn't afford to do that – who'd pay the bills? And what with the docks all closing, she'd be having to go for interviews before long, and that'd look just great, wouldn't it? Who'd give her a job then?

And then there was Richie.

Richie . . .

How had it come to this?

'Look, if you're coming in, then hurry up, you dopey cow,' the woman suddenly snapped, grabbing her roughly by the arm. 'Or d'you want all my neighbours to see you and guess your dirty little secret?'

Chapter 10

'You shouldn't have come out in this, Lorna. It's blowing a blizzard out there.'

'I'm all right, Mum. I'm just sorry to be such a nuisance, bringing all this washing over.'

Lorna did her best not to wince with pain as she hoisted up the pillowcase full of dirty laundry and dumped it onto the old-fashioned, scrubbed wooden draining board in her parents' kitchen.

'Especially after you and Dad letting me stay here so long, and me only just going back to . . .' She was about to say *Richie*, but just stopped herself from blurting out his name. '. . . the flat. And now I'm back again.'

'Don't be so silly,' said Shirley, picking up the pillowcase, ready to empty it on the floor. 'You know you're always more than –'

'No, leave it!' Lorna snapped, snatching it away from her.

Seeing the surprise at such rudeness on her mother's face, she added with a little laugh in her voice: 'Really, Mum. I'll do it. You've done enough for me already.'

'OK, but I was only going to sort out the whites from the coloureds.'

'Honestly, Mum.' Lorna held on to the pillowslip as if it were full of the most precious jewels, rather than soiled and crumpled bed linen, but she was doing her best to sound casual, light-hearted, as if it didn't matter to her in the slightest who had hold of the thing. 'I wouldn't have bothered you at all, but what with the weather being so bad it's no use me even trying to dry anything indoors. And I can't bear going in that Launderette at the bottom of the flats any more.'

'Not very clean?'

'It's not that. You should see the horrible lot that've started hanging round there.'

'Horrible?' Shirley asked absently; she was eyeing the pillowcase, itching to get her hands on it. She could get that lot done in no time: washed, rinsed and spun, then on to the clothes horse in front of the fire to dry off – just right for ironing. If only Lorna would let her. But she knew how touchy her daughter had been since she'd gone back to the flat, so decided not to push her. If only she'd not gone back there; if only she'd stayed here where she belonged. Maybe then she wouldn't be looking so pale and worn out; it was as if the life was being drained right out of her.

'Types you definitely wouldn't like,' Lorna said, interrupting Shirley's thoughts. 'If it's not the tarts – schoolgirls by the look of some of them – sheltering from the cold while they're waiting for, you know, blokes, keeping warm by the dryers, it's other young kids doing deals. It's obvious it's drugs. I reckon they've got to be working for someone older, because where are they going to get the money to deal in that stuff? You should see them, Mum.'

'In the Launderette? Never?'

'I'm telling you.'

'Wherever are their parents, letting them get up to nonsense like that? And in a public place. If they have to get mixed up with that sort of disgusting behaviour, at least let them keep it away from decent people. Why haven't the police been called in?'

Lorna felt the familiar panic that came over her whenever she realised she'd said too much. Having the police sniffing around the flats would definitely not please Richie. 'It's not really that bad, Mum,' she said with a little shrug. 'And it's only because of all this snow. Once the weather improves –'

'Snow or no snow, what's the world coming to when respectable people, minding their own business, have to mix with the likes of them? They want their backsides tanning and being sent straight back to school. No, borstal, that's what they need.'

Shirley pushed the twin tub over to the sink, attached the rubber hose to the single cold tap, and started filling the washing machine's drum. 'And I don't know about those lowlifes not wanting to be outside in this weather, it's you that shouldn't be out in it. You don't look well to me, Lorna. And it's about time you had a machine of your own, anyway. You should have one of those automatics, make things a bit easier for yourself.'

'I know I should, Mum. And I really don't mean to be a nuisance. Maybe I'll be able to get one after Christmas.'

Shirley turned round, intending to tell her not to be so silly, that she had nothing to be sorry about, that she couldn't be a nuisance if she tried, and that she'd never, ever, not be welcome, but when she saw the state of the bed sheet that her daughter was obviously trying to shove into the machine before she saw it, the words turned to dust in her mouth.

Shirley made a grab for the now sopping wet sheet and heaved it back out of the drum. 'What on earth's happened here?'

Lorna's forehead pleated into a deep frown. 'I, er, had

a really bad period. I woke up in the middle of the night, about three o'clock it was. I looked at the clock.'

She was speaking so softly Shirley had to strain to hear her, but Shirley knew immediately from the way she was adding in all the unnecessary little details that her daughter was hiding something.

'And it was everywhere. I was in a right mess. I had to throw my nightie away. Wrapped it in newspaper and put it down the chute. Rinsed it through first, of course. But the sheets, they're new, so I couldn't afford to throw them out. It was really heavy, Mum.'

'You're saying all that came from a heavy period?' She shoved the sheet back into the machine, wiped her hands on her apron and put her hands on her daughter's shoulders. 'Lorna, that looks more like a haemorrhage. Did Richie get the doctor for you?'

'No, he was working.'

Shirley let her son-in-law's middle-of-the-night absence pass by for the moment. She had more important things to deal with. 'Well, I'm telling you, this isn't right. No wonder you look washed out if you're losing like that. Now you promise me, you get round there as soon as you can, all right? Just for my peace of mind.'

'No, really, I'm fine.'

'Well, this hardly looks fine to me.' Shirley poked at the sheet, pushing it under the water, with the laundry tongs. 'And I meant it, darling. You could never be a nuisance to me. I only meant why doesn't Richie buy you a machine? Not that I don't want you using mine.'

Lorna stared down at the brightly tiled floor, unable to look her mother in the eye, unable to speak for fear of what she might say.

'He's all right driving about in that new car of his.

You need him to realise how hard you've been working. You're in that dock office first thing of a morning, then rushing about in the lunch hour doing your shopping, then flying home and waiting on him hand and foot. And him turning up when he feels like it.'

'Mum –'

'No, just let me finish, Lorna.' Shirley put her finger under her daughter's chin and lifted it until she had no choice but to meet her mother's gaze. 'Look at yourself: you're worn out.'

'Mum, please . . .'

'I know I said I'd never interfere, and even when you turned up here so upset that night I never asked any questions, but I'm going to break my rule just this once. I'm going to say this, and I want you to listen: Lorna, *you don't have to stay with him.*'

Lorna gnawed at the inside of her cheek. She had so much she wanted to say, but how could she? How could she say: *Mum, you have no idea what my life is like, what I've been reduced to, how a life that any average person would consider abnormal has become normal for me; how bit by bit, day by day, I've been reduced to a pathetic coward who can barely lift up her eyes, never mind stand up to the bully who made me do something I know I'll always regret*? How could she put her mum and dad through that? It would not only shame them, it would be dragging them down to the sordid level where she had found herself.

She just wished she was a little girl again and could stretch out her arms and her mum would pick her up, hug her close, and make it all better again.

'I really mean it, you *don't* have to stay with him. You were fine back here with me and your dad, weren't you? You never wanted for anything; we never started treating you like you were a little girl again. We let you come and go as you wanted. We didn't even bad-mouth Richie, when the Lord knows –'

'Mum, don't.'

'And while we're on the subject of Richie: what sort of work does he do that has him out of the flat at that time of the morning? Three o'clock? What is he, a flaming milkman? Lorna, do you actually know where he was last night?'

'Don't, Mum, please.'

Sighing helplessly, Shirley turned off the tap, disconnected the hose, and then closed the lid of the machine.

The water began swooshing rhythmically as the twin tub set about loosening the blood from Lorna's bed sheet.

Shirley sighed. 'That's it, I've had my say, so come on, let's go through to the other room and cheer ourselves up. I've got in a few bottles for next week; we can give the ginger wine a go.'

Lorna followed her mother listlessly into the living room, and dropped down onto the red velvet, deep-buttoned sofa – a new addition to their home that Joe had intended as a surprise for his wife, but which he had had so much trouble getting up to the flat, that not only did Shirley know about it, but so did the rest of Lancaster Buildings.

Shirley looked at her daughter. With her head tipped sideways on the wide, cushioned arm, the dark bruises of tiredness under her eyes, and her unusually messy, now almost white-blonde hair, she was a picture of exhaustion. Why couldn't she have found herself a decent husband, a real man like her father, and not a gutless bully?

'Here, drink this.' Shirley handed her a glass. 'And you really must promise me you'll think about seeing the doctor. You might well need a course of iron tablets if you're losing like that.'

Lorna folded her legs under her, curled up against the plump velvet of the sofa and sipped the spicy wine.

'This reminds me of Christmas when I was little.'

'What does, darling?'

'The taste of this ginger wine; Dad used to let me have a tiny drop in the bottom of one of those little medicine glasses. Remember?'

'Course I do.' Shirley was smiling. 'How could I forget?' She tapped the side of her head with her finger. 'It's like a photograph album in here. From the day you were born, I've got pictures of you all stored up.'

As happy memories of days out at the seaside, Christmas mornings, starting school, prize days, learning to ride bikes and balance on skates, came flooding into Shirley's mind, the pain now in her daughter's face, as she sat beside her on the sofa, became all the more heartbreaking. It was so hard for her to keep smiling when she felt more like bursting into tears.

'I saw Phyllis this afternoon,' she said brightly, topping up their still almost full glasses. 'She's so pleased her Denise is still going with Terry Robins.'

'I bet she is. He's a nice bloke, and he's doing really well for himself.'

'So Phyllis said. But she's a bit worried about her Chantalle and Maxie. They're a pair, those two. She reckons they're too young to be going to these clubs they hang around in, and I suppose what with all these drugs about nowadays, it must be a worry having kids that age. But Phyllis said: what can she do? They're not babies, and they're both earning a living. But I said to her, if they're still under your roof, Phyllis, you've a right to know where they are and what they're up to. And what with the terrible things you read in the papers . . . And now you say, Lorna, that they're even selling that muck down the Launderette . . .' She frowned, thinking what it would be like to have a child involved with such things.

Lorna sipped her ginger wine and said nothing.

'There's something I want to ask you, Lorna.'

'Yeah?' Her voice was little more than a whisper.

'About Richie.'

'Mum –'

'I don't know how else to say it. He's not involved in anything like that is he?'

'Mum!'

'Lorna, you can't blame me. He's driving round in a brand-new car, wearing different clothes every time you see him. Phyllis keeps going on about what a good living he's making and how he's always treating her. Then seeing you looking like this: worried, tired out.' She watched Lorna gnawing anxiously at her thumbnail.

'I know it's not people's way to interfere round here, but I am your mother, Lorna. I can't help but worry.'

Lorna carried on worrying at her nail.

'Please, tell me if you can, love. What's going on? What's the matter?'

'Nothing.'

'Is he in trouble?'

Lorna shook her head.

'This is me you're talking to, your mum, remember? Tell me, Lorna. Don't bottle it up, you'll go making yourself ill.'

It was getting harder for Lorna to stop herself from

weeping. Her stomach ached so badly and her ribs were so sore.

'I mean it, I can't stand seeing you like this.'

Lorna closed her eyes, knowing she had to say something. 'It's knowing I'm going to lose my job,' she finally blurted out. 'And it's nearly Christmas. I feel useless.'

Shirley stroked her gently on the cheek. 'Why should you feel useless? It's not you closing down the docks. And anyway, a few minutes' bus ride and you can find yourself a job in any office in the City. If dopey old Denise, love her, can find herself such a good job, and –'

'Denise is working in a West End record company because she's having it away with a bloke in a pop group.'

Shirley stiffened. 'I'll ignore that sort of talk, Lorna, and put it down to you feeling poorly. But if she can do it, then a clever girl like you certainly can.'

'Clever? Me? I think you're getting me mixed up with someone else. Because, if you must know, I'm the stupidest person in the world.'

That was it, the dam broke. Lorna started sobbing.

'Oh Mum,' she wailed, 'what am I going to do? I'm so unhappy.'

'What is it, love?' Shirley folded her arms round her daughter's heaving shoulders.

'I didn't have a heavy period, I lied to you, I . . . I just had . . .'

'Tell me.'

'Mum, I was pregnant.'

'Oh no, my poor little love. Not again.' Shirley rocked her in her arms as if she were still a toddler needing comfort after grazing her knees. 'But you're young, and when that happens, it's usually because –'

'No.' Lorna pulled away and shook her head; now she was really sobbing. 'It wasn't a miscarriage. There was this woman. She was over in South London. She looked clean, but I didn't want to, Mum . . . but she said . . .'

'What woman? Try and calm down so I can understand what you're saying.'

'She . . . She got rid of it.' Lorna stared into the middle distance as her words came spilling out. She was breathing in great gulping sobs, and her chest heaved as she wept. 'It was vile. I was so scared. But Richie told me if I didn't, I'd have to get out again. He said he didn't want a brat hanging round him, getting under his feet.'

Shirley could feel her stomach knotting with pain for her child – and with hatred for Richie Clayton. 'He said what? After you'd already gone through all that?' She stood up. 'You stay there, Lorna, I'm going to get my coat on, and I'm going round yours to sort this out once and for all. He'll be lucky if I don't kill him stone dead.'

'*No, Mum!*' Lorna sprang to her feet, swiping the snot and tears from her nose with the back of her hand. 'Don't, please. You don't know what he's like, how he gets.'

She took hold of Shirley's arms. She had to stop her leaving the room. 'I've got to sort this out for myself. Please. You've got enough to worry about.'

The words had come out before Lorna could stop them. She could've bitten her own tongue. Why had she said that? Sorry as she felt for herself, the last thing she wanted in the world was to do anything, ever, to hurt her mum. Lorna knew how she hated anyone thinking she wasn't *right as rain, bright as a button, fit to conquer the world.* Why had she said that?

'What's your dad been saying?' Shirley's voice was flat and detached.

'Nothing, he's not said a thing.'

'So what did you mean? *I've got enough to worry about*?'

'You know how worked up you get over Christmas,' she improvised, 'wanting everything to be nice, and everyone to have a good time. It's only a week away. You've got more than enough to worry about, without me.' Lorna covered her face with her hands to hide her tears. 'Please, Mum, please, leave this to me.'

'Lorna,' Shirley pulled her close, 'come here and give me a cuddle.'

She felt Lorna flinch.

'What is it? What have I done? Is it . . .' What could she say? '. . . your stomach?'

'No, it's . . . I just tripped and hurt my ribs, that's all.'

Shirley rubbed her forehead with her hand. 'Lorna, we've got to do something about all this.'

'Listen. The washing machine's just stopped. I'll go through and sort out the next load.'

'No, you sit down.' Shirley's voice was weary, a tiredness that came from a mother's impotence to sort out her child's agony. 'You put your feet up and have a rest. I'll do it.'

'No. I'll –'

The telephone started ringing.

'Do as your mother tells you.' Shirley eased her daughter down onto the sofa, picked up the phone from the sideboard and handed her the receiver. 'You can do me a favour: sit there and take that call, and I'll go and sort out the washing.'

Lorna took a deep breath. 'Hello, East 3212,' she sniffed, as Shirley disappeared out into the kitchen.

'Mrs Clayton?'

'Speaking.' That was strange: it was for her.

'Don't you care what your old man gets up to?'

'I'm sorry? Who is this?'

'I'm a mother, that's who I am. And I've been watching you, *Mrs Clayton*, seeing what sort of a person would ignore what a bastard like Richie Clayton was up to. I saw you just now, going up to your mum's flat with your bag of washing, like a good little wife. Thought you Wrights were meant to be a so-called respectable family. Well, let me tell you, Mrs Clayton, there's nothing respectable about your bastard of a husband. He's out every night schtupping my fifteen-year-old daughter, Rita, and now the fucker's gone and put her on the game.'

The woman paused for her to reply, but all she got from Lorna was a gasp of shocked incredulity.

'Don't put on that old shit for my benefit, you must know what's going on. Me, I have to hear it from my neighbours, because Rita won't see me, won't even talk to me. She's completely besotted with the arsehole; he's got her fucking brainwashed. But I'm telling you, if you don't put a stop to him, then I'll tell my old man, and he'll put a stop to him all right. With an iron bar.'

'Look, Mrs –'

'No, you look. The only reason I've not told him so far is I don't want him doing anything silly and getting nicked. That whoreson's not worth him dirtying his hands on. But I'm giving you fair warning: if you don't do something right away, then I'll have no choice. I'll have to tell him, and I won't be responsible for his actions. An iron bar can do a lot of damage.'

With that she slammed down the phone.

Lorna felt as if someone had just whacked her with an iron bar.

Fifteen years old? *Fifteen*?

Shirley came back in the room, a strained smile on her face, wiping her wet hands on her apron.

'Who was it, love?'

'Nobody. Wrong number.'

'Richie, how much do you love me?'

Rita propped herself up on one elbow amongst the tangle of grubby sheets in her increasingly fetid room in Upper North Street, and traced patterns with her fingertip on Richie's naked chest.

He batted her hand away impatiently.

'What?' he asked, rolling over and snatching up his trousers from the mess on the floor by the bed. He rooted around in his pockets until he found his packet of Players.

'I said: how much do you love me?'

'Rita, don't start getting on my nerves, girl. You know I can't stand you being annoying. And you know how I get when I'm upset.'

'But, Richie, if you love me lots and lots, you'll want to buy me a really nice Christmas present, one I really want, and I know exactly what I want.'

'Listen, you silly, daft bitch.' Richie shook the flame from the match, dropped it to the floor with the other debris, and took a long pull on his cigarette. 'You just shift your arse out of this bed, get out there on the street and earn me some money, or you'll get a present all right. You'll get a fucking broken jaw. Understand? Clear enough for you?'

'Richie, don't be mean to me.'

He closed his eyes – moody, clingy little tart. What was it about birds? Why did they always have to get like this? 'You've not exactly been raking it in, have you?'

'You know I'd do anything for you, Richie, but there's just not that many punters about. It's the weather. They don't want to do it outside when it's snowing. It's not my fault. If I was working somewhere where they all had their own motors, I'd be earning you a fortune. I'd do anything to make you happy, Richie. Don't be cross with me.'

The slow smile that spread over Richie's lips had Rita in ecstasies. He was pleased with her! 'What?' she squealed happily. 'Tell me: what are you thinking?'

Another stupid question, but he'd let that one pass – this time, anyway. 'Get your war paint and your clobber on, Rita, we're going out in the car.'

Now she was really excited; Rita jumped out of bed and started searching around for something reasonably clean.

'Where, Richie? Where are we going?'

'Cable Street. I reckon it's finally time that I branched out. And I just know there's going to be a lovely long queue of lorry drivers just dying to spend their money on giving themselves a nice Christmas treat with a fresh little bird like you.'

Chapter 11

Phyllis shivered as she stomped along the passage. Christ, it was bloody perishing. She hated Henry doing this early morning job in the markets. She liked him bringing in a regular wage, but the thoughtless bastard woke her up early every single day, crashing and bashing about as he got ready. He was so sodding selfish. And this morning, what had he done? To make matters worse, he'd gone out and left her with no milk; used up the last drop in his rotten flask, so she'd had to get her coat on and go and see if the buggering milkman had bothered to come yet.

Jesus, she could flatten Henry, the stupid git.

She opened the street door the tiniest crack, so she could just about put out her hand and reach the bottles without freezing her arse off, but the moment she poked out her hand, the unmistakable sound of Mrs Elliot, at full, very unpleasant volume, echoed in Phyllis's ears. What on earth was she doing out and about at this hour?

Mrs Elliot obviously thought the same about Phyllis. 'You're up early, Mrs Parker,' she hollered.

'Yes, Mrs Elliot,' Phyllis said, sighing resignedly and grabbing one of the bottles. She straightened up. 'And so are you.'

'Difference is, I'm working, of course; busy as a little bee, I am.'

At what, thought Phyllis, haunting houses? But she wasn't going to get any more involved, not in this weather, and certainly not at this unholy hour, so she just flashed the weakest of smiles and said: 'Lovely, glad to hear it.'

She was just about to close the door, when Mrs Elliot, surprisingly fleet-footed for a woman of her age, bounded up to the top of the stone steps and stuck her beak determinedly into her neighbour's hallway.

She obviously didn't realise just how tempting it was for Phyllis to slam the door shut and to trap her interfering nose firmly in the jamb.

'Yes,' she went on, 'got myself a right cushy little number, I have. Cleaning. Up the City. It was my Mavis's idea. "Get yourself a little job, Mum," she said. "You only have to do it for a couple of weeks. Then spin them plenty of old flannel about Christmas having been so hard for a poor widow woman, and, you wait and see, they'll have a whip round for you, and you'll wind up getting yourself a nice little bonus. Then, soon as you've got it safely in your bin, you can tip 'em flipsy and tell them what to do with their poxy job. Let them find some other mug to mop their floors and scrub their steps."'

Phyllis closed her eyes in disgust, as Mrs Elliot's hacking laughter turned into an unpleasantly bronchial fit of coughing.

'Clever girl, my Mavis,' she eventually gasped.

'A total genius,' said Phyllis flatly, not bothering to hide either her displeasure at being obliged to share Mrs Elliot's germs, or her complete lack of interest in the woman's half-witted nonsense.

Mrs Elliot narrowed her eyes. 'At least she's a bloody sight brighter than that Richie of yours.'

Now that did attract Phyllis's interest. She opened the door wide and stuck her face right up close to her neighbour's nasty, sneering, thin-lipped chops.

'Whatever you're hinting at, Mrs Elliot, you'd better not have been spreading any rumours about my family. Do you understand me?'

Mrs Elliot was enjoying herself too much to allow a feeble threat to silence her.

'I see,' she said, all mock concern for what she was determined to turn into Phyllis Parker's Big Predicament. 'You've not heard, have you?'

She tutted sadly. 'Oh dear, but then they do say the family's always the last to hear about these sorts of things. Or rather, the last ones who'll ever *believe* such bad things about their own.'

'Mrs Elliot, I'm freezing my bits off standing here listening to you, so will you just spit out whatever poison you've got going around in that cesspit of a mind of yours and let me get back indoors in the warm?'

'There's no need to take that sort of a tone, Mrs Parker.'

Phyllis moved towards her; it would have been so easy to reach out and put her hands around the interfering old hag's scraggy chicken neck . . .

Sensibly, Mrs Elliot backed away until she was halfway down the steps. 'The thing is,' she said, with a sanctimonious sniff, 'and remember, I'm only telling you this for his own good – is that your *nephew's* been getting himself busy down Cable Street.'

'Do what?'

'Cable Street. And, if you want my opinion, I reckon he wants to mind himself. Them Maltese don't mess about, you know. They use knives and razors, and coshes, and even, so I've heard –'

Phyllis slammed the door so hard that even next door's windows rattled.

*   *   *

Antonio Diaz was a short, slim, dapper little man, with a carefully trimmed moustache, black, pomaded hair, and a rather high-pitched voice, but what he lacked in size he made up for in reputation. He was a known face, and a hard one at that.

He had moved in on the owner of Lil's, one of the small coffee shops dotted along Cable Street, several years ago, declaring to the owner that from now on he would be using the place as his office.

'Lil's Twenty-Four-Hour Coffee Shop and Tea Rooms', the establishment's full designation, was a surprisingly prim name for what had become more of a crooks' parlour than a café, twenty-four-hour or otherwise. But it was warm, if filthy, and somewhere for a man such as Diaz to sit down and rest his legs, while keeping an eye on business. Equally important was the fact that it gave Diaz the perfect alibi whenever the law came nosing around: *I was just having a coffee and sandwich, officer, ask anyone here, officer.*

It would have been no good asking Lil, however. No one could remember anyone of that name ever having anything to do with the place, it having been run for the past twenty-odd years by a huge Glaswegian – imaginatively known as Jock – who had jumped ship after a fellow stoker had been found with his head stoved in with a coal shovel.

Jock never had any trouble with his customers, and the place's reputation for orderliness – if not cleanliness – generally meant that the police over at Leman Street left well alone. The thinking being that it was more convenient to know where Diaz, and his bull-necked minders, were to be found if they fancied rounding them up in order to add a few more collars to their tally if the charge sheets were looking a bit thin. It was certainly easier than causing unnecessary aggravation.

Since the day Antonio Diaz had blessed Lil's with his 'custom', he had never looked back. His business – running a stable of girls close to the docks in what was known to be a notorious red-light district – was booming.

Some days, Diaz's toms couldn't deal with their mixed bag of punters quickly enough; they smiled seductively, wiggled their backsides, beckoned with cheaply bejewelled fingers, did their business, collected the cash, and moved on to the next one.

That next one might be a lonely seaman from some far-off, undreamed of land, fresh from a long voyage, cut off from female companionship; or a businessman from the nearby City, out slumming, in search of a rough bit of how's-yer-father with no strings attached; but, most likely, the punter would be one of the real bread-and-butter trade: the lorry drivers.

There were scores of them.

Officially they were out collecting and delivering cargoes from the docks, going back and forth between the massive warehouses, and supplying the early morning wholesale markets with everything from bananas to smoked haddock, but from the number of trucks and vans lining the side turnings and parked up on the waste ground around Cable Street, it was clear that taking a break from the daily grind involved something a touch more intimate than the drivers having a nice cup of tea and a cheese and pickle roll.

With business so good, and with his young wife expecting their fourth child any day, Antonio Diaz should have been a very happy man, but, from the angry expression on his face and the stiffness of his olive jaw, he was anything but happy.

The two large, threatening-looking men who stood respectfully by the food-stained table from which Diaz conducted his business didn't know how to answer him.

Diaz, in a frighteningly calm voice, asked them once again. 'I said: why does this meaningless piece of dog shit believe he can bring his girls over here? Onto my patch?'

One of the men made the mistake of not only answering him, but also of contradicting him.

'No, you've got it wrong, Mr Diaz,' he began. 'He's only got the one girl working for him. He's got no real trade to speak of. And she's more of a kid really. Can't be any more than –'

'Did I ask how his trade was doing?' Diaz was on his feet, his head barely reaching the breast jacket pocket of the man he had just interrupted.

The man gulped. 'No, no, you didn't, Mr Diaz.'

'Did I ask the age of the insolent fucker's whores?'

'No, Mr Diaz.'

'Did I ask how many he has working for him?'

Wisely, the man said nothing more; he just clasped his hands in front of him and stared down at his boots.

Diaz sat down again. He thought for a moment. It was time he found himself some new girls; half of his current crop had the clap, and the other half were looking like the lazy, stringy old boilers they all seemed to become after they'd been working on the streets for a year or two. Maybe this idiot could do the job for him, save him the trouble.

'What chance is there of him bringing in more?'

The two men's minds whirled. How to answer that one?

'I want the truth.'

The one who had already spoken flashed a pleading look at his equally bulky companion, who then took a deep breath and said in a resigned so-kill-me-now tone of voice: 'The truth, right. There's a good chance, I reckon, Mr Diaz. A really good chance. He's cocky. And he's stupid. If he's not stopped right away, he's the sort who'll get confident. Before you know it, he'll be bringing in all sorts.'

Diaz nodded. Let him bring in some fresh meat, and he would take it off him: toys from a child. 'Good. That's exactly what I want him to do.'

When he saw their puzzled faces, he felt smug. That's why he was the boss – he had the brains. And they were the grafters – the mindless muscle.

'For now,' he offered as his only explanation.

Denise looked at her friend. It made her feel so sad; the time was when Lorna was up for anything. She would try anything new, and have a right laugh doing it. But now, sitting here in her brand-new flat, stuck up here in her prison in the sky, she was more like a rag doll with all the stuffing ripped out of her. Or, more likely, with Richie on the scene, a rag doll with the stuffing knocked out of her.

'Come on, Lorn,' she pleaded again, 'it's only a flipping interview.'

'Yeah, I know. And it's in the West End.'

'That's the whole flipping point: it's in the West End, and it's at *my firm*. We'll be working together. It'll be really great.' She put on a miserable face and said in a wheedling little voice, 'I don't half miss seeing you every day, Lorna. Having a laugh together and that.'

Denise was going to add that Lorna just *had* to come and work there with her, because Denise would go mad if she didn't. She couldn't stand the other girls in the office. They were a snooty load of toffee-nosed bitches who could barely bring themselves to talk to her, never mind crack a joke with her in the ladies. But she didn't want to put her off.

'And now the dock office has closed, and what with the expense we all had at Christmas, you must be completely boracic, and you can't keep borrowing off your mum and dad all the time. They can't be finding things easy either. You've said as much yourself.'

'You know I didn't spend a penny over Christmas; I was in bed, ill, all over the holiday,' Lorna said, reinforcing the lie she had told everyone. A lie to explain not only why she hadn't been round to see anyone, but also covering up the fact that even if she had gone anywhere she'd have been by herself, as Richie had been somewhere else, and probably with someone else.

She paused, trying to think of any sort of a reason why she couldn't work there, and quickly came up with what had to be the most obvious reason of all: 'And it's a record company,' she said, as though that absolutely clinched it.

'Lorna, I know what sort of a company it is, I do flaming well work there. But that's what makes it so great.' Now it was Denise who was improvising. 'Next year, you'll be able to get everyone cheap LPs for their Christmas presents. Your mum loves the Supremes.'

'Yeah and Dad loves Perry Como, but –'

'No, Lorna, no more buts. I'll be round at half-eight tomorrow morning, and I'll expect to see you in this.'

She handed Lorna a shiny black carrier bag, embellished with gold, stylised writing. 'And I'll bring some bleach round later on and touch up those roots of yours.'

'I have let them grow through a bit,' said Lorna, unconsciously touching her hair, as she peered into the bag as cautiously as if she had been told that it might contain a bomb. 'But I've not felt up to doing them. I've got all the stuff in the bathroom; I should really do it this eve–'

She stopped speaking as she pulled out first the jacket, then the trousers of an elegant, cherry-red suit. 'Den, it's gorgeous, but I can't take this off you. It's much too good. It's brand-new.'

'I know it is, you cheeky thing,' said Denise brightly. 'And I've got absolutely no intention in hell of giving it to you. But that doesn't mean you can't have a lend of it, now does it?'

'No, I'm sorry, I can't.' She thrust the bag back into her friend's arms. 'I really am.'

Denise shrugged. 'Me too.'

As Lorna saw Denise out of the flat, and stood waving to her as she walked along the wind-whipped balcony, she felt sick to her stomach.

How could she have gone for the interview? What would she have told Richie? That she was going for a job at the record company where Terry had already got Denise all nice and cosy and settled? He'd have loved that. He hated Terry Robins's guts.

For that matter, Richie hated the guts of anyone making a decent life for themselves; he just couldn't resist sneering and belittling anyone who grafted, or who made any sort of an effort to better themselves by hard work.

Mugs, he called them.

But it didn't seem to stop him letting Lorna go out to work. Just so long as it was somewhere he didn't mind her working, of course, somewhere like the docks.

But the docks were closed now, so what was she supposed to do – starve? Worry the life out of her poor mum and dad, who were trying to sort out their own lives now her dad didn't have a job any more either?

And what did it matter what Richie thought, or what Richie approved of? He was hardly ever there any more to find out what she was doing, or if she was all right, or whether she needed anything. He didn't care that she felt deserted and alone, grieving now for two unborn children, weeping bitter tears into her pillow every night as she imagined how things might have been. How they *should* have been.

And where did he go when he disappeared for days, even weeks at a time? What was he doing?

Things she didn't even want to think about.

Lorna stood there, her breathing growing more rapid, watching Denise waving her goodbyes as she went to get into the lift.

'Den,' she shouted. 'Wait. OK still for the morning?'

'Fantastic!' Grinning broadly, Denise rushed back to Lorna and shoved the carrier bag in her arms. 'Half-eight sharp, and don't you dare let me – or yourself – down. Promise?'

'Promise.'

And Lorna meant it. She was going to start putting her life back together.

Chapter 12

Terry was feeling great. The Spanners had been asked back to the Canvas – *again* – and here they were, sitting in the dressing room, getting ready to go on the stage. But despite the place now being more familiar to him, his mouth was still dry with excitement. This was working, working well, really well. For the very first time, he felt that it wouldn't be tempting fate to believe that it was all going to go exactly the way he wanted it to, the way he'd dreamed of: that the band would make it, and that before long he'd be a star, up there with the big ones – the Beach Boys, the Stones, even the Beatles.

'Hi, Terry.'

He took a breath, and – slowly and deliberately – finished tying his shoelace. Only then did he look up and make eye contact with the person whose annoying voice was all too familiar to him.

It was her.

'Chantalle. I won't say it's a nice surprise. And how exactly did you get back here? You need the All Areas pass for the dressing rooms.'

Chantalle poked out her tongue and flashed the laminated card she had lifted from her sister Denise's handbag. 'I have my ways,' she giggled, provocatively eyeing the other members of the band. 'And if she couldn't be bothered to come tonight, then . . .' She shrugged and turned down her mouth.

'You know she's not been well.'

'No, Terry, I don't. But what I do know is that she's

totally feeble. She should be like me, fit and healthy. I'm never ill.' She winked at Michael, the drummer, as she ran her hands down over her hips. 'I'm in really good nick.'

'Listen to me, Chantalle,' said Terry, plucking the pass from her hand, while doing his very best not to touch any part of her body, 'we're trying to get ready. This is an important gig.'

'Leave her be, Tel. She's all right,' said the drummer, returning Chantalle's wink.

'And she's also my Denise's little sister. And she's a right little stirrer and all.'

Terry took a moment to consider his actions then put his hand on Chantalle's shoulder and steered her across the cramped and seriously overcrowded room towards the door.

'Please, Terry,' she said, stopping to stroke the neck of the bass guitar that stood propped against the single, illuminated, rather tatty dressing table, 'let me stay. I won't get under your feet. I promise.'

'And I promise that if you don't get back out there into the club, I'll call security and tell them you're under age, and –'

'*Terry!* Don't be mean, you know I was seventeen last –'

'Yeah – officially too young to be in this club, Chantalle. Now, if you promise to behave, you can go back out there and enjoy the rest of the evening. Or would you rather I had you chucked out?'

She pouted sulkily. 'Got no choice, have I?'

'Good, now don't try and pull another stroke like that, or I'll tell your mum what you've been up to.'

'Like she'd care.'

'Chantalle, I'm warning you.'
'All right, keep your hair on, I'm going.'

Chantalle wandered back into the crowded club. She was doing her best to look miserable and resentful, but, despite her intention of making Terry feel sorry for her, she couldn't help but be thrilled she was actually in the Canvas Club again. It was a fabulous place. Fabulous.

But, even better, who was that over by the men's lavs? This was even more fabulous: it was Richie!

'Hello, Rich. Richie, it's me.'

Richie lifted his head and moved his gaze up from the pool of beer he had just spilled on the bar, and directed it at the person who had just spoken to him.

He took a moment to focus.

It was Chantalle.

''Lo, darling.'

'This is great,' she bubbled, pushing out her 36Bs. 'I was dreading having to stand here alone, listening to the band, and fighting off all the fellers. Now I can pretend I'm here with you.' She dropped her chin and peered up at him through her lashes. 'You don't mind, do you, Rich?'

'No, no, that's fine, Chantalle, just fine.'

His breath stank of booze, and his eyes were kind of swivelly, but Chantalle didn't mind; he was the best-looking bloke in the whole club – the Spanners included – and he was wearing the best clothes, and had the loveliest darkest, long, curly hair. She'd be stupid not to pretend she was with him, even if he was her cousin. No one else need know.

'Here, Richie, the band's coming on in a minute. Let's get to the front. We might as well, seeing as we're here.'

'Right,' said Richie, putting his arm round her shoulder

and guiding her in an aimless zigzag through the crowd. 'Might as well.'

Chantalle, taking over the navigation to the stage, and taking Richie firmly by the arm, put on her girliest of voices. 'Where's Lorna, Richie? Having a pee or something?'

'No.' Richie laughed to himself as he formed and sharpened an idea in his mind, an idea that he was going to share with Chantalle. 'You know what they say, darling: Saturday night's for the old woman, Friday night's for the tart.'

'You're really funny, do you know that, Richie?' simpered Chantalle, parking him next to her, right at the very front. 'And I think you're ever so good-looking. I always have.'

'You trying to get off with me, young Chantalle?' asked Richie, narrowing his eyes as he tried to concentrate on her fresh young face. 'Whatever would Auntie Phyllis have to say about that, do you reckon?'

'Richie,' she said, brushing the side of his cheek with her lips. 'I know we're related and everything, but it's not illegal, is it?'

Richie had a moment of clarity, a vision that made him grin. 'Is that right?' he said, stroking her bare arm from shoulder to wrist.

She nodded and said something, but at that moment the Spanners started playing. The music was loud and electric.

Richie shook his head. 'What?' he shouted into her ear, but didn't wait for a reply. 'Blimey, Chantalle,' he went on, 'you can't hear yourself think with all this row. Let's go outside for a fag. I could do with a bit of fresh air, and we can have a proper talk.'

Terry, dazzled by the stage lights, squinted down into the darkness. Was that Richie Clayton disappearing with Chantalle? With his jacket draped round her shoulders? Christ, if it was, he could only hope that the bastard wasn't thinking about giving her any dope. Phyllis would be sure to blame him for letting her be there, and it would cause all sorts of trouble between him and Denise.

'Oi! Terry!' hissed the rhythm guitarist. 'Will you give it a bit of attention, here? It's your middle eight.'

The night air was so cold that the breath came out of their mouths like steam from an overboiled kettle, and the icy wind whipped and snapped the rubbish about their ankles, as they stood there surrounded by puddles of goodness only knew what in the grotty back alley behind the Canvas. But Chantalle, shivering in her bottom-skimming mini dress, with Richie's jacket slung around her shoulders like a trophy animal skin, could have been standing in the cool shade of a coconut tree on a gorgeous Caribbean beach with the sun pouring down on her lovely young flesh.

She was in paradise.

She could hardly believe it: Richie had just said she was *beautiful*!

'I'm telling you, darling,' he muttered, 'plenty of men would pay good money to have a beautiful girl like you.'

'*Have* me, Richie? Whatever do you mean?' Chantalle couldn't stop herself from grinning. She loved all this attention, loved Richie saying she was desirable, loved the idea of . . . of *doing* it – at last. It was something she'd been wanting for ages. Or rather, had been thinking about for ages.

'Richie.'

'Yeah?'

'Give us a snog. Go on, please.'

Richie was grinning like a fool. 'Chantalle, I'm shocked.'

'Why? Come on, Richie, please. I'm not a kid any more. Just a little snog.'

'I really don't know what to say.'

'Then don't say anything, Richie. Don't say anything at all. Just . . . Oh, Richie, *please*.'

Richie packed Chantalle off home in a cab – he even paid for it – and went back into the Canvas. And now, just as he had been for the past hour and a half, he was leaning on the tiny bar in the corner of the club, oblivious of the Spanners and the wildly enthusiastic response they were getting for every song they played, for every encore they generously agreed to bestow on their adoring fans.

Richie didn't even notice when the band finally came off stage, and the DJ started spinning his discs again.

In Richie's drink- and dope-befuddled brain, in his strange alternative universe, time was telescoping, and meaning was shifting.

He took a while to respond to the ever more persistent taps on his shoulder.

'*Richie*. I said: what was all that about?' Terry ignored the stares and whispers of the adoring girls huddling around him, as he stood behind Richie and hissed into his ear.

'What?' As Richie turned round to face him, Terry saw the unmistakably glazed and unfocused stare brought on by all the gear that Richie had obviously been throwing down his throat all night.

'Concentrate, Richie. I watched you, I saw you, when

I was up on stage. You were taking Chantalle somewhere. Where? What were you up to? Where is she?'

Richie felt a warm glow pulsing through his veins. Terry was all right. A good bloke. He smiled at him. 'I was getting her a cab, wasn't I, mate?'

'Why? Where was she going?'

Richie turned away, back to his drink. He picked up his vodka and orange and half emptied the glass in one long gulp. He took his time answering.

'We're all chaps together, ain't we, Tel?' he said eventually, his back still turned to Terry. 'You know and I know, mate, what that little prick-teaser's after all the time. Practically had to fight her off, didn't I? Trouble is, she's very persuasive. The sort what can't get enough of it. Right good with her tongue, though, she is, had it right down my throat, and . . .' He laughed nastily. 'Well, what could I do? You have to give these little whores what they want. You know that.'

'You filthy animal, Richie. You're her fucking cousin.'

'Cousin?' Now Richie was giggling. 'Is that what you reckon, Tel? You want to have a word with our Denise, mate.'

Terry shook his head. 'I know you're pissed, Richie. Stoned. Both maybe. But haven't you got any shame? Don't you realise what you've done? Snogging a kid who's not only your own fucking cousin, but she's only just seventeen. What does she know? What's going to happen next, eh?' He shook his head. 'It makes me feel like puking when I think what the likes of you are capable of. But you've crossed a line this time, believe me.'

'I reckon you're right, Tel,' Richie grinned. 'Might be a good idea if I go home to the missus tonight, eh?

Probably be a bit awkward going round Auntie Phyllis's. That lot'd give me a right earache.'

Richie Clayton stumbled from the club, with a discreet helping hand from the two oversized security men summoned by Terry Robins.

With the state he was now in, it took Richie nearly half an hour to find a taxi willing to take him, but it was a half an hour that, with pharmaceutical help, had melted into a blur of lights, cars, and grin-inciting memories of the look on Chantalle's young, fresh, sexy little face.

He'd have her working on the street for him in no time, no problem at all – she would lick the dirt off his boots if he said so – but, if he could persuade her and little Rita to do a double act, he'd be able to clean up. He'd be able to move on to more upmarket punters, the ones who'd be glad to pay for something a bit special. But, for now, he'd be doing all right just extending his business in Cable Street.

No, fuck all that *extending* lark – he'd take the bastard place over.

He'd run the whole thing; him, Richie Clayton.

'Oi, pal, I said: whereabouts in Poplar do you want?' The cab driver looked in his rear-view mirror and studied the drunk in the back seat. What a state. Still, that fiver he'd handed over had certainly sweetened his decision to pick him up and risk him spewing his boots all over his nice clean upholstery. The driver didn't want to know where a young bloke like him got that sort of money, but he did need to know where the useless piss-head was going. Where he lived. If anyone would have him indoors in this state.

'Well?'

'Yeah, yeah, all right. I wanna go to Chrisp Street,' slurred Richie. 'No, I've changed my mind. I wanna go to Whitechapel. Cable Street. Got it?'

The driver flashed his eyebrows in a knowing, but dismissive way. 'Fair enough, pal, you're the boss.'

The cab driver didn't blink an eye as he pulled into Cannon Street Road and spotted the first of the 'girls' standing in the freezing night air on the corner of Cable Street.

It was the drunken idiot's own business if he fancied a bit of the other with a brass, he supposed, but, honestly, what the bloody hell had things come to when a young, good-looking bloke like him had to go paying for it – drunk or not? And, knowing the reputation of the old brasses round this way, he'd wake up with a lot more than a hangover after schtupping one of them. He'd be visiting the clap clinic for months and dipping his dick in disinfectant before his regular bird would have him anywhere near her again.

It was barmy: when he was that age, he was beating them off with bats, and that was back in the flipping 1940s, so what was all this old toffee about the Swinging Sixties, when girls were meant to be as up for it as the fellers were? It was all a bloody mystery to him. It was true what they said: the world had gone mad.

He pulled into the kerb to let Richie out, and wondered, for a brief moment, if he should ask him for the five and a tanner fare, or whether he should just let it go?

He'd let it go. The bloke had enough problems. He'd make do with the fiver he'd already pocketed.

'Cheers,' the driver said, putting the cab back into gear, but definitely not putting on his light. He didn't want to go picking up any old sorts round here. His missus would kill him if she got even a whiff of tom. And, make no mistake, she would; she had a nose like a sodding terrier that one. 'Be lucky, pal.'

As the cab pulled away, Richie reeling backwards, grabbed hold of a lamppost to steady himself. 'I am, mate,' he called after the taxi. 'Luckiest bloke in the world, me.'

It took Richie a moment to sort out in his head why he was actually standing there, swaying gently. He knew he had to think quickly – the rain had just started and he was bloody freezing. The cold concentrated his mind: the Maltese. He'd come to have it out with the Maltese. He had to go to the all-night café.

And, what do you know, he was standing right next to it – magic!

'Nice cuppa tea,' he said loudly, staggering through the door. 'And two slices of toast. Oops.' He grinned foolishly as he brushed against a large, dark-suited man, who was standing with a similarly huge companion by a small corner table occupied by the much smaller figure of Antonio Diaz.

The big man looked down his nose at Richie and was about to say something, but the owner of the café got in first – the last thing he wanted was for this stupid young drunk to pick a fight with one of the Maltese minders. They were complete headcases, blokes who didn't think twice about putting blokes through the plate-glass window. *His* plate-glass window.

'Sit down and behave,' he said to Richie, waving his grubby-looking tea towel at an empty table, 'and I'll sort out your tea and toast for you.'

But Richie wasn't in the mood to be told what to do. He propped himself against the counter and pointed at the minder. 'He should watch where he's standing. This ain't Malta, you know, mate, it's England. *My* country.'

The owner rolled his eyes – terrific, not only drunk, but a lairy drunk. It was going to be one of those nights.

'Listen, moosh, you either keep your trap shut and behave or you're out.'

Richie blinked and dragged his thoughts together. No, he didn't want that – didn't want to be thrown out. He had to talk to the little Maltese bloke. The pimp with all the girls. Tell him his plans. Hang on, that was him. In the corner. With the big fellers. He had to work out what to say. Needed a bit of time.

Clinging to the counter, Richie affected a deep bow, almost tipping himself onto the floor. 'My apologies, sir. Hope you'll accept them.'

The minders exchanged a look, and then turned to Diaz for instruction. He simply shook his head and kept on eating.

Reluctantly the man accepted Richie's apology. But if Mr Diaz hadn't been there, he'd have ripped the bastard's head right off his skinny little shoulders. But Mr Diaz didn't like unnecessary trouble, didn't like drawing attention to himself, liked to keep private. But he'd have him later.

Richie winked over his shoulder at the owner. 'See, mate, sorted.'

Diaz hadn't looked up once from his fried egg sandwich.

Chantalle might not have had the drink and drugs inside her that Richie had consumed, but when she eventually bowled into the room she shared with Denise at almost three o'clock in the morning, she was buzzing with excitement. How could she have just gone home after what had happened to her tonight?

Despite her promise to Richie that she was going straight back to East India Dock Road – he hadn't wanted to get rid of her, he'd said, he just didn't want her getting into trouble with her mum for being out late, *he was so thoughtful* – she had waved goodbye to him and had immediately redirected the driver to drop her off at a party she'd been invited to in a turning off Grove Road near Victoria Park.

And now, having danced and drunk cheap cider with a load of kids for the past couple of hours, she was even more entranced by Richie's worldly ways and his gorgeous good looks. Why mess about with that lot when you could go to a gig in the Canvas, go outside with Richie, and then be put in a taxi?

She flicked on the two-bar electric fire and snarled over her shoulder at her sister: 'Don't pretend you're asleep, Denise. I saw you turn over.'

'For Christ's sake, Chantalle, turn that light off, will you, and don't be so selfish? My head's killing me. You know I'm not well.'

'Leave off moaning.' Chantalle unzipped her tiny dress, stepped out of it, and let it fall to the floor. 'If you weren't so pathetic, you'd have seen Terry's best gig ever.'

Shading her eyes from the light, Denise propped herself up on her elbows. 'What did you say? Have you been to the Canvas?'

'You didn't need your pass, did you?'

'If you've been chasing my Terry –'

'Look at yourself, Denise – red nose, puffy eyes, hair all over the place. And look at me.' She sat at the dressing table, dressed only in the flimsiest of bra and pants, and began peeling off her false eyelashes. 'Do you honestly think I had to do much chasing? It's been a fantastic night. A long one too.'

Denise snatched the alarm clock from the bedside table. 'It's nearly three o'clock in the morning. Have you been out with him all this time?'

'Well, I did spend some time outside. Round the back of the club. You know, where everyone goes to have a . . .' Chantalle left the words dangling in the air.

Denise threw back the covers, grabbed her coat from the wardrobe, and pulled it on over her baby-doll pyjamas.

'Blimey, it must be a miracle,' said Chantalle, putting on a suitably surprised face. 'I thought you were meant to be ill, Den.'

'I was,' she said, zipping up her knee-length boots, 'but now I just feel sick.'

As her sister stormed down the stairs and out into the freezing cold night, Chantalle shrugged nonchalantly and continued getting ready for bed.

'Oh well, if you won't let me finish what I was saying, Denise, you're bound to get the wrong end of the stick.'

Richie was just finishing his fourth cup of tea – he was so thirsty he could have drained the whole urn – when Antonio Diaz stood up, wiped his mouth daintily with an immaculately ironed handkerchief, and left the café followed by his two minders.

Richie frowned. What was going on? Where was he going? He hadn't even talked to him yet. He had to discuss business, let him know what was what.

He lurched unsteadily to his feet and hurried after them. The café owner did consider asking him to settle his bill, but decided that he was just glad to be shot of the little runt. It was enough to worry about, keeping Diaz and his crew sweet, without having a drunk kicking off in front of them.

Richie stood on the pavement – the combination of strong tea, toast and fresh air sobering him up a bit – impatiently waiting for a line of fruit market trucks to pass by, watching in frustration as one of the big Maltese blokes unlocked a sleek black Bentley that stood just across the street.

'Come on, come on,' Richie muttered.

As the final truck passed, he couldn't believe his luck. The two big ones got in the car, but the little one didn't. He just leaned on the roof and bent forward to say something to them through the window. He was staying behind – by himself.

Richie scooted across the street and tucked himself into the shadows of the dripping, dank-smelling railway arch.

'You sure you'll be all right, Mr Diaz,' he heard one of the big ones say. 'I don't mind hanging on for you.'

'I'll be fine, thank you. The street's getting busy with market traffic; there are plenty of people around. No one will start trouble now.'

'If you're sure you don't need any help.'

'Listen to me, the day I need help going to see my woman, is the day I retire.'

'I'm sorry, Mr Diaz, I never meant –'

Diaz laughed. 'Go on, off you go, I'm frustrated enough with Mrs Diaz having her baby any day without you keeping me any longer. I need my recreation.'

With that he slapped the Bentley on the roof, pulled the collar of his navy cashmere overcoat up about his ears, stuck his hands deep into his pocket, and strode off towards Dock Street. It was there that he had his latest bit on the side settled in a little flat in a dilapidated-looking building. The flat, with its utter sumptuousness and the good taste of its luxurious furnishings, would have shocked anyone who only knew the area as a run-down red-light district. But Antonio Diaz liked to look after not only his personal comfort, it also suited him to have secrets, and Dock Street was the last place anyone would have thought him to have a flat – for himself anyway.

He had just put his key in the front door when Richie pounced.

Pinning him in a headlock, Richie dragged him backwards along the street to the arches.

Diaz felt the touch of cold metal on his cheek. Whoever it was had a knife.

'OK, OK,' gasped Diaz. 'There's no need to hurt me. My wallet's in my inside pocket. If you'll just let me –'

'Keep your money, *Mr* Diaz, you're going to need it a lot more than me. You see, I'm going to be taking over this pitch from now on, you Maltese ponce. Just thought I'd be polite and let you know.'

Diaz stiffened. He'd been jumped by that young fool who had brought the girl over to work on the street. A bloody amateur.

'I think you already have a girl on my pitch.'

'*Your* pitch? I told you, it's mine from now on.'

'Don't get excited, Mr . . . ?'

'Clayton, Richie Clayton. Remember that name, you squeaky-voiced little runt.'

'Oh, I will, Mr Clayton, I will.'

Chapter 13

Denise hitched up her coat, grabbed the top of the locked side gate and clambered over. She was too angry to notice the biting cold wind, the splinters sticking out of the wood, or even the fact that she was out on the streets of Poplar, by herself, in boots and her baby-dolls, at nearly half-past three in the morning. All Denise wanted to do, all she could think about doing, was putting her hands around Terry Robins's throat and shaking him till his bloody teeth rattled.

Him and her little sister. Who the hell did he reckon he was? And what did he reckon *she* was – his supposed girlfriend – an idiot or something? She'd show him what it was like to cross Denise Parker. She'd have him begging for bloody mercy.

She crept along the alley that lead to the tiny, paved yard at the back of Terry's house. Even though it was the middle of the night, and the depths of winter, there was still plenty of light coming from the streetlamps, and from the security arcs protecting the stock in the timber firms' yards that lined the canal running along the back of the house.

She bent down and searched the paving slabs until she found some bits of slate that had fallen from the roof. She hadn't done that for years, not since she and Lorna had last played hopscotch, and had collected the slates for markers. Things had been a lot simpler back then. If she'd rowed with her bloody sister when they were kids, she just used to clout her one round the back of the head.

Come to think of it, that wasn't such a bad idea now; it might be worth doing exactly that when she went back home. It might not do the conniving little tart much good, but the sound of Chantalle yelling the place down would certainly make Denise feel a whole lot better.

She straightened up, blew on her fingers to warm them up, then took aim and shied the chippings at what she could only hope she'd rightly identified as Terry rotten Robins's bedroom window.

By the time Terry was finally roused by the sound of slate hitting glass she had almost run out of ammunition.

He pushed up the sash window and stuck out his head. Despite his breath forming clouds in the freezing night air as he yawned and shuddered from the cold, and the little-boy-lost look of his bed-tousled hair, Denise could find no sympathy for him whatsoever; she was going straight for the kill.

'Oi, you, get down here. I want a word.'

'Den? Is that you?' he hissed. What on earth could she want at this time of night, especially when she was ill? Maybe she was delirious. He'd heard of that happening if your temperature went too high. 'Is everything all right?' he asked, and then added hurriedly, 'And do you think you can keep your voice down a bit, please?'

'Yes, it's me,' Denise answered slightly more quietly than she had begun, but she wasn't finding it easy to control either her volume or her anger. 'And I said I want you down here. Now.'

In no time at all, Terry appeared at the back door, with his jeans pulled on over his pyjama trousers, his dad's old army greatcoat – his makeshift extra blanket in this cold weather – sweeping the floor round his feet, and with a very puzzled expression on his face.

'Come in, Den.' He was rubbing his eyes and shivering. 'But, honestly, you've got to keep it down. Mum'll go spare if we wake up her and Dad.'

Denise followed him through to the kitchen. 'I'll do my best, *Terry*,' she muttered murderously, 'but I am very, very upset, and I'm not sure how long I can keep it down for.' Her jaw was so rigid with temper that it ached.

Terry closed the door with a soft click, turned on the light and leaned towards Denise, ready to kiss her.

Denise responded by shoving him away. Not only was she surprisingly strong for such a small person, but her action was so unexpected that Terry completely lost his balance and went staggering backwards across the lino, his sock-covered feet slipping and sliding like an unathletic, trainee ice-dancer.

It was only by grabbing hold of the cooker that he just managed to stop himself from crashing into the table and waking up not only his parents but everyone else in the house as well. He could just imagine how thrilled his mother would be if the Turners – the other couple, plus their three little kids, who shared the house in Burdett Road with the Robins family – came storming in to find out what the commotion was all about.

'Christ, Den, you could have really hurt me. I know you're not feeling too good, but have you gone barmy as well?'

'No, Terry, I've not gone barmy, but I think you must have.' She moved closer and began stabbing her finger into his chest. 'I've just had a little chat with our Chantalle, and, you could say, I'm not very happy about it.'

'Oh.' Terry scratched his head, clearly embarrassed,

but also confused. 'You've found out, have you? But I don't see why you're having a go at me.'

Denise threw up her arms. She wanted to scream. Why hadn't she realised before what a class-one bastard he really was? What sort of moron had she been to believe all those sweet little things he whispered in her ear while they were making love on the sofa in his front room while his mum and dad snored away in their bedroom. *How* stupid was she? He'd just been using her. She was the one who deserved a clout round the back of the head – for being such a fool, for being taken in by nice, loving Terry Robins. To think she'd even dreamed about getting engaged to him one day – to Terry lying sodding buggering bleeding Robins. She'd rather get engaged to Jack the bloody Ripper; at least she'd know where she stood with him.

She put her hand to her forehead; she was sweating and shivering all at the same time. She'd wind up with pneumonia at this rate. She might even die. Not that he'd care. He probably wouldn't even go to her funeral.

'Den, I don't think you're very well. Let me help you. Sit down, eh? I'll make you a drink.'

He put out his hand to her, but she slapped it away.

'Get off me, you creep.'

'Please, tell me what's wrong.'

'You really don't see why I'm having a go, do you?'

'I'm sorry, Den, but no, I don't.'

'You're priceless, you are, Terry Robins. You disappear out the back of that place with my little sister. *My little sister*. And then you reckon you don't know why I'm having a go at you?'

'*Me* disappear out the back with her?' The shock had made Terry forget he was supposed to be whispering. He clapped his hand over his mouth and cast a wary glance up at the ceiling as though he could see right through the plasterboard and into his parents' bedroom to check that they were still asleep.

He should have been concentrating on Denise.

She took a single step forward, raised her arm and landed a flat, open-handed slap right across his face.

'Oi! That bloody hurt!'

'Good. Shame it didn't hurt as much as this.'

With that, Denise launched herself at him like a dried lentil out of a schoolboy's peashooter.

Terry took his chance and grabbed her by the arms – he wasn't risking another slapping – pinned them to her sides, and steered her firmly towards one of the kitchen chairs.

'Den, I'm not putting up with this. You just sit down there and tell me exactly what's going on, what exactly you think you're talking about. Because I haven't got the first clue.'

Denise wasn't sure if she felt hurt, or if she felt angry, but she knew one thing she felt and that was dizzy. Really dizzy. She was actually glad to be sitting down.

'Terry – Christ, I can hardly stand to say your name – Chantalle is my little sister.' Her bottom lip began to tremble. 'I know she can be a mare at times, and act all flirty and that, but she's still only a kid.'

She dropped her chin until it touched her chest. 'I know all about you and her. She told me about going out the back of the Canvas tonight . . . last night . . . Oh, you know when I mean. You should do, you were bloody there.'

Terry closed his eyes and shook his head. This had

the stink of Richie Clayton all over it. Well, sod him; he wasn't taking the flack for him.

'Denise, I swear on my life, on my mum's and dad's lives, that I haven't been anywhere near your little sister. Well, not like that. I saw her last night, sure. She had your pass and even managed to blag her way back stage to the dressing rooms. But I never touched her. Honestly, Den. On my life.'

'But she said she went round the back of the club, down the alley, and –'

'Listen to me, Denise. It wasn't me she went out the back with. It was Richie.'

Denise shook her head. 'No, you've got it wrong. It can't have been.'

Terry curled his lip. 'I know. Bit hard to take, eh? But it was definitely Richie. I talked to him after he came back inside. You know, all that kissing cousins stuff makes my stomach turn. Can't understand it.' He grimaced. 'Just the thought of kissing my cousin Barbara, even if she didn't look like the back end of a bus, makes me want to chuck up.'

Denise, tears streaming down her face, rose unsteadily to her feet. She wobbled for a moment, and Terry tried to make her sit down again, but she wouldn't have it. She lurched over to the kitchen door and stumbled out into the backyard.

'I've got to go,' he heard her call from outside.

Terry smacked the table in exasperation. 'Den, you're not well. Hang on. I'll get my shoes and a jumper, and walk you home.'

He strode over to the door and stared out into the night, intending to make her wait inside while he got dressed.

But he was too late. The backyard was empty. She was gone.

'And don't worry about apologising, will you, Den? I mean, it's only daft old Terry. I don't need an apology, do I? Just trample all over me and accuse me of all sorts. Human doormat, me.'

He went back inside and filled the kettle. He was getting fed up with that family.

The whole bloody lot of them.

Lorna started at the sound of the front door opening. Only Richie and her mum had keys to the flat. She hadn't seen Richie for weeks; he didn't even know she had a new job, and it wasn't likely that her mum would be out on the streets at – she glanced at the bedside clock – half past three in the morning in the perishing cold.

Unless it was her dad coming round because her mum had been taken ill again.

She threw back the blankets and swung her legs out onto the bedside rug.

'Who's there?' she called, shivering as she searched around for her housecoat.

The only reply was the sound of the front door smashing back on its hinges, and then of someone staggering along the hall towards the bedroom.

It was Richie.

He was still drunk, but, unluckily for Lorna, had sobered up enough since his earlier encounters with Chantalle and then with Antonio Diaz in Dock Street, not just to flop down on the bed and fall fast asleep.

He had other ideas about what he wanted to do, and, as he pulled roughly at her nightdress, tugging it up round her thighs, and then thrusting himself into her without a word, Lorna realised she was still too scared of him to try to stop him.

The self-realisation disgusted her almost as much as he did. After all her resolutions to get her life together – the new job, the clothes on loan from Denise, her new attitude – she had been reduced to this again.

She wouldn't go on like this. She couldn't. She would get away from him once and for all.

Since the moment Denise realised what had really happened – that it wasn't Terry, but *him* who had been with Chantalle – she had been crying. Not only was he Lorna's husband, he was . . . Jesus, it was too vile to put into words – even in her own head.

She was still weeping as she stood, shaking and shivering with fever, in the doorway of her bedroom – the bedroom she had shared with her little sister since Chantalle had grown out of the crib in her parents' room, and had been promoted to the folding toddler's cot beside Denise's 'big girl's' bed.

Chantalle might be seventeen years old now, earning her own living as a switchboard operator in an office in Leadenhall Street, and actually looking more like a twenty-year-old, but she was still Denise's little sister. And, much as Denise would have liked to give her a slap every bit as hard as the one she had given Terry – *oh God, Terry. She'd just left him there in his kitchen* – Denise still loved her, and would do all she could to protect her.

And now this had happened and Denise hadn't been there to stop it. Hadn't been there to stop Chantalle from snogging that vile, devious animal. How could even someone as low as him do that to his own half-sister?

Denise took a deep breath, wiped her nose with the back of her hand and sniffed loudly.

'Chantalle.' Denise pulled back the bedclothes and shook her sister by the shoulder. 'You've got to come downstairs with me. I've got to talk to you about something. Something really important.'

'Denise, do you mind? I'm trying to get my beauty sleep.'

'I mean it, Chantalle.'

She opened one eye, and saw her sister's puffy face and tear-stained cheeks.

'What's up with you then?' she asked, in her usual *I-couldn't-actually-give-a-toss-but-I'm-just-doing-you-a-favour-asking-you* tone.

'It's about Richie.'

A sly smile twisted around Chantalle's lips as she propped herself up against the pillows. 'So, you've realised at last that I wasn't trying to pull your dopey Terry then? As if I'd have any interest in that one. You're safe there, Den.'

For once, Denise showed no inclination to rise to her sister's snide comments.

'This is serious, Chantalle. Come downstairs, please. I don't want Mum or Dad hearing what I've got to say.'

Although she could tell that Denise really meant it, Chantalle didn't have it in her to drop her cocky façade. 'Not scared I might take Richie away from your gormless mate Lorna, are you? Even though I could,' she snapped her fingers, 'just like that.'

Denise turned and began walking away. 'I'll be down in the kitchen.'

When Chantalle eventually deigned to appear, Denise was

standing by the back door, staring out into the dark, taking in lungfuls of icy night air, trying to clear her head.

Chantalle took her cigarettes from the pocket of her turquoise towelling dressing gown, lit herself one without offering the packet to her sister, and slumped down at the table.

'What's the big deal then?' she asked unenthusiastically.

Denise couldn't face her. 'There's something you don't know, Chantalle.'

'Bloody hell, Den, you're not going to start telling me about the birds and bees, are you? It's a bit too late for all that.'

Denise spun round. 'What do you mean?'

Chantalle rolled her eyes. 'What I mean is, Denise: you can't talk to me like I'm a little virgin any more, because I did it. Last night. With Richie.'

Denise knocked the cigarette from her sister's hand. 'Tell me you didn't, Chantalle. Please.'

'What? Tell you me and Richie didn't have it off? Sorry, Den, but we did. And he was great. He had me up against the wall in the alley. I bet everyone could see us and all.'

Denise grasped the side of the table. 'No.' The room was swimming round her like a fairground ride.

'Why not? It's not illegal. Cousins can even get married. Did you know that?' Chantalle clapped her hands to the side of her face. 'Oh, sorry, forgot – he's already married to dozy drawers. Still, divorce is always a possibility. It's getting more and more common nowadays.'

'You didn't, Chantalle, please, say you didn't.'

'What are you getting so hot and bothered about? I am seventeen years old. And don't tell me you and Terry don't do it. Mind you, must be hard fancying someone like him. Now, Richie, he's a completely different kettle of fish altogether. He's well tasty, and so sexy, Den. Makes me feel randy just thinking about him. Does just thinking about Terry make you feel randy? Bet it don't.'

Denise couldn't look at her. 'What have you done? Richie's your brother.'

The colour drained from Chantalle's face, leaving just two spots of bright pink on her ashen cheekbones.

'You're lying. Because of Lorna. Trying to make me feel I've done something wrong.'

Denise shook her head, and hurried out into the backyard.

Chantalle stood there in a daze, listening to her sister heaving and retching.

Then she ran upstairs to their bedroom and threw herself onto her bed.

When there was finally nothing left inside her stomach to throw up, Denise walked unsteadily back inside, and stuck her head under the single cold tap at the kitchen sink. Then she drank cup after cup of the icy water, but didn't think she would ever get rid of the vile taste in her mouth; didn't think she would ever get rid of the vile images in her head.

She could only pray that Chantalle had had the brains to make him use a rubber.

With a supreme effort, Denise locked up, turned off the lights, and hauled herself up the stairs.

She paused on the landing outside their room, listening to her little sister sobbing as if her heart would break. Then she went inside, sat down on Chantalle's bed, and stroked her hair.

'Don't worry,' Denise whispered, 'he won't get away with this, Chantalle.'

'You won't tell Mum, will you?' she wailed, her words muffled by the pillow she was hugging to her like a life preserver.

'Course I won't, and, I promise, I won't let him anywhere near you again. He's got me to deal with now. But if he's stupid enough to try anything, *anything*, I'll cut the bastard's bollocks off for him.'

Chapter 14

The watery, pale winter dawn was doing its feeble best to break over the horizon as Denise stood outside Lorna's flat, shivering from the cold and from the temperature she was still running. What she wouldn't have given to be tucked up in her bed, but she had to do this, and she had to do it now.

She hesitated, finger hovering over the doorbell, thinking about the awful things she was going to have to say, when the door suddenly opened.

Denise jumped back in shock. Lorna was standing there in the hallway, fully dressed.

'How did you know I was here?' Denise managed to say before being bent double with a noisy coughing fit,

Lorna looked nervously over her shoulder towards her bedroom, stepped out onto the balcony and pulled the front door shut behind her.

'I saw you walk past the kitchen window. I was making a cup of tea.'

'Why are you up and dressed this early on a Sunday morning?'

'I've got plans. Anyway, you can talk. Look at you. You should be home in the warm.'

'I'm all right, and I'm sorry to bother you, Lorn, I know it's really early,' Denise apologised, her words tumbling out in a burbling rush, 'but I came round on the off chance that you'd be up, and, seeing as you are, can we have a talk?'

Lorna whipped another nervous look over her shoulder,

and checked with a good tug that the door was secured, that it was still pulled to, a barrier between her and what was inside.

'Sorry, Den,' she whispered. 'I can't really. He's in there. Asleep.'

'We can go for a walk, can't we? Go on. Please. It's really important.'

Lorna bit down on her bottom lip. 'I don't know, Den. And you shouldn't even be out.'

Denise blew her nose loudly. 'Trust me, Lorna, I wouldn't be here if it wasn't important, would I?'

'I suppose so. But, really, I can't be long. He was drunk out of his head again last night, and, knowing him, he'll be wanting a fry-up as soon as he gets out of bed. And if I'm not there he'll do his nut.'

She didn't mention that her plan was to act as sweet as pie to Richie – including providing a full cooked breakfast and a winning smile – until he got out of the flat for his usual Sunday lunchtime skinful, and then, while he was out, she was going to pack up every one of her possessions and get out of there for good.

'It won't take long. Promise.'

Lorna took a deep breath. 'I know your promises, Denise Parker.'

'I'm not a kid playing games, Lorn. This is serious.'

Lorna said nothing, she just studied the black patent toes of her ankle boots and gave a small, almost imperceptible, shrug.

'Cross my heart, you've got to hear this. That's why I came over. I should be going round to Terry's if I was going anywhere with this cold on me – to apologise for something I did, but that's another story. This *had* to come first. Really, honestly, and truly, Lorna, it's that important.'

'If it's so important, tell me now.'

'I don't think that's a good idea. Just go and get your coat.'

Despite Denise's protestations that she was contagious, Lorna linked her arm through Denise's and they made their way along the balcony towards the lifts.

'He's not changed,' said Denise, running her fingers along the icy metal rail that was supposed to stop would-be suicides from tipping themselves over the top and down onto the solid concrete 'play area'. 'When he was still living at home – properly, full time, I mean, not just treating the place like a dosshouse – he used to have Mum flapping around after him of a Sunday morning like she was running a caff just for his benefit. He'd finally manage to drag his lazy carcass out of bed after being out boozing all night, and grace us with his presence down in the basement. The kitchen's meant to be the heart of the family, isn't that what they say? Well, when he was in it we'd all be walking on pins. He is such an arsehole.

'Anyway, we'd all make do with a bit of toast, but not him. He always had to have the full plateful to *help his hangover*. Should have seen the fuss. Mum always having to make sure his bread was fried *properly* on both sides, that his eggs *weren't too runny*, and that the bacon was *all nice and crispy*. Everything had to be just right for her precious Richie, didn't it? You know, Lorn, Mum's got a lot to answer for. She turned him into a bloody monster.'

'I don't think he needed much help from your mum,

Den. And now you know she was living with all that guilt about him really being . . . you know.'

Denise opened her mouth, but the words just wouldn't come. Christ, what was she going to say?

'Where's this bloody lift then?' was what she eventually came up with.

Lorna snuggled closer to her. 'Christ knows, but blimey, it's cold, Den. Feels like it could start snowing again.'

Denise could feel her heart pumping; she knew she had to get it over with, had to actually say it out loud.

'Look, Lorna,' she began, 'I didn't come to talk about Richie's breakfast, or the horrible weather, or even how long the lift takes to get here. I came to talk about something much more serious than any of that. It's to do with our Chantalle.'

'Chantalle?'

'Yeah. I don't know how to say this, but –'

The arrival of the lift interrupted her, announcing its appearance with a loud, metallic ping.

Lorna put her finger to her lips to keep Denise silent.

The doors shooshed open to reveal a urine-fragranced space, deserted save for a milk crate full of empties.

Denise laughed ruefully. 'Didn't think anyone else was as daft as us, did you, coming out in this weather at this time of a Sunday morning?' She ushered Lorna into the lift. 'Tell you what, instead of walking the streets and me developing full-blown double pneumonia, let's get a bus up to the Lane, and we can go in a nice warm coffee shop and get ourselves a cup of tea and a hot salt beef beigel. How about that for a proper breakfast?' Denise saw the doubt on her friend's face, and jumped in before she could refuse.

'And we can talk about you borrowing a few more of my outfits for the new job. It's great working together, eh, Lorn?' She managed a little grin and lifted her shoulders in a show of excitement. 'Really fantastic.'

'I told you, Den, I can't be long. I've got to get back.'

Denise said nothing more until the lift stopped on the ground floor and they had stepped out onto the wide open, windswept space that linked the flats to Chrisp Street's deserted market square.

She was no longer grinning. 'When you hear what I've got to say, Lorna, I can't see you being in much of a hurry to go back and cook for that bastard. I can't see you ever wanting to go back to him ever again.'

Buttoning her coat right up to her throat, Lorna smiled ruefully as they began making their way up to the main road. 'How many times have I said that before?'

'Trust me, Lorna, this is bad.'

Lorna stopped dead, pulling Denise to halt next to her. 'OK, he can't hear us now, there's no risk of him jumping out on us – so tell me.'

'It's not easy.'

'It never is with Richie.'

'It's just . . .' Denise shook her head. This was too hard. It was the worst thing she'd ever had to do, and she felt like shit.

The rumbling sound of an approaching engine made her look up. 'Look, Lorna, there's a number fifteen. Come on and I'll buy you that breakfast. We needn't be long.'

They began running for the bus stop.

'And I'm telling you, I know you weren't keen going on working up the West End, but you're going to be so glad you've got that job, because you're never going to want to take another penny off of him again.'

Despite the cold, and the dirty, yellowish white of the snow-filled sky, the bus was packed with surprisingly cheerful people. They were all making their way to Petticoat Lane market, going in search of bargain fruit and veg, and bits of cheap toot to help balance their January books after too much overspirited spending at Christmas time.

Lorna and Denise sat on the packed upper deck, smoking in self-absorbed silence, Denise coughing and spluttering as she went over and over how she would tell her friend about what had happened, and Lorna staring out of the window, wondering what on earth her drunken, scheming bully of a husband could possibly have done that involved Chantalle.

If he'd got her caught up in the drugs that Lorna was sure he was involved in, or in thieving from the last of the bonded warehouses down at the docks, then that really would be it this time. She wouldn't let him pull Chantalle into his clutches. She would grass him up, no matter what he threatened to do to her. It might actually be enough of a final straw for her to tell her dad of him. The thought of Richie getting a good slapping almost made her happy.

They got off the bus at Aldgate and walked through the maze of bustling side streets jammed with stalls and shoppers.

Denise took a deep breath. 'I won't make you wait any longer. Let's go into that caff.'

While Lorna fetched them drinks, Denise claimed the only empty table in the furthest corner of the steam-filled room; it was over by the coat pegs where no one else wanted to sit and be bothered by customers hooking and unhooking their things from over their heads.

'Right,' said Denise.

She handed Lorna a cigarette, lit it for her, then leaned as close to her as the table would allow. 'There's no other way for me to say this, and no way to dress it up nicely, delicately, prettily, or any other way. Chantalle lost her virginity last night. Up against the wall, in a stinking alley, out the back of the Canvas Club, while Terry was inside playing with the Spanners.'

'But you said this was to do with Rich–' Lorna clapped her hand over her mouth, stopping the words. Her eyes widened in horror and she shook her head.

'I'm so sorry, Lorna. You had to know.'

'No. You must be wrong.'

Denise flopped back in her chair, puffed out her cheeks and dragged her fingers down her face. 'That's exactly what I mean. It was Richie; he schtupped his own half-sister. What a classy bloke, eh? Makes me feel so proud I could stick a knife in him.'

Lorna rose unsteadily to her feet, her face now as pale and clammy as Denise's was flushed by fever. 'I think I need some air.'

Denise took her arm and led her towards the door.

The fat café owner grinned at his line of damp-coated customers. 'Had a bit too much last night, did you, darling?'

Lorna spun round and jabbed her finger in his fat, pudgy face. 'A bit too much? I've had more than that, I've had more than you could even imagine, *darling*.'

Outside in the busy street, Lorna leaned against the window, not even noticing the chill against her back of the condensation pouring down the glass. She squeezed her eyes shut.

'How could he have done that to her, Den? How could even he stoop so low?'

'I don't know how he could do it to her, or to you. All I know is I could kill him stone dead.' Denise saw the café owner glowering at them through the streaming window, and touched her friend gently on the arm. 'Come on, let's get away from here.'

'All right, Den, but I'll tell you something: you won't have to bother to kill the bastard, because I'm going to get to him first.'

They moved through the streets in a blind daze, not even noticing the Plate Man attracting his usual crowds with his acrobatic juggling displays using full, genuine china dinner services – gravy boats and soup ladles included – a sight that would usually have entertained them for at least a good ten minutes before they strolled off to look for the next free diversion.

They continued along Brick Lane and round into Club Row without a second glance at the exotic delights of the Snake Man, who would drape a fully grown boa constrictor round your neck for just a single sixpence, or for free if you were a pretty young woman like Denise or Lorna. Even the fluffy yellow cuteness of the piping, cheeping, day-old chicks in their makeshift wire pens – which would usually have had the girls sighing and cooing, working out how they could so easily build a hen coop in Denise's backyard, before they moved onto the orange boxes full of velvet-tummied puppies just begging to be petted and kissed – didn't warrant so much as a break in their step.

But then, without warning, Lorna stopped in her tracks, causing a minor collision of shopping-laden passers-by.

'I'm so ashamed I ever had anything to do with him.'

'You're ashamed? How do you think I feel? He's my own brother.' Denise could taste the bile in her throat.

'Den, I'm going home.'

'But say he's still there?'

'I said home, not to the flat. Not to that pig.' Lorna started to cry for the first time since Denise had told her. 'I'd already planned to pack up all my stuff this afternoon, but he can have the lot of it. I can't go back there. Den, I want my mum.'

'Hello, Mrs Wright, is Mr Wright in?'

Shirley, hands covered in flour from the apple pie she was making, stood in the doorway smiling. 'No, sorry, babe, he popped out for the Sunday papers and a nice hot loaf from Alice's.' It wasn't usual for Denise to want to speak to Joe, but Shirley wasn't one to interfere, though she was one to help. 'Anything I can do for you? Everything all right?'

'No, not really, but hang on a minute.' Denise leaned back and called along the balcony. 'You're OK, Lorn, your dad's not in.'

'All young couples have rows, darling.' Shirley topped up her daughter's teacup and pushed it to her across the kitchen table. Delighted as she was at the news that her daughter was leaving her husband – that was something a respectable woman such as Shirley would never have believed she would find herself thinking – she didn't want to start discussing her business in front of Denise, even if they had been friends since they were little more than toddlers. It wasn't right. 'Even me and your dad sometimes fall out, and you know how easy-going we are.'

'Mum, it was more than a row.' Lorna flashed a look at Denise who was sitting opposite her, a handkerchief clamped to her streaming nose. 'But please don't ask me the details.'

'Course I won't. That's private. You know I'd never poke my nose in where it's not wanted.'

'Don't be silly, it's just . . .' She shrugged. 'Mum, do you think I can stay here for a bit? Till I get a place of my own? With this new job I'll be able to put a bit away and find somewhere to make a fresh start.'

And this time she meant it. If what he had done hadn't been so vile and disgusting she would have thanked Chantalle for making her see the light at last – to realise she had to be really serious about rebuilding her life, a life away from him.

'Lorna, it's not even an issue. This is your home, and it always will be. You can stay here for as long as you want. You know that.'

Lorna bowed her head and nodded miserably.

'We've been down the Lane,' sniffed Denise, filling the silence.

'Have you, love?' Shirley asked, obviously distracted. 'That's nice.' Then she went on: 'Lorna, I don't think it's a very good idea to tell Phyllis about this. Not yet. It's up to you, of course, but I think it'd be better if you don't.' When Lorna didn't reply, Shirley continued, her voice even, measured, 'You see, if she knows there's trouble between you and Richie, on top of everything else, it might be too much for her.'

'On top of *what* else?' asked Denise. God, her head hurt.

'She was that upset over Chantalle, Denise, I can't begin to tell you. She was sobbing on the phone.'

The girls looked at each other. Christ, surely Chantalle hadn't told Phyllis?

'How do you mean?' asked Lorna warily.

'What have I gone and said? You two must have been down the market.' Shirley rubbed her hand over her forehead, leaving a trail of flour. 'I wondered why Denise never said anything.'

Lorna gulped as all sorts of horrible visions filled her head. '*Mum?*'

'Sorry, girls, I'm all over the place. Look, Den, your mum, she phoned me earlier to see if I knew anything. I hate being the one to tell you, love, but your Chantalle, she's gone missing.'

Denise sprang to her feet, her sore head forgotten. 'She's what?'

'Phyllis said she left a note saying she was sorry, she couldn't explain, but she didn't want anyone looking for her. Most of her clothes have gone, and some old school bag of Maxie's.'

Denise felt her legs begin to wobble.

Shirley put her hand on Denise's shoulder. 'Sit back down, eh, love? You're not well.'

'No, I can't, I've got to go and see Mum.'

'I'll come with you.'

'No.' Denise was staring at the table. 'Thanks, but I'd better go alone.'

'Weren't you meant to be going round to see Terry?'

'He'll have to wait.'

'I can go round there if you like.'

Denise nodded absent-mindedly as she pulled on her coat. 'Thanks, Lorn, if you don't mind.'

*   *   *

'So you see, Tel,' Lorna gulped back the bitter taste that kept rising in her throat, 'it was even worse than you thought. A bit more serious than them having a snog.'

Terry shook his head, and picked distractedly at the arm of the sofa – his mother's pride and joy that stood in front of the fire in the front parlour, the sofa where he and Denise made love. After what Lorna had told him, the thought made him feel oddly queasy. 'He actually had Chantalle, up against the wall, out the back of the Canvas? *His own little cousin?*'

'It gets worse, Terry.'

'I can't think how, Lorna, I honestly can't.' He wanted to wrap his arms round her, and make her feel better. She was such a decent girl: kind, generous, a really good friend to Denise, and she didn't even realise how good-looking she was. How had she ever seen anything in Richie Clayton? She could have had her pick.

'Can't think how, son?' repeated Mr Robins, Terry's smiling, ever-friendly dad, as he popped his head round the parlour door. 'Not whether you can manage another drop of shandy, surely?'

He pushed open the door with his knee and presented them with a tin tray that held two foaming half-pint glasses. He winked at Lorna.

'Oi, oi, young Lorna, you're looking a bit sheepish. I've not got to tell that friend of yours you're after her feller, now have I?' His smile broadened into a grin. 'Good for you, Tel. You've got Denise, the nice little redhead, now you've got Lorna, the gorgeous blonde. How about going for the brunette next?'

'*Dad.*'

Mr Robins handed Lorna a glass. 'Least ways, I told his mother it was shandy. We all know it's larger and a touch of lime, really, but that's our little secret. She'd be after me with the yard broom if she thought I was encouraging you two into bad ways.'

He gave the other glass to his son. 'Seriously though, Lorna, it's very nice to see you again, sweetheart. You make sure it's not so long next time. And I think it's right kind of you coming round to let our Terry know that young Denise is feeling poorly. Good friend I call that. Especially coming out in this filthy weather.'

He ruffled his son's hair fondly. 'Terry's always saying we should get a telephone put in. Perhaps we should, eh, son? Now you just give me a call if you want anything more.' He laughed happily to himself. 'But no use trying the phone, eh? Not till we get one! But till then I'll be out in the kitchen with Mrs Robins. You know I reckon I could sneak two more of them *shandies* past her easy enough if you fancy them.'

'Sorry about that, Lorna,' said Terry the moment his father had closed the parlour door.

'That's all right, Terry, you don't have to apologise for him; he's nice, normal.' She took a sip of her drink. 'You know, with all this rubbish with Richie going on, I'd almost forgotten what being normal was.'

She knocked back the rest of the lager in three quick gulps and stood up. 'I'd better get off now, Tel.'

'But you said there was something else.'

'No, it's not important. I wasn't thinking straight.'

Terry did his best to smile at her. 'Try not to worry too much, Lorna. Everything'll work out, you just see if it doesn't.'

'Do you reckon?'

'Yeah. I know you'll be fine, because you deserve to be.'

Denise shoved open the street door, which, as always, had been left on the latch.

'Mum, where are you?'

'Is that you, Denise?' she heard Phyllis call from the front room. She sounded terrible, really distraught. And what was she doing in there? They never went in there unless someone important came round, like the insurance man, or . . .. Jesus, it must be the police.

'Yes, Mum, it's me.' As Denise stepped into the over-furnished, lavender-polish-scented room, all she could focus on were the two uniformed officers sitting on the wooden-armed easy chairs that faced each other in front of the gas fire in the blocked-up cast-iron grate. One of them, the man, was drinking from her mum's best bone china tea service. She never got out the best china. Ever. Even at Christmas. And why didn't the woman have a cup?

Denise ran her fingers through her hair. Why was she thinking all this nonsense?

'Thank God.' Phyllis launched herself across the room and wrapped her big beefy arms tightly round her daughter. 'I thought you'd gone missing as well.'

After covering her hair with damp kisses, Phyllis let go of Denise and stepped back.

Denise saw that her mother's eyes were red and puffy from weeping. She looked old.

'I'm so sorry, Den. I shouldn't have said it like that, shouldn't have just blurted it out . . .'

'It's all right, Mum. I already know. I've been round Mrs Wright's with Lorna. She told us.'

'Mrs Wright's? Lorna?' The male officer asked.

'Lorna's my best mate. She's married to my . . . to my cousin. Richie Clayton. Mrs Wright's her mum. Shirley. Me and Lorna, we'd been shopping. Down the Lane.' Denise could have slapped herself. Why was she blabbing her mouth off before she even knew what was going on? Why couldn't she just keep her trap shut for once?

The policeman looked at Denise's empty hands. 'Doesn't look like you bought very much, miss.'

'Too many people. Couldn't see anything. And I don't feel well.'

'Right.' He put his cup down on the floor and picked up his notebook from the wooden arm.

'So, let's see. Your cousin, he'd be?'

'Richie,' said Phyllis. 'Richie Clayton.'

'And his wife. She's Lorna?'

Denise nodded.

'If I could have their address, please . . . ?'

Denise closed her eyes. Should she tell them that Lorna wouldn't be there? But then her mum would know and she'd get even more upset. Sod him; Richie would have to sort this out for himself.

'They live over in the new tower block. The flats at the back of Chrisp Street market.'

Chantalle shivered. She felt cold, damp, exhausted, and completely and utterly alone.

She had been sitting on her bag in the doorway of the shop in Piccadilly since she had arrived there just before dawn. It was now midday, but the sky still hadn't brightened from the dull, leaden yellow it had turned at first light. It was one of those sleety winter days when it would never really get light, and then the gloom would just sort of merge into dusk and it would be night-time again.

She counted out her money for the fifth time.

Still only fifteen shillings and a few coppers whatever way she counted it. She should look for somewhere to get some food, and she could go into the ladies and have a wash and comb her hair through. And warm up.

But if she shelled out on a meal, how would she manage getting in to work tomorrow?

As if she could face seeing anyone she knew ever again. It was as if she were wearing a placard saying exactly what she'd done, a sign of shame for everyone to read: *Whore. I did it with my own brother so I might as well do it with you.*

But if she didn't go in to work, what would she do for money? Even if she wanted to get a different job, how could she with nowhere to live?

And how could Richie have done this to her?

And what if she got pregnant?

When she was younger, she and all her schoolmates had really believed that you couldn't fall the first time you did it with a boy, but then Kay Spencer, a girl in the third year, had proved that little theory to be a complete load of rubbish.

If it happened to her, there'd be no pretending she was on holiday with her auntie as Kay's family had done when they'd packed her off to the mother and baby home to have her child taken off her. No pretending it was her little niece or nephew as her own mother had done with that scumbag Richie.

She might be pregnant, right now, sitting in a shop doorway like a tramp. A little tiny life forming inside her, not knowing that its mum was a useless, stupid slag who went with her own brother.

If only she could go home, but how could she stand being under the same roof as him? And say her mum ever found out? She hid her face in her hands and began to sob pitifully.

'Excuse me?' It was a friendly northern voice. Male, but soft and caring. 'Are you OK, lass?'

Chantalle, unable to speak through her tears, looked up at him and shook her head.

'I thought not. Now, let's start off properly: what's your name?'

'Chantalle . . . Turner,' she said hesitantly, pausing long enough for him to know she was lying. Chantalle wasn't her real name, he'd put money on it. How would a kid like her wind up with a name like that?

He held out his hand to her. 'Here, up you get. You must be frozen stiff sitting on that cold pavement. And there's no need to look at me like that. I'm a respectable married man, I am. You just think of me as a fairy godfather who doesn't want to see a damsel left in distress. Upsy-daisy, move yourself, I'm going to buy you a Sunday lunch you'll never forget.'

In normal circumstances, the boldly handsome Chantalle would have tossed her wild red curls and told the expensively, if slightly flashily dressed man to *fuck off and leave me alone, you old pervert*, but these weren't normal circumstances, and there was something about his smile, and the offer of his hand – not to mention the cold and damp that had bitten right through to her bones, and the shock and desperation that were scrambling her judgement – that made her simply nod self-pityingly and accept this strange man's hand and his simple offer of kindness.

'Thanks,' she said softly.

'That's all right,' he said, pulling her to her feet. 'They do say that's what you have to do sometimes: accept the kindness of strangers.'

She looked at him through narrowed eyes. It was as if he could read her mind.

'May we come in, sir?'

Richie, tightening the belt of his bathrobe, peered at the two uniformed officers through his thick fringe of black, sleep-tangled hair.

'Why?' he said to the man, the one who had asked the question. 'What do you want? It's bloody Sunday.' And where the hell was Lorna? He'd kill her when she got back; having his sleep disturbed like this, and not being around to warn him that the law was on the sodding doorstep.

'It's about a Miss Chantalle Parker.'

The female officer noted the shifty look that clouded Richie's face at the mention of the girl's name. He was hiding something.

'May we, sir?' she asked.

'It's not very convenient.'

'We won't take too much of your time,' she said with a smile, easing past him and into the hallway.

Richie spun round and practically threw himself between the nosy cow and the sitting room. 'Come in the kitchen,' he said as casually as he could manage, 'it's much cosier in there.'

'And perhaps your wife would like to join us,' she suggested.

'Yeah, I'm sure she would.' Richie tried a smile. 'When she gets back from visiting her mother.' He turned to the male officer. 'But you know how women like to gas. She might not be back for bloody hours. Talking about knitting and shopping and that.'

The twitch in the female officer's right eyebrow was so slight that only her colleague – accustomed to the gesture of irritation – noticed it.

'I promise,' said Richie, offering the two police officers a cheery wave from his front door as they walked back to the lifts. 'First word I hear from our little Chantalle, and I'll be right on the blower to you.'

He gave a conspiratorial chuckle. 'And if she thinks she's going to hide out here to punish Auntie Phyllis because they've had a row over something silly or other, then she's got another thought coming. Now, you two get back to that nice warm police station out of all this rotten weather, and thanks for your interest and all your help.'

With that he gave another little wave and shut his front door with a controlled slam, leaving the two police officers to shake their heads in wonder at such mind-numbingly bad acting.

The little slime ball might not have known where his cousin was, but now they were both convinced he had something to hide, and they'd be back to find out exactly what.

Richie didn't bother to wash or shave, he just got himself dressed in record time, dug out his stash from under the bed – he'd have to find a proper place to keep his gear if he was going to stay in the big time – and drove like a maniac to Cable Street.

As soon as he got there he went in the telephone box and made a couple of calls. He stomped up and down in the cold, smoking and waiting impatiently until, at last, a dull grey Morris pulled up next to him.

Within moments a large amount of drugs were exchanged for a large amount of money, the deal was done, and Richie was off on his next task – pulling his girls off the street.

'What's going on, Richie?' demanded Sal. 'We've only been out here for just over an hour. I don't know about you, but I need the dough after Christmas. What's going on?'

'None of your business, is it, Richie?' said Rita, making sure she got in the front seat next to him, and glaring at the other four – Sal, Trish, Pauline and Pamela, who were all squashed in the back seat – daring them to challenge her.

'Nothing wrong, is there, lover?' Rita cooed, stroking his cheek proprietorially. 'Nothing serious, is it?'

Richie pulled away from her. 'There's too many law about. Now get your hands off me, I'm trying to drive.'

'It was strange, Mr Diaz,' said the ox-sized minder, whom Diaz had sent out from the café to observe what Richie was up to. 'Those girls who turned up an hour or so ago, he's just taken them away again. Maybe he's thought better of trying to move in here. But I shouldn't think so, he seems too much of an idiot.'

Diaz said nothing. He just lit a skinny little cheroot that, in his tiny hand, looked more like a full-sized Cohiba robusto.

'But before he bundled the five of them into the car he was up under the arches. Did a really big deal – and I mean big for him – with one man.' He shook his head. 'In broad daylight. Must think he's invisible.'

'Or invulnerable.' Diaz nodded with satisfaction. 'I knew that fool wouldn't be able to control himself, wouldn't be able to resist getting too big for his cheap boots.'

The minder smirked. 'You can be sure he'll have Fuller on his tail now. These are wholesale quantities we're talking about.'

'Good,' said Diaz, tapping the ashes from his cigar. 'The more involved, the more confusion. Always good for cover, and a pleasing situation when you value your privacy.'

Ray, as the man had introduced himself to Chantalle, seemed to be well known in the hotel where he had taken her for lunch. In truth, the place was a bit dingy and faded, but it had only been a few moments' walk from Piccadilly, and Chantalle had been so pleased to be out of the cold that she wouldn't have cared if it had been a complete tip. And anyway, it wasn't as if she'd had much experience of hotels. Maybe they were all like this behind their posh, excluding doors.

'That's better,' said Ray, as she finally put down her knife and fork after clearing her plate. He had eaten nothing, but had sipped at a single half-pint of Harp lager. 'You look human again. Pretty in fact. Like a picture.'

Chantalle smiled.

'And, do you know, you're truly beautiful when you smile. A lot of men would really go for you, Chantalle, especially with that gorgeous red hair of yours. Irresistible, that.'

Chantalle's smile disappeared.

'Not shy, are you? Good-looking girl like you should be used to compliments, and proud of your looks. How old are you, twenty?'

'Seventeen.' She shouldn't be rude to him, not after he'd bought her a meal.

He nodded, apparently pleased by her age. 'Got a boyfriend, have you?'

She shook her head, as much to get rid of visions of what that animal had done to her last night as to say no.

'Had a row at home?'

She didn't respond.

'Look, Chantalle, I'm not going to sod about, love. You need somewhere to stay, and I've got somewhere that I'd be happy to lend you; I'm a landlord, you see, for my sins. But you're not a kid, and you know and I know that, as always in life, there's a catch. You'd have to do a bit of work in return. For your rent like.'

Chantalle looked steadily into his eyes. She was grateful to Ray; he was offering her a solution, and so long as he didn't want her to do something even more awful than Richie had made her do, then she'd do anything that meant she could earn some money, have somewhere to live, and never ever have to go back home and face him ever again.

She almost laughed. *Was* there anything that could be more awful than what that bastard had done to her last night?

If there was, she couldn't think of it.

Ray was surprised at just how easy it was to persuade her of the sense of his proposal. He'd risked wasting the price of the meal only because she'd looked so fresh for a kid on the streets. And here she was, agreeing to work for him – not that he'd actually told her what he had in mind, of course, but how naïve could a kid of seventeen really be nowadays?

'What do you want?' Henry, who had been sitting alone at the kitchen table, staring into his empty cup, lifted his head and glared at his so-called nephew with loathing in his eyes.

'Not that it's anything to do with you,' Richie said cockily, 'but I'm looking for our Denise.'

He'd actually gone round to East India Dock Road to tell Phyllis that she had to look after some money for him – the fat wedge he'd just picked up in the drugs deal in Cable Street, and didn't want to keep it up at the flat in case the law came round sticking their noses in again – but he wasn't telling Henry that. But, come to think of it, he'd better see Denise as well, had better straighten her out with a few quid before she went blabbing to Phyllis about Chantalle. That silly little cow was bound to have told her precious sister what they'd done.

And she also might know where that silly tart Lorna had got to, before she started mouthing off to anyone. Bloody birds, they couldn't keep a secret if you taped their sodding mouths shut for them.

'Do you know where she is?'

Henry ignored him.

'I said, *Henry* –' Richie's voice was low, menacing – 'do you know where Denise is?'

'I'm here,' said Denise, from the top of the stairs that led down to the kitchen, 'but I've got nothing to say to you.'

She had just turned to walk away, when Richie sprang at her and grabbed her by the arm.

'Oi, I want to talk to you.'

'Well, I don't want to talk to you.'

Richie raised his hand and smacked Denise – whack! – across the side of her head.

Henry was on his feet before Denise could even scream.

He locked his arm round Richie's neck and dragged him backwards down the stairs.

'If you make a single sound and wake Phyllis I'll snap your neck just like the scrawny chicken you are.'

'Since when did you care about Phyllis?' sneered Richie, swaggering to the last.

'Not that I have to answer to you,' said Henry, tightening his grip on Richie's throat, 'but whatever trouble her and me have had in the past – and will probably have in the future – that woman's suffering, suffering like I've never seen before. And I don't want her upsetting any more. Got it? So you listen to me, boy. You are not wanted round here. Just get out and don't you dare let me set eyes on you again.'

With that, Henry shoved him up the stairs. 'And God help that lovely little wife of yours, that's all I can say.'

'And God help Phyllis having to be married to the likes of you. Even if she did only want a mug to be a father for her kid, I reckon she deserved something better than a prat like you.'

Chapter 15

Richie blinked at the bedside clock. Fuck! Half-past eleven. He'd overslept again. That bitch still couldn't have come home or she'd have given him a call for breakfast nearly two hours ago.

He heaved the bedcovers angrily onto the floor.

And he had a hangover.

What did the stupid cow think she was playing at? The police had come back yesterday, questioning him, wanting to know why she was staying over at the Buildings with her mum and dad, asking him what he had to say about what had happened between them, and was she friends with Chantalle, and was Lorna's leaving anything to do with Chantalle – like any of it was anything to do with them.

As Richie sat on the edge of the bed, drawing down the smoke from his first cigarette of the day, he could just imagine her old man sticking his oar in, suggesting all sorts to the thick-headed coppers who no doubt jotted down every single word in their little notebooks. There was nothing the likes of Joe Wright enjoyed more than getting other people into trouble. The only sodding straight docker in the whole of East London, and he had to have him for a bloody father-in-law.

Richie scratched his chest through his grubby string vest and raked his hair out of his eyes. He had to get moving, had to get back on track. He had things to do, people to see. He needed energy, needed a buzz, needed that edge.

He stubbed out the remains of his cigarette in a pretty china bowl on Lorna's dressing table, then dug out his suit jacket from a heap of clothes on the floor by the wardrobe. He searched through the pockets until he found two slightly crumbling lavender-blue pills, tossed them into his mouth, groped his way through to the bathroom and put his head under the tap.

He screwed up his eyes and let the water run through his hair and over his face, then he twisted round until his mouth was positioned right under the gushing stream. He drank greedily, gulping down the drugs as if they were the answer to every question he had.

He knew they were his last, that he had to restock quickly, that his customers wouldn't appreciate being kept waiting.

He pulled the damp towel off the doorknob and rubbed it over his head. Maybe he should keep his new supply over at Rita's until this crap with the police and Chantalle had blown over. Until she either turned up at East India Dock Road with her tail between her legs, crying like a baby and begging Phyllis and Henry to take her back, or the coppers found her dead in a canal somewhere, washed up like the bit of rubbish she was.

Rita clambered inelegantly from Richie's silver Zephyr and joined the two other girls, Sal and Trish, who were already standing on the pavement. She looked nervously up and down the street.

'Are you sure this is all right, us coming back, Richie? Yesterday you seemed so dead set against us being here. You said the police were –'

'You're not questioning me, are you?' Richie, still sitting comfortably in the driver's seat, made no attempt to duck his head so he could actually make eye contact with her as he spoke – she didn't matter enough for that.

'No, course I'm not questioning you.' Rita tugged at the hem of her tiny skirt. She was cold, and her thighs were turning red and had started itching like mad. Before long they'd look like two blocks of corned beef fresh out of the tin, like some old lady who'd been sitting too close to the electric fire. And her toes were numb. If she wasn't careful she'd get chilblains. She had asked Richie if they could have the heating on in the car, but he'd said no, because he was wearing a heavy overcoat and didn't want to feel uncomfortable.

All in all, she was fed up.

'But you said the law was sniffing around because of Chantalle,' she whined, 'and –'

'And?'

'And it's freezing out here, Richie.' She knew she sounded moany and pathetic, and Richie hated that, but she couldn't help it; she was scared. She'd heard so many stories about what it was like in borstal and in prison and in places like that. And about how the other prisoners treated you when you'd never been in before – never mind what she'd heard about the guards. She swallowed hard. Why couldn't Richie have just left her working for him in the flat in Upper North Street? She was good at it, and earning him more than enough, and, while it might not have been very glamorous, at least it was warm.

'Honestly, Rich, it's really freezing.'

'Have you finished?'

She nodded.

'Good, because this cold weather means there'll be plenty of blokes about, all wanting to treat themselves to a nice little warm-up. So I'll be expecting you three to do well for me today then. Really well. There's things I need to buy, so you won't disappoint me, will you? 'Cos if you do, I'm going to be ever so upset.'

Trish nudged Sal, who mouthed an obscenity at Rita. Why couldn't she just shut her trap? Winding him up like that.

'Course we won't disappoint you,' they chorused as if they'd been practising three-part harmonies.

'That's the spirit, girls. I'll be in the caff when you need to bring me your dough. And make sure there's plenty of it.'

He turned the key in the ignition and engaged the clutch, then, as a departing shot, he called to them out of the window: 'And if them two other lazy mares haven't shown in the next half-hour, I'm going round after them. So perhaps one of you wants to give them a ring before they get me all worked up and angry.'

Leaving the girls to get on with things, Richie drove the fifty yards along the street to Lil's.

He bought himself a mug of Jock's industrial-strength tea, settled himself at a table in the front window, and directed a sarcastic smile over his shoulder to the back of the café where Antonio Diaz was sitting with two of his heavies.

As they stared back at him – stony-faced and tight-jawed – Richie didn't understand the actual words they exchanged, although he guessed they were speaking Maltese, but, from the look on their faces and the tone of their voices, he reckoned he had a pretty good idea about what they were feeling: totally, completely, without-a-doubt fucked off that he was back on the scene.

He'd made a mistake panicking like that yesterday just because the police had shown. He should never have run off; it looked weak. But he'd make up for it today, all right. And he'd soon have those pathetic Maltese nonces sitting on it and wriggling. They'd be more pissed off than they'd ever been before. Richie had plans, big plans: he was going to have at least half a dozen more girls working the street by the beginning of February, and by the summer he'd have shown those foreign cowsons exactly who was in charge. He was not only going to be one of the big boys, he was going to be *the* big boy – the biggest of them all.

He smiled – genuinely this time. He should get himself a minder. Maybe he'd start training young Maxie for the role, he was a big enough bastard, built like a brick shit-house. And, he laughed unpleasantly to himself, he liked keeping things in the family.

Antonio Diaz considered the young fool sitting at the front of the café. Did he really believe that he could just sit there insulting him? He had given the boy leeway, hoping that he would bring more pretty youngsters into the street, like the first one he had brought there. Diaz was looking for fresh young girls and had planned to pluck them from him like ripe fruit from the pomegranate tree. But then, when he had seen the worn-out creatures he had turned up with yesterday, Diaz had changed his mind. He had no need to take such women from anyone; they could be found on street corners anywhere. Diaz prided himself on replenishing his collection with healthy stock. That was his reputation – it kept his customers coming back for more. He would have to rethink what he intended to do about young Mr Clayton being on his patch.

It was now mid-afternoon and was already growing dark;

Richie had to squint through the lowering gloom to be sure what he was seeing going on right across the street from the café. He considered a moment, slowly sipped some of his tea, then put down his cup on the table, and stared harder through the smeared, greasy window at the little drama being acted out before him.

What he saw made Richie laugh so hard, he nearly choked.

Talk about keeping it in the family!

His 'uncle' Henry, the bloke who'd had the cheek to grab hold of him, the cheek to tell him to get out of his own mother's house, had just climbed out of the cab of his fruit and veg truck and – this was almost too good to be true – he was actually trying to negotiate a bit of business with *one of Richie's girls*.

This really was better than anything he could ever have hoped for. He'd show the pathetic old fucker the price of upsetting Richie Clayton.

He got up from the table and sighed happily, savouring every single moment. He treated Diaz and his cronies to a cheeky wink, then strolled outside.

'Oi, Uncle Henry!' he yelled. 'Over here. Fancy a cuppa?'

Henry Parker leaped back from Sal – the young woman whose left breast he had been fondling as part of his negotiations – like an ill-trained electrician trying unsuccessfully to mend a faulty ring main.

Henry was the only member of the Parker household who had gone to work that day. Denise had stayed home to look after Phyllis and to nurse her cold, and Maxie, ever the opportunist, had taken all the to-do about Chantalle as an excuse to skive, claiming he was too upset about his sister to able to concentrate. Phyllis had been only too glad to have the two of them where she could see them.

But now, the combination of nervous tension and boredom was getting to them.

Phyllis was pottering about in silence, peeling spuds, carrots and onions and frying up some mince, promising in her heart that she would do whatever God wanted if only Chantalle would just turn up and sit down to share the cottage pie with them as if nothing had happened. She was exhausted with worry and lack of sleep.

Denise was doing her best to help – getting rid of the peelings, mashing the potatoes, making yet more tea – but Maxie was just being a pain. He sat at the kitchen table, flicking through the early edition of the evening paper, with his long, muscled legs sticking out from under the cloth not thinking or caring if they might be in anyone's way.

'Even bloody work would be better than this,' he whispered miserably to Denise as she got on with her mashing, and as their mother stared up aimlessly through the shallow basement window at people's passing feet. 'This is giving me the right hump.'

'Grow up, Maxie,' snapped Denise. 'If you actually did something instead of just sitting there, perhaps you wouldn't be bored.'

'What do you want me to do, go out searching for the selfish cow? We all know she's just gone and pissed off with some bloke or other. You know how she is with fellers. She's a right scrubber.'

Denise narrowed her eyes. She'd have loved to have seen the look on his smug, rotten face if she told him what was really going on with Chantalle, but she kept her thoughts to herself. The fewer people who knew the truth the better as far as Denise was concerned – it meant that there was less chance of her mum having her heart shattered.

'Mum,' he whined, shoving back his chair and standing up, 'all right if I pop round Graham's for a bit?'

'What?' asked Phyllis, her voice flat, distracted.

'Christ, Maxie,' snapped Denise, 'can't you try for once, for Mum's sake?'

'What can I do? We're sitting about here like it's a bloody funeral or something. Well, I've had enough. I'm going round me mate's now and I'm going in to work tomorrow. Even that poxy office is better than this.'

'You wanted the day off, so just sit down, Maxie, and shut up.'

Denise and her brother were still glowering at one another when they heard the street door open above them.

Phyllis hurried over to the stairs that led up from the basement kitchen to the hallway. 'She's come home, I knew she would.'

But it wasn't Chantalle who appeared in the doorway. It was Richie.

'All right, Auntie Phyllis?' he said, swaggering down the stairs. 'Wondered if I could join my family for a bit of tea.'

'Why aren't you eating at home with Lorna?' asked Phyllis, her voice dull, as she made her way wearily back to her watching post by the window. 'She'll be worrying where you've got to. We should be with our loved ones at a time like this.'

'Right. So where's Uncle Henry then?'

Denise stared at him; if she had had something heavier than a potato masher in her hand she would have crowned him with it. 'Dad's working, where else would he be?'

'What?' Richie winked conspiratorially at Maxie. 'Till this time?'

'Shut up, Richie,' snapped Denise, 'and you can stop grinning, Maxie.'

Phyllis threw up her hands and spun round to face them. 'Stop it, you three. Right now. This is no time to argue. And no time to be clever with one another. Richie, where's Lorna?'

'How do I know?'

'What?'

Denise stood up and went over to her mother. 'They've had a bit of a row, Mum, that's all. Lorna's round at Lancaster Buildings with her mum and dad till it all calms down.'

Richie flashed his eyebrows at her. 'And that's why I'm round here for me tea, Auntie Phyllis. If I'm welcome, that is. There's no food in the flat, see. Nothing. Bloody disgrace, it is, a bloke going hungry after a hard day's work.'

'Denise, set an extra plate for Richie.'

Denise stomped over to the maid-saver, grabbed a plate and slammed it down on the table in front of Richie. 'Come round because you wanted something to eat, did you?' she hissed into his ear. 'And there was me thinking you'd come round to see how we're all doing and if there's any news about our Chantalle. I hope it flipping well chokes you.'

Joe kissed Shirley on the lips, and then pecked Lorna on the top of her head, then he handed his wife a brown-paper carrier bag with string handles.

'There you are, babe. There's a nice bunch of chrysanths in there, a bottle of advocaat, and a bottle of lemonade.

I'm going to make snowballs for my two best girls after tea tonight. Just the way you like them.' He dug into his pocket and pulled out a little jar. 'With cocktail cherries and everything.'

'You shouldn't have, Joe,' said Shirley, setting the bag down on one of the kitchen chairs while she finished dishing up the lamb chops. 'Wasting your money on us like that. You should spend it on yourself for a change.'

She turned to Lorna. 'Here, darling, put these flowers in a vase for me.'

Joe smiled at his daughter. 'How do you think that seeing my family being happy and enjoying themselves is wasting money? This is how it should be, Shirl, us all together, being a proper family. I'm telling you, I'm going to make the most of all this while we've got our Lorna here with us, and while we've got the redundancy money to treat ourselves and, anyway, we've got something to celebrate – Harry Martin from the pigeon club just told me he's got me that job with him on the demolition. So let tomorrow take care of itself.'

'I'm so pleased for you, Joe.' Shirley returned his smile and threw her arms round him, but inside she was weeping. She'd known for days that he'd guessed, that he could always tell when she was feeling bad again. It wasn't fair, wasn't fair on any of them, but it broke her heart knowing how much her pain hurt her beloved Joe.

Chantalle was scared, scared and alone. Her room wasn't too bad, not really, a bit dingy and damp, though definitely better than some of the other rooms in the house that she'd been given the job of cleaning – she couldn't understand how those girls lived like that – but it was so lonely. When she'd been at home she was always desperate to get away from everyone else and from all their noise so she could read a magazine in a bit of peace or listen to her transistor radio. But now she would have given anything to have heard Denise screaming at Maxie to keep his hands off of her new shampoo, while her mum yelled blue murder at her dad to wipe his boots.

It was the loneliness that had made her tell Ray all that stuff about herself.

And all that stuff about Richie.

She closed her eyes. She shouldn't have drunk that wine he gave her. She hadn't even liked it. She'd never have said all those things otherwise. If she hadn't been drunk, and if she hadn't been so lonely, and if she hadn't been terrified that she might be carrying her own brother's baby . . .

At least Ray didn't know her full name or where she came from. That was something.

Her thoughts were interrupted by a sharp knocking on the door. She didn't hesitate to answer it; she scrambled off the narrow bed, sending the nylon bedcover crackling and slipping onto the lino-covered floor.

'Coming,' she called, glad of the distraction, not even considering who it might be.

'Ray,' she said, flinging open the door.

'You're very trusting, lass,' he replied. 'Say it'd been someone else? Someone not quite so friendly as yours truly?' It was a serious question, but he flashed her such a generous smile as he handed her a fancy, straw-covered bottle that it just sort of passed by without comment.

'Thanks,' she said, peering at the foreign writing on the label.

'Best Chianti, that. You'll love it.'

The room was too small for any furniture other than

the narrow single bed and the rickety chair that doubled as a wardrobe and bedside table, so Denise wedged her pillows against the wall and they sat sideways on the bed, using it as a sofa.

Ray took a corkscrew and two plastic cups from a brown-paper carrier bag and set about opening the wine.

'And how are you coping, Chantalle?'

She shrugged. 'You know.'

'Bored?'

'Yeah.'

'Thought so. Cleaning the flats is all right for some girls, but a bright little button like you needs something more challenging to occupy her time.'

'I usually work in an office.'

Ray pulled a disapproving face as he gave her one of the cups. 'That's for people with no ambition. I'm talking about proper work, enjoyable work, a job where you can earn good money and have a good time into the bargain.'

Chantalle sipped the wine. It tasted like cold, overstewed tea that had been left for far too long in the pot, and had then been mixed up with weak blackcurrant juice. It was horrible.

She took another sip.

'What sort of work?'

'Escort work.'

Chantalle sat up straight. 'No. No, Ray, I won't.'

'Why not? I bet you don't even know what it involves. It's nothing nasty, Chantalle. Remember, I'm a respectable married man, I'm hardly going to get involved in anything dodgy, now am I?' He smiled winningly. 'I wouldn't dare try. If I did, my Anita would kill me.'

He pulled out his wallet and showed her a picture of

a woman standing in the street outside a terraced house; she was using her hands to shade her eyes from the sun as she looked into the camera. It was impossible to make out any of her features.

'That's her. My Anita. She was an escort when I met her.'

Chantalle said nothing; she just carried on studying the slightly faded black and white image.

'I was a lonely businessman in a strange town. I went into this club – I'd been recommended to go there by the concierge in the hotel where I was staying. Nice little place. Respectable. I had a drink and was hoping for a bit of company. And that's when I saw her. We spent a smashing evening together, chatting about this and that, having a laugh.'

'Did you have a screw as well? Or was that extra?'

He snatched the photograph from Chantalle and put it back in his wallet. 'I don't know why you're so high and mighty. You told me you went with your own brother.' His voice had changed; it was hard, cold.

'But I told you, I didn't I know he was –'

'That doesn't make it any better, now does it? Doesn't make it right.'

'I didn't know.'

'You could still go to jail. You do know that, don't you, Chantalle? But I can protect you. Act sensibly, my little love, and I'll look after you. But start playing the giddy goat and, well, anything could happen to a young girl like you alone in the big city. Especially if you're –' he looked pointedly at her stomach – 'in a certain condition. But I can even arrange for someone to help you out of that particular bit of trouble, should it come to it.'

He put his arm round her and gave her a squeeze. 'You

know it makes sense, sweetheart. You listen to your Uncle Ray, he'll take care of everything.' He took a long gulp of wine. 'And let's face it, darling, you've not exactly got a whole lot of choices now, have you?'

Henry stood at the top of the stairs staring disbelievingly down into the kitchen. He could hardly credit it. Richie, that useless piece of troublemaking scum, was actually sitting at the table – *his* table – eating alongside Denise and Maxie, as if he had every right to be there. He had more neck than a fucking giraffe.

Henry took a deep breath and started down the stairs. 'All right, Phyllis?' he said, glaring at Richie. 'Any word?'

She shook her head without turning away from the window.

'No, Dad,' said Denise, fetching Henry's dinner from the top of the stove, where she'd been keeping it warm for him between two tin plates over a saucepan of hot water. 'Nothing.'

She leaned forward and said quietly so that her mum couldn't hear. 'The police popped back again earlier, but only to have a look through Chantalle's things in our bedroom. But she hadn't left that much behind. I don't think they got any clues or anything.'

'Right,' said Henry, picking up his knife and fork, but not attempting to touch his food. 'You're being a good girl, Denise, helping your mum when she's got so much on her mind.'

'She'll have even more on her mind if she finds out what you've been up to, won't she, Henry?' grinned Richie from across the table. 'Here, Auntie Phyllis,' he called to her, 'you'll never guess who I saw today.'

'Don't let's go bothering your aunt when she's already got so much on her plate,' warned Henry, pointing his knife at Richie.

'You seem nervous, Henry,' said Richie. 'Nothing wrong is there?'

Slowly, Phyllis turned until she was facing the table. She stared at Richie as if she had had trouble understanding what he had said.

'Nothing wrong?' she repeated. '*Nothing wrong*? His daughter's gone missing, it's the middle of winter, it's snowing again, and we've got no idea where the poor little bugger's got to. Are you mad?'

'I was only having a laugh, Auntie Phyllis.'

'A laugh?' exploded Henry, making a grab for him across the table.

'Don't! Stop it! Both of you,' shrieked Phyllis. 'Please, just this once, can't you all just stop it?'

'It's him,' sulked Richie. 'He winds me up.'

'Well, perhaps we'd all be better off if I wasn't here,' snarled Henry throwing down his knife and fork.

'Do you know, I reckon you're right for once, Henry,' said Richie.

Phyllis watched in tearful silence as Henry grabbed his coat from the banister and stormed off up the stairs. 'I'm going over the Blue Boy for a pint,' he shouted down from the hallway.

She stared at Henry's empty chair; her family was falling apart.

'A pint? You sure that's all you're going out for?' Richie called back.

Denise picked up her dad's dinner and put it back on the stove. 'Mum, would you mind if I went out for a bit?'

Phyllis turned to face her daughter, moving as if she

were in too low a gear. 'No, course I don't mind. You go. It'll do you good to get out. Go and see Terry. But wrap up warm.'

'Can I go out an' all, Mum?' asked Maxie, not wanting to miss out on such an opportunity.

'Yeah, go on, son. But not too late, eh?'

He didn't need a second chance, he was on his feet and halfway up the stairs before his mother had finished speaking.

'And, Maxie?' Phyllis called after him.

'What?' he snapped with a sulky wag of his head.

'If Graham's mum's heard anything from that big mouth Mrs Elliot, you tell her you don't know what she's going on about. All right?'

Phyllis waited until she'd heard the front door slam, and then watched through the high window as her son and daughter walked off in the yellow glow of the streetlights, in different directions along the road. Only then did she speak, when she was sure it was just her and Richie left in the house.

'Richie,' she said, still staring up into the street.

'Yes, Auntie Phyllis?'

'Why can't you just keep your gob shut for once?'

Terry welcomed Denise with wide-open arms and a concerned, pitying expression.

'Come in, Den,' he said, leading her through to the front room. 'You know Lorna came round to see me, don't you?'

Denise said nothing. She just dipped her chin, frightened to speak in case she started crying. In case she blurted out something she shouldn't.

'How are you feeling now?'

'All right,' she said softly. 'Throat's still sore.'

'You shouldn't have come out. But I'm glad you did.' He sat her down on the sofa, made sure the door was shut properly, then sat next to her and put his arm round her shoulders. 'She told me, you know.'

Denise stiffened. 'She told you what?'

'What that bastard did to Chantalle.'

Was Lorna out of her mind?

'Yeah. I mean, how could he, Den? Not bad enough she's only seventeen and all the rest of it, but he's a bloody married man – or supposed to be. It's disgusting. And how about Lorna? How must she be feeling? No wonder poor old Chantalle's gone on the missing list.'

Denise gripped his hand tightly in hers. 'Terry, did Lorna say anything else?'

'Like what?'

'I don't know, anything.'

'How do you mean?'

'What's wrong with you, can't you even remember that far back? It's not bloody last year we're talking about.'

'You've lost me, Den.'

'Not started taking drugs in all your fancy nightclubs, have you? Gone and done your head in like that pig, Richie. I'm not stupid, I know what goes on: young girls throwing themselves at anyone with a guitar in his hand.'

'Don't start on me, Denise. I'm only trying to be helpful.'

She let go of his hand, threw back her head and took a deep breath. 'I'm sorry. They all kicked off round home again tonight, and I've just about had enough.'

'So that's why you did me a favour and decided to come round and see me, is it?'

'Don't be stupid.'

'I reckon I must be. I thought it was because you wanted to spend some time with me, not because you wanted to get away from that lot having another row.'

'*That lot* are my family.'

'You must be very proud.'

'Leave off, Terry.'

'No, Denise, you leave off. I'm getting fed up with all this. I've got feelings as well, you know.'

'Aw, poor little you,' said Denise, jumping to her feet. 'It must be bloody awful being such a sensitive little soul.'

'Where are you going?'

'Home. I'd rather be with *that lot* than with you any day.'

Chapter 16

Despite the fact that spring was, supposedly, just around the corner, the weather was still no warmer, but Shirley – due to a combination of pain-killing medication and a blind, raging fury at Richie Clayton for inflicting such sleep-depriving, appetite-killing pain and despair on her beloved daughter – didn't notice either the slush-packed gutters or the gusting flurries of snow which were showing no sign of letting up night or day.

But the weather could have offered her clear blue skies, brilliant sunshine, and eighty degrees in the shade for all Shirley would have noticed. For now, all she could focus on was the job she knew she had to do. Not only was she was going to make sure that her daughter had nothing more to do with Richie Clayton ever again, but she was also going to watch every rotten, conniving move he made. She was determined to get the proof about what he was up to – which she was certain was going to be something far worse than the two-bob petty thieving he used to be involved in – and she would make sure that she did something about it, something that would put a stop to him once and for all.

She would get him put away.

Shirley had no qualms about what she was doing; any rights he might have had to his mother-in-law's loyalty had been forfeited a very long time ago.

During the past weeks, as she had watched and waited, Shirley's attitude to Richie Clayton had hardened even more. She hadn't actually been very surprised by the activities in which she had witnessed him taking part, she had been more sickened and revolted by them. She had always known what he was like, of course, although she had managed to bury most of that knowledge, in the self-deluding way of an anxious, doting mother protecting her beloved daughter. But it was the everyday, almost banal reality of his sordid, nasty existence that had really shocked her – and the fact that he was so open about it all.

He was shameless. He had no sense of respect for himself or for others. He was, quite simply, a disgrace of an excuse for a man.

He would appear each morning – usually at around eleven, but sometimes much later – strutting out of the main doors at the bottom of the tower block as if he were the cock of the walk. He'd be dressed in what Shirley guessed were probably expensive, but flashy-looking suits, and always with his shoes unpolished, and wearing fat, horribly gaudy ties, with his hair curling down over his collar like a cheap spiv.

Sometimes he would have a girl with him, the one Shirley had found out was, as she had suspected, Rita Thomas. It had been difficult to tell if it really was her at first, what with all the muck she had plastered on her face. But, by 'accidentally' knocking into her one day last week, while Richie had been in the newsagent's buying cigarettes, Shirley had got a good look, right up close, and had seen that, yes, it was young Rita.

God help her. She wasn't much more than a kid.

It made Shirley's stomach churn to think what that child had experienced since she'd been involved with Richie Clayton.

Later that same week, when she'd been watching him

as he sat in a café over in the red-light district in Cable Street, Shirley had seen Rita's father, Mickey Thomas, approach his daughter and try to talk to her. But rather than having a loving family chat, or even exchanging a few civil words, there had been a lot of angry shouting and desperate pleading – shouting on Rita's part and pleading on her father's. It had all come to a very unpleasant conclusion when Rita, screaming like a banshee, had thrown up her arms, shoved her father hard in the chest with both hands, and, the crowning insult, had spat in his face.

Mickey Thomas had walked away, head bowed, a defeated man. Since then, Shirley had seen no more of him. She could only suppose that Rita's family had abandoned her to the sordid life she had chosen: living in a tiny room in a house in Upper North Street, and working on the streets for Richie Clayton. That family must have been as dejected as Lorna.

Shirley didn't blame the girl; Rita was young, foolish, and, as she herself knew from bitter experience, Richie could certainly turn on the charm when he wanted to. She didn't even blame Rita's parents. Shirley of all people understood how hard it was to tell your child what to do – even if you were only trying to guide them through life in the most gentle and caring of ways, they would still do what they wanted.

No, she could do no more than sympathise with them, and imagine the 'if onlys' that those poor people were putting themselves through, just as she had done, when Lorna had been so determined to marry the revolting bit of work that was Richie Clayton.

On other mornings, Shirley would watch him emerging alone from the tower block, although he would still follow his usual routine: breakfast at a café on the East India Dock Road, then into his silver Zephyr, either to check up on Rita and the four other girls she thought were working for him in Cable Street, or he would go and sort out some other – undoubtedly illegal – bit of business, maybe down by the docks or even as far afield as Soho.

It had not been easy for Shirley to organise her programme of spying on her son-in-law, in fact, it had taken some considerable ingenuity on her part to figure out even how to begin following him. She was, after all, a middle-aged mum, who, if she were honest, was not feeling that well at the moment, hardly James Bond material. So she'd had to come up with a plan, something plausible, that wouldn't arouse Joe's suspicion about what she was up to, and that also wouldn't be too physically trying.

Then it occurred to her: she'd follow him by car.

The only trouble was, she didn't have one. Not many women did in Poplar. Nor, for that matter, did that many men.

Joe had actually taught Shirley to drive a few years ago, when Lorna was still at school, a rare thing for women to achieve in those parts. He had even gone as far as looking for a little runabout for her own personal use. But not wanting him to waste his hard-earned money on her, or to be seen as a snob by her neighbours, Shirley had claimed to have found driving a waste of time. There were buses at the top of the street, for goodness' sake, and at least two markets within easy walking distance. What more could she want?

So, to fulfil her plan, she had to become a born-again, really enthusiastic motorist. And that's exactly what she'd done.

Claiming it would be oh so useful as she hadn't been

feeling at all well lately – and that bit hadn't been a lie; she and Joe both knew she hadn't been right since before Christmas – she'd gone on to argue that a car would be absolutely ideal for picking up Lorna from Mile End Station, when she came home from work on dark, freezing-cold evenings.

But Joe hadn't co-operated, and had, at first, been a bit put out by the very idea. His was adamant: if Shirley needed anything, he would be there for her, especially if she was feeling poorly again, and the Lorna argument carried no weight at all. Not only was a big girl like her perfectly capable of getting the bus along Burdett Road, it wasn't even as if she were travelling alone. Now she was working with Denise she had ready-made company for the journey.

But Shirley had persevered, and had finally come up with the clincher when she had said how much she would truly value having a bit of independence, that it would make her feel less like a spare part, and that would make her truly happy.

And so it was that after only three days of planting the idea in her husband's head – that her having a car made such a lot of sense for all concerned, and that it was actually nonsense for her not to drive – Joe had come home with what he called a safe-as-houses, no-nonsense, bomb-proof little Austin for her exclusive use that had barely made a dent in the redundancy money.

But then Joe had panicked, and had insisted on paying Billy, a solidly trustworthy mechanic he knew from the docks, to give the vehicle a final, just-in-case, who-knows-what-might-happen, let's-just-be-safe-rather-than-sorry once-over before he was eventually satisfied with it. Only then had Shirley been allowed to actually get in the thing and drive it.

Even that hadn't been the end of it. It had taken over thirty circuits around Victoria Park, with Shirley driving the car and Joe riding shotgun, to satisfy him that his wife wasn't going to crash the thing the moment she touched the accelerator pedal.

Then, and only then, had Joe finally agreed to let her go solo.

He was such a good man, and he cared so much about her, and Shirley really did love him – that's why it killed her to lie to him, but she had no choice. She had to do something about Richie Clayton, something that would stop him before it was too late, before he stretched out his tentacles and suckered their only child back into his vile world.

She had no doubt that he was perfectly capable of ruining their daughter's life utterly and completely, totally and for ever, and Shirley was not going to let that happen.

Shirley parked the little beige car in Mansell Street, turned off the engine, threw the tartan travelling rug over her legs, and poured herself some coffee from her flask.

She looked at her watch – half-twelve. So long as she was home an hour before Joe, in good time to make his tea, she was prepared to wait for as long as it took.

'Ready to go to lunch?' Lorna asked, tapping on Denise's desk to attract her attention.

'I'm not very hungry to tell you the truth, Lorn.'

'Nor am I, but I wouldn't mind going out for a walk. How about you?'

'Good idea.' Denise tossed the pile of post she'd been half-heartedly sorting onto her desk and levered herself up out of her chair. 'Let's go over to Soho Square and get a coffee in Gino's.'

The girls hunkered down into their coats, heads down against the wind, and arms linked, as they pushed their way through the lunchtime crowds, determined to make the most of their precious hour away from work – their precious hour trying to make sense of things without the distraction of having some idiot standing over them wanting an answer to some meaningless question *as soon as possible, if you don't mind.*

But it wasn't easy.

'We're a right miserable-looking pair,' said Lorna, catching sight of their grim reflections as they passed a shop boasting a *Maxi Winter Sale!* of *Gorgeous! One Off! Mini Dresses!* at *Never To Be Beaten Prices*!

'Are you surprised, Lorn? Let's face facts here: you're separated from your husband, a bloke who not only happens to be one of the nastiest bastards ever born, but, oh yeah, this is a nice touch, he's my half-brother, and he's abused my sister in the worst possible way anyone could ever come up with. Even the worst possible pervert on this earth. And now – hoo-bloody-ray – she's run off God knows where, and I think my mum's about to have a nervous breakdown.'

'Sorry.'

'What're you apologising for? You're one of the arsehole's bloody victims.'

'Don't say that, Den. I won't think of myself in that way. I might have done once, but I'm stronger now. Now I'm away from him, out of his clutches, not having to listen to him telling me I'm worth less than a bit of rubbish day in day out. No, he's lost his power over me. It used to be that everything he did to me made me weaker, but not any more. Now it's as though I can see him for what he is: a pathetic, pitiful coward. It's not me who's weak any more, it's him. I can stand up to him. I know I can. I'd look him in the eye and –'

Denise was horrified. 'You're not telling me you'd ever want to see him again, surely?'

'No, but I wouldn't mind creeping up behind him and bending a great big heavy frying pan right over his head.'

'That sounds tempting, and, do you know what, if I thought it would bring our Chantalle back, I'd be more than happy to volunteer for the job myself.'

'You'd have to get in the queue behind me, Den.'

'Seeing Terry?' asked Lorna absently, as she stared at the bare-armed, darkly handsome man, wrestling with the hissing, steaming espresso machine.

'Not tonight.'

'That's five nights in a row you've blown him out.'

'Yeah, I know, but what with worrying about Chantalle and everything, I've been more concerned with keeping Mum company, trying to keep up her spirits and that, rather than worrying about how Terry's doing.'

'That's all very thoughtful of you, and I know she must be really going through it, but can't your dad sit with her?'

Denise looked at Lorna as if she'd just lost her senses. 'Dad? Are you kidding? He's about as much use as a one-legged man in an arse-kicking contest.'

'It's not easy to disagree with you on that count, Den, because to be truthful, apart from my dad, I've not met many men who are much use. But Terry, he's a good bloke. A really nice feller. Don't go neglecting him, or you might wind up regretting it.'

'He can look after himself.'

'I'm sure he can, but I mean it: don't make the mistake of taking him for granted, Den, or you'll lose him. And decent blokes like him don't come along that often.'

Shirley's supposition had been right: Richie did have four other girls as well as Rita working for him. Admittedly they looked a bit older – and a bit rougher, if she were honest – than young Rita, but they still weren't that much more than kids. And look at what they were doing: working on the streets, risking disease, unplanned babies, and God alone knew what sort of treatment at the hands of dirty old men – men old enough to be their fathers, if not their grandfathers.

And it wasn't only that – as if that weren't bad enough. Shirley had noticed something else going on. It was something she wanted to be sure about, because, if she was right, it didn't mean that Richie Clayton was any more disgusting than she'd thought he was – she'd always known that about him – but she would have something on him that could put him away for a very long time. Because that something was drug dealing.

It wasn't a very comfortable thing for a decent woman such as Shirley to admit about the world, but she knew that as far as running prostitutes was concerned the local law didn't seem that bothered. Just taking a casual look at this street said it all: pimps were openly putting girls to work, and where was it? It was just around the corner from the police station. No one in the flats across the road was batting an eyelid about the carryings on, and the cafés were serving up their meat pie and two veg followed by syrup pudding and custard as if everything was perfectly normal.

Shirley could only be grateful that she had avoided Richie Clayton's world up until now; she only wished the same could have been said for Lorna.

She watched as Richie came out of one of the cafés and spoke to one of the girls; he then showed out to a well-built, but pale-looking man standing under the arches, and crossed the street to speak to him.

She waited a few moments to make sure that Richie was absorbed in conversation with the man, then she snatched the rug from her legs, hurriedly tied an old paisley headscarf over her neat, blonded hair, and pulled on a shapeless rayon mac. It was a coat she had bought especially, in Watney Street market, a place where she never usually shopped, where she wasn't known as a woman who would never wear such an unfashionable garment. Next, she heaved two bulging bags off the back seat, bags full of odds and ends she'd brought with her from her own larder – the final touch in the disguise that she knew would make her invisible to the likes of Richie Clayton and the punters who frequented the area.

She took a deep breath, locked the car, and crossed over into Cable Street.

With her shoulders bowed, no trace of her usual, carefully applied make-up, and with her eyes fixed firmly on the pavement, Shirley shuffled along in the dowdy, flat, zip-up boots she'd bought from a dusty window display in a run-down branch of Bata's.

Making sure everyone could hear the efforts of her progress, Shirley came to a wheezing halt by one of Richie's girls.

'Hello, dear,' she mumbled, a perfect picture of down-trodden womanhood. 'I hope you're planning to get yourself inside in the warm soon. You'll catch your death standing about in that skirt. And there's some nasty germs around at the minute.'

The girl tossed her head, making an obvious show of ignoring her. But that didn't matter to Shirley; all she wanted was to be seen as a worn-out, elderly woman, so she could watch, listen and learn, and maybe even spread a few traces of doubt in at least one girl's mind about what she was doing with her young life.

'Been terrible weather,' she said, making a real performance of transferring her shopping from one woolly gloved hand to another, all the while keeping an eye on Richie, who was still standing under the railway arches talking animatedly to the pale-faced man.

'See him, the bloke over there,' Shirley said to the girl, waggling her head in Richie's direction. 'Bet you don't know what he is.' She didn't wait for an answer; she didn't expect one. 'He's what you call –' she lowered her voice conspiratorially – 'a pimp. And, do you know what he does for a living? I'll tell you. He gets young girls going on the street for him. Doing all sorts of, you know, *things*. With strange men. For money. Then he pockets the lot!'

She spoke as if she were sharing a truly surprising secret with the girl. 'Can you believe it? Who'd be daft enough to have a bloke do that to her?'

She took a moment, then added slyly: 'I know you're probably just waiting here for a friend, dear, probably planning on having a nice little bite of lunch somewhere, but I'd be very careful hanging round these parts if I was you. Because it's not only men like him, you see, darling.

There are some real tough men round here. Men who have run this place for years, Maltese fellers who wouldn't think twice about putting a knife in someone's guts. I'm telling you, they won't tolerate the likes of him, that one over there, getting in on the act. If he's not careful, you know what'll happen, don't you?'

Shirley leaned closer, throwing caution to the wind, no longer caring if the girl might notice she wasn't actually a dear little old lady – not that she was likely to, as she was doing everything to avoid eye contact with Shirley.

'They'll have him,' she breathed into the girl's ear. 'Just grab hold of him one night when he least expects it. Then they'll do him in, chop him up in little bits, and feed him to the pigs on a farm somewhere, or chuck him down on the marshes for the crabs to pick over.'

Worried she might have gone too far, Shirley straightened up. 'You see all about that sort of thing every week in the Sunday papers. Shocking.'

The girl sneered and stepped away from Shirley, obscuring her view of the arches.

On the pretext of easing her aching muscles, Shirley put down the shopping bags, stuck her fists into the small of her back and stretched her neck, craning it until she regained sight of the two men doing their business.

She saw Richie take a wad of money from the big, pale-faced man and then hand him a thick packet from his inside pocket in return – exactly as he had done with a procession of other men the day before.

There had been a lot of gossip on the estate about Richie Clayton being involved with drug dealing, but then there always was gossip in any small, tight-knit community where privacy was a luxury that had to be fought for. But here was the proof of her own eyes.

Shirley could only wonder how many lives her so-called son-in-law was responsible for ruining, and could only hope that her little talk might frighten this young, misguided girl into at least thinking about what she had got herself mixed up in, and that she might decide that the best thing she could do was to get herself as far away from Richie Clayton as was humanly possible.

'I don't believe this,' said Shirley to the girl. 'Do you know what? I think that man over there's selling drugs. In broad daylight. I'm going right round the police station to tell them.'

The girl snorted unattractively, pulled herself up to her full, high-heeled five feet nine and glared down her foundation-caked nose at Shirley. 'Look, I don't know what church or other do-gooders' mob you're from, Grandma – we get so many of your type round here it's hard to keep up – but I wouldn't bother if I was you. The bloke he's just done the deal with is Jimmy Kramer.'

Shirley looked blank.

'DI Kramer?'

Still she looked blank.

'Detective Inspector. He's an off-duty copper.'

Shirley blinked. 'He's what?'

The girl laughed maliciously. 'And you can save your breath with all your snidey remarks and all. You can't shame me into being a good little girl. I screw men for money. All right? But I screw him over there, Richie Clayton, whenever and wherever he fancies it, because I love him.'

The girl took a packet of cigarettes from out of the cap sleeve of her cheap nylon blouse and lit one with icy cold, shaking fingers. Then she stared hard, defiantly, right into

Shirley's eyes. 'I don't even care that he brags he's done it with his own little sister. In fact, I find it quite exciting. How about *that* then, Grandma? What would they make of that up the Mission Hall or wherever you come from? Send him straight to hell, would they?'

Without saying another word, Shirley picked up her bags and hurried away, the girl's words crashing and ricocheting around in her head.

With his own sister? That's what she had said.

Shirley had to get back to the car; she wouldn't give the mocking little madam the satisfaction of seeing that her legs were about to give way with the shock.

Terry stood with his arm round Denise in the sound-proofed practice studio, waiting for the rest of the Spanners to finish tuning up.

He pulled her closer to him. 'Don't worry, Den, you'll hear from her soon. You know your Chantalle, she always lands on her feet.'

Denise wriggled out of his arms, pulling away from him. 'Leave off, Terry. Go on, they're waiting for you.'

'I'm not leaving you like this. I can see you've been crying again. Look at your eyes.'

'There's nothing wrong with my eyes. I'm tired, that's all. Really tired. In fact, I think I'll go home. I shouldn't have come here in the first place. I don't like to think of Mum sitting there in the chair just smoking and drinking tea all night.'

Terry shrugged. 'If that's how you want it, Den.'

He was going to add – *So we'll forget we haven't seen each other for nearly a week, shall we? And that we were meant to be going out for something to eat afterwards. And, if you ask me, it's a pity your mum never worried so much about any of you lot before. Because perhaps then all this business with Richie and Chantalle wouldn't have happened.*

But, true as all that might well have been, there was no point saying any of it. It would only start another row, and rowing was all they seemed to be doing lately. If Denise hadn't been in such a state over her sister being missing, he might have had the guts to pack her in. But he couldn't, not while all this was still going on. Sodding Richie Clayton. How could one bloke cause so much trouble?

Because he was a useless, selfish bastard, that's how.

Terry clenched his fists, his nails digging hard into his palms, as he watched Denise pull on her coat and then disappear through the double doors.

He couldn't help himself; despite everything, he loved her; loved her more than was good for him, and, if he were honest, loved her a lot more than he liked her.

Especially at this precise moment.

Richie sat at the window table in Lil's, too lost in a greed-filled world of his own to notice Shirley, who was now sitting opposite the café in her car, staring across at him. Neither did he notice Antonio Diaz and three of his heavies, who were studying his every move from their table over by the counter.

All Richie could see was money, the money he was counting into neat piles onto the tea-stained Formica table in front of him, and all he could hear was the sound of the pound notes as he peeled them, with a snap, one by one, from the fat wad that DI Jimmy Kramer, the man under the arch, had handed him in exchange for the drugs.

It was unfortunate on Richie's part that he was so preoccupied. If he had been paying a bit more attention to what was going on around him, he might have heard Diaz – a man who had decided that he had wasted quite enough time waiting for Clayton, the cocky little fucker, to bring in some decent-looking toms for him to poach – instructing one of his men to get another message through to David Fuller in the nick.

This time it was an urgent message advising him that a certain individual, by the name of Richie Clayton, was now openly taking over yet another part of Fuller's drugs business – and doing so while he, Fuller, was rotting away in Her Majesty's establishment at Parkhurst. Worse, it was no longer nicking the trade with a few no-marks on the estates, he was now taking over a part of Fuller's business that included one of his very best customers – DI Jimmy Kramer – a customer who came with the very special bonus of offering a handy line in quasi-official protection that was second to none; a customer it would make very good sense for Fuller to look after, to keep safely for himself for when he got out.

And, the message from Diaz would continue, where were the men who were meant to be minding Fuller's business for him? Not only was Clayton taking the piss out of him, so were Fuller's so-called friends who were meant to be looking after his interests while he was otherwise engaged. It was obvious to everyone on the outside what the lazy sods were doing – they were staying at home in their nice warm flats and letting the customers come to them. And that not only meant that the regulars would be neglected – all ready for Clayton to take them over, as easily as shooting fish in a barrel – but also that the only customers they would keep were kids. No self-respecting grown-up would be seen visiting a flat of a known dealer. Trouble was, kids had big mouths, especially when they had a few uppers inside them.

They were all making a fool of David Fuller and in Antonio Diaz's humble opinion, and speaking as a respectful friend, that was why it was time for Davey to put a stop to all the liberty-taking – particularly from that amateur hood Richie Clayton, before there was any more damage done to his reputation. And if he could be of any help in the matter, then he, Antonio Diaz, would be only too pleased to be of assistance.

Diaz took the navy silk handkerchief from his top pocket and wiped his forehead; it made his already high blood pressure soar, having to waste even a moment speaking about the piece of scum who had been fool enough to threaten him.

It was bad timing on Richie's part that he chose that exact moment to lift his head and notice Antonio Diaz.

With a broad, mocking grin, Richie waved a wide fan of banknotes in his direction. 'Good to see my business doing so well, eh?'

Diaz turned his head away and hissed through his teeth, 'Get that message through now, and just make sure everyone knows that Fuller's got it in for that whoreson.'

Two days after he had done his deal with Richie Clayton, Detective Inspector Jimmy Kramer, a picture of pale-faced, thick-set, crop-haired brute force, was about to push, or rather barge his way through the swing doors of the Sail and Compass, when he felt a hand grip his shoulder.

He spun around, ready to lash out with his fists, but

he could only stare in disbelief at the person who had dared touch him. It was a short, wispy-haired bloke in a dark, sober suit and old-fashioned tortoiseshell spectacles, who looked as if he would have been more at home in an accountant's office than standing outside a rough, dockside East End boozer.

'What?' growled Kramer, even more surprised when the man didn't remove his hand.

'I have a message for you, from Mr Fuller.'

And his voice! He sounded like an undertaker who'd swallowed a whole bag of plums. Kramer wouldn't have been surprised if he'd whipped out a bowler hat, a rolled umbrella, and a bloody pigskin portfolio. He was a City brief, it was the only explanation.

'He has requested that you conduct your *business* with no one other than one of his representatives.'

'Leave off. You having a laugh? There hasn't been one of *Mr* Fuller's *representatives* anywhere near here for months. We've all been having to travel bloody miles till this new geezer showed up.'

'Things are changing. Going back to how they were. And Mr –' he consulted the tiny scrap of paper that he was holding in his hand – 'Clayton will no longer be operating from the arches.'

'Oh yeah?'

'Yes. It's all being arranged. And Mr Fuller would also appreciate it if you returned to your old business relationship with him . . . with his representative . . . as soon as possible. As we speak, in fact.'

Kramer pulled a face of mock fear. 'What if I don't? You won't hurt me, will you?'

'No, DI Kramer, but the associates of a certain Maltese gentleman have been kind enough to agree to oversee the smooth transition of things, until they return to the status quo, and I can't speak for them, I'm afraid.'

The veins in Kramer's neck bulged with fury as he watched the dapper little man turn on his heel and walk off into the night as if he were strolling, at his leisure, through the noble byways and alleys of the Square Mile.

He'd show David fucking Fuller what it meant to try to put the frighteners on him.

Much later that night Richie Clayton was stretched out on his bed thinking about the trade he was building up with the likes of Jimmy Kramer – trade he'd been only too glad to mop up when Fuller's blokes got lazy – but he was also wondering if he should stick with knocking out LSD and speed, or if it was time to move on to something a little more ambitious.

He'd been thinking for a while now about the possibility of moving into big-time dealing: shifting proper, grown-up quantities of some of the serious gear, and tonight he'd made a tentative first move in just that direction, which could open up all sorts of exciting opportunities.

He and Rita had been taken to a new, members-only nightclub in Soho, by Bernie Watts, a well-off wholesale greengrocer, who, for some unfathomable reason, favoured Pamela Logan, definitely Richie's ropiest brass. In fact, Bernie Watts was her best and most regular customer. He would turn up like clockwork, twice a week, after the early morning market had closed, driving his big, shiny Daimler, and then reward himself for a job of work well done, with a job well done by chubby-thighed Pamela Logan.

And yet there he was in the nightclub, sitting with

Nina, his wife, a good-looking woman, who had real class about her.

Still, it wasn't for Richie to question a punter's tastes, and the evening at the glamorous club had turned out to be an eye-opener in more ways than one, especially once Bernie had pointed out a man to him with almost awe-struck discretion.

Richie had studied the man, and had been gripped when he saw just how powerful someone could get in the dealing game – if they got stuck in to it big time.

OK, Richie wasn't exactly messing about selling little bits and pieces as it was, but he was greedy for more. He wanted the money the big dealer had, the power, and, not least of all, he wanted the respect that man had so obviously demanded.

The trouble was, it would mean getting involved with some really hard people. Richie didn't mind the violence involved, of course, but only if it meant that it was other people getting hurt.

Yet despite his reservations, his greed, and all the Scotch and champagne he'd consumed, eventually gave him the courage he needed to approach the man. The moment Bernie and his wife had made their way onto the dance floor, Richie left Rita giggling into her drink, and went over to speak to him.

The man had been a bit standoffish at first, hadn't seemed that interested in talking, but Richie put that down to natural caution on the man's part, and had persevered asking him for advice and even for a few possible contacts.

The man would have none of it, and had insisted on keeping his distance, even getting a little irritated, but Richie had eventually persuaded him to at least accept the damp cocktail napkin on which Richie had scribbled down his address. Only then had he excused himself and made his way back to Rita.

As he'd sat down next to her, Richie had been beaming; delighted with his progress. He had made the first move on the road to real success.

Had all that really happened only a few hours ago?

He rubbed his hand over his eyes and looked at the dial of the alarm clock glowing in the dark.

Nearly half-three. He'd usually have drifted off to sleep at least an hour ago, but his brain was buzzing with all his plans.

He also needed the lavatory, as he was a bit more pissed than he usually allowed himself to get when he was out doing anything to do with work, but he had enjoyed seeing that snooty little bitch of a waitress in the nightclub come over all smiley and fluttery – obviously well impressed – when he had ordered the second, then the third bottle of champagne, and had told her to keep the change. *Nearly six quid!*

Richie had liked playing the big man, liked showing that he was really getting there.

He rolled over and punched his pillows into shape. His nose wrinkled; they had an unpleasantly musty whiff of staleness about them. Maybe he should find himself a new bird – a classy one, not some little scrubber like Rita, one more like Bernie's old woman. Get her to move in with him, and let her look after the place a bit. Change the bedclothes and that.

He threw his arm across his face.

Lorna always kept the place decent enough, and she would have looked the part on his arm at that club tonight. The stupid bitch could have had the life of Riley if she'd stayed with him, if she hadn't gone running back home like a frightened schoolkid.

He rolled onto his back again. Fuck her. Fuck all of them. He didn't need birds, they needed him. Richie Clayton.

He was just slipping his hand into his underpants, half dozing off, half woozy-headed from all the booze and dope flowing around his system, when he could have sworn he heard the front door opening.

It was the door.

Talk of the devil: it must be bloody Lorna.

Fantastic.

He smirked to himself: he wouldn't say no to her. He quite fancied a bit of the other with the silly whore, and it'd save him doing the job himself . . .

He hauled himself upright and stretched out for the switch on the bedside lamp.

He never reached it.

The first blow to the side of his head knocked him out stone cold. It was the third blow that killed him.

'Sorry,' Sergeant Murray said with a world-weary sigh. 'Can you repeat that, please?'

It was nearly four o'clock in the morning, and this was all he needed. As if the drunks in the cells hadn't been bad enough tonight. He'd just got himself a brew and a plate of milk chocolate wholewheats, and was about to settle down – at last – at the duty desk with the crossword, and now he had himself a mumbler. He knew it'd be some jealous old goat, with some trumped-up complaint against their better-off neighbours, who didn't have the guts to come right out and say so in daylight, but had stayed awake bearing grudges and had decided to disturb him with their tales of exaggerated slights and imagined disorderly conduct. That's what it usually was at this time.

That or someone with a missing husband or wife, whom they wanted tracing, but without the embarrassment of actually having to come in and report it, and so avoiding identifying themselves as the shamed and abandoned spouse. 'They'd mutter on something about being a *concerned friend*, who'd *rather not give my name, thank you.* But expect the force to sort it out for them all the same.

The great British public? Great British bleeding nuisances, more like.

'Look,' the sergeant said a little impatiently, 'if you think that talking like that to disguise your voice makes any sense, let me tell you: there's no point. You're wasting your time. This is the local nick, not the Secret flaming Service. We've not got the phones tapped, and we've not got someone listening in on another line.'

He sighed again, bored and uninterested. 'You can speak quite freely to me.' *Or you can go and boil your head if you prefer.*

He dunked one of the wholewheats into his tea, bit off half of the soggy chocolate biscuit and waited. They'd either cough up or hang up.

There was a brief silence, and then a slightly husky, slightly effeminate voice began speaking.

'There's been a murder,' the person said. 'A local drugs dealer. Do you want the details?'

Sergeant Murray took a gulp of tea to clear his mouth, snatched up a pen and started scribbling as if his life depended on it.

Murder? Drugs dealer?

He could only wish that the phones *had* been bloody bugged; if he got any of this wrong he'd be for it in the morning.

Chapter 17

'So, let me see,' said Detective Sergeant Mackenzie. 'How long exactly is it that you've been living back here with your parents, Mrs Clayton?'

Lorna, her hands shaking as she gripped her teacup, raised her head and looked through red-rimmed eyes at the policeman seated across from her on the other side of the fireplace.

'Since around Christmas time.' Her voice was low, barely audible. 'You can go out in the kitchen and ask Mum. Or Dad. Either of them. They'll tell you.'

DS Mackenzie affected a puzzled frown. 'We already know you've been staying here, Mrs Clayton, from the time of the Chantalle Parker investigation, so why do you sound as if you don't think we believe you?'

'Why should I think that? I only meant that they'd know the exact date.'

'Why's that then, love?' It was the more junior officer speaking, a female DC; she was standing up behind her boss, who, earlier, on being shown into the living room by Joe, had taken the only other armchair as an unspoken matter of right. 'Special day for them, was it?'

'They said it was a great day. The day they'd both been waiting for.' Lorna looked away as her eyes filled, yet again, with hot salty tears. 'A day to celebrate.'

'Really?' She sounded casual. 'Didn't they like your husband then? Not care for him very much?'

Lorna nodded. 'That's right. They both hated me being with him. I reckon they knew he was a no-good all along.

When I think back, I think they despised him from the very beginning.'

She paused to swipe her nose with the back of her hand, and, as she did so, she realised what she's said.

She looked up anxiously, her gaze going from the man to the woman. 'But they never said anything to me about him. Not at the time. I mean they never tried to influence me, or interfere, or to try and get me to leave him or anything like that. They knew I'd come to my senses eventually. And they're good people. They wouldn't hurt anyone. Anyone round here will tell you that.'

Lorna stopped speaking and gulped down some of the now almost cold tea. She was just making things worse. The way she was going on, she was making it sound as if her mum and dad really had it in for him, as if her dad had gone round there in the middle of the night and had done him in with his docker's hook. But how would they know that her dad, huge as he was, would never do anything like that? Know he was too gentle, far too gentle, to harm a fly? That he was a real man, a decent man? Nothing even remotely like Richie.

'And what made you –' it was DS Mackenzie again, this time making a big show of consulting his notes – '*come to your senses*, as you put it?'

'He was a bully. Especially when he'd had too much to drink. And he pushed me too far, and I had enough. So I left.'

'How did he push you too far?'

'I told you: he was a bully.'

'OK, we'll leave it at that – for the moment.'

He paused, playing for a few moments with his pencil: first tapping it on his knee, then against his teeth. Only when he saw Lorna actually begin to squirm, did he continue.

'Now, Mrs Clayton, what can you tell us about the large quantity of what we suspect are illegal substances that we found at your flat?'

All these questions; Lorna was beginning to feel dizzy. 'I told you: it's not my flat, it's his, or rather it *was*. I suppose it's the council's again now. Aw, I don't know. I live here – here, with my mum and dad. This is my home, not that place. That was never my home. Not really.'

'OK. Let's move on again,' he said stiffly. 'Do you know anyone, apart from yourself, of course, who has fallen out with your husband recently? Maybe someone who might have something to do with those substances we found in your – sorry, in *his* – flat?'

This time Lorna said nothing, she just stared down into her lap, and moved her cup round and round in its saucer.

'Well, Mrs Clayton?'

'I was just thinking.'

'Anyone at all? Anyone who used to visit regularly?'

Slowly Lorna lifted her chin until she was looking at the woman. 'How did he die?'

'You mean no one's explained yet?' she said, sounding genuinely surprised.

Lorna gnawed at her bottom lip. 'When the policemen came round from the local station to tell us what had happened – early it was, just as me and Dad were getting ready to leave for work this morning – they said he'd been found dead. That it looked as if he's been . . . murdered.' She swallowed hard. 'My legs sort of folded under me, and I passed out. When I came to, I was stretched out on the settee over there.' She lifted her chin, indicating the sofa that stood against the far wall. 'And the policemen weren't there any more. At first I thought I must have been dreaming, having a nightmare. But then I saw Mum and Dad's faces, and I knew it was true. He'd been murdered.'

'And then?' the female officer asked gently.

'Dad said there'd be a lot of questions, things we'd have to answer, and he asked me if I wanted to know the details before the police came back to talk to me. But I said no.'

'Why was that?' Her voice was soft, caring rather than challenging.

Lorna looked away. 'Didn't think I could face it.'

'But now you've changed your mind?'

Lorna nodded at her.

'Right, the facts as we know them, are –'

Before the woman could continue, her boss interrupted her.

'His skull was bashed in, Mrs Clayton. Probably with the length of heavy wood we found on the rug beside the bed.'

His mouth curled open into an odd semi-smile, showing yellowing, uncared-for smoker's teeth.

'Funny really, it looked more like a rolling pin than a weapon. More suited to pastry making in a back kitchen than to a murder scene.'

He took another long pause, openly assessing Lorna through narrowed eyes.

'Ridiculous, it looked, like something you'd expect to see in one of those cartoon fights between a violent, drunken husband and his angry, vengeful wife.' His strange half-smile disappeared, and he continued in a slow, deliberate monotone. 'Except this wasn't make-believe, Mrs Clayton; it was real blood splattered all round that bedroom – your old bedroom. And all-too-real shattered bits of skull and flesh stuck to the wood.'

He then added briskly: 'From the violence of the blows, it's likely he died fairly quickly. And as to whether it was murder or not, I'll tell you something for nothing: if it wasn't then it was the freakiest kind of accident I've ever heard of, or the weirdest kind of suicide.'

Lorna just managed to reach the bathroom before sicking up the five cups of sugary tea that had made up the contents of her now completely empty stomach.

'That was a bit brutal, Mac,' the female officer whispered to her colleague, as they listened to the lavatory flushing, and to Shirley tending to her sobbing daughter.

'I wanted to see her reaction, Gina.'

'You always did have a way with women, you smooth-talking charmer.'

'That's enough sarcasm, thank you. Inexperienced as you are, even you should know you usually don't have to look any further than the immediate family.'

'Sorry, *sir*, and, of course, I am aware of that, but I only meant that considering the sort of business he seems to have been involved in, isn't it far more likely to be someone he's upset in some deal or other than a domestic? In fact, if you ask me, his dealing is probably the reason his wife left him in the first place.'

'Glory be, I'm working with a genius.'

She didn't rise to his taunting. 'And these are just decent, ordinary people, while he sounds a right slag, a typical –'

She suddenly stopped speaking and turned round to face the living-room door. She had heard Lorna come back into the room.

This time she had both her parents with her.

'Do you really need to ask her any more questions?' Joe said firmly, but quietly.

'Quite a few actually,' said DS Mackenzie, with an arrogant tip of his chin. 'This is a murder investigation, after all. And, like I said, a considerable amount of what we believe to be illegal drugs have been found in your daughter's flat.'

'I keep telling you: I don't live there any more.'

Joe pulled Lorna close to him as he appealed to the policeman.

'I know you've got your job to do, but is there any chance you could come back later? This has all been a terrible shock to us, and you can see how upset my wife and daughter are. I'm sure we'll be far more use to you when we've had a chance to get some rest.'

The detective sergeant snapped his notebook shut, stuffed it in his pocket, and stood up with a nod.

'All right,' he said, 'we'll be back tomorrow. Expect us some time late morning. And make sure you're all here.'

Jimmy Kramer sat at the sticky, plate-littered kitchen table, in his pigsty of a flat on the Whitechapel Road, and lit yet another cigarette from the butt of the one he had just finished smoking.

He'd called in sick, knowing he was too wound up even to think about chancing going in to work and letting slip something he shouldn't. He had a terrible temper on him, and he knew the trouble it could get him into, just as he knew he had to calm down, think things through, and take control of his situation before somebody else did it for him.

He'd got out of the shit before and he'd get out of it again, but he had to think straight, had to get his mind organised, had to work it through.

He tossed four lethal-looking black and green capsules into his mouth, picked up a bottle of vodka from the floor, and emptied the last few remaining measures into a cracked china mug that wished him *All The Best From Broadstairs* in a fancy, curlicued script. Then he swigged at the liquor, swallowing down the pills in a single gulp.

He'd be fine. He'd work it out.

Then with one of the mood swings his more junior colleagues had learned to be so wary of, Kramer threw back his head and began laughing hysterically.

Of course he could work it out – he was a bloody brilliant, fantastically experienced detective, wasn't he?

On the balcony outside the Wrights' flat the DC flashed a questioning look at her boss.

'That was . . .' she paused, '. . . very good of you, leaving them in peace like that.'

'No it wasn't,' he said, pulling up his overcoat collar as they walked towards the lifts. 'I mean, Jesus Christ, Gina, it suddenly occurred to me that there we were wasting our time wondering who got rid of some monkey little bastard, some useless piece of shit, who, from all accounts, the world's a lot better off without, when we could be in the Coach and Horses doing some serious damage to a meat pie each and a couple of pints. I've not had much more than a manky cheese and pickle roll since breakfast, and my belly's beginning to think my throat's been cut.'

Gina rolled her eyes in frustration. He might be able

to sod about taking his time with an investigation, but he didn't have to worry about getting his promotion like she did. It was always so much easier for blokes in the force. So she'd have to kid him along; persuade him that they needed to put in a few more hours, do a bit more spadework before they called it a night.

'I know what you mean, Mac, but think: it's not going to take Sabre of the bloody Yard to sort this one out, now is it? Nice tidy case, all done and dusted in no time. And wrapping up a murder *and* a drugs investigation double fast? Imagine the gold stars that'll bring in. And that never does any harm, now does it? And think of all the nice pictures of you coming out of the court – justice done for the community and all that. So let's just bite the bullet and get stuck in, eh?' She waited for his response, but when none came she added: 'And there are a good two hours till closing time.'

'Always the sensible one, eh, Gina? But there's no rush, and I can hear a light and bitter calling my name from afar.'

'But his family only live a few streets away.'

'Oh yeah?'

'Yeah. His aunt and uncle: Phyllis and Henry Parker.'

'Delightful invitation as it is – going round to see yet another grieving family – not tonight, eh, Josephine?'

The lift arrived and he went to get in, but Gina grabbed him by the arm.

He flicked impatiently, almost crossly, at her hand, but she hung on to him.

'Mac, why don't we go and have a quick word with Mrs Barker then? She only lives along the landing here.'

'Mrs who?'

'Doris Barker, the woman the station sergeant reckons runs all the fencing on the estate.'

'What, the one who no one's ever actually managed to collar for some reason?'

'Yeah, that's her.'

'Bloody hell, Gina, I know how sodding keen you are, but I am *not* getting involved with a mob of geriatric old hoisters, right? They can come out here and offer you a case of bent Scotch right under my strawberry-coloured hooter, and I would still not waste a single moment of my precious time doing uniforms' work for them. Got it?'

'Got it, *sir*. But the fact that they *haven*'t nicked her – doesn't that make you think she might be a snout? And if she is, who knows what we might find out. Women like her know what's going on in their patch – they have to – and you can guarantee what a woman of her age is going to think about drug pushers. It needn't take long. And she might have something fresh in her mind that she'll have forgotten by the morning.'

The idea that the woman might be willing to grass made sense to Mackenzie, and, loath as he was not to be heading for the pub, he gave in – albeit reluctantly.

'Maybe a few minutes wouldn't hurt, seeing as we're here.'

'Great, then after that, perhaps we could pop round to the Parkers?'

'No.'

'Well, how about going over to Clayton's flat?'

'Gina . . .'

'We could have a look at how they're getting on sifting through all his stuff.'

'Don't push your luck, sweetheart.'

* * *

Joe stood in the kitchen doorway, watching his wife buttering bread at the table.

'Did she take it for you, Joe?'

'Yeah, but she took some persuading that taking a sedative off the doctor wasn't the same as taking drugs off a bloke on a street corner.'

'She's upset, that's all; what with everything that's happened.'

'I know, but at least she's getting some rest now.'

'Thank goodness for that. She looked exhausted.'

'She's certainly been through it, poor little thing. But now he's out of the picture, it won't be long before we get our old Lorna back.'

'Thanks for doing that for me, Joe. I was frightened that if I went in her room with her I'd just sit on her bed and start crying all over again, and set her off as well.'

He gripped the sides of the doorjamb. It was all he could do to stop himself from punching the wall just thinking about what had happened, what that evil pig had got their child mixed up in.

'She's done enough crying over these past few years, Shirley, and that bastard's still making her cry even when he's stone-cold dead in the mortuary.'

Shirley said nothing, so Joe just stood and watched the tranquil domestic scene being acted out in front of him: his wife getting on with things – as she always did.

Most people would have seen nothing out of the ordinary, but just standing there watching her making him the ham sandwich that she'd insisted he would have to eat to keep up his strength, and brewing a pot of tea for them to share, made Joe's heart swell with love for her. She was still as beautiful as the day he'd met her, but there was a pain in her eyes that tortured him. If only he could take that away for her, he would be a truly happy man.

'Shirl.'

'Yes, love?' she said turning her head so that she could look at him over her shoulder.

'Is there anything . . .'

'Anything what?'

'Anything, you know . . . that you want to tell me?'

'There is one thing.'

'Yeah?'

'If you don't go in the other room and sit down in the armchair and eat this sandwich, and relax for at least ten minutes, then you'll have me to deal with.'

He took the plate from her and kissed her gently on the forehead. She was an amazing woman; with everything she had to worry her, here she was acting as if she didn't have a care in the world except making sure that everyone else was all right.

Doris Barker stood on her doorstep, looking the two coppers up and down, thinking what she should do, but, in the end, she knew she had no choice. Even though the last thing anyone could ever accuse her of was being a grass – and it certainly wasn't her way to speak ill of the dead – for Richie Clayton she would make an exception on both counts. He was a special case, and special cases needed special treatment.

'Come on then, in you come. I've just had a cup of tea, so if you don't mind, I won't make another one.'

Mackenzie flashed a look at Gina that told her she'd pay for this later. Then he smiled a sickly smile at Doris Barker, and nodded his thanks as she ushered them through to her kitchen.

'You sit there,' she said, directing them towards two low wooden chairs, and perched herself high above them on a stool by the breakfast bar. Doris Barker was nobody's fool, and she intended to keep the upper hand, both literally and metaphorically, all through this particular meeting.

She looked down at them and began.

'I'll tell you all about Richie Clayton.'

'Make sure you note this down. Accurately,' Mackenzie barked at his female colleague, winning himself a look of contempt for his discourtesy from Doris Barker.

'Tell me if I go too fast for you, dear,' she said to Gina by way of making up for the man's bad manners. She might not like coppers – even well-behaved, young female ones – but Doris couldn't abide rudeness.

'Thanks, Mrs Barker, I will.'

'Well, let's begin. He was a thief, a drug peddler, and a pimp. He had girls working for him down Cable Street.'

She nodded towards the notebook. 'And I mean girls, not women. They get them hooked on that rubbish, and then they've had it. No chance of getting away from them then. I know that young Rita Thomas's mother has been driven half out of her mind since her girl got involved with Clayton. And I know she wouldn't mind me telling you, because she's tried going to the police about it already.' She dabbed at her nose, surprisingly daintily for such a big woman, with a lace-edged hankie. 'For all the good that did her. Anyway, I should have asked earlier but I'd still like to know: why are you talking to me?'

Gina smiled politely at her. 'It's because the Wrights are your neighbours, Mrs Barker. We wondered if you'd seen or noticed anything . . .' She shrugged. 'Anything unusual maybe. Say, for instance, if –'

Mackenzie narrowed his eyes maliciously at Gina, butted in, and went rattling on with impatient haste: 'The reason we're speaking to you is that the person who reported the incident was female. Clayton was involved with drugs. And,' he improvised, wanting to get the interview over as soon as possible, and before the Coach and Horses closed for the night, 'as your opinion of that particular trade is well known locally, and is now more than obvious to me as well, you seem an obvious person to speak to.'

Doris Barker took a moment to consider the ignorant man sitting in front of her, in *her* kitchen, with his number nines planted on her nice clean floor. What a prat he was. Still, it was all in a good cause.

'I don't talk to the law very often, or very willingly – no one does round this way – but you're right, I don't like drugs or anyone who has anything to do with them. I've got a daughter to think of. And I don't want that filthy stuff being sold round here. So I'll tell you all about the rubbish the likes of him have introduced on to this estate, shall I?'

She didn't want him telling her what he did and didn't want to hear from her, so she didn't wait for his answer.

'You know that kid who jumped off the top of the Eastern?'

Mackenzie nodded, obviously bored, although he had no idea what she was going on about.

'He was on drugs. That LSD they reckon it was. And I heard that Richie Clayton was tied up with money trouble, a lot of money trouble, right up to his neck in it. He owed a big supplier of the disgusting stuff. The bloke who sold it to him so he could sell it off to the kids round here.

Our kids. And the word is, it's more than something to do with that Fuller and the ones he's left to carry on his so-called business for him.'

'Fuller?' asked Gina, looking up from her note-taking with a questioning shake of her head.

'Do you mean David Fuller?' said Mackenzie, leaning forward.

'Yeah, that's him. Got banged up a while back. He brought the drugs round here in the first place. There's a copper from up the West End, Jameson's his name. Strange little bloke – very neat fingernails; look like they've been shaped with a file.' She shuddered at the thought of such an unmanly aberration. 'But never mind all that. He's the one you want to talk to. He'll tell you all about David Fuller.'

Mackenzie was now looking very much more interested in what Doris Barker had to say.

'And what do you know about David Fuller, Mrs Barker?' he asked.

'Nothing, but like I told you, if you need to know about him, you ask Jameson. Now, if you'll excuse me, I've got some clearing up to do in here.'

Looking round the gleaming, pristine kitchen, they knew they were being dismissed, and that any further questioning of the blunt-speaking woman would be a waste of all their time, so they kept what they had left of their dignity and said their goodbyes.

As Doris bolted and chained her front door behind them, she puffed out her cheeks and shook her head.

A lot of what she had just told the coppers was a complete load of old fanny – made up and embellished from a mixture of gossip, hearsay, and rumour. But so what? If it had allowed her to bring that animal Fuller into the picture alongside Richie Clayton then it had been worthwhile. Good riddance to the pair of them, the death-peddling scum.

'In you get, Chantalle,' said Ray, his soft northern tones cajoling and soothing, as he held open the passenger door of the sleek, low-slung Jensen sports car.

Chantalle did so, exactly as he'd taught her, with an elegant, sideways glide.

He smiled to himself as she leaned forward and let her stole drop from her shoulders, while she studied her reflection in her handbag mirror, carefully checking that her make-up and teeth were perfect.

He'd done well with this one; she was a fast learner. She was even beginning to sound the part, losing what had been to his ears the nerve-jangling edge of her broad, twanging cockney accent. She was no Mandy Rice-Davies maybe – he couldn't help it, he still preferred blondes, despite the problems that little madam had caused everyone – but she did have more than a touch of the Christine Keeler about her. She was earthy in a sexy, groin-stirring sort of a way. He might even get a taste for redheads if they all had bodies on them like this one.

Chantalle put the mirror back in her bag, and, as she tucked it down by her feet, she felt something silky on the floor.

'And what are these?' she asked in her newly acquired, more neutral accent, and dangled a pair of tiny, scarlet lace panties between her thumb and finger.

Without missing a beat, Ray took them from her, stuffed them into the pocket of his green velvet jacket, waggled his eyebrows and grinned.

'That Anita . . .'

'Are you really expecting me to believe they belong to your wife?'

'Chantalle,' he reprimanded her as he turned the key and the car purred into powerful, throbbing life, 'I'm shocked. Who else would they belong to?'

'You're a git, Ray,' Chantalle tutted amiably.

She was speaking to him, but she was looking out of the side window at a huddle of girls who were all firing envious looks at her, as they stood in the drizzle at the bus stop, all wishing they were her.

She enjoyed the feeling, just as she was beginning to enjoy her job. She had been so relieved when she discovered she wasn't pregnant, and so pleased with all the new things Ray had bought her, and the nice little flat he had moved her into, that everything seemed if not perfect then certainly more than OK. She didn't much like what she usually wound up doing with most of the men she was hired to accompany for the evening, but she did like the attention they paid her beforehand. And the presents they gave her. All in all, it wasn't a bad life. Not really.

She turned and smiled at him. 'You must take me for a right berk, Ray. I'm not some little innocent, just off the banana boat, remember.'

'Language, Chantalle. Remember our gentlemen enjoy the company of ladies, not of foul-mouthed little guttersnipes.'

'So sorry, Raymond,' she drawled, sounding for all the world like Eliza Doolittle after Professor Higgins had finished with her.

'And gentlemen don't appreciate ladies being sarcastic either.'

His admonishment was half-hearted. Chantalle had proved too much of a success with his clients for him to risk upsetting her. And with her feisty nature he knew she'd be perfectly capable of telling him to fuck off, and then disappear for good off to Park Lane with one of the Arabs who seemed so keen on her. She'd probably do that one day in any case, but for now she was earning him plenty so he wanted to keep her sweet.

'You look lovely this evening, Chantalle. Black suits you.'

'Thank you, Ray; how kind of you to say so.'

He flicked her a sideways glance, checking for any hint of mockery. But no, she was just slipping back into role. Good girl.

'I told you escorting was perfect for someone like you, Chantalle,' he said. 'And I know you'll love the gentleman you're going to meet tonight. I'm taking you there personally, because it's a bit special.'

'I wondered why you didn't just send a cab as usual.'

'It's a private dinner party, in a gentleman's club in St James's. Very discreet. I know it's a first for you, but I can trust you to behave, can't I?'

'Ray, stop the car. Now.'

'Don't be silly, Chantalle. There's nothing to be scared of.'

'I'm not scared, you silly sod. Just stop this car. *Now.*'

'OK, OK, calm down.' He pulled the car into the kerb outside Leicester Square tube station, sending up a spray of water that just missed the news vendor's stand.

'Give me some money, Ray.'

'Now hang on, Chantalle, if you think –'

'Ray, I just want a bit of spare change. I've got to get an evening paper.'

He looked through the rain-pitted windscreen at the stand. It had a display of the West End Final edition of the *Evening Standard*.

Almost the whole of the front page was taken up with a photograph of a handsome, dark-haired young man, and above the picture was a huge banner headline:

MURDER VICTIM NAMED

Chapter 18

Mrs Elliot, the Parkers' irredeemably interfering neighbour, hurried frantically along the East India Dock Road, with her shopping basket on wheels dragging behind her, bouncing and swerving over the cracked and uneven flagstones as if it were a reluctant dog. She'd spotted a uniformed policeman, a local man known to her by sight, striding along with a weedy-looking plainclothes companion, who she guessed must be the detective – a man called Jameson – that everyone was talking about.

The men were about to climb the flight of steps that led up to Phyllis and Henry Parker's front door, but she was determined to stop them before they touched a single bit of shoe leather to the weatherworn stone. If they went inside, they might be in there for hours, and Phoebe Elliot didn't much fancy standing outside on the pavement all morning, waiting for them two to finish nattering on with that miserable pair of bleeders.

She had been right about the plainclothes man's identity. It was DI Jameson, and he was now in operational charge of the Richie Clayton investigation. Within a few hours of Mackenzie opening his mouth and mentioning the name David Fuller to one of his superiors, the case had been taken right out of the unenthusiastic detective sergeant's hands.

It was strange the way it had taken him: Mackenzie had been left feeling oddly disappointed. Up until then he hadn't been all that bothered about the case, despite it involving one of his profession's most prestigious double acts of crimes to be solved, namely drug dealing and murder. But that was because he had thought it only involved a no-mark, petty thug called Richie Clayton – hardly a contender to challenge the Krays' authority in the world of organised crime – and so he had dismissed it as small time. He'd thought of it as something that could be done and dusted at his leisure, between trips to the Coach and Horses, and pleasant afternoon visits to a pretty little dark-haired PC he'd spent too many weeks cultivating, like a gardener with a hot-house orchid, to let her lose interest through lack of attention. And then there was Mrs Mackenzie; she expected him to spend at least the occasional few hours at home between shifts.

So he had thought that Gina, a few of the other junior officers, and a bunch of uniform noddies could do the legwork for him, then he'd step in, wrap it all up with a nice tidy bow, and Bob would be your auntie's live-in lover. He'd get the praise and glory without the hassle of having to work for it.

It hadn't been a bad plan – not until Fuller's name came into the frame, and he was no longer involved. Now Mackenzie found he really resented being excluded – no, not excluded, elbowed out – and especially by a limp-wristed West End nancy boy like Jameson. Mackenzie hated being shown up by anyone, but when it was the likes of Jameson doing the showing up . . .

But he knew that regrets were pointless. Jameson had taken over and, as far as DS Mackenzie's contribution to matters was concerned, that was his lot. From now on, he wouldn't get a look in. He'd had it made very clear to him that Jameson was only interested in using people he'd worked with before, and even then he kept apart from his team most of the time, preferring, as far as possible, to work solo.

Mackenzie had also heard whispers that Jameson was a weirdo in other ways: he took his own food in to work as he wouldn't use the canteen because he thought the food was *greasy and unhealthy*; the bloke was rarely seen in a pub, and, if either of those things weren't strange enough, he had never been seen with a woman. Ever. Mind you, he hadn't been seen with a man either for that matter.

It wasn't natural; someone like him had no place in the force, and that made it even more irksome. Still, perhaps he'd find a way to express his thanks to the runty little DI from the West End for getting him chucked off the case. But, for now, he had another plan: to take some leave and lie low for a bit.

'I've heard you're interviewing women about this Richie Clayton business,' said Mrs Elliot, tapping Jameson on the shoulder. She was puffing and wheezing from the effort of rushing to catch up with them. 'Well, I can tell you a thing or two about him – the horrible, lowlife, thieving bugger – I can tell you plenty in fact.'

Jameson turned round. He didn't look at Mrs Elliot, but at the hand that was about to start tapping him again, and shooed the polluting, repulsive thing away, as if it had a life independent of the rest of the old woman's body.

'If you don't mind . . .' He took a breath and shook his shoulders like a slightly damp dog. 'Please, don't touch me.'

'Suit yourself. Anyway, the name's Elliot. Mrs Phoebe Elliot. I'm a widow woman, and, *God help me*, I live next door to that mob.' She jerked her head sideways to indicate the Parker residence. 'And what a crew they are. For a start, there's their Chantalle, she's gone and –'

'Take Mrs Elliot's details,' Jameson hurriedly interrupted her by giving orders to the uniformed officer. 'And make an appointment to speak to her later.'

As he spoke he brushed at the back of his coat, where the woman had touched him, reaching over his shoulder with long, pale fingers.

'Yes, sir,' said PC Jennings flatly, taking out his notebook.

Ted Jennings was getting fed up with this. He knew he'd picked the short straw when they were deciding who'd be accompanying the Weed from the West End – as his colleagues had christened Jameson – and the older coppers had all started laughing at him when he had been assigned to the job. They told him he'd have to start acting like a nursemaid, make sure he looked after the bloke, save him from getting into trouble on the mean streets of Poplar. But rather than acting as the little milksop's minder, what was he doing? He was standing in the street, taking notes like some bloody female civilian clerk, from a mad old hag who probably thought she was being burgled every time a floorboard creaked in the night.

And what the hell did she think she was doing now?

What Phoebe Elliot was doing was snatching his notebook from him.

'You don't need to make no appointment to hear what I've got to say, young man,' she said grandly, snapping the book shut and handing it back to the constable with a wave of her hand.

'I can save you wasting your time and effort chatting to people who don't know what they're talking about.

You mark my words, you don't need to bother looking no further for the murderer than amongst them Maltese fellers over in Cable Street. That Richie Clayton had toms working for him over there. On their manor. Right under their noses. What a mug. Everyone knows they won't put up with little squirts like him treading on their toes.'

Jameson, genuinely torn between keeping his appointment with the Parkers, and his detective's instincts for picking up useful snippets of information whenever and wherever they presented themselves, struggled with his dilemma. He liked to conduct his affairs in an orderly way, in both his personal and professional life, but this might actually be important.

He took a long moment to weigh it up, then, finally, he snapped at the old woman: 'How do you know this?'

Mrs Elliot looked shocked at such ignorance in a senior officer. Bloody outsiders, they might as well be from Timbuktu for all they knew about the way of things.

'It's traditional, innit?' she said enunciating each word carefully, loudly and slowly, as if Jameson were a particularly stupid child, and, as she did so, leaning far closer to him than he cared for. 'They run the toms over there, see. The working girls. The brasses.' She lowered her voice and mouthed: 'The *whores*. It's been their patch for years. Since they come over here from foreign parts in the 1950s, and all settled over in –'

'No, Mrs Elliot.' Jameson was practically quivering with frustration. Why did it always have to be like this when he ventured into the East End? 'I wasn't asking for a history lesson. What I meant was: how do you know about Mr Clayton's involvement?'

'Well, why didn't you say so?' she tutted impatiently. 'Bloody hell, some people.'

She rolled her eyes at the constable in a gesture of cockney unity against this twit of an interloper, parked her shopping trolley securely against the Parkers' railings, and folded her arms.

'Listen to me, young man. I know a lot of things about what goes on. And I know some of the girls who that light-fingered little crap house rat put on the wrong road in life and all. And I know their families. So tell feller-me-lad here to sharpen his pencil, and I'll tell you who they are and where they live. And that's just for starters, way before I get on to the time when I caught him trying to rob my gas meter.' She let out a dry, snortling, humourless laugh. 'And would that mother of his believe me? If she had, perhaps things would have been different. He should have had a good hiding when he was a kid, that would have stopped him.'

When DI Jameson and PC Jennings finally escaped Mrs Elliot's clutches they were almost thirty-five minutes late for their appointment with the Parkers. This obviously displeased Jameson, but Phyllis and Henry didn't seem to notice their tardiness. As for Jennings, the time was of no consequence to him whatsoever. He was so miserable being with Jameson that every single minute seemed to last a quarter of an hour anyway. It was like working with a human robot, but one thing that did surprise Jennings about DI Jameson was that, for such a finicky man, he didn't waste time standing on any sort of ceremony or bothering with any of the niceties when it came to interviewing the Parkers. In truth, Jennings was a bit shocked by the man's brusqueness, considering he was dealing with the poor sods at such a terrible time for them.

Jameson had sat himself at the head of the long deal table that stood in the centre of the Parkers' big basement kitchen, facing across to Henry at the other end, and with PC Jennings on one side of him and Phyllis on the other. He sat up very straight, with his fingers primly interlinked on the table in front of him.

'You probably realise I know the following facts, Mr and Mrs Parker,' he began, 'but I will state them for the record. I understand that Richard Clayton was not, in fact, Mrs Parker's nephew, but was her son.'

Phyllis's chins wobbled as she struggled to fight back her tears. 'My Richie is lying dead in a mortuary, I can't even bury him, and what do you do? You drag up the past. Well, thank you very much for pointing that out. I really appreciate it.'

She dabbed at her eyes with the hem of her apron. 'I suppose that at least it's a good job my old man already knows, or I'd be looking a right charlie now, wouldn't I? On top of everything else. Call yourself a copper?' She slapped the flat of her hand on the table. 'You're useless.' She pointed an accusing finger at him. 'Tell me, if you dare – our Chantalle, what are you doing about her? No, don't bother to answer, because I already know. Nothing, that's what. You couldn't care less if I lost all my kids.'

Jameson showed no sign of emotion. 'As a matter of interest, Mr Parker, when did you find out about Richard's real relationship to your wife? Was it recently?'

Henry blinked very slowly. 'Just because I don't talk like you, *Detective Inspector*, it don't mean I'm a fool.'

'Thank Christ we've got away from all that for a couple of hours,' said Denise.

'You're not kidding,' agreed Lorna. 'I don't know how much more I can stand. Mum's looking terrible, and I think Dad's coming close to chucking that new copper, that Jameson bloke, over the balcony. He's so rotten toffee-nosed, he puts your teeth right on edge just looking at him.'

The girls were sitting on the top of a bus on their way to the Roman Road. Denise had planned for them to go to Chrisp Street – mooching about in markets had always been one of their favourite distractions – but Lorna had persuaded her otherwise. What with all the stories appearing in the papers every day, she couldn't bear the thought of bumping into anyone they knew, and being expected to answer all sorts of questions, or knowing that people were whispering about them behind their hands as they walked around the stalls, and worst of all, of course, was the fact that it was so near the flat.

Over in Bow they'd just be a pair of strangers walking through the market.

'It's overwhelming,' Lorna went on. 'Every day the coppers come round, wanting to know some ridiculous thing or other that can't be any use to them. I mean, Den, how does the fact that I've not got any kids after being married for four years help them find out who did it?'

'Who brought that up?'

'Guess.'

'He's got a cheek, that Jameson.'

'I don't know why he doesn't get on with his job and leave us all alone.'

'He's caused murders indoors. It's getting more and more like a bloody madhouse. Maxie don't hardly get out of bed, and Mum's latest thing is fretting that they've completely given up looking for our Chantalle. Dad said she had a right go at Jameson yesterday morning.'

'Bet he didn't like that.'

'No. And I don't suppose he liked it much when Mum went on about them not letting her set a date for . . .' Denise hesitated, wishing she hadn't said anything.

'Date for what?'

'The funeral. You know. For *him.*' She shuddered. 'It's something to do with the coroner having to release the body.'

Lorna frowned. 'Blimey, Den. Do you know what, he was my own husband, but it's not even occurred to me to think about anything like that? Not even crossed my mind.'

'Don't you dare start feeling guilty about anything to do with that animal, Lorna.'

'Don't worry, I won't. It might sound a shocking thing to say but if I didn't feel so sorry for your mum I'd put out the flags and let everyone know that I'm glad he's dead. That I'm really free of him at last.'

'I suppose he was her child when all's said and done.'

Lorna stared out of the window. The sun was out for the first time in what seemed like weeks, but her mind was on things very far away from taking pleasure in the first hints of spring filling the air.

'I wonder what it must be like,' she said, 'having a child, and being able to forgive them anything.'

Denise raked her fingers through her mass of red curls. 'I doubt if she'd feel like that if she knew the full story.'

'But she doesn't.'

'No, thank Christ.'

Lorna took out two cigarettes and handed one to Denise. 'So there's no word at all from Chantalle?'

'No, not a dicky bird. I'm beginning to wonder if there ever will be.'

It was eight o'clock in the evening, and Jameson was sitting in his office, systematically going through the beige cardboard files stacked in a pile on one side of his desk. As he finished studying each one in turn, he placed it on the smaller pile on the other side.

He was spending as little time in the incident room they had set up in Poplar as he could get away with, preferring to come back to his own office whenever possible. He felt right in his West End base. Despite the sordidness of the sex industry, and the regular flare-ups of violence that raged between the gangs competing for control of the rich pickings the area boasted, he liked it there. Enjoyed feeling close to the places where he liked to escape to: the open green spaces of the parks, the cinemas and theatres, the museums and galleries. They were the places that, for him, represented civilisation – the civilisation he had joined the police force to protect from the likes of those who lived east of the City, the place his father's second wife had come from. His self-appointed stepmother.

She was a woman with a gravel voice, figure-hugging clothes, and bleached hair, and she made his father laugh out loud like a fool – something Jameson's mother had never tolerated while she had been alive and running their once-orderly home. She represented everything he loathed, and had disgusted him more than anything or anyone had ever disgusted him before or since.

He had just opened the file he had compiled on Henry Parker, when the telephone rang.

'Jameson,' he said bluntly, with most of his mind still on the relationship between Parker and his wife's purported nephew.

'Meet me in the Pig and Pound in half an hour,' a man's voice said.

He flipped the file shut. 'Who is this?'

'I've some information about . . .' There was a brief silence. 'Let's say: recent events.'

'OK. In half an hour, but –'

'But what?'

'Where's the Pig and Pound?'

Jameson had been sitting by the door of the noisy, bustling pub for twenty minutes, and was seriously thinking about giving up on his informant, whoever he was, when a man shouldered his way through the sea of people and winked at him.

'You're here then,' the man said.

'And you're Kramer,' replied Jameson.

Kramer was taken aback. 'How do you know who I am?'

'You were around when I was on the Fuller case.'

'And you remember me from then? You could only have met me a couple of times. We exchanged less than half a dozen words.'

'I make it my business to remember all sorts of things and all sorts of people, and anyway, you remembered me.'

'Your picture's always in the paper. Bloody wonderboy, you are.'

'I'll take that as a compliment, but I don't think you're here to give my professional record your approval.'

'No, but I'm sure a top-notch tec like yourself will have

figured out that I might have some information about this Richie Clayton turnout.'

He nodded.

'Don't waste words, do you, Jameson?'

'What's the point?'

'Look, I might not be a college boy like you, Jameson, and I might not work up the West End, but I'm more shrewd than you'll ever be. So, before I start, I want your word that if you want this information, you keep your trap shut and just use it, all right? No attribution, not even a hint.'

'You'd take my word?'

'Funny enough, yeah,' Kramer laughed mirthlessly. 'Based on your reputation, believe it or not. I know that you're as different from me as it's possible to be, and my word's worth shit.'

Jameson sighed, for him, an unusual display of emotion, but this case was getting to him. It really wasn't the way he liked to work. But he'd be a fool to let this opportunity go, and it wouldn't hurt to hear what he had to say.

'Go on. You have my word.'

'You don't interfere with me in any way; I keep working, and you don't even acknowledge you know me. Deal?'

Jameson considered. 'I'll get us some drinks, and think about it.'

He came back to the table over ten minutes later, his skills at attracting barmaids not being very sharply honed. He put the double whisky in front of Kramer, and kept hold of the half-pint of bitter.

'What's in it for you, Kramer?'

'Someone took the piss.'

'So this is a fit-up?'

Kramer leaned back in his chair and sneered at Jameson. 'I told you, I'm not stupid.'

Jameson took a sip of bitter. He found the glass very thick, unpleasant to drink from. 'OK, deal,' he said simply.

Kramer's lips twisted into a smile as he leaned forward. 'OK. It's a bloke called Antonio Diaz you want.'

That name again.

'Before Fuller got sent down, Diaz was into pimping, nothing else, but then, when Fuller's boys failed in their duties, let's say, and left his patch open to all-comers, Diaz thought he might as well take the opportunity to move in on the dealing. Well, he started really coining it, didn't he? But then, up pops silly nuts – Richie Clayton Esquire. You could say he was a naïve kid. Or you could say he was the daftest fucker ever put on this earth. He actually thought he could just move in. Girls, drugs, the whole schmeer. Diaz didn't much care for that sort of behaviour, so he topped him. Well, him or his gorillas.'

'And you have proof of this?'

'I've got proof.'

Kramer also had all of Diaz's girls so terrified that they'd swear to anything he told them to.

Jameson hated being in the pub, hated the smell of the drink and the smoke, and hated men like Kramer, who had no right to call themselves police officers, but he realised that by agreeing to meet him he had hit the jackpot. Kramer had talked for nearly two hours, giving him enough to go on to build a case so watertight it could float all the way down the Thames, from the docks to the Southend estuary, without springing a single leak.

Jameson left the pub first, glad to get away, and eager

to get back to his files. He'd said good night to Kramer, very formally, but hadn't shaken his hand. That suited Kramer. He left twenty minutes later, after another couple of drinks, and walked off along South Molton Street with his chin in the air and a swagger in his step. He liked this area, and knew it was where, by rights, he would live one day, in a bachelor pad down one of those little alleyways with all the flowerpots. Nice.

Getting Diaz collared for the murder and the drugs was also nice – very nice. It would send exactly the right message to David Fuller. He wouldn't mess around making any more threats about who he should and shouldn't do business with. And that was enough for Kramer – for now. In fact, he didn't actually much *want* to point the finger at Fuller; no, he quite fancied the idea of having a little meeting with him, and discussing the possibility of becoming one of his 'representatives' as that weaselly little lawyer had put it. Well, his *only* representative really. More of a chairman of the board than an employee.

And, anyway, when all was said and done, it would be a bit stupid pointing the finger at a man who had enough on you to put you away on charges ranging from everything from corruption through to conspiracy.

Despite it being unmarked, the three men sitting by the counter in Lil's immediately recognised the big black saloon that pulled up outside as a police car.

One of the two minders with Antonio Diaz jumped to his feet. 'Surely, they've not come to round up the girls? No one told us they were doing a raid today.'

Diaz ground out his cigar in the tin ashtray, until the end was frayed and ragged. 'Why do I pay my contribution –

on time, always in full – if they can't even be bothered to send someone round with a message to warn us?' he demanded, waving his arms in anger. 'What do they think I'm paying for – charity? And look at her over there. Why do I have to put up with this?'

Diaz held his head in his hands.

Four policemen were getting out of the car – two uniforms and two plainclothes – and one of his girls was still standing on the pavement opposite looking for punters. She hadn't even noticed them.

Well, he'd teach her: he wouldn't lend her the money to pay her fine. He'd let her go in Holloway for a stretch, that'd concentrate her mind on things.

'Paul,' he said, to the other minder, who was already walking towards the door to check that the girls had managed to spirit themselves away. 'Leave Chrissy there, let them take her in.'

The man grasped the door handle then looked round to answer his boss over his shoulder. 'They'll only be putting on a show for some posh visitor round the nick. Bet they've got the mayor in there or something. So they can go back and have tea in the office and all say what a good job they're all doing.'

He was about to turn the handle to open the door, when someone did it from the outside.

Diaz's eyes widened. The police were ignoring the girls – they were heading straight for him.

Jameson had been sitting opposite Diaz in the interview room, off and on, for over five hours, and he still looked as fresh as someone who had just showered and shaved and was looking forward to a relaxing day ahead.

It was a trick that Diaz wished he could emulate. He

was sweating; his clothes felt as if he'd slept in them; and he'd run out of decent cigars. Oliver Timpson, his idiot of a brief, had brought him in a flat, hinged tin full of some unspeakably awful cheroots that Diaz, ordinarily, would have consigned straight to the rubbish bin.

He was just concentrating on lighting his third one, when Jameson judged that he'd been softened up enough; it was time to test the water.

'So, Mr Diaz, David Fuller –'

'What?' Diaz's head snapped up as if a switch had been thrown.

'I said: David Fuller.'

'Ow!' He dropped the match that had burned down to his fingers.

Jameson could barely suppress a smile. *Bingo.*

'Look what the fool made me do,' Diaz complained, showing his hand to Oliver Timpson.

'You seem agitated, Mr Diaz. Is there something about the name David Fuller that upsets you?'

Diaz's lawyer shifted in his chair. 'OK, Antonio,' he said quietly. 'Don't lose your temper.'

'Don't lose my temper? Shut up, Oliver, and speak when you're spoken to.'

'When someone is locked away in prison, Mr Diaz,' Jameson went on, 'spending all those long hours stretched out on his bunk thinking, it isn't unusual to become obsessed with matters on the outside. Maybe becoming unhealthily focused on the idea that someone on the outside is doing something bad to you. Taking advantage. Doing something they wouldn't dare do if you were still a free man.'

'What has he been saying?' Diaz's eyes were bulging with fury.

'You have an unusually high-pitched voice, Mr Diaz,' said Jameson calmly. 'Some might say almost like a woman's. We thought it was a woman, who –'

As Diaz lunged across the table, his hands out ready to throttle him. Jameson moved neatly to the side and gripped the man's wrists with surprising strength. 'Don't even think about doing anything so foolish, Mr Diaz.' He turned to the lawyer. 'Perhaps you should have a word with your client, Mr Timpson. I think he might be needing some serious advice.'

Jameson was disappointed not to have anything further with which to charge David Fuller – this time. But he knew he'd finally nail him with something really big, a lot bigger than the few piddling charges he'd been able to make stick two years ago. But they had at least got him put away. He was, however, satisfied with the outcome of events in other ways. He was gratified that just a matter of weeks after being called in on the Clayton case, he had had Diaz formally charged, and refused bail. And, for now, Jameson could say good riddance to the East End; although he would have to spend an hour there next week, attending Clayton's funeral.

But he wasn't going out of sympathy with the family. For Jameson, this funeral was nothing to do with paying last respects. He saw it as an occasion were the heady mix of sentimentality and bravado might well throw people off their guard, might encourage them to say things they would, in other circumstances, never dream of saying.

So, reluctant as he was to return to the place, the funeral was too good an opportunity to miss. Who knows, some of the mawkish fools might have something to say, a few titbits to offer, about the good old days when they were such close pals of good old Davey Fuller's.

'Hello, Mac, good to have you back.' Gina put down a cup of tea on his desk.

DS Mackenzie looked at her as if she were stark staring mad – bringing him a drink and being pleasant. What was going on?

'Have a good leave?'

He narrowed his eyes at her. 'Fabulous. How could it be otherwise? Two weeks in the pouring rain in County Cork, and all I catch are two fish and a stinking cold. What more could a man ask for when he takes a break from work? Still, could have been worse, I suppose: could have had the old woman and kids with me.'

'I might have something to cheer you up.'

'What? Won the pools and decided to give me the winnings?'

'If I had got the big one, do you think I'd give you so much as a five-bob postal order out of it?'

'No, not really, but we can all dream.' He sipped suspiciously at the tea. It was stewed and foul – vintage canteen – nothing unusual there. 'So what is it?'

'It's about that git who nicked our case.'

'What, Jameson?'

'Yeah, him.'

'Gina, why would I want to hear that big jessie's name ever again?'

'You know I wasn't exactly thrilled about getting pulled off the Clayton job either, but that's why I was so interested when I went out for a drink with some of the girls from West End Central.'

'Let me be straight with you. I am probably less

interested in what the members of your witches' coven have got to say for themselves than I am in Jameson.'

'Will you listen? One of the girls was in the Pig and Pound, over in South Molton Street, and she couldn't help it, but she overheard a certain conversation going on. A conversation between that yob Jimmy Kramer and, you'll never guess.' She paused for effect. 'Jameson.'

'Him in a pub with Kramer? Never. She made a mistake.'

'No, she didn't. She got a good look at both of them.'

'So why did she tell you?'

'Because we trained together, and she's a good mate. She knew what had happened to us with him and the Clayton case, and so she thought I might appreciate hearing the information, maybe using it somehow, that's why. You see, women know –'

'OK, save me all the solidarity bollocks.'

'I thought you'd be pleased.'

'Darling, I am fucking delirious. Now what's her name, this mate of yours?'

'Jenny Bryant.'

'Gina,' he said, springing from his chair and taking her face in his big, rough hands, 'you are a living doll.'

Then he kissed her, noisily, smack on the forehead, let her go, and made a beeline for the door.

'Does this mean you'll be recommending me for –'

'Not now, love, I'm busy.'

As the black cab turned into Grange Road, Lorna shivered. Despite it being a bright spring day full of daffodils, and the promise of even better weather to come, she felt a chill run right through to her bones.

'You all right?' asked Denise in a voice so low that Lorna could barely hear her.

'Yeah, but I feel such a hypocrite.'

'I know, me too, but thanks for doing this, Lorn. It's so important to Mum.'

'Why else do you think I'm here? It's certainly not for him.'

Lorna pulled on her gloves, easing down each finger in turn, giving the job far more attention than it required, but it was good to have a distraction, an excuse to not have to look Denise in the eye. 'I was really relieved when Phyllis didn't insist I went with her and your dad and Maxie in the funeral car. I couldn't have handled that.'

Denise sighed sadly. 'She's too upset to know if you, Dad or anyone else is in the car.' She ducked her head to look out of the window – they were nearly there. 'Do you think your mum and dad'll come?'

'They were getting ready to when I left to go round yours earlier.'

'I've not even thought to ask, sorry, Lorn: how is your mum?'

'Not good, that's why they're making their own way here. Dad's driving them so they can shoot off if she feels rough.'

Denise stared vacantly out of the window. 'Good idea.'

'Yeah.'

Shirley and Joe were actually already there. Shirley had wanted to arrive early so they could get a place at the very back of the crematorium, because she didn't want to upset Phyllis by causing a fuss if she had to slip out. And that she might have to was a real possibility; the new drugs the hospital had given her were making her feel so queasy, she couldn't be sure how long she could last without having to rush outside.

But getting into the chapel in the first place wasn't as straightforward as she'd imagined. As she and Joe had made their way slowly along the gravel path from the main gates, with Shirley hanging onto her husband's arm for support, they saw a huge crowd of people already gathered outside the doors. They were definitely there for Richie's funeral because his was the only one scheduled that morning.

When she thought about it, Shirley wasn't that surprised by the number of people there – Phyllis was a well-liked woman and she had plenty of friends who would want to pay her their respects, but she was surprised that they were all so early, and that she recognised so few of them.

She spotted DS Jameson – hardly a friend – straight away. He was lurking to one side of the doors, studying the crowd, looking for all the world like a scrawny commissionaire anxiously eyeing a potentially rowdy queue at the cinema. And there was Phoebe Elliot – of course. How could she have resisted the combination of someone else's sorrow and the chance of a free feed? And over there was a huddle of big, tough-looking men from the docks who had worked with Henry and Joe over the years. But as for the rest: strangers, every one of them.

Shirley beckoned for Joe to bend forward so she could whisper into his ear.

'Joe, who do you think all those people are?'

'From the look of those bags and all the kit they've got with them, I reckon they're reporters and photographers.'

'What, from the newspapers?' She moved even closer to her husband, not much liking the idea. 'Do you really think so?'

'Yeah. It's strange, you read things every day in the papers about tragedies and crimes and accidents and that, but you forget that all those stories, what they're about is ordinary people, ordinary people like us who've got caught up in something . . . something, I don't know what you'd call it, something extraordinary, I suppose. And all through no fault of their own.' He kissed Shirley on top of her head. 'Come on, let's go back to the gates and wait for Lorna so I can get her to walk round the back way to the chapel. We don't want them bothering her when she arrives.'

Once she had settled down, Shirley didn't feel too bad, and thought she might well be able to stay till the end of the service, but, just after the minister began speaking, Joe stood up and insisted they went outside.

'I'm sorry, Shirl,' he said, as he stood outside the chapel smoking his third cigarette in a row. 'If we'd stayed in there a minute longer I would have had to have got up and said something. All that mealy-mouthed crap that that minister – supposedly a man of God – was spouting. It was obvious he'd never even laid eyes on the little tosser.'

'Calm down, Joe,' she said. 'They'll hear you.'

'Calm down? *I want to welcome you here to celebrate the life of Richard, a dear husband, cousin and nephew.*' Joe spat out the words as if they were poison. 'Was the bloke out of his head? I don't know who he thought he was talking about, but it certainly wasn't any Richie Clayton I knew.'

'Joe, please,' Shirley soothed him. 'Think of Phyllis.'

'I am.' He threw down the cigarette and ground it out furiously beneath his heel. 'And that poor woman must be –'

'Ssshh, Joe, listen. The doors are opening.'

Phyllis and Henry appeared first, leading the congregation outside to the accompaniment of a wheezing version of 'Abide With Me', that had Joe's hackles rising nearly as high as when the vicar's sanctimonious eulogising had gone as far as saying that *Richard* would be sadly missed by all who knew him.

Sadly missed? If the bastard had been buried instead of cremated, Joe would be dancing on his grave.

There was a look of real relief on Phyllis's pale, tear-stained face when she saw Shirley standing there with Joe. 'Look at you,' she said, holding out her arms to hug her old friend. 'You're all right, thank God. When I couldn't see you inside, I thought you'd been taken bad. I couldn't have stood that.'

She gave Shirley a squeeze, then let her go and turned to Joe. 'Give us one of your fags, mate. I smoked all mine on the way here.'

Joe lit one for her, then offered the pack to Henry.

'You are sure you're all right, Shirl?' asked Phyllis, narrowing her eyes against the smoke.

'I'm sure. I just needed a bit of air, that's all.'

'Couldn't stand the stink of all them lies, more like,' muttered Henry.

If Phyllis heard what her husband said, she didn't show it. She just closed her eyes and drew the smoke into her lungs.

She didn't even react to the mass of strangers, who were now streaming outside and pressing towards the four of them, shouting questions, demanding comments, and popping flashbulbs in their faces. All Phyllis could think of was Richie, the child she'd left behind in that bare, lonely chapel.

'Henry,' said Joe, folding his arm protectively round Shirley's shoulders, 'have you seen the kids?'

'Lorna's over there with Maxie, waiting by that big tree, and Denise is walking up to the gates with Terry.'

'Right, come on, let's round them up and get away from here before we're all crushed.'

Joe and Henry flanked Shirley and Phyllis, and attempted to move forward, but it was as useless as trying to steer a courteous route through a rugby scrum.

'If you don't let us by,' snarled Joe, 'I might start knocking them expensive-looking cameras on the floor by mistake.'

Despite his size, Joe's threats had no effect on the scandal-hungry pressmen; for them the Clayton case, with its rich recipe of drugs, sex and murder, was as irresistible as catnip to a ginger tom.

'What're we going to do now?' said Henry.

'Christ knows,' said Phyllis with a gulp. She was beginning to feel scared.

'Don't worry,' said Joe, hugging Shirley to his chest with one arm and beckoning wildly to a group of men standing by the chapel doors with the other. 'I can see the cavalry.

'Over here, boys,' he yelled. 'Help us and the kids out of this.'

The men he called to were the dockers who had worked with Joe and Henry. They'd been hijacked by the minister, who still had a whole bucket load of platitudes left in him, and was only too keen to bestow them on anyone who would listen. Regardless of the fact that all they wanted to do was get out of the cemetery and over to the pub, the men, mostly of Irish Catholic descent, had been raised to defer to a dog collar, and so had been too polite to say so.

Joe and Henry's predicament was a stroke of luck for them: not only did it give them a perfect excuse to escape the vicar's self-important ramblings, it also gave them an opportunity to be of use to the two men they had known for so many years. That was a good feeling – being of use – especially when not one of them had a single idea how else to express their totally conflicting feelings of being, on the one hand, completely gutted by what had happened to the families concerned, but, on the other, being so glad to see the back of the nasty bit of work they had just watched being committed to cremation that, if they valued their mortal souls, they'd have to go to confession at the earliest opportunity.

'Sorry, Reverend,' said a big, tow-haired man. 'People in trouble over there. Got to go.'

A dozen wardrobe-sized men, who lifted heavy weights for a living, proved too much for the mostly beer-bellied, frequently deskbound reporters, and the dockers found it easy to provide an escort to the cars. The pressmen still called out their questions, and the photographers, delighted by the dramatic scene, snapped away at the procession as it marched purposefully towards the gates – but at least they all did so from what they judged to be a safe distance.

The dockers then formed a circle round the two families so they could get into their cars with some sort of dignity.

One of the men, who was keeping an eye on a

particularly aggressive photographer, noticed a pretty young girl in a smart black suit, trying, and failing, to get past the camera-wielding bully who was refusing to give up his place in the vanguard.

'Oi, you!' the docker hollered, pointing at the photographer. 'Move over and let her get past or you'll be taking a close-up of my fist.'

'Charming,' sneered the man with the camera, stepping to one side to let whoever it was through. Realising how attractive she was, he fired off another hail of bulbs as the girl twisted sideways and edged by him.

'Thanks,' she said to him over her shoulder, pausing just long enough for him to get a good shot of her, then she slipped through the ring of dockers with a smiled *thank you*, bent forward and looked in the windows of all the cars, scanning the passengers.

When she found who she was looking for, she hurried forward and rapped on the window of the undertaker's big black Daimler.

'Mum,' she shouted through the glass, 'I thought I'd missed you.'

Phyllis practically threw herself out of the car. She could hardly believe her eyes.

'Chantalle!' she screamed, wrapping her arms round her daughter. 'Look at you, you're alive.'

'Who's that with you, Mrs Parker?' a voice called from the mob.

'Give us a smile, darling,' shouted another. 'And we'll get you on the front page with a figure like that.'

'Oh, Chantalle, how did you find out about today, love? I didn't know where you were. I tried so hard to –'

'Mum, it's been all over the papers.'

Phyllis dropped her chin. 'I deliberately haven't been

looking at them. All them terrible lies they've written about our Richie.'

Nobody else got out of the cars; they just watched while Phyllis and Chantalle hugged and talked to one another. Even Mrs Elliot didn't butt in, but that was only because she was too busy giving an *exclusive* interview to yet another one of the journalists.

After just five minutes, the pressmen saw Chantalle start shaking her head, and Phyllis start crying. Then a bright red sports car pulled up out of nowhere, Chantalle shook her head once more, got inside the car, and waved out of the window at Phyllis.

The car roared off, and that was it: Chantalle was gone in an explosion of flashbulbs and a frenzy of shorthand, as photographers got their front-page specials, and reporters scribbed down their fevered fantasies about the possible identity of the mysterious, red-headed beauty who had made such a sensational appearance at Richie Clayton's funeral.

The original plan had been for the cars to take everyone to the Blue Boy, but, in the end, only Henry and Maxie wanted to go there, and then only for a drink, having no interest at all in having any of the food Phyllis had asked the landlord to lay on.

Shirley hadn't felt well enough to go to the pub, and, as Joe had no intention of leaving her alone indoors, they both went back to the flat.

As for Phyllis, she had gone straight up to bed to cry herself to sleep. Despite Chantalle's promises that she was just fine and that she would be in touch very soon, Phyllis found herself even more upset that her daughter wasn't going home with her than she had been during the service for Richie. She had lost her son once, but it was as if she had lost her daughter all over again.

Terry, after having a few words with Denise, had surprised everyone by literally running away from the cemetery, disappearing along the road towards Plaistow. Joe had tried calling after him, to persuade him to get in one of the cars, but he hadn't even turned round to say no.

And the last time any of them saw anything of Mrs Elliot, she was going into the pub opposite the cemetery gates with four of the journalists.

That left just Denise and Lorna, who decided that a drink was a very good idea, but they certainly didn't fancy going in the Blue Boy, so they'd headed along the Commercial Road and went into a quiet little pub in Three Colt Street.

'So are you going to tell me what happened with you and Terry?' said Lorna, putting a vodka and lime on the table in front of Denise.

'He said he had something really important to tell me.'

'And?'

Denise took a swig from her glass. 'It was hardly the time and place, was it?'

'I don't know. Depends how important it was.'

Denise sighed heavily. 'There's this really big record label, right. They contacted him some time last week.'

'And?'

'They're interested in taking over the Spanners' current contract, and giving them some proper deal. Three albums or something.'

Lorna raised her glass. 'That's fantastic. First good news in I don't know how long. Which label?'

'I wasn't even listening, to tell you the truth, Lorn.

Like I said, it was hardly the time and place, but he kept going on, telling me it was their big break, that he had to give them an answer today, but he'd give it all up if that's what I wanted him to do.'

'What did you say?'

'I told him to do whatever he wanted.'

'What did he say to that?'

'Nothing. That's when he legged it.' She shifted in her seat. 'There's no need to look at me like that.'

They sat there in silence for a while, sipping their drinks.

'How are you doing, Lorn?'

'How do you think I'm doing? Look at me, a widow at twenty.'

'I meant, do you want another drink?'

'Sorry, I was just thinking how upset Terry must have been.'

'Whose side are you on? You're supposed to be my friend, not his.'

'This is not about sides, Denise. This is Terry's future. *Your* future.'

Denise said nothing. She stood up and went to the bar for more drinks.

When she came back she said softly, 'Lorna, can I tell you something?'

'After what we've been through together? I don't think there's anything we couldn't share.'

'I'm thinking about leaving my job.' She paused. 'And Terry.'

Lorna tried a rueful smile. 'I do hope you mean that Terry's thinking of leaving his contract.'

'You know what I mean: I'm thinking of leaving my job and breaking up with Terry as well.'

'But why?'

Denise shrugged. 'Pop music. Nightclubs. Blokes with guitars. Drugs. Groupies.'

'But that doesn't make any sense. Look, I know these past weeks have been terrible, but . . . You're upset, that's all.'

'No, it's not that. It's a world I don't want anything to do with any more. And now Terry's been offered this really good deal, I couldn't ask him to give it all up for me. I've got no right to hold him back.'

'I don't understand.'

'You saw Chantalle back there.'

'Yeah, it was really good to see her, and looking so well. More than well, she looked lovely.'

'Them blokes from the papers seemed to think so and all. But where do you think she's getting the money to get herself done up like that? That suit wasn't from Richards.'

'Den, I know what you're thinking: she runs off in clothes off the market, and then turns up a couple of months later looking like she's been dressed in Bond Street. There's obviously some rich feller involved, probably old enough to be her dad. But it wasn't anything to do with clubs or pop music, and certainly not Terry, that made Chantalle run away. It was Richie. He did that to her.'

'Maybe.' She knocked back the rest of her drink in a single gulp. 'I just don't know what to think any more.'

'But Terry's such a nice feller.'

'Yeah, a really good bloke. So everyone says.' She stared into her empty glass. 'But do you really believe he can stay that way? With all that temptation he's going to have dangled under his nose every single night?'

*   *   *

'James Kramer?'

'Yeah?' Kramer had been half asleep when the bell had gone, and had opened his front door without even thinking about putting on the chain. He really would have to stop taking so much gear every night. It didn't only fuck up his brain, he was using up all the stock he was meant to be selling. If he carried on like this, he wouldn't wind up living in a posh mews flat, he'd wind up broke in some bloody gutter somewhere.

He rubbed his fists into his eyes, trying to wake up. 'What do you want?' he asked the two men.

'I'm sure even a copper as disgraceful as you is familiar with official procedures, Kramer, but we have to go through the formalities.'

That pulled him round quicker than a cold shower. 'Hang on, you're not telling me –'

'Yes, Kramer, I am. We're Old Bill, just like you're supposed to be.'

'And what? You think you can come round here, to my home, and start mouthing off like –'

'James Kramer, I am arresting you on suspicion of supplying Class A drugs, and anything you –'

Kramer's eyes darted from one man to the other. 'This is Jameson's doing, innit? I'll have him, so help me. I'll kill the bastard.'

'Jameson, eh?' the man said raising an eyebrow at his colleague. 'There's that name again. But,' he turned back to face Kramer, 'actually, we were given your name by DS Mackenzie.'

'Oops,' said the other police officer, 'shouldn't go mentioning any more names or you might get someone else in trouble.'

'Yeah, silly me. It'd be terrible if we got Mackenzie all upset as well, wouldn't it? And what with mentioning Jameson's name like that, we might as well just start reading names out of the phone book, way we're going on. Before we know it, we'll be getting everybody in trouble.'

He put his hand on Kramer's shoulder, and leaned right into his face. His voice had changed; now it was low, intimidating. 'And that wouldn't do, would it? But whoever it was fingered you, Kramer, I don't think you should go making murder threats like that in front of two police officers, do you? Especially not ones who have got a special job to do – investigating corruption in the force.'

Chapter 19

Although it was still warm and sunny outside, the living room felt cheerless, so Lorna flicked on the standard lamp that stood in the corner by the door.

'Dad,' she said gently, 'do you want a cup of tea?'

'Is that you, Lorna?' Joe's voice was thick with sleep.

'Yeah, you must have dropped off in the chair.'

'What time is it?'

She looked at her watch. 'Ten to seven.'

'You're late.' There was an unmistakable hint of panic in his voice. 'Nothing wrong is there?'

'No, everything's fine. I popped round Den's after work to sort out about going to the pictures this evening.'

'I was only going to have a quick five minutes,' Joe said, rubbing his hands over his stubbly chin, 'before I put the tea on.'

He went to get up, but Lorna stopped him.

'There's no rush. I put my head round the bedroom door and Mum's out like a light.'

He looked relieved.

'Tell you what, Dad, you sit there and I'll make you a cup of coffee to wake you up. Then we can do the tea together.'

She took off her jacket and threw it over the back of the armchair. 'How's Mum been today? Any better?'

Joe bowed his head and scratched at the back of his neck. 'No, not really.'

His sadness made Lorna want to weep; she knelt on the floor in front of him. 'Not even a bit?'

He shook his head. 'No.'

'She's not going to get better this time, is she?'

'I don't know, love. I just know she's really ill.'

'What did the doctor have to say?'

'Your mum said she didn't want him to come today. Said there was no point.'

He threw back his head and stared up at the ceiling. 'Said she was fed up being pulled about for nothing.'

'But at least she's still taking the tablets the hospital gave her. That's something.' Then he nodded, tried to say something but couldn't. He covered his face with his hands, trying, but failing, to hide his tears from his daughter.

'Oh Dad. What're we going to do?'

'I don't know, babe,' he sobbed. 'It's doing me in, seeing her like this. It's like she's decided it's all over, that she's finished with things.' He swiped at his tears with the back of his hand. 'All the life's draining away from her.'

He reached out and touched Lorna on the side of her face. 'I shouldn't be going on like this in front of you. You've had so much to put up with, and you've coped with it all so well – and look at me. But I truly don't know how I'm going to get by without her.'

'I know, Dad.' She stood up, and took her jacket from the back of the chair. 'I won't be a minute with your coffee.'

Joe stood up as well. 'No, you're all right; I'll make it. It's not doing any of us any good, me sitting here feeling sorry for myself. And I'll get the tea on as well while I'm at it. You go and get yourself ready for the pictures.'

'Would you mind if I didn't have anything to eat? I'm not feeling very hungry.'

'Nor am I really.'

'Shall we have a sandwich or something later on?'

'OK,' he said, sitting down again. 'I'll leave something out for you in the kitchen to have when you get back.'

'I don't think I really fancy going out. Den won't mind.'

'Please, love, go out for a couple of hours and enjoy yourself. Your mum would hate to think you were staying in because of her.'

'I'm not, I'm staying in to be with you.'

'Why?'

'You're not telling me you wouldn't like a bit of company?'

Joe took his daughter's hands in his. 'Lorna, I'm going to be straight with you. There are some things I've been meaning to say to your mum – private things – for some time now. And I think I should say them soon. And it might as well be tonight.'

'Don't, Dad,' she pleaded, screwing up her eyes against the tears.

'There are things that have to be faced. That I have to face. So, please, go out with Denise tonight and give me and your mum a bit of time together.'

'I heard you moving about, Shirl,' Joe said, helping his wife to sit up amongst the heaps of pillows she now needed to support her if she wanted to get any sort of rest, 'so I made you a cup of tea.'

'Ta, Joe. What time is it?'

'Just gone half-eight.'

'Have I been asleep all that time?'

'Yeah, my little sleepy head.'

'I'm sorry, it's all these pills. They knock me right

out.' She reached out, and, with a huge effort, managed to ruffle his hair. 'And you've been all by yourself since this afternoon.'

'I'm big enough and ugly enough to cope with things for a few hours, and anyway, you need your rest.'

'Never ugly,' she said, managing a smile. 'Did Lorna get back from work OK?'

'Yeah, fine. Then she went to the pictures with Denise.'

'That's nice. I'm glad she's gone out; she's been such a good girl to us, she deserves a bit of a treat. But you must be ever so bored, Joe.'

'How could I be bored with you, Shirley Wright?'

She took a tiny sip of tea, but could barely swallow it, and had to struggle to control her breathing.

Joe took the cup and saucer, and flapped around, unsure what to do, until she eventually got her breath back again and was able to talk.

Her words came in short, laboured bursts. 'Why don't you pop over the Blue Boy for a pint and a chat with the chaps?'

'Shirley, I'm not leaving you when you're like this, and anyway, it's you I want to talk to.'

'I'm not much use to you.'

'Don't say that. Don't ever say that.'

'But I've not got a clue what's going to happen to the Hammers next season.'

'Shirley, I'm being serious.'

'Sorry, Joe, but I'm not much company at the minute. I've not exactly been doing anything very exciting these past few weeks.' She produced another weak smile. 'All I could talk about is the crack in the ceiling over there. I've seen enough of that to know it inside out.'

He stared up at the ceiling. 'I've never even noticed it.

I'll fill it in and paint it for you. Would that make you feel better? It wouldn't take me long. And I wouldn't disturb you or anything.'

'Joe, you are a big, daft 'apporth, and I do love you.'

He looked around the room he had shared with his wife for so many years, as he searched for the right words. He knew he would never find them, but he had to say something.

'Shirley,' he said, unable to put it off any longer. 'I woke up again that night.'

'What night was that?'

'You were getting out of bed and I asked you what was wrong. You said you wanted a drink. I said I'd get it for you, but you wouldn't let me.'

'Good. You do too much for me as it is. But, it must be these pills confusing me, I still don't know what you're talking about.'

'Shirley, don't mess about. If we can't be straight with one another now, then when can we be?'

She shifted on the pillows, grimacing from the pain of the movement.

'You OK?'

She nodded.

'You went out, didn't you?'

'I honestly haven't got a clue what you're on about, Joe.'

'Think back: that night, it was nearly six months ago now.'

He noticed a flicker of something – pain? fear? recollection? – clouding her face for a brief moment.

'You said you didn't fancy anything to drink after all,' he continued, 'and got back into bed. Then you waited until you thought I was asleep, and then you got up. I was awake, but you'd been so determined that you didn't want any help, I didn't interfere, didn't want to upset you.'

'You'd been working all day.' Her voice sounded distant as she remembered. 'And I'm not helpless. Well, I wasn't then.'

Joe flinched at the truth of her words. 'Once you'd got up, I really did fall asleep. I heard you go into the kitchen and turn on the light, and that was it. I drifted off. You're right, I had been working hard, but I woke up again.'

'Did you?' she asked in a low whisper.

He nodded. 'It must have been an hour or so later. When I turned over and realised you weren't in bed, I got up to sit with you, but you weren't in the kitchen, or the living room. You were gone. I was terrified, couldn't understand what had happened to you, why you hadn't woken me up if something was wrong. So I pulled my coat on over my pyjamas and went out to look for you. I didn't know what else to do. But I only got as far as the balcony. Then I stopped.'

He lowered his gaze away from her. 'Shirley, I saw a woman walking across the courtyard, back towards the flats.'

'Did you recognise her?'

'It might have still been pitch-dark, but of course I recognised her.' He raised his head. 'It was you. I knew right away, even though you were wearing a coat I'd never seen before.'

'It was rayon,' she said, staring blankly across the room. 'A mac. I bought it down Watney Street market.'

'I went back inside. I thought that if you'd been so determined to go out alone, then it was something you had to do. And if you wanted to tell me then you would, when you were good and ready. So I got back into bed and waited for you. But you were a lot longer than I'd expected you to be, even if you'd used the stairs instead of the lift. And then, when you came into the bedroom, you weren't wearing the coat, just your nightdress, and when you got under the covers you were icy cold. And . . .' he sighed wearily, 'there was a smell of smoke on you.'

Joe took her hand. 'You burned the coat in the bottom of the rubbish chute, didn't you?'

She looked at him and nodded sadly. 'I shoved it in a pile of old newspapers and threw a match on it. The rayon went up like a torch.'

A big, fat tear plopped onto her pale, dry cheek. 'I'm so sorry I lied to you, Joe.'

'You didn't lie to me, Shirl, you couldn't if you tried. You just weren't ready to talk about it. But it doesn't matter because I know where you were.'

'What?' Shirley tried to sit up.

'It's all right, there's no need to get upset. As me and Lorna were getting ready to go to work the next morning, those two coppers turned up to tell us what had happened to Richie.'

'Joe, please –'

'Ssshh, I told you: it's all right.' He stretched out beside her on the bed, looked deep into her eyes and tenderly stroked her hair. 'I knew right away what you'd done.' He touched his lips to her forehead. 'And if the law had got even close to you, I was going to say it was me who did it. And I wish I had. Wish I'd had the guts to do that for Lorna.'

'It wasn't only for Lorna, Joe. It was for a lot of people.' She closed her eyes, breathing in the scent of him, the man she loved. 'There's so much you don't know. He had to be stopped.'

'Like what?'

'I wanted to tell you, but I didn't know how. Didn't know what you'd say, what you'd think of me.'

'Don't get yourself worked up, love. Everything's going to be OK, I promise.'

'I want it to be OK, Joe, I really do, so would you do something for me?'

'Anything, darling, you know that.'

'Go round in the morning and fetch Phyllis. I've got to talk to her about Richie.'

'No, Shirley, don't do that. Just leave well alone. If you go raking through the ashes, you don't know what you might disturb.'

'Please, Joe, I've got to. And I've got to tell you the truth about him and Chantalle.'

'Enjoy the film, Lorn?' asked Denise, as they walked along the Commercial Road back towards the Eastern. 'I didn't think it was nearly as scary as they said, but I did like Mia Farrow's haircut. I might get mine cropped like that. What do you reckon?'

'Sorry, Den, what did you say?'

'What's up with you? You're miles away.'

'I keep thinking about my mum.'

'Mum said she was poorly again. That bad, is she?'

Lorna nodded. 'Yeah. I can't seem to concentrate on anything else. Nothing else seems important any more.'

'I know what you mean. It's not the same, but I keep thinking about Terry while I'm meant to be working. Good thing I'm only temping or they'd have me out on my ear.'

'I miss working with you, Den.'

'Me too. We used to have a right giggle, didn't we?

Perhaps we should go and find something together in the City. The agencies there have always got loads of jobs.' She laughed. 'I mean, if they're desperate enough to give me a different temp job every few days . . .'

They walked along in silence for a bit. Then Denise asked casually, 'You've not bumped into Terry at all, have you, Lorn?'

'No. He's not dared show his face at work since the Spanners signed that new contract. And there's nowhere else I'd see him. How about you? How long is it since you've seen him?

'Over two months now.'

'Any chance of getting back with him?'

'Are you kidding? The queue to be a Spanners' girlfriend must be about two miles long, and me, the genius big mouth that I am, what did I do? I dumped him. It'd be great to get back together, but you know me, I was never one to beg.'

'He begged you often enough, Denise.'

'That's different.' She smiled wistfully. 'If we do get to work together again, bagsy it's not in a record company.'

'Deal.'

'Fancy going down Salmon Lane for a Chinese?'

'I'm not really hungry. Do you mind if we go straight home?'

Phyllis stood awkwardly by Shirley's bedside, wishing she had some sort of rule book to tell her what to say at moments like this, but that, unfortunately, was a luxury she didn't possess. She'd just have to busk it.

'And how are you this morning, Shirl?'

'As you can see, Phyl, not too good. I think this is nearly it for me, not much time left.'

'Don't go talking silly.'

'Not silly, just truthful.'

'Shall I make you some tea?' asked Phyllis, trying to sound cheerful.

'No, thanks. I'm trying not to drink too much. It's uncomfortable having to get in and out of bed to go to the bathroom.'

Phyllis nodded solemnly. This was so wrong: a woman like Shirley going through all this. A woman who would do anything for anyone. A woman who never hurt another soul in her whole life.

'There's something I have tell you, Phyl, before I go.'

Phyllis wanted to weep. 'Don't waste your energy, Shirley love. Whatever it is, we can talk about it later. You're getting yourself all out of breath. Why don't you rest for a bit while I go through and have a bit of a tidy round for you?'

'This is too important to leave, Phyl. Please, sit down on that chair and just listen. I'm warning you: it won't be easy. But once I've told you, you can try and put things right for Chantalle.'

'Chantalle? *My* Chantalle?'

Shirley nodded, and Phyllis, frowning, sat down to listen.

'No!' Phyllis shook her head angrily, her eyes wide and fearful. 'You're wrong, Shirley. My Chantalle would never have done that. Never.'

'Please, Phyllis, listen to me. *She didn't know what she was doing.* Not when it happened, she didn't. I reckon it was as good as rape. He might not have forced himself on her in that way, but he didn't tell her he was her brother. She didn't have a single clue. Not at the time. But when she found out the truth, that's when she ran off. I can't imagine what was going through that poor kid's mind.'

'This is like a nightmare.' Phyllis tugged at her lip. 'Drugs, and whores, and him beating up your Lorna . . . I've not wanted to believe any of it before, thought everyone had him wrong, had it in for him. I knew he was up to a bit of this and that, but . . . but now you tell me he did that to my little Chantalle. God forgive me for what I'm about to say, Shirley, but if this is true then I'm glad he's dead. If I met them blokes who did him in, I'd shake them by the hand.'

'Take *my* hand, Phyl. There's something else I've got to tell you . . .'

Not many of the congregation had set foot in St Anne's during the five years since Lorna and Richie's wedding, but they had all made sure they were there today. There were a lot of people who wanted to say their goodbyes to Shirley Wright, and to pass on their sympathy to her almost inconsolable family, Lorna and Joe.

Shirley had left instructions that nobody was to wear black, that the music should be cheerful, and that everyone should smile as they remembered the laughter they had shared with her over the years. And they had done their best to do as she had asked. But the moment the organist began to play the joyful opening chords of 'All Things Bright and Beautiful' to accompany the arrival of her coffin – a hymn Shirley had loved since she had first sung it at Sunday school – and a shaft of golden sunlight had angled down through the high church windows down onto the flower-decked, blond oak casket, her wish for happiness and laughter was too difficult for the congregation to honour.

They marked the death of Shirley Wright in the only way they could: with tears, pain, and, in Joe's case, with anger at God for taking away such a good, beautiful, tragically young woman, from the family who loved her with all their very being.

With Richie's funeral still fresh in their memories, it was difficult for the mourners not to compare his bleak, soulless dispatch with the heartfelt, flower- and tear-filled occasion they were at today. And when the cortège moved on to the cemetery in Plaistow for the committal, the comparison became even more pointed. There were no reporters or photographers, no undignified scrums, no bodyguards of burly dockers, just a chapel full of people regretting the passing of a dearly loved woman.

'If you're sure you're ready, Dad, I'll ask Malcolm to ask for everyone to be quiet.'

Joe nodded and threw back the last of his brandy. 'I'm ready.'

'Bit of hush, please, everybody,' hollered Malcolm Danes, the landlord of the Blue Boy, tapping the side of a glass soda siphon with his lemon-slicing knife. 'Joe wants to say a few words.'

Joe walked over to the bar, nodded his appreciation at Malcolm, turned, and stood there straight-backed and damp-eyed.

'First of all,' he began, fighting to keep the emotion from his voice, 'I want to say thank you to everyone for coming. I know Shirley would have been very proud to see so many of you here today. I also want to say that I couldn't have been a happier man than I was being married to my Shirley, but the tragedy of a happy marriage is that it can never have a happy ending.'

As Joe continued to speak, the rest of the jam-packed pub stood listening in respectful silence. The only sounds apart from his voice were those of soft weeping, intermittent sniffs, noses being blown, and of Phyllis whispering 'Excuse me' as she made her way through the crowd to stand with Lorna.

When she reached her, Phyllis wrapped her arm round Lorna's shoulders and held her close until Joe had finished what he had to say with a lifting of his glass and a final, simple: 'To Shirley.'

'To Shirley,' repeated Phyllis, squeezing Lorna to her. 'May she rest in peace, God love her.'

'Phyllis, can we go outside a minute?' asked Lorna quietly.

'Course we can. Come on, a bit of air wouldn't do either of us any harm.'

They stood outside on the pavement, leaning against the ornately tiled pub wall that felt soothingly warm from the heat of the late afternoon sun.

Lorna sipped at her drink, not even noticing what it was. 'Mum told you, didn't she?'

Phyllis felt a chill run right through her, and she clamped her hand over her mouth as if her fingers could seal in the truth.

'It's all right, Phyllis. Me and Den have known right from the beginning.'

Phyllis clutched the window ledge for support. *Christ Almighty, surely Lorna and Denise didn't know what Shirley had done? They couldn't.*

Phyllis wasn't sure what to say. What could she say? Nothing. So she just fumbled around in her bag, searching for her cigarettes.

Lorna didn't seem to notice her discomfort, or maybe she did, and just chose to ignore it.

'At first, I didn't think you knew,' she said. 'But then, about two weeks or so ago, something changed, and I realised Mum must have told you.'

Phyllis handed Lorna a cigarette, took one herself and lit them with trembling hands.

'Told me what?' she asked, desperately trying to sound relaxed.

'About what Richie did to Chantalle.'

'You mean that he –'

'Yeah. I won't give it the dignity of spelling it out, but I wanted to be sure you also knew about –'

'What?' Phyllis was coming very close to screaming. 'What else is there to know?'

'How Chantalle honestly and truthfully had no idea about the way they were really related. It wasn't her fault. You do know that, don't you? Richie's the one to blame. He did that to her without telling her he was her own brother. I'm sorry, I know he was your son, my husband, but I wanted to make sure you realised he wasn't worth a light and that Chantalle wasn't to blame for what happened.'

Phyllis closed her eyes and offered up a silent prayer of thanks that Lorna hadn't found out her mother's secret, that she had taken it with her to the grave, that only she and Joe now knew the whole truth, and they would never ever let it hurt Lorna.

'Yes, sweetheart,' she sighed, patting Lorna's shoulder. 'I know about Chantalle. Your mum told me.'

'I'm glad, because I keep thinking about what he put her through.'

'Not easy, is it? It haunts me night and day.'

Lorna finished the last of her drink. 'He was a bad person. A really bad person.'

Phyllis nodded sadly. 'He might have been my own flesh and blood, but after I found out what that dirty bastard did to my little girl, I'm glad . . .' She paused; she'd said enough. 'Come on, let's go back in and get another drink. I think we could both do with one.'

She pushed open the door and was about to usher Lorna inside, when she saw Joe standing over at the bar. He stood almost head and shoulders above everyone else, but with his tear-stained cheeks, and the strain around his eyes, he still looked as vulnerable as a child. It was then that Phyllis knew she had to make sure that she put a stop to all this once and for all. Knew she had to stop Richie hurting anyone else, that she would never let his sickness infect Joe, or Lorna, or Chantalle, or the memory of dear, sweet Shirley ever again.

She put a hand on Lorna's arm. 'Hang on, pet, let me say one more thing before we go back in there.'

Then, quite calmly and deliberately Phyllis said: 'Lorna, I'm glad that those men did that to him. I'm glad he's dead. It's no more than he deserved. Your mum was brave enough to tell me, brave and kind enough to let me understand why my Chantalle ran off like that. And because of that I'm going to be able to help her. I'm going to make sure I find her and bring her back home. Make everything all right for her. Sort it all out.'

She hugged Lorna to her chest.

'I know you miss your mum, darling, miss her more than anyone can ever understand, but you'll never be short of a friend with our Denise around. And, you remember, while I'm around you'll never be short of a . . .' She smiled ruefully. 'Do you know, I nearly said *mum*. But don't worry, I know I could never match up to Shirley, wouldn't even dream of trying to take her place. But I'm here whenever you need me.'

'Thanks, Phyllis. That's really kind of you, and I think I might be taking you up on it as well. I'm going to need a lot of help getting Dad and me through all this. It's so hard. I'm glad Mum's not in pain any more, but – I know it sounds selfish – I just wish she was here with us, wish it more than anything.'

'It's hard all right, darling. Now, are you ready to go back in, to see how your dad's doing?'

Lorna nodded and stepped inside.

She was leading the way through the crowd towards the bar when she felt someone tap her on the back. Thinking it must be Phyllis she turned round, but was surprised to see Phoebe Elliot standing there.

'Excuse me bothering you on a day like this, dear.'

'Yes, Mrs Elliot?'

'I just wanted to say –'

'What?' snapped Phyllis, grabbing the woman by the arm, and ready to throttle the old cow if she dared say a single bad word about anyone or anything. 'What did you *just want to say*?'

'If you don't mind, Mrs Parker,' Mrs Elliot said haughtily, removing Phyllis's hand from her sleeve, 'I just wanted to say, to young Lorna here,' she turned to face her, 'Lorna, your mum . . . Shirley . . . She was all right.'

'Thanks, Mrs Elliot,' said Lorna, touched more than she would ever have imagined by the woman's terse but uncharacteristically kind words. 'She was, wasn't she?'

Postscript

1983

Chapter 20

'I'm so glad you felt up to coming out for Mum's birthday, Lorn.'

'Would I have dared miss Phyllis's seventieth? She'd have been after me like a rat up a drainpipe.'

Denise grinned. 'Here, wouldn't it be great if you went into labour tonight and the baby had the same birthday as Mum's.'

Lorna's hands went protectively to her bulge. 'Don't say that, Den. I've got over a week to go, and Robert'd pass out if anything happened too early. You know what he's like – everything has to be done by the book, all nice and orderly, everything in its place.'

Denise's gaze strayed – yet again – back to the television that had been propped rather precariously above the optics. 'That Terry's still a good-looking bugger,' she said admiringly.

'Never saw it myself,' teased Lorna, nudging her friend in the ribs. 'Remind me, which Goodbye Tour is this? Their sixth or their seventh?'

'Fifth actually.' Denise glanced sideways at Lorna and said smugly: 'And I bet I know something else that you don't know.'

Lorna rolled her eyes, but still went along with the game. 'What?'

'Terry wrote this song for you.'

Denise was more than gratified by the look of complete astonishment on Lorna's face.

'Don't be daft, Den,' she said, looking around as if

every customer in the whole pub was staring at her. 'Everyone knows he wrote "Getting There" for an old girlfriend. For you.'

'I know that's what everyone thinks, but he told me different. And it's not even a love song. It's about a girl he really admired. You.'

'You're barmy.'

'You just listen to the words properly, when it's nice and quiet, and then you'll –'

'Oi, Denise,' yelled an elderly-looking man, interrupting her from his table in the corner. 'Tell Vince here that you used to go out with that Terry Robins.'

'That's right, Vince, I did,' she hollered back. 'For once in his life, Dad's not trying to flannel you.'

Henry glowed with pleasure at pulling off such a coup. 'And he wrote this song for you, didn't he, babe?'

'That's right, Henry,' Lorna butted in, 'he did. He wrote "Getting There" for your Den.'

'Wrong,' Denise hissed at Lorna under her breath, 'he wrote it for you.'

'Blimey,' Vince called back. 'You could have been a rich woman, Denise. What's the matter with you, not keeping hold of that one?'

Denise winked at a fair-haired man who was standing with two other men just along the bar from her and Lorna. 'I'm doing all right with my Kevin, thanks very much.'

Kevin winked back and chuckled.

Phyllis, on the other hand, pursed her lips. 'Will you stop stirring things, Henry,' she snapped, widening her eyes and jerking her head towards her son-in-law, by way of a not-very-subtle signal for her husband not to upset Kevin.

'And you, Matthew,' she went on, turning her attention

to the new landlord, who really hadn't got the measure of his clientele yet, 'will you turn that racket off and start the karaoke? I go to all the trouble to get it in and what do you do with it? You leave it in the corner. I'll remind you, young man, this is meant to be my birthday, not a night in round the telly.'

Lorna snorted into her glass. 'Doesn't your mum mean *not a night in round the Terry*?'

Denise giggled. 'I wouldn't be surprised, knowing how protective she is of Kevin.'

'But then I suppose she was the one who insisted on having the telly brought in, in the first place.'

'No one could ever accuse Mum of being logical.'

'But I think she's being a bit stern with that new landlord.'

'Matthew?'

'Yeah. He looks scared of her.'

'Do you want to argue with her? Tell her to behave?'

'No thanks.'

'And that poor bleeder Matthew definitely doesn't.'

They watched with increasingly ill-concealed amusement as Phyllis supervised the hapless man's efforts to assemble the karaoke equipment, and then her dismissal of all his hard work as next to useless. This was followed by her obsequious request for Kevin to help out his poor old mother-in-law, and – less gently – to *get the sodding thing* working before she thought better of things and went home to spend her birthday all alone. And, she supposed, they'd all like that, wouldn't they?

'I've not laughed like this for ages, Den.'

'Well, you should come over more often. But if you will live across the river, just because it's where his lordship comes from . . .'

'It's only bloody Surrey. You drive through the tunnel and you're practically on our street doorstep.'

Denise didn't look convinced. 'Don't think I can do that, Lorn. You know me, I cross the Thames and I get earache. It's not right, East Enders crossing the water.'

Lorna beamed happily at her friend and kissed her on the cheek. 'You might have turned into a moaning old cow, Denise, but I do miss you.'

'And I miss you as well.'

'Not really surprising, is it, what with all the things we've been through together.'

Denise shook her head, remembering. 'Richie; then Chantalle; then your mum; and then your dad getting so ill almost straight after.'

'I'll never forget what Phyllis did for me back then. Taking me in for all those months when Dad was in hospital. She was so kind. So generous.'

Denise sniffed back the tears that were threatening to spill onto her cheeks. 'You went through so much.'

'Here look at you – the booze is making you sentimental. They weren't all bad times.'

'You're right. They weren't all bad times by any stretch of the imagination.' Denise, making use of her inherited Parker family ability to change her mood like a weather vane with a screw loose, was now smiling cheerfully at her memories. 'Mum really can be a good old stick when she wants. And she's always been fond of you. Always said you were a nice girl.' She paused, frowning. 'It's me she's always had a go at.'

Lorna smirked wickedly. 'I wonder why.'

'And now you're having the baby, she'll be even worse. You know what she was like with my pair when they were little.' Denise patted Lorna's swollen middle. 'She can't wait to get her hands on madam here.'

'I know, she was saying to me earlier that she still can't understand why I waited so long to have one.'

'Well, when you think of it, things have changed so much. Most of her generation were grandparents by your age.'

'Thanks! She was nearly as old as me when she started.'

'You know Mum, one rule for her . . .'

'But you're right, Den. A lot of things have changed.'

'Yeah, girls actually get *pregnant* now. They don't have to whisper about being in a *delicate condition*, or say that they're *expecting*.'

'And they don't have to put up with being dragged off to some mother and baby home if they're not married. Like that poor Kay from school. Remember her?'

'Course I do. Wonder what happened to her.'

'Don't suppose I'd recognise her now. All I can remember is a girl with pigtails and mousy-brown hair.'

'Don't suppose she'd recognise us either.'

'Don't suppose she would; we're hardly girls any more.'

Lorna laughed. 'Do you mind? I'm barely out of my teens. Thirty-plus-a-bit-too-much-loose-change, that's me. Oh, but of course, that means you're thirty-six as well.'

'Don't remind me.'

'And there's a lot more changed besides us getting older. Look at your mum and dad, bless them.'

The girls turned and watched them jigging about on the stage, stifling their laughter as Phyllis and Henry belted out their truly original karaoke rendition of 'New York, New York'.

'It's taken them nearly forty years to call a truce,' chuckled Denise.

'Nice, though.'

'Yeah, it's good to see them happy.'

'And talking about change: look at this place. The old pub doesn't look much like the Blue Boy since Malcolm sold it to these new blokes.'

'Old pub, Lorna? You might have those in Surrey, but this, if you don't mind, is a yuppie wine bar, complete with its charming gay owners – don't tell Mum that bit – who have an excellent cocktail selection available, and, usually, very firm views on taste, but who have been kind enough to let her turn it back into a rotten old boozer complete with light ale, jellied eels, and karaoke for the night.'

'Like you said, Den, would you argue with her?'

At that moment, the song came to a denture-rattling, climactic end. Lorna joined in the wild applause for the birthday girl and her husband, while Denise stuck her fingers in her mouth and whistled enthusiastically.

'Why don't you come back over here and live, Lorna?' she said, clapping her hands above her head as her parents took their bows. 'Robert could get you one of those places they're doing up down Wapping, right on the river they are. Fantastic views.'

'You look after yourself, Denise. You could be living in one of those if you'd married Terry.'

'I'll leave the high life to our Chantalle, thanks very much.'

'Here, did you see that picture of her in the *Evening Standard*?'

'What the one with her standing by Simon Le Bon outside that nightclub? How gorgeous does she look still?'

'I know, I could hardly believe it. But I suppose once a model . . .'

'Mum's got it up on the mantelpiece – not that she's even heard of Duran Duran. Right there it is, next to my wedding photos, and the one of Maxie graduating from music college.'

She touched Lorna on the arm. 'Hold up,' she wailed, as the backing track to 'My Way' began. 'Mum and Dad are only doing an encore. It's just like Old Blue Eyes is up there on the stage.'

'What, Old Blue Eyed Dirty Mick from Itchy Park who used to sing for drinks outside the pub when he'd run out of meths?'

'That's the feller,' grinned Denise.

'Seriously, Den, don't tell me you don't sometimes wonder what your life could have been like.'

'Lorna, if I'd have married Terry he wouldn't be Mr Big Shot Bloody Pop Star doing yet another goodbye concert, now would he?'

'Do you really think he'd have given it all up for you?'

'I'd never have asked him to, Lorn. He'd have resented me for the rest of our lives. Mind you, that's not what Mum reckons when she gets the hump with me when she's been minding the kids in the school holidays and they've been playing up.'

'She loves having the boys.'

'Course she does, but you know how she leads off: *I could have had the life of Riley, a bit of comfort in my old age, if you'd have married that Terry Robins. Servants, that's what we would have had.*'

'You and Kev are hardly on your uppers, Denise, with four market stalls and a fleet of trucks to your name.'

'Yeah, but you know Mum.'

'Yeah, she's a real one-off.'

'Do you still think much about your mum?'

'Every day.' Lorna paused, thinking about Shirley, and also about the two babies that she would never hold, but who still came into her thoughts; maybe not as often as her mum did, but the thoughts were still there.

'She'd have been really happy for you.'

'I know: proper career, lovely feller.' Lorna raised her orange juice in salute to Robert, a smartly dressed, good-looking man, who was standing at the bar with her dad and Denise's husband, Kevin. 'Look at him, love him.'

'I'd love him all right, handsome great big bugger. Good job, nice manners, thinks the world of you . . .'

'He'd be perfect if he didn't expect a round of applause every time he does something indoors. And if he didn't keep pestering me to marry him.'

'Don't knock marriage, Lorna. Look how happy I am. Well, most of the time – like everyone.'

'No, not everyone, Den. Never forget you're one of the lucky ones.'

Denise considered for a moment, thinking back to another lifetime. 'You know, I honestly forget you and Richie were ever married. Seems like a dream or something.'

'Dream? Nightmare more like. Who wants to remember that bloody awful mess?'

'It all seems such a long time ago.' Denise drained her drink. 'I still don't know how he could have done all those things. It makes me feel ill to think about it. My own brother.'

'Why should you feel bad? What was it you used to say

to me? *Don't you go feeling guilty when it's him that's at fault.*'

'Talking about guilt . . .' Denise looked along the bar, smiled at Kevin and mouthed 'All right, darling?' Then she leaned forward and whispered to Lorna, 'Terry still phones me.'

'No!'

'I'm telling you.'

'But you've never said anything before.'

She shrugged. 'Wasn't exactly a secret, but, you know . . .' Then she grinned. 'How do you think I knew that song was about you?'

'I thought you were having me on.'

Denise flashed her eyebrows.

'You crafty cow, Denise. Here, have you ever been tempted?'

'No. Well,' she shrugged again, 'maybe once or twice. When the kids are driving me mad; or when one of the blokes who runs the stalls calls in sick and I have to cover for them and get up in the early hours of the morning while it's still dark; or when Kevin wants me to do the wages, because he's got to go off somewhere and sort out some business deal or other; or when . . . Of course, I'm bloody tempted. I'm only human. But can you really see me as a rock chick? Mind you, I wouldn't half like to give him one again. He was always really great at –'

'Ssshh, heads up, Den. Here comes Phyllis.'

'Your turn, girls,' said Phyllis, jabbing her thumb towards the makeshift stage.

'Come on, Den,' giggled Lorna. 'It'll be a laugh.'

'You sure about this, Lorn – with you in your condition?'

'I'm *pregnant*, remember, Denise,' she said, letting Phyllis shoo her along, 'not delicate.'

'If you're sure.'

'You're scared.'

'Scared? Me? Are you having a laugh?' sneered Denise.

'Well, don't keep us all waiting,' said Phyllis, shoving Denise unceremoniously onto the stage. 'Get up there and give us all a song. They've heard the best, now let 'em hear the rest.'

The backing track started and Phyllis thrust the microphone into Lorna's hand.

'Yeah, come on Den,' said Lorna, 'let's show them what rock chicks are really made of.' She threw one arm in the air, and began belting out the first line of the song.

'Go on, girls,' hollered Phyllis, clapping along. '"I Will Survive!"'

'How're you doing, Lorn?' asked Denise, looking dubiously at her very pregnant friend wiggling away energetically to the music.

Lorna winked. 'I'm getting there, Den, I'm getting there.'

Joe stood with Robert, the man he hoped would marry his little Lorna one day very soon and become his son-in-law, and Kevin, the decent, kind sort of a feller, who had been brave enough to take on Denise, and watched the girls – as he would always think of them – singing and laughing. He knew how proud and happy Shirley would be.

He raised his glass and smiled, and his eyes filled with tears as he remembered – just as he always did and always would – and made a silent toast: *To Shirley*.